AESTUS

BOOK 1: THE CITY

S. Z. ATTWELL

ISBN 978-1-7354790-0-2 (Paperback Edition)

ISBN 978-1-7354790-1-9 (MOBI)

ISBN 978-1-7354790-9-5 (EPUB)

Library of Congress Control Number: 2020914183

This is a work of fiction. Any similarities to real persons, living or dead, are not intended by the author. Any references to historical events, real people, or real places are used fictitiously. Characters are products of the author's imagination.

Cover design by Books Covered Ltd

Formatted using Vellum

Printed and bound in the United States of America

First Edition: August 2020

Published in Somerville, MA

S. Z. Attwell

www.szattwell.com

Bismillah

Secondarily, to those who are brave, and true, and stand up for what is right.

1

---

15 years ago

Jossey scrambled up the side of the condenser pod and sat under the desert sky, looking up at the glitter of stars.

She winced at the squeak of Tark's shoes on the sleek metal curve of the pod. This one was older, maybe a century or more, but still in good condition. "Ship-shape," Father would say, though the phrase meant nothing to her. It was one of those strange things grown-ups said.

The steel pod gleamed in the starlight. She hoped the Onlar wouldn't see two figures sitting here.

Tark plunked down beside her, floppy hair shoved out of his face. "You scared now?" he hissed.

"Shut up." She was, but she didn't dare show it. Tark was thirteen and didn't let her forget that she was only ten. She pretended to be nonchalant, but strained to hear over the soft whooshing of the condenser motors.

She wasn't quite sure she believed the Onlar existed, always half-wondered if those were stories made up to keep children obedient, like the monster under the bed, but if Father caught them...

But the *stars*.

They seemed to move, to shimmer, in the burning air above the horizon. Even at midnight it was hot, like the slow glowing of an oven that has been left open to cool. The land was punctuated by rock spires and deep canyons that Tark said the Onlar used to hide during the daytime.

Above her rose a massive arc of stardust and shining distant regions, seeming to twist its way across the July sky. She reached out her hand as if to touch it.

Father used to jokingly say that the atmosphere hadn't exactly turned to Venusian fumes after the years of extreme heat began. (She didn't know what Venusian meant, but it sounded bad.) Instead, it seemed to have expanded in the heat, an enormous bubble wobbling and making the stars appear to shimmer and dance, glittering orange and pale shades of pink, melting into the horizon.

Tark glanced over his shoulder at the deep hole in the side of one of the spires. The glint of machinery shone there in the starlight. The elevator. The pair had snuck out upside using it, the result of hours of Tark exploring the City's abandoned upper tunnels with his friends. It was a crankshaft model from the old days, nearly rusted beyond repair, and just unsealed enough for a group of boys to be able to break in.

Of course, none but Tark had been brave enough to risk a trip in such a rattling bucket up to the surface, or, really, anywhere. None but Gavin, his best friend.

And his little sister.

She looked up again, searching for the moon, and slid to the left. Tark gripped her arm. "Careful." She glanced down and saw, beneath her dangling feet, the edge. It was a twenty-five-foot fall. She shivered and scooted closer to her older brother.

* * *

They were up there because Jossey had asked to see the moon.

She'd seen it in videos, of course. She'd also seen paintings her father had done, from memory, of the surface when it hadn't been quite so hot. There was one of a sunset. There was even one of a tree, a tiny scrublike thing Father had seen once as a boy, rising out of the sandy ground.

From time to time he would talk about it in wonder, the insistence of life on survival aboveground. The pictures lined the interior of their small living chamber, next to the portrait of the rose Mother had given him on their wedding day. (None of them had ever seen a rose. It was a symbol of Mother's family.)

But Jossey had never seen anything other than the daylight sky, and that only when Father let her tag along on Engineering trips up to the surface, telling her that she needed to pay attention to the machinery and to leave the landscape to Patrol.

She had seen something white in the sky on that trip, and Father had explained to her that that was the moon, and it was often out at night, and she had stared because it looked like a little planet, floating up there in the blue. She had asked if it was cool up there, and Father had said he didn't know.

So she had asked to see the moon. And Tark, who never said no to his little sister, and who explored the scariest tunnels, even the ones the guards didn't want to go into, shrugged and said, "Okay."

Now they were sitting on top of a condenser pod, the sweet-smelling night air drifting past them. Tark's eyes were bright, almost silver, under a mop of blond hair.

"There it is," he whispered. He pointed a skinny arm across

the canyons, across the darklands to the east. The moon floated low on the horizon, a few days past full, looking faded as time carved a shadow into its yellow face.

Jossey stared at it, amazed. It was like an entire world was there in the air before them.

It was so beautiful that Jossey forgot all about the Onlar, forgot about Father, forgot even that Tark was holding her wrist so she wouldn't slide off the pod. She was brought back to reality when his hand tightened over her arm.

She started to complain, but he hushed her, gray eyes enormous in the faint light as he stared past her.

Then she turned to look and she wasn't sure which of them was screaming.

* * *

Patrol found her the next day, draped across the base of the machine under the burning summer sun, nearly dead from dehydration. She had a massive bleeding cut across her eye and her femur had partly splintered on impact with the machine. Surgeons later told her it was a wonder she had survived.

For weeks, while she recovered in the hospital, Jossey screamed about green eyes, but otherwise refused to talk about what she had seen.

And despite their best search efforts, Tark was gone.

2

PRESENT DAY

The tunnels were burning.

Jossey stood watching the condensation running down the rough-hewn walls in the flickering light, waiting for the shuttle to come and take her deeper underground, to the safe zone. The fans were on down far below, a constant blasting in the background, but the air was barely moving. She fumbled in her bag for the tin of water, reassuring herself for the fifth time that it was there. Sweat poured from her, and from the other workers staring dead-eyed at the floor or wall, waiting for the evening transport to arrive.

It wasn't like the shuttle to be this late. Storms were already rocking the atmosphere above them, and the thunder could be heard, dully, above the fans deep in the tunnels. She hoped she had enough water to last if the transport were delayed again.

Jossey checked the red safety gauge on her wrist. 110 degrees, and that was cooler than it had been earlier in the day, before the storms. She wiped at her forehead, tried to make herself more comfortable without actually opening the tin; water had to be strictly rationed.

The ground beneath them shook as thunder sounded above. The storms had arrived earlier than ever this year, and she hoped she was up for another week in the solar plant. At least they paid well, she thought, and someone had to do it. Even if they had to deal with the awful transportation. Her giant duffel was uncomfortable against her long-ago-injured leg, which still ached when the pressure was low like this. She hiked the straps further onto her shoulders, grimacing.

She glanced around. The two solar crews were scattered in clumps, some sitting on their bags, some huddling near the walls and morosely watching the condensation drip. At least today there'd been a bit of respite: one of the families in the other solar crew had just had a baby, so the new father had brought some treats up top with him.

Just about anything to take their minds off the start of the storm season and their daytime banishment from walking the solar farm border, with its slightly cooler canyons. It was dangerous during electrical storms, especially with all that tall metal equipment out there.

Not that the canyons were that safe either, but at least they were outside, not cooped up in the control box.

Despite the blazing heat, it was always hard to come back down after a day above. Jossey especially hated this shuttle stop and how dim it was. To save energy, the City had cut the lights up near the surface, and workers were expected to bring their own illumination for "emergency purposes." That meant that the end of their shift found them all huddled in a blazing hot tunnel next to the only light source from here to the first safety gate hundreds of feet below.

Try to walk from here and you'd be in pitch darkness all the way down, with only your little clip-on red safety light to illuminate the path, following the spiraling edge of a pit with a guardrail that Jossey didn't trust to keep a bus on the road.

She shook her head and tried not to think about the darkness below them.

Usually it didn't bother her; she slept on her long journey down into the earth. But she did wish the transport would be more on time, because –

Her safety gauge pinged and began to glow a faint orange. Beginning of sunset. She fidgeted and looked around. The transport's delay was now more than just annoying.

Another twenty minutes and the sun should be fully down. She hoped Patrol would be manning the outside tunnel entrance tonight.

A faint clanking sounded farther up in the tunnels, barely audible over the noise of the fans. The transport, she thought, relieved, peering into the dimness, but the noise sounded off somehow, as if one of the tires were worn down almost to the rim. She covered her other ear and squinted, straining to make out the sound.

Then there was a sharper sound, almost like a backfire, that resounded up and down the tunnel.

Someone next to her, Adams she thought, sighed. "New driver," he grumbled. "They always run the gears too hard."

Jossey glanced at the time. Twenty-six minutes late. Too close to the risk window. Much too close. She could hear the atmosphere rumbling above her, elemental, sounding as if the storms were about to break.

There was a horrible mechanical screech from very close up the tunnel and the clattering sound came again. Everyone's heads shot up as the transport shuddered its way into view.

"Finally," muttered an old man who had taken up refuge on one of the half-hewn benches and was fanning himself with his workman's cap. Jossey half-smirked. He was a machinist with her solar crew. She'd never heard him utter a word.

She looked over toward the approaching vehicle as people started shifting, gathering bags, getting into a semblance of a line.

Her smile disappeared.

The entire transport was listing to the side. The lights in the interior were dim, and the driver seemed not to see the waiting group, inching forward, then slamming on the brakes, as if just realizing they were there.

Jossey's skin prickled. The driver looked...not right. He was middle-aged, probably ex-Patrol, tasked with the boring yet necessary job of shuttling workers to the surface to keep the condensers functioning. He was one of several; Jossey thought she recognized him, but today he looked wild-eyed at them as if they weren't there, as if he thought he were seeing things.

She glanced at the tires, but it was too dark in the flickering single light at the stop to see if anything was wrong.

The door swung open and they shuffled on. The driver didn't look at them. His face was a strange shade of gray; Jossey blinked and hoped it was the poor lighting.

She waited until everyone else from her crew was on, counting them off. Then she climbed on, dragging her heavy bag, and took a seat near the front. The door hissed shut and the yellowish lights inside the transport buzzed and flickered.

With a rumble and a clunk, the transport trundled downward into the underground night.

The headlights barely pushed back the inky blackness, two beams slicing across the jagged hewn rock walls and into nothingness beyond. Jossey held her bag tightly, feeling distinctly on edge.

Usually the darkness was familiar, a fact of life to those who lived underground, and she knew that Patrol should be operating for another hour or so. But the tunnel's stone walls seemed discolored, like the driver's face, and she shook her head, concentrating instead on her own reflection in the darkened windows: her eyes shadowed, the left brown, the right an icy blue-green, a scar slicing across her brow and her eye and coming to rest on her cheek.

Her face was thin, almost pinched, with a pointed jaw and pale skin; she was barely twenty-five but she felt much older. Her uniform read SOLAR CREW 23 – LEADER, reflected backward in the glass. She always felt dry, exhausted, when she came down from the blistering heat of the outside.

She frowned and turned back to the view through the windshield, staring ahead into the tunnels. The driver still seemed to be on autopilot, big hands clumsy on the wheel, heavy shoulders hunched. The other passengers seemed nervous as well – normally some of them made light conversation, but this evening they were dead silent.

The transport shuddered as the driver overcorrected for no discernible reason and veered to the left. He gripped the wheel so hard his knuckles turned white, and slowed down to a snail's pace.

Jossey felt the juddering of the brakes beneath her feet, could smell the dust from the tunnels as it filtered through the transport's old intake system. Before them, the headlights disappeared quickly, swallowed up into total blackness.

On the boundary of light and dark, through the dusty windows, she thought she saw movement.

If the Onlar come, don't move. Make yourself small. They can see you in the dark.

Jossey turned away, spine tingling, before she could let herself look too closely at the darkness.

She watched the driver's hands nervously. The air felt cooler down here, the humidity lessening as they descended, but she felt clammy and strange and cold, skin prickling.

She glanced around, thought maybe others had the same consuming urge to get out and run.

But they were trapped inside their little bubble of half-functioning light.

The transport hissed as it clanked its way deeper into the earth.

The lights continued to buzz and flicker, and she realized she could hear a strange dragging sound. It was almost as if a piece of the transport had come off and was bumping against the rocky floor of the tunnel behind them. She stood, hesitant, and approached the driver.

"Um, excuse me – "

The driver nearly jumped out of his seat at being addressed, but kept his eyes focused on the tunnel ahead. Jossey jumped too, startled. The passengers behind her shifted uneasily.

Over the eerie silence, she heard a steady whispering coming from him. She realized he was muttering what sounded like some kind of prayer.

"Excuse me," she began again. "I hear something, there's some kind of – "

The driver hunched further, away from her, and began to mutter more feverishly.

She paused, listening more closely. She couldn't identify the sound. It didn't quite sound like metal. It was almost as if a heavy bag had caught on the fender. Someone's belongings, maybe, left behind at the stop. She frowned, trying to make it out.

Something else: a scraping. Slight. Persistent.

The clammy feeling was worse now.

She stepped forward again, opened her mouth to try again.

At that moment, with a clunk and a thud, the dragging noise ceased.

3

At the sound, the driver flinched as if someone had struck him with one of those Patrol wands. As Jossey watched, he half-glanced over his shoulder, face gray and eyes wild.

Before she could look back to see what had been causing the noise, he stomped on the accelerator.

The transport, much too old for this type of treatment, groaned and hissed as it picked up speed. Jossey frantically grabbed for a handhold and whipped around, but the transport didn't have a back window.

She suddenly found she did not want to see whatever had fallen.

She staggered as the transport hit the beginning of a curve and her bag tipped to the floor, spilling the contents everywhere. She yelled for the man to stop, using her foot to scoop her things into a pile while trying to keep her balance. She couldn't afford to lose anything, not here.

Not in the dark.

"Sir!"

The driver ignored her.

"Leave it, leave it," he was muttering under his breath.

"Sir!" Someone joined in. Now the crowd on the transport seemed terrified. "Stop the shuttle!"

The ground rumbled beneath them and the headlights wove wildly as they bumped over the rocky tunnel floor, careening into blackness. Jossey looked out the right-side window as they turned a corner, behind them, and thought she saw something in the distance, a long shape, on the tunnel floor.

Jossey turned back to the driver, pleading, joined by a chorus of voices. "Please! Stop the shuttle!"

Suddenly the driver began to gurgle, a wheezing sharp gasp seeming to come from somewhere deep inside.

He reached feebly for the dash controls, then slumped forward, motionless.

People started screaming. The young woman behind Jossey was whimpering, holding her bag in front of her like a shield.

The driver's foot was stuck on the accelerator. Jossey abandoned her bag and stumbled forward, hitting her shoulder sharply on one of the hold-bars as she dove to the floor and shoved the man's foot off the pedal. There was no brake pedal, none that she could see.

One of the other solar crew, a tall young man with glasses, pulled his way forward, stepping over people's spilled belongings, and touched the man's neck.

"He's breathing," the passenger announced.

"Get him out of the way!" Jossey gasped, grabbing for the steering wheel. It was heavy, rubber-coated metal, and it jerked out of her hands as she tried to pull the transport into a straighter course. The young man complied, manhandling the driver to the floor, as she flailed for the wheel. Everything was shaking; she could barely sit down without falling.

She looked frantically for a brake, an emergency stop, anything. The transport was rattling too hard for her to make out the labels on the dash, the light above the driver's seat flickering over the dashboard. Her teeth were shaking in her head as the tires bounced over the rocky tunnel floor.

"Anyone know how to stop this thing?" she yelled, looking over her shoulder. A sea of silent, gray faces met her. She looked at the young man. "You?"

He had pulled himself to his feet and was holding onto one of the bars. He shook his head, staring at the unconscious man on the floor.

"Well, try!"

He examined the instrument panel, then grabbed a lever and yanked on it. A horrible hissing sound, and the door swung open. Beside him she could hear the loud reverberations of tires on rock, bouncing back into the vehicle.

"Try another!" She gripped the steering wheel, feeling the vehicle shuddering as it bounced over the rock.

Somewhere, even over the noise of the transport, she could hear rushing water – an underground river, one that helped keep the City functioning, currently flooded by the summer storms. She knew that meant they were nearing the top of the giant spiral and the pit. There was a slight up-incline close to here, she remembered, and then a steep drop. If they could hit that up-incline they might be okay.

She gritted her teeth, took her eyes from the road and looked at the instrument panel. Still nothing that said "brake." "What kind of stupid system is this?" she hissed.

The young man pressed another button. With a groan, the transport shuddered, then the brakes engaged. He staggered, reaching desperately for the nearest handhold; Jossey felt the wind leave her as she was slammed into the seatbelt.

Sparks flew outside the windows, steel shrieking against steel. In the headlights, Jossey could see the arm of the spiral approaching, a steep incline to the right, with a drop-off hundreds of feet into a frighteningly deep pit. The guardrail looked extremely flimsy against several tons of solid steel. She closed her eyes and prayed.

The bus rolled more and more slowly, then shuddered to a stop and went silent as the engine disengaged.

Then the vehicle turned off, leaving them in total blackness.

4

IT WAS PITCH BLACK INSIDE THE TRANSPORT. PEOPLE WERE shrieking, gasping, their voices ringing off the glass and walls. The noise, the terror in their voices, was overwhelming. Jossey dropped to the floor and fumbled for her belongings. The knife, where was her knife? Had she packed it? Had she forgotten it?

She collided with a seat and sat still, trying to breathe, trying to orient herself. *Calm down. Remember the procedure.*

They come in the dark. They can see you.

The scar across her eye began to throb. She'd seen one of Them, a long time ago. She'd lived. Tark, her brother –

Calm down calm down calm down

The air was thick with fear. Jossey could feel the waves of prickling heat rising in her chest, choking her.

Procedure. Follow the procedure. Team leaders, instruct the others.

She fumbled for the safety light around her neck. Water, she needed water.

"Find your lights," she managed to croak.

Her cord was tangled. She frantically yanked and heard something snap, fall to the floor.

Circles of red light blossomed around her, one by one, like

so many giant eyes floating in the blackness. In the dimness, she saw her safety light, a dark lump on the floor. She picked it up carefully, pressed the button.

It glowed in her cupped hands like a coal. She resisted the urge to shove it in her pocket, keep whatever might be outside in the darkness from seeing it.

Calm calm calm you have to be calm

Faces crowded around her, shadowed and foreign in the dim reddish light, eyes watching her expectantly. They were too close. She tried to maintain eye contact.

Her Engineering team members all knew what had happened to her, to her brother.

They'd never seen one of the Onlar, the creatures from the aboveground world.

But she had.

"Are you the team leader?" It was the young man who had helped her stop the transport. He was crouching in front of her, watching her face. In the dimness, his glasses shone eerily. One of the lenses was cracked. She blinked, shoved away the image that came to mind.

The question, the urgent tone, knocked some sense back into her brain. She closed her eyes, willing herself to calm down, and thought for a moment. Patrol should be alerted that a transport hadn't arrived, should come looking for them. But the driver needed medical attention. And the gates below were due to close soon. Once they closed for the night, it was up to the discretion of the City's Council whether to send out a team to retrieve anyone.

"Well?" demanded one of the older workers from the other crew. PERKINS, his uniform said. He was tall and balding, with a craggy face and a perpetually combative manner. She remembered him being argumentative on previous transport trips.

She tried to keep her face expressionless.

"Hold on, I'm thinking." She got to her feet and turned to the dashboard, carefully stepping over the driver. The radio should be around here somewhere. She deeply regretted having never listened to her father when he tried to show her how these vehicles worked.

She held the glowing light over the dash and inspected it. There – a radio! She pushed the button, listened.

Nothing.

"The engine has to be engaged, I think," the young man said quietly.

Jossey looked down at the driver on the floor. He was breathing, but shallowly.

She sat carefully back in the driver's seat, felt around for the ignition. The keys were still there. She turned them.

A sputtering sound, then a grinding of metal. The noise in the blackness was horrific, like giant claws scraping the stone walls.

She shut the engine off, petrified. If the Onlar were in the tunnels already –

Her watch beeped. The sun was fully down now. Jossey shook her head, held it in her hands, staggered out of her seat.

The others watched her with what looked like pity and not a little fear. They knew her story. But she was the leader of Solar Crew 23 – the rest weren't likely trained for such emergencies. The other crew's leader was out sick, she knew.

That left just her to take care of nearly three dozen people.

She sat on the floor, tried to collect herself. The heat was making her feel sick.

"You try," she gasped out, waving the young man toward the driver's seat. He seemed competent enough.

He gave her a worried look, sat down and tried. The engine made a *chunk chunk chunk* sound and a foul stench began to fill the transport.

"Shut it off!" yelled Perkins. "You're ruining the – "

There was a loud hiss as the stench intensified. And then, with a very final-sounding clunk, the engine fell silent.

The two crews staggered out of the transport, coughing, waving away the fumes. The railing wasn't ten feet away, a thin line barely visible in their safety lights. Jossey, one hand still pressed to her eyes, tried to wave them into a group at the front of the bus.

She poured some precious water onto a cloth and covered her face.

"We can't stay here," she said through the cloth. "There's no shelter. Even if Patrol makes it way up here, even if Council allows it – we'll probably be toast if the Onlar find us. Or if we run out of water. It's still" – she glanced at her wrist gauge – "eighty-five degrees, give or take."

Perkins opened his mouth, and she gave him a steely glare.

One of his team members, a very young junior Engineer whose name Jossey recalled as Sally, spoke up. "I can't," she said firmly.

The old machinist had followed Jossey's example with the cloth. "What do you mean, you can't?" The air stank of whatever chemical had been put in the ancient transport. He coughed wetly. "If They don't get us, this stuff in the air might."

"I – " The girl looked at the railing, and beyond to the enormous chasm. "I can't walk...down, I mean."

"She's my niece," Perkins said, stepping forward. "Scared of heights." He glanced around the group. "I imagine she's not the only one. Am I right?"

There were a few murmurs, but the group stayed silent. "And you want us to walk all the way down in the dark? Next to that?" Perkins gestured to the guardrail.

"Like I said, there's no shelter, and no water," Jossey said quietly. "We're about as unsafe as we can be here. Do you hear that?"

The group, floating spots of red in little clusters, paused. Over the sound of the rushing water from the underground river, Jossey could hear the beginning of a faint wailing coming from deep below.

Tunnelsong, it was called. It happened when the cooler night air began to sink into the pit. It was the final warning that darkness had fallen above.

The group looked at her soberly.

She repeated herself. "We have to move."

The group shuffled around. They weren't protesting. But she could hear mumbling. It was probably a matter of time.

"Line up," she ordered.

She counted them off into teams of five. They hovered in little clusters of light, throwing eerie shadows on the tunnel walls.

"Each group, choose a leader. The rest of you, lights on your backs. Any weapons you have on you, grab them now. No water until I say so, or unless you've reached stage-four exhaustion. Understood?"

"Understood," they responded.

The groups probably had no weapons worth using, she thought grimly, but it should give them something to occupy their minds.

As they mutely dug around in their bags, she turned to the young man who had helped her stop the transport.

"Come with me," she muttered.

He followed her to the back to the transport.

She looked at him appraisingly. He was tall, maybe late twenties, with long, tied-back dark hair. He had removed his broken glasses, and his face looked entirely different than she had imagined.

Long silver eyes observed her silently as she struggled to process the change. Before, he had been one of the group, another bored-looking Engineer nose-deep in the latest scientific texts; she couldn't even say with confidence how long he'd been working the other crew. But now –

Something about him was oddly familiar. She couldn't put her finger on why. Maybe a former classmate? Someone she'd served with before?

She shook her head. More important to their current situation, he seemed remarkably calm.

She also did not miss the ease with which he handled his heavy pack.

He looked faintly bemused at her frank assessment, and seemed to be waiting for her to speak. She blurted out what was on her mind. "Are you former Patrol?"

He blinked, and lowered his bag. "Apprenticed, once upon a time," he admitted. "I didn't do so well in training. I decided I was more useful as an Engineer."

"Well, I hope you've remembered something of your training," Jossey said quietly. "What's your name?"

"Caspar."

She opened her mouth. He looked uncomfortable. "I know who you are."

Jossey didn't meet his eyes. She motioned to the back of the vehicle. "We need to get the stretcher out. Are you up for carrying the driver?"

He gestured in assent.

Jossey knew enough about transports to know that somewhere near the back there should be an emergency stretcher. She held the safety light up and shined it over what looked like a rusted sign. "MEDICAL EMERGENCY ONLY," it said. She could barely make out the lettering – it had faded over the decades, maybe longer. She realized she had no idea how old this transport was. It could be from her great-grandparents' time, for all she knew.

"Caspar, give me a hand with – "

Frowning, she paused and looked more closely, held up a hand as Caspar obligingly took up a position on the other side of the heavy door. He waited patiently.

She held the orb nearly to the metal, squinting in the darkness. There were flecks of something – it was hard to tell what color they were in the reddish light. She moved the light slowly down the door toward the fender.

Jossey nearly gasped as the light vanished into three gouges each as wide as her thumb.

She made a strangled sound. The fender was halfway off, more deep gouge-marks scored into the metal. The base was twisted where it appeared to have been dragged along the ground.

Where something had held onto it, she thought. Something that had fallen onto the floor of the tunnel.

She could feel the blood draining out of her face; her scar throbbed and her eye teared up. Her hands were suddenly ice-cold despite the heat.

"Don't," Caspar said under his breath, gesturing toward the circle of reddish lights floating near the front of the transport.

She half-laughed, shakily. She didn't think she could scream if she tried.

Perkins glanced over irritably and Caspar waved. He turned back to Jossey. "We need to hurry," he said.

Deep behind them in the tunnel, Jossey thought she heard something. The clink of a rock. A trickle of gravel.

She whipped around, stared into the blackness. Part of her wanted to turn up the brightness on the safety light. Part of her wanted to switch it off entirely.

"Can we get back into the transport?" she muttered.

"Not with that chemical floating around." Caspar shook his head. "Forget about the Onlar – it might kill us. I have no idea what the Founders put in these things back in the day."

She realized she was shaking. "I saw it. It looked dead."

"What?"

She pointed to the fender. "It wasn't moving. I saw it."

She had a sudden memory of bright green eyes, glowing in the darkness. And the terror on Tark's face.

"It didn't move," she repeated, almost frantically.

"Let's get a move on!" shouted Perkins, making her jump.

"Stupid loudmouth," she muttered under her breath. She wanted to yell something back, but she didn't want a crowd of jumpy people to get angry and shout and give themselves away even more. Not with rocks maybe moving in the tunnel above them.

She was having a hard time breathing all of a sudden.

She glanced at her wrist gauge once again. The final night shuttle was late too. She didn't want to think about why.

5

It felt like hours before they managed to organize themselves and start downward into the earth. Every movement, every sound, was making Jossey anxious, and despite her calls for speed, they descended at a snail's pace into the deep, carrying all the extra water they could find in the transport's cargo boxes.

She clutched the handles of the stretcher, the strain tearing at her shoulders. Caspar carried the other end. Jossey had taken first shift – she figured she'd have a mutiny on her hands if she didn't, since many of the group wanted to just leave the driver for Patrol to recover.

Barbarians, she thought, but she understood their logic all too well.

They can see you in the dark.

She gritted her teeth and shuffled her way over the rocks, following the faint trail of red bobbing lights before her. To his credit, Perkins had managed to organize the group and was acting as point.

The instructions were to be as quiet as possible. But at least one person was stumbling on rocks every so often, knocking them over the edge of the cliff with a nerve-jangling clatter. It took all Jossey's self-control not to shout at them.

Behind her, she could feel the night breeze in earnest. And she could hear the slow dribble of rocks, occasional enough that she thought maybe she was hearing things.

She hoped.

Without safety lights, the darkness of the tunnel was absolute. With them, it was dim, but she could make out the wall and the figures of the thirty or so people shuffling down into blackness.

It was impressive, she thought, how the human eye could adjust.

Caspar, carrying the other end of the stretcher, glanced back every so often as if to make sure she was okay. She wasn't, but she gave him a brief smile before focusing on blocking out the pain in her arms.

A trickle of night air hit Jossey, and the smell of the desert. A memory flashed before her – the moon, floating on the horizon. And the rustle of bleached hair in the wind.

She shook her head frantically, stopping in her tracks, hands white-knuckled on the stretcher.

At the sudden jerking stop, Caspar turned around, eyeing her. "You okay?"

Her face felt white. Her leg burned with the memory of THAT pain.

The screams in her mind were so loud she almost wondered if they were real. But Caspar just looked at her, quizzically. She tried to smile. "Yes," she managed. "Let's keep going."

"We can stop."

She thought about the rocks in the tunnel and shook her head.

They would probably need a water break soon, however. They'd already covered quite a distance, even at such a slow pace.

She was calculating how much each person would need when a shriek tore out of the darkness up ahead, a terrified sound like a wounded animal.

Caspar jerked around and met Jossey's eyes. Without a word, they set the stretcher down and sprinted toward the source of the noise, staying well to the left of the crowd. Jossey's wrists were numb, and she shook them as she ran.

Sally sat on the edge of the cliff, clutching Perkins' ankle. Apparently her foot had slipped over the side in the dark at a point where the ledge had eroded. She was sobbing. Perkins was awkwardly patting her on the head.

"She's on my Engineering team," Caspar muttered to Jossey as they pushed through the crowd. "New kid. Never been aboveground before."

"Apparently she's never been tunnel exploring either," Jossey whispered back. "Not doing so great in the dark." She glanced over her shoulder, at the maw of the tunnel behind them. "I thought I hear– "

He gave her a look. She clamped her mouth shut.

Sally was in hysterics. "I can't go. I can't." She scooted back against the wall, sat there with her hands pressed against the rough-hewn stone, hyperventilating.

Jossey shouldered her way through the crowd and crouched in front of the young woman, Perkins hovering protectively.

"Sally," Jossey said as gently as she could.

"I can't," Sally whimpered. "We have to wait for a transport."

"We need more light," Perkins barked.

"That's not a good ide– "

"Who do you think you are?" He rounded on her. "We're all Citizens here."

Jossey remained crouching, glaring up at him.

"She's team leader," the old machinist said.

"For your crew, maybe," Perkins said. "My team leader's sick today, and I'm a Senior Engineer, so guess that makes me in charge."

"Can't you feel the night air?" Jossey said coldly, standing up and turning to Perkins, ignoring the pain in her bad leg. She twisted her fingers in the faint breeze.

He was half a head taller than her, but she held her ground, crossing her arms. Sally looked back and forth between them, wide-eyed.

"I guess you should know," Perkins finally said, smirking. "Aren't you the girl whose brother – "

In an instant, Jossey's face went from concerned to frozen, stonelike. She looked sharply away from Perkins.

"No extra light. None." She smiled twistedly at him. "Try not to fall." To Sally, she said, "Get up."

Sally looked at her, openmouthed.

Jossey stalked back to the stretcher. "Let's go."

Perkins had turned away from her and was grumbling to one of his fellow workers. Sally was still on the ground, huddled against the wall, head in her arms. Jossey shook her head and stretched, preparing her arms for carrying the driver again.

In the darkness behind them, there was a light clink as something rolled out of the tunnel and struck the stretcher.

Caspar spun.

Jossey, without turning around, gave him a look.

Then she reached up and switched off her safety light.

6

THEY CAN SEE YOU IN THE DARK.

Jossey sidestepped into the blackness, slipping off her pack and leaving it on the ground so it couldn't get in her way.

In the faint dimness she saw a tall shape near the tunnel wall, nothing more.

She had been facing away from the creature when she had turned off her light; she hoped it would not notice her disappearance, especially not with all the other lights up ahead. Her breathing felt ragged, her head pounding and starting to spin as the heat and darkness and fear converged, and she regretted not drinking more water before they started down into the earth.

Too bad, she told herself. *Move.*

The railing had to be behind her somewhere. She could feel the nighttime circulation from the pit, a wall of air rushing downward.

It got stronger the closer you were to the edge. She shivered.

Her hands were clammy as she reached backward into darkness for the metal rail, her eyes on the creature, watching it for signs of movement.

There was no rail.

Jossey tipped backward, flailing, stepping into empty air, white-hot terror stabbing through her core.

She tried to scream.

And then she couldn't breathe at all as her upper back hit the rail with a solid thud.

Her hands shot out sideways and found the metal bar that separated her from a five-hundred-foot fall, closing over the rail in a desperate vicelike grip. Her left foot slid forward and she pulled her right foot up over the edge, scrabbling for solid ground, her already-sore arms burning as she held on.

She sagged against the rail, eyes closed, trying to breathe, trying not to whimper.

Jossey let the cool night air wick the sweat from her forehead and tried not to think about the hundreds of feet of blackness below her or the creature before her, tried not to think about how clammy her hands were and how easily she could slip off this railing. The ground beneath her feet was pebbly. Eroded, she thought. From below, she could hear the faint reverberations of tunnelsong rising.

Jossey gritted her teeth, then bent her right knee and felt behind her with one tentative foot for the edge of the cliff to see how far back it was, how much maneuvering room she might have.

She bit her lip to keep from shrieking as her toes disappeared over the edge in the blackness. She lost her balance again, dropping to her right knee, hard, on the stone.

A foot. A foot between her and the pit.

Focus. You can do this. You have to do this. Team leaders, you are responsible for your group.

Jossey hauled herself back up to a standing position, entire body rigid.

Her hands shook against the rail. She tried to slow her breathing, forced herself to open her eyes.

You are the team leader.

The group seemed to have slowed, a sea of bobbing red lights to her right and dead ahead.

There it was. The creature, too, seemed to have slowed.

Its green eyes were dull, not the brilliant color she remembered, as if it too were hiding in the dark.

She heard the snick of claws as the Onlar unsheathed them, and saw the dullest of gleams, red in the eerie light.

She remembered turning with Tark to find a blaze of white hair and two green almost-flames where eyes should be, a creature, its voice shrieking, endlessly, so close to her face that she could smell its foul breath. The image burned in her memory like the desert moonlight. She remembered Tark's arm around her, trying to drag her back, and then the creature's claws had flicked out toward her face and she remembered nothing more.

Jossey squeezed her eyes shut, tried to clear her mind. *Now. You are here now. Not there.*

When she opened them at last, the creature had inched forward. It stood still, intently, as if studying the group. As she watched, it began to follow them.

She carefully – very carefully – released the railing with slippery hands and dropped to her knees, crawling forward until she was well clear of the edge.

* * *

By the time anyone else seemed to realize it was there, the Onlar was close to the head of the group.

Then someone turned and saw it, full in the face, and there were screams and sounds Jossey had never before heard from human beings as people clawed at each other, trying to get away.

Safety lights fell to the ground, scattered on the tunnel floor, rolling and sending running shadows flying across the blood-colored walls as people tried to hide in the darkness.

The creature slashed at the crowd with its claws, but it was staggering, pulling itself forward on what Jossey thought was a broken leg, toward the person yelling for them all to stop.

Toward Perkins.

Jossey broke into a sprint, running to the cover of the tunnel wall.

She inched her way along the stone, knife gripped in her fist, heart beating in her throat. It wasn't much of a blade, compared to what Patrol carried – her father had given it to her, and Mother hadn't approved of weapons, even after Tark – but it was something. At most, she thought, the others might have wrenches on them.

She didn't know what even her knife could do against one of the creatures, not after the stories she'd heard. Their bite was deadly, it was common knowledge; no one bitten had ever survived it. As for those They took with them...

Sometimes they only find bones.

She willed herself to move, keep going forward, but her feet felt frozen to the ground.

The creature's eyes were lit a brilliant green now, like two almost-flames in its face. It was panting, its blazing eyes fixed on Perkins, pointing at him with claws the length of a man's forearm. Its hair was matted and stuck out at odd angles.

She could see no face, just eyes.

Perkins turned and saw the creature.

The creature hissed and pulled itself forward.

Perkins backed up against the guardrail. His face was a horrible shade of gray as he shouted for help, fumbling in his bag.

From one of the dark corners of the tunnel, some brave crew

member threw a rock at the creature; it struck it in the back and the creature let out an enraged howl, but it kept stumbling toward Perkins, leg dragging along the ground.

Perkins shouted for help, again, desperately.

Jossey could see Sally in the shadows, her eyes shut, shaking as she pressed her hands over her ears.

The safety lights glowed softly, dotting the tunnel floor like a galaxy of blood-red stars. A part of Jossey noted that in another situation, they might be beautiful.

In that moment, something occurred to her.

She made her way to her abandoned pack and dropped to the ground, wincing as she hit her sore knee.

She tore open the bag and fumbled through its contents. The rough ground bit further into her knees and she ignored the pain, rifling through as fast as she could.

Did I leave it on the transport?

She let go of the knife, which hit the floor with a clattering sound, and dug in with both arms.

At the noise, the creature whipped around, blazing eyes trained directly on her.

Jossey's breathing caught and she forced herself to stay calm as the creature looked back and forth slowly between her and Perkins.

Where is it where is it where–

She had a horrifying mental image of the little metal tube rolling down the aisle of the transport, and realized she didn't know if she'd gotten everything back.

The interior of her duffel was a mess of unidentifiable objects, sharp and dull and different materials, all jumbled together in darkness.

And she might have about three seconds before –

The creature snarled, blazing eyes locked on her.

Jossey's fingers closed around a long metal object. She yanked it triumphantly out of the bag.

A utensils holder.

Out of the corner of her eye, she saw Caspar and a man from her crew brandishing stretcher poles. They shouted at the creature. She didn't know what good the poles could do.

Why weren't we armed? she thought furiously to herself.

The Onlar ignored them, focusing back on Jossey.

She stared it straight in the eyes as she scrabbled frantically in the endless bag with her arm, fingers half-numb and icy cold.

The creature made a gurgling sound and lurched in her direction.

Then, suddenly, her hand found the raised printing she sought.

She ripped the tube out of the bag, twisted off the top and pressed the button.

With a *pssssssst* and a loud crackle, the emergency flare shot out gleaming pinkish-red sparks and then hissed, blazing bright, so bright it was almost as if it were suddenly daylight underground.

They can see you in the dark, she thought. *But what about in the light?*

The creature howled at the brightness, throwing an arm up in front of its eyes. Staggering, it turned and lunged in Perkins' direction, claws extended. Perkins didn't move, frozen to the guardrail.

Jossey looked away from the light and hurled the flare at the creature.

The creature dragged itself toward Perkins, still covering its eyes, swiping viciously ahead of itself into open space with enormous jagged claws. What sounded like gargling came from its throat.

Perkins still didn't move. Jossey, still half-blinded by the light, scooped up the knife and broke into a sprint, shouting for Perkins to run.

The creature swung around, claws extended toward her face.

7

JOSSEY HADN'T EXPECTED SUCH QUICK MOVEMENT. SHE SLID TO the ground as she dodged underneath the claws and found herself looking straight into a pair of green almost-flames for the second time in her life.

The creature hissed, barely balancing with its bad leg, and stabbed downward with its enormous claws. She jerked her whole body to the side, felt them jab into the ground beside her. She could hear Perkins' horrified voice, Caspar shouting, others she didn't know.

She scrabbled for the flare, felt it sear into her hand as she wrapped her fingers around it, just below the flame.

Then she thrust it upward toward the creature's face as it leapt on her.

8

EVERYTHING WAS DARK.

Jossey wasn't sure she was still breathing.

Everything was dark, and heavy, and she felt as if one of the tunnels had collapsed on her. Something was warm, all over her hands and her arms, and she wondered if maybe it was her blanket overheating again. She tried to shake her head, but found she couldn't move.

Something smelled terrible, rank. Something very close. She could feel it filling up her nostrils. From somewhere high above came the murmur of voices.

She tried to speak, but she couldn't find the air. Her chest felt as if someone were standing on it.

In the darkness, she felt a slight breeze, drifting across her left hand. Just barely. Desperate, she tried to move her fingers.

The voices above her stopped. She tried harder. One finger felt half-broken.

She gritted her teeth and forced it to move.

There was a muffled exclamation from above, and then the weight was being pulled off her, and with a sharp pain in her chest and a gasping rush of cool air to her lungs she could breathe again.

She lay there for a moment, choking, inhaling dust, then rolled over and groaned as pain seeped through her body. Wherever she was, it was very dark, with an odd flickering in the air. She wasn't home, she thought.

The ground beneath her was rocky, gritty. It smelled of dirt and that rank odor. Next to her hand, the remains of a flare smoldered on the ground, bits of hot ash scattered and glowing gently.

She rolled onto her back again and blinked up at the half-familiar faces staring down at her, four images resolving into two and then blurring again. Her head was killing her. "What's going on? Who are you?"

The younger man's brow furrowed. She didn't think she recognized him. The older one was white as a sheet. He looked more familiar, if blurry. Percy? Patrick? She could not remember.

She turned her head to the right and jumped, leaping backward with a shriek.

An Onlar was lying facedown next to her, very definitely not breathing. Jossey pushed herself to a sitting position, inching away from the Onlar, and cradled her head in her left hand as the light from the flare wavered in and out, pulsing unpleasantly in the background.

She realized she was gripping a knife in her right hand. The blade and her arms and torso were covered in blood.

She leaned over and was violently sick on the stone.

The reddish light from the flare was still flickering over the tunnel walls as she tried to collect herself. Why was one of the creatures from the aboveground – She tried to remember. Her head throbbed where she had struck it against the tunnel floor.

"You saved us," the older man said quietly. Perkins, she thought she remembered. She opened half an eye, wincing, and looked up at him. "Who are you?" she repeated.

"Don't you remember?" The younger one.

His uniform said SOLAR CREW 35. Not her crew, then. Sharp silver eyes probed her face. "The accident? The transport?" he said urgently. "How many fingers am I holding up?"

At the word "transport," memories came flooding back, along with a surge of adrenaline that made Jossey grip the knife so hard she thought the handgrip would cut her palm.

She wobbled as she scrambled to her feet, ignoring his question, and felt herself pitch sideways. The two men grabbed her shoulders and forced her to sit.

"Don't move," the older one, Perkins, said. "We think you took a nasty hit to the head." He cleared his throat. "Caspar and I – " He glanced at the younger man.

Caspar. That's right.

"Where are the others?" she demanded. "What happened? Did Patrol – "

Perkins gestured further down the tunnel, where the red light dissolved into blackness.

Caspar spoke up. "They ran when the thing attacked you." He cleared his throat. "We, ah – " He looked away.

"We thought you hadn't made it," Perkins said gruffly. "We told them to wait further down so they wouldn't...have to see anything further."

She closed her eyes for a moment, trying to process it all.

"Don't!" Caspar's voice was sharp. She blinked, startled, and tried to focus on his features. It made her dizzy.

"Don't close your eyes," he said more gently.

"I – "

"We have to get you on the stretcher. Patrol doesn't seem to be coming."

"The driver?" she asked weakly.

He looked sober. "That" – he gestured to the Onlar – "got to him on its way up to Perkins." He frowned. "Usually they don't bother to chase us this far down without larger numbers."

"Why?" She tried to keep her vision steady, gripping her head in her left hand. *Concussion*, she thought. Her right hand still wouldn't let go of the knife. Her left felt strangely numb, detached, although she knew she had probably burned it badly.

She glanced at it. It was white, as if she had dipped it in chalk. Second-degree, she estimated, maybe third.

"Where's the group?" she asked a second time.

"You need a doctor," Caspar said, frowning.

Perkins got to his feet. "I can go get the stretcher. You okay to move?"

Jossey gestured in assent, but she was struggling to sit straight. "Do I have to?"

Perkins picked up what looked like an improvised weapon and walked off. Caspar stayed, watching her face.

"We're not far from the first checkpoint," he said. "We can call Patrol from there. You did a good job getting us this far, Jossey."

"What checkpoint?"

"Patrol has them in the tunnels."

"They do?"

"I don't remember much from my apprenticeship, but I remember the endless check-ins." He gave half a smile. "It should be around here somewhere."

"Huh," Jossey said distractedly. She stared at the knife in her hand. *I should clean this,* she thought. "The poor driver. I wonder–"

Caspar reached out for the knife. Her grip tightened even further.

"Jossey."

She shook her head. "I can't." Her wrist was trembling.

"It's okay. It happens to many of us." He smiled ruefully. "It happened to me."

"You?" Her hands were starting to shake now from the adrenaline. And she could feel the searing pain of the burn from where she had held onto the flare.

"When I was an apprentice. I was fifteen, maybe sixteen. When we were first attacked in the tunnels, I...might have hidden behind a rock spire. The commander had to pry the knife out of my hand." He cracked a grin. "I think that's the only Patrol-related injury I have."

She laughed shakily and focused. Her wrist relaxed, just barely.

With a clatter, the knife fell to the ground, making her jump.

Caspar picked up the weapon, glanced at it, then casually wiped it on his uniform. Jossey looked away, horrified.

"Sorry," he muttered. "Habit."

They both looked up as footsteps approached.

It was Perkins. With him was Liam, the silent blond giant from her crew. The stretcher looked like a toy in his arms.

Some people from the group had followed, keeping well back as they eyed the dead Onlar on the tunnel floor. Sally was at the front. Her hands flew to her mouth as she saw the creature.

She broke from the group and ran to Jossey's side.

"I'm so sorry," she cried.

"Keep your voice down!" Perkins hissed.

The young woman's gaze flew to her uncle, stricken. In a whisper, she continued. "This is all my fault. If I hadn't screamed – "

Jossey shook her head, instantly regretting it as pain lanced through her skull. She gripped her forehead in her hands. "Please don't," she managed.

Sally wiped at her face and took a step back. "You saved our lives," she said, gingerly reaching out and touching Jossey's shoulder, flinching when Jossey winced in pain.

Perkins gently drew his niece away. She wept into his shoulder.

Others weren't much better off, Jossey saw. One was supported by his neighbors, face white as he eyed the dead Onlar. He was injured, probably while running. His crew members helped him onto a makeshift second stretcher. Several people looked to be in shock.

"Get everyone water," she muttered to Perkins. To her surprise, he did as she asked without complaint.

Caspar took one of the canteens, slit it open with the knife. Jossey tried to protest, but he gave her a look that silenced her.

"Put your hand in this," he said.

"What?"

"Just do it."

She put her burned hand into the half-canteen. It was full of cool water. Her hand was still shaking, but she focused on keeping it still.

"This is all the water we can spare," Caspar told her. "But you need to cool that off."

"Are you a doctor too?" Jossey half-joked.

He grinned. "Just got into too many adventures as a kid."

"You probably won't feel that burn fully for a while," he added. "Adrenaline is a beautiful thing."

Liam placed the stretcher on the ground next to Jossey. "Thank you," he said. His normally stonelike expression cracked into a smile. She smiled back.

"Here," Caspar said, glancing at Liam. He stood up and moved aside. "Be careful with your head."

"I'm fine," Jossey muttered. She gingerly climbed onto the stretcher, trying not to spill the water or move her head too quickly. She stared at the ceiling as they slipped someone's bundled emergency blanket under her head, and tried not to look as the Onlar was unceremoniously shoved to the side of the tunnel.

The creature's arm slid down its body, and the claws hit the floor with a clicking sound that made Jossey flinch and close her eyes against the wave of fear that threatened to overwhelm her.

Caspar's voice said, "Don't sleep!"

She opened her eyes and stared resolutely at the ceiling. "I'm not."

"Good." He turned to Liam. "Let's go. Carefully."

Suddenly he sounded much older; there was something dark to his tone.

Jossey wanted to look at him, see what had changed, but she found she felt less sick if she simply looked up.

9

THE REMAINDER OF THE GROUP WAS WAITING FOR THEM AS THEY neared the curve in the tunnel. Jossey tried to smile as people murmured their thanks. An Onlar attack wasn't unheard of against Patrol – was fairly common – but the last attack on a transport had been before Jossey had been born.

None of these people had been prepared for this, she thought.

None, she suspected, but Caspar. He seemed exceptionally calm, nothing like the terrified Patrol apprentice he said he had once been. And maybe Liam, whose granite-like back forged ahead into the gloom. She was glad they were the ones carrying her. The rest of the group clustered together like tunnel bats, jumping at every sound.

They made their slow way ever downward.

Jossey faded in and out of awareness, focusing on keeping her eyes open, pinching herself when necessary. Her hand was beginning to burn.

Really burn. Like she had dipped it in fire.

She tried to think about something else, and her mind drifted to Tark.

If he were in this situation, she thought, he'd probably be having a great time. Onlar, the dark, a broken-down transport...that kind of thing was almost all he and his best friend Gavin used to talk about. They used to play Patrol all the time. Sometimes they would take her with them, though not into the outer tunnels.

She half-smiled.

Tark had never been afraid of the dark, of the tunnels and the stories their teachers told, even as a child, she remembered. He'd just laughed whenever the teachers tried to scare them into staying within the City bounds. Every year the speech was the same.

She remembered the last one she'd heard with Tark, before he'd moved on to middle school.

"The Onlar are vicious killers," Teacher Peterson had told them, striding dramatically across the front of the primary school's classroom, as if his words were not frightening enough. He was a tall, angular man, with a face like a horse, as Mother had said.

Eight-year-old Jossey did not know what a horse was, but she thought it must be scary, like Teacher Peterson.

"There are three levels to this City," Peterson nearly shouted, spittle flying from his mouth. "The inner level is usually safe. The outer level you may only enter *with* your parents, or an adult. And you must never, ever go outside the main gates without Patrol. Do you understand?"

Jossey knew that Tark and Gavin snuck outside the gates on a regular basis when Patrol wasn't looking. Patrol couldn't be everywhere, and often the boys weren't missed for several hours. When she'd caught on, they'd bribed her with sugar gems and the promise of a tunnel adventure to keep her quiet.

Onlar, Peterson went on, was a word that meant "They" or "Them" in the Old Language. Creatures of the aboveground.

They hid during the day. But at night...

Jossey was in her third year of primary school, and she'd heard all of this before, but some of the others clearly hadn't. Little Benny Kingman looked petrified, and clutched his sister's hand under their adjoined desks.

Tark, though, seemed less than impressed. He yawned from the back of the classroom, earning giggles from Gavin and a withering glare from Teacher Peterson.

"Do you know WHY you must never go into the tunnels, Tark?"

Tark sat up straighter, but looked evenly at the teacher. "Because the Onlar might take you."

"That's right," Peterson snarled.

Tark looked unfazed. "I've heard Patrol only finds bones," he said, grinning.

Gavin raised his hand. Peterson pointedly ignored him.

"Stand in the corner, Tark," Peterson said. "This is no laughing matter."

Tark shrugged and wandered over to the corner.

Jossey watched him go, wide-eyed. The class was almost over. If he got in trouble again, Father might not let either of them go on the Engineering trip he'd promised them.

Peterson returned to the front of the classroom, looking disdainfully at the motley group of children. They shuffled their feet under his gaze.

He flicked the switch on a projector, and the terrifying features of an Onlar filled the screen, far too close-up for Jossey's liking. Beside Jossey, Benny whimpered.

"THIS is an Onlar," Peterson announced unnecessarily.

Jossey pretended to be brave, looking coolly at the screen while secretly hoping the lights in the inner tunnels wouldn't flicker on the way home.

"Beyond the City gates, the tunnels are off-limits except by special permission, as I said," Peterson continued. "Once you are adults, if you are Engineers, you may take shuttles to the surface. These shuttles are specially designed to – "

Gavin's hand was now fluttering. Peterson sighed and turned from the screen. "Yes, Gavin?"

"What if we took swords with us? Or – or – " He dissolved into giggles.

Tark cracked up. "Yeah, what about if we dressed like Onlar and – "

"Out of my class. Out!" Peterson roared. "Demoted for the day!" Muttering under his breath, Peterson stalked over to his desk.

Tark and Gavin whooped and raced out of the classroom, laughter trailing behind them.

The other children were stock-still, eyes enormous, watching Peterson scribble something into his notebook. Demoted for the day was a severe punishment – it meant no field trip points. And they desperately wanted to go to the City's chocolate-processing plant on Friday. Jossey squirmed, hoping that being Tark's sister wouldn't put her spot in danger.

There were slight whispers as Peterson got up again, but the class fell dead silent as the teacher turned and looked at them. Jossey shrank in her chair.

"Anyone else?" Peterson demanded.

Chocolate field trip or no, Jossey timidly raised her hand.

Something had been puzzling her for weeks. Tark's answers hadn't been sufficient, and were, she suspected, probably made-up.

She gulped as Peterson glared down his narrow nose at her.

"Teacher P-Peterson," she half-squeaked, "how do the Onlar – that is, how do they survive aboveground if they don't have uniforms like us?"

Peterson's face was like stone.

"They hide in the canyons," he said finally. "There are caves up there. And even so, the Onlar are adapted to the heat."

She thought for a moment. Caves made sense. But –

"What does ad-adapted mean?"

Before Peterson could respond, the class bell had rung, and Jossey's question had gone unanswered.

Now, Jossey watched the tunnel ceiling above her, half hearing Caspar and Perkins' low conversation.

"They'd have to examine the body," Caspar said.

Jossey's ears perked up. Patrol would probably be interested – they'd want to know how and why one of the Onlar had managed to get past the defenses at the tunnel entrances and attack a transport. Those were normally heavily secured – the transports went through a gate at the surface before picking up passengers, who took an access tunnel directly from the solar farm to the transport stop.

Her thoughts went to the second transport, the one that was supposed to have come in behind them.

There was always a final backup shuttle, in case anyone had to stay for any reason at the solar plant. Otherwise, they'd be stuck up there for the night, sealed into the metal box. She'd had to do that once or twice.

It had been a truly awful experience – she hadn't slept a wink, every shadow moving under the moonlight a potential threat, maybe an Onlar coming to attack their solar plant. She'd sat by the window, staring off into the moonlit desert landscape. Once, she'd thought she'd seen a pair of green eyes staring back at her from a cliff.

A desert cat, her then-crew-leader had guessed. She'd hoped so.

What if the transport –

"What – " Her mouth was dry, and the word came out as a croak. Caspar glanced down at her.

She tried again, cleared her throat. "What happened to the other transport? The night one?"

Caspar shook his head. "Don't think about it." He glanced over at Perkins. "Doing all right?"

The answer was a grunt.

"The Patrol box is somewhere up here," Caspar said to Liam. "Let's slow down a bit."

"Would Patrol even come get us, do you think?" Jossey said softly, hoping the rest of the group wouldn't overhear. She knew that after nightfall the Council might refuse to send Patrol up into the tunnels. It was too dangerous. And escorting an entire group of unarmed civilians...

"My uncle is on the Council," she added hopefully.

"Is he?" Caspar glanced down at her.

"Yes. Pyotr Sokol. He's – "

" – Minister of Intelligence," Caspar said. "Yes, I know who he is." He smiled a little. "I think everyone does."

"Well then maybe – " she said hesitantly.

Liam cut her off. "I see something up ahead."

Caspar slowed down, peered into the dimness. Jossey couldn't see anything. But Caspar whistled. "There it is."

10

A BOX, ABOUT THE SIZE OF JOSSEY'S HAND, GLOWED A FAINT turquoise in the tunnel wall, barely illuminating the rock around it. Caspar grinned. He and Liam gently lowered the stretcher to the ground.

Caspar went up to the glowing box. "Let's see if I can remember how to do this," he muttered.

He reached out and put his hand on the box. It began to glow more brightly. A strip of red appeared around the edge.

"Is it working?" Perkins asked.

"Hold on." Caspar frowned. He punched a couple of buttons. "This one's an older model." Something lit up, flickered, then faded. He groaned. "I can't remember the code."

"Great," Perkins grumbled.

Jossey watched from the ground, curious. She'd been in the tunnels a few times, mostly when Tark had taken her exploring, but had never seen one of these. Maybe Patrol didn't have them so close to the City.

Caspar looked lost in thought for a moment, then his silver eyes lit up and he pressed another sequence of buttons.

A green strip appeared around the edge, and the box crackled loudly.

"Identify yourself." The tinny voice resounded around the tunnel.

Caspar quickly pressed another button. The volume dropped.

He leaned in toward the box. "Level P-45, quadrant four." His voice was calm, assured. "I'm an Engineer with solar crew 35."

P-45? Jossey squinted, her head pounding.

The other crew members silently gathered around, watching.

"What is your situation?" The voice was young. Jossey guessed a new recruit.

Caspar glanced at the rest of them.

"We are a transport party, two solar crews, total about thirty people. We've been attacked, one Onlar down, one driver down, several injured. We need immediate help," he said.

"Stand by."

There was a click. A few seconds of silence.

There was a second click, a faint rattling sound.

Then the tinny voice spoke again. It was calm, measured.

As if the person on the other end were reading from a script.

"We regret to hear of your situation, Engineer, but the Gates have been closed."

"I understand that, but – "

"You are advised to remain where you are," the tinny voice continued. "Take shelter. At first light Patrol units can be sent to the surface and evacuate you along the way."

Caspar stared at the box.

It crackled, and went silent.

Someone choked. Jossey turned but couldn't see who. Their safety lights had been on for over two hours, and were beginning to dim.

She reached up and switched hers off; they might need them later. She watched others silently do the same.

Liam's jaw tightened, and he stepped forward as if he wanted to physically reach the person on the other side of the box. Perkins put a warning hand on his shoulder.

"Don't," Perkins rumbled.

The Patrol dispatcher on the other side of the box had sounded like he was rattling off the day's menu or announcing an evacuation drill – "Citizens, remain calm," that type of thing – rather than giving them what was essentially a death sentence.

Jossey looked at her safety gauge. 10:02 PM. Sunrise should be around 5:00 AM.

Seven more hours in the dark, most likely. Enough water for about four hours.

No one moved for a long moment.

Jossey made to get up, but found she could not.

She sank back to the ground, hand over her face. Perkins gruffly handed her his water canteen, and she drank from it gratefully. It wasn't quite as hot down here, but she'd calculated the water rations. They'd used some to treat the injured, and she'd used up all of her own after fighting the Onlar. Her burned hand was currently dipped in her ration.

Seven hours, she thought again. She looked up at Caspar, feeling dizzy.

Perkins exploded before anyone else could.

"You can't do that to an entire transport!" Perkins yelled. "Do you hear me? We're Citizens! We pay your wages!"

The tinny voice did not react. The box still glowed a faint green, which meant it was connected.

Caspar held up a hand.

Toward the box, he said calmly, "We do not have enough

51

water, even without considering the Onlar. Do you understand me?"

The voice repeated, firmly, "The gates are closed."

Jossey tried again to get to her feet, tried not to drop the water container. Her hand was nearly screaming in pain.

"Our team leader is injured," Caspar said, seeing her trying to stand. He shook his head at her, frowning. "We cannot wait for rescue. Do you – "

"Again, I am sorry, but – "

The voice did not sound particularly sorry.

Caspar's face stilled. "Give me your superior," he said slowly.

His tone – Jossey looked up sharply at him. There was something about it, something she had not heard before.

As if he expected unquestioning obedience. His long silver eyes were narrowed.

She felt a sudden chill.

He started to type in a code.

"You have no override authority – " the box squawked.

"There is a Council family member in this crew," Caspar said coldly. "Maybe you are familiar with Pyotr Sokol."

There was a pause. A slight crackle.

Then a different voice, crisper. "Solar crew 35? Your first name for our records?"

"Caspar."

Silence.

"I'm very sorry for the confusion. We can immediately send a transport retrieval team." The voice was crisp, polite. And afraid, Jossey thought.

She'd never considered her family connections to be important. Her father hadn't wanted anything to do with the Council, had just wanted to be an ordinary Engineer. She had always found it distasteful that being the niece of Pyotr Sokol would get her special privileges, though Tark had had no such reservations.

She'd always mumbled her last name when called upon in Engineering school, had always ignored the glances and whispers, had made sure she'd earned her crew leader position.

But if this would save them, she was all for it.

"Engineer, please stay with the com box. And stay alert. There may be more Onlar. The retrieval team should arrive within thirty minutes."

"Thank you."

A click, then silence in the tunnel.

Perkins almost clapped, but restrained himself, looking around at the black entrance to the tunnel above them.

Caspar sighed and came back over to the stretcher, crouching beside Jossey. She smiled at him. "Thanks," she whispered. "I don't know what P-45 means, but I'm glad you remembered it."

"It's a standard check-in number. It's on the box." He pointed to the glowing tiny symbols at the base. "It gives them your location." He smiled ruefully. "It's pretty much the only thing I remember. And, of course, how to sound authoritative." He grinned.

She laughed, flinching as her headache worsened. "You're good at that."

"Sorry to interrupt." Perkins was standing there. "Hadn't we better set up a perimeter?"

Caspar snapped to full attention. "Yes. Right." He glanced down at Jossey. "Excuse me."

They walked off. Jossey rolled onto her side, making herself as uncomfortable as possible, so she wouldn't sleep.

She looked down at her uniform, at the Onlar's blood everywhere. She felt itchy all of a sudden, felt the need to dunk herself in a tank of water. If only that were allowed down in the City.

Instead, she covered herself with a thin blanket Sally had brought her from someone's bag, trying not to think about her ruined uniform.

Her vision was a little better now, but she still saw stars if she moved too quickly. Her hand was aching. She wasn't sure which was worse.

Perkins and Caspar's voices approached again. She turned carefully to see that the group was now two circles, the inner one women and older men, the outer one younger men. Liam, who was the biggest of the group, was positioned closest to the upper tunnel exit.

"Good," murmured Jossey.

She felt clammy all of a sudden as Caspar and Perkins sat down next to her. Something felt wrong.

"I don't feel – "

Caspar took one look at her face, grabbed the nearest canteen, and shoved it into her hand. "Drink," he ordered.

"I need a doctor," Jossey mumbled, pushing it away. "That's someone else's water."

"It's my water. Drink it." He looked frantic. "Perkins – "

Perkins looked back and forth between them. "Sally!" he barked.

His niece hurried over.

"Keep her awake. Tell her stories. Poke her in the shoulder. Anything. We have to keep watch," Perkins said.

"Make her drink the water," Caspar added.

Jossey sighed and tried to drink. She choked, took another sip, tried not to spill any.

Sally looked apprehensive, but sat down next to Jossey. "Tell me about – your childhood," she said cheerily.

Caspar looked concerned, but satisfied. He and Perkins walked farther off and began to converse in low tones.

Jossey groaned. The last thing she wanted to do was to talk

about her childhood. But Perkins had a point. She took another swig of the water and coughed.

"What do you want to know?"

Sally smiled, a little shyly. "Did you ever go tunnel exploring?"

Jossey laughed. "Will you tell on me?"

Sally was trying not to laugh aloud as Jossey told her the story of the time Tark had snuck an entire live tunnel bat family into their living quarters and hid them in his room for two days before Mother discovered them.

Jossey smiled too. She'd forgotten some of these silly stories, had purposely buried them.

She was grateful to Caspar for the extra water, though she felt guilty as he sat on the ground, looking exhausted.

He looked over, and she looked away from him awkwardly before taking another swig of the water.

Maybe she'd try to save some for him.

She realized it was hard to see him, even with her eyes adjusted to the dimness. With a shock, she realized that it was hard to see, period.

Was it her concussion? she wondered, frantic.

Then she realized that it was the safety lights.

They were fading.

No one seemed to have noticed. But with those off, they'd probably be sitting ducks...again. The Onlar could move silently, on padded feet, even when injured. Even in numbers, she'd heard.

"Caspar," she croaked. "Perkins."

They didn't seem to hear. Sally looked at her, frowning.

She gestured for the junior Engineer to go get them.

They got to their feet in an instant as Sally came running,

looking over at Jossey with alarm. Jossey beckoned to them with her good hand, barely able to raise her head off the makeshift pillow.

Caspar got there first, dropping to a crouch. He shoved dark strands of hair out of his face, concerned silver-grey eyes peering into hers. "Are you all right?"

"The lights," she croaked. "They're going out."

She gestured to Perkins. "We need to turn them off. All but the outer circle. Patrol gave us half an hour. It's been ten minutes. At this rate, we might have ten minutes of solid darkness if we don't turn some off."

The Onlar had attacked in maybe three minutes.

"I can tell them." Sally stood up.

She disappeared into the circle.

One by one, the lights in the center faded to blackness.

Caspar got to his feet. "Everyone needs a swig of water. And we should enforce absolute silence. Without enough light – "

He didn't have to complete the sentence.

"I've got the outer circle," he said to Perkins. Then he looked down at Jossey. "And you – "

She smiled wanly. "I'm closest to the bottom of the circle. They'll probably come from above."

He looked soberly at her. "Just don't make any noise."

She handed him the water. "Drink."

"No."

"I'm in charge."

Something like a smile passed over his face.

"You're out of commission," was all he said.

Before she could say anything else, he disappeared into the dimness, leaving her with the water.

She lay there, waiting, as her hand continued to burn and the lights faded even further. Some of them began to flicker.

The group was completely silent as one, then the next, vanished into blackness.

It had been forty minutes since they'd called for rescue when the final one went out.

11

To the group's credit, they stayed quiet.

She could hear people scooting closer to one another in the darkness, but no screaming. No speaking.

She could hear the occasional semi-frantic breath, the occasional low murmur.

But for those, she thought, she could almost be in a tunnel in darkness all alone, just her and the heat.

The blackness was absolute. Somewhere below she could hear tunnelsong, but it was fading, probably as the temperature gradient stabilized and the tunnels began to cool. She had a faint memory of reading about this process in a textbook. It was the only diagram she'd ever seen of the pit.

Behind the walls, deep in, she could hear the rush of the underground river. They were closer to the City than she'd realized, she thought.

But still not close enough.

She wondered if her uncle knew she was out here. He would have to, she imagined – he was Minister of Intelligence. If so –

A sound came from somewhere in the tunnel. A faint hissing.

She jumped, alarmed, trying to pinpoint where it was coming from.

She heard gasps from around her, muffled exclamations. Against orders, lights flared, like a dozen floating tiny stars in the darkness.

The sound was audible over the river. She couldn't identify it.

Ignoring the pain in her head, she sat up. She saw Caspar get to his feet, Liam as well.

Caspar murmured something, and Liam handed him Jossey's knife.

Jossey couldn't breathe. It was too hot, and the hissing was getting louder. The rest of the group jumped to their feet as one. Perkins stiffened, fumbling around as if for a weapon.

There was a sudden loud sound, and a reddish glow appeared. It threw into sharp relief a group of shadows clustered along the tunnel walls, as if waiting, directly behind her group.

12

JOSSEY CLAPPED HER HAND OVER HER MOUTH TO STOP FROM shrieking, staring at the shadows. She counted at least ten, twelve. Maybe more.

It was a long moment before her muddled brain caught up with her and she realized the shadows were just that. They were from her own group.

Shakily, she started to laugh, unable to stop herself.

The group looked at her wide-eyed, glancing back into the tunnel with terror on their faces.

Then, with a faint hiss, one of Patrol's ultra-quiet personnel shuttles came into view.

It stopped, bathing the group in its military-grade red headlights and illuminating the entire tunnel. Jossey blinked, half-blinded.

She was still half-laughing, and it quickly turned into hyperventilating as the shock of the evening started to catch up with her.

She couldn't unsee the shadows on the tunnel walls, black

against blood-red. She'd really thought –

She curled into a ball, turned away from the light.

"Jossey."

Caspar was standing over her. "Jossey!"

She hadn't heard him approach. She looked up at him, trying to calm down, trying to breathe normally.

"Patrol is here." He looked worried.

She tried to smile.

The shuttle pulled smoothly to the side of the tunnel. All silent, of course. Patrol had top-of-the-line technology, second to almost nothing in the City. The hissing came from its propulsion system, Jossey guessed. It was a newer model, designed to transport upward of forty people, and had a driver's pod at each end so it didn't have to turn around in the tunnels. Its silvery panels could be switched to blackest black in an instant.

A nearly-inaudible click, and the first side panel opened.

Her breathing slowed as she watched them exit the vehicle.

The six men all wore dark clothing, standard-issue: chest- and leg-plates and shoulder armor with looser coverings for their limbs, and masks that concealed the top two-thirds of their faces. Some had arm guards as well.

They could see her, she thought, but she couldn't see them. She shivered.

They did not acknowledge the group. They waited silently, hands resting casually on their swords. Each agent was tall, broad-shouldered.

In their hands, the weapons almost seemed fragile. She knew Patrol's swords were forged specifically by Council-appointed smiths; civilians could face imprisonment or worse if found in possession of them.

Tark had always been fascinated by them. But once, he'd come back to their living quarters, pale and shaking. He'd gone

61

straight past Jossey and locked himself in his room. She thought she'd heard him crying.

When she'd gotten him to come out at last, he'd put on a brave face, talking about how cool the Patrol swords were and how much he wanted one.

"They're so cool. They can slice through an Onlar," was all he would say.

Now she eyed the agents warily. She'd never felt comfortable around most of them. Only –

Suddenly, the agents straightened, went very still, as a seventh man stepped out of the vehicle.

He carried his sword on his back, almost like an afterthought, and his commander's uniform was ridged with extra strips of armor along his back and enormous shoulders. His mask concealed everything but his mouth.

He dwarfed his men by a good half-foot.

"The Tiger," muttered someone in awe. Jossey stared.

Whereas the others moved with crisp efficiency, he gave the impression of darkness, of barely-restrained power. He strode over to his men, who snapped to attention.

With no more than a gesture and a few words that Jossey couldn't quite hear, the agents fanned out immediately, turning on their red night-lamps, two of them heading toward the upper end of the tunnel.

Two medics appeared from the shuttle, supplies in tow.

The commander turned and surveyed the tunnel, the cluster of exhausted men and women sitting closely in rings, a few of their safety lights barely illuminated. They watched him silently. He waved one of his medics toward them.

Caspar stood next to Jossey's stretcher, and in a clear voice that carried, he said, "We need medical attention."

The Tiger's blank mask turned toward the sound. The

commander held up a hand to the Patrol agent next to him, who had been speaking.

Jossey was still staring at the man as his masked gaze fell on her.

13

THE COMMANDER'S ENTIRE BODY SEEMED TO FREEZE.

He gestured urgently to one of his men, then strode over to the stretchers, half-glancing at the injured man on the other one before stopping before Jossey's.

TSKOULIS, his name badge said.

Not bothering to acknowledge Caspar or Perkins, the Tiger crouched beside her and tore off his mask, wavy dark hair falling forward with it. His handsome, tanned face was flushed, frowning, dark eyes narrowed as he focused on her.

"Jossey? What are you doing here?" he demanded.

She smiled wanly at him. "Hello, Gavin."

Commander Gavin Tskoulis, Tark's childhood best friend, paled a little as he took in her damaged hand, the blood all over her uniform.

"Medic!" he shouted.

The closest medic was working on another patient. His head shot up at the commander's voice.

"Now! Leave him! Priority one!"

Priority one was for people who were dying.

Jossey tried to laugh, tell him he was being overly dramatic, but he looked stricken.

"What happened to you?" he asked.

"It's not my blood," she mumbled.

Perkins was staring openmouthed at the man. The Tiger's reputation preceded him, thought Jossey.

"She killed the Onlar," Caspar said. He was watching them, arms crossed, silver eyes cool.

The Tiger tore his attention away from Jossey, looking up at the newcomer, then straightened, eyes unreadable. "Who are you?"

"Caspar Savaş. Solar Engineer with Crew 35. I'm the one who called Patrol."

The Tiger reached out and shook his hand. "Commander Gavin Tskoulis. What happened? We got a priority call, but they didn't tell me – " He trailed off, expression dark.

The medic arrived and laid out his supplies. "Excuse me, sir," he said to the Patrol commander, who moved aside, glancing down at Jossey.

"She saved all of us," Caspar said to Gavin. "Took a direct hit from the Onlar." He gestured to the occupant of the other stretcher. "It's a good thing you brought medics."

Perkins stepped forward. "We're very grateful for your help, Commander, sir."

The Tiger smiled, but his gaze was deadly serious. "How did this happen? The creature got past the upper gates?"

Perkins and Caspar explained quickly.

Jossey tried to listen as the medic worked on her.

The man shined a light into Jossey's eyes and made a noise that she knew well.

"It's not good, is it?" she asked quietly.

"We need to get you down to the City," the man said. "Did you touch the creature?"

"Yes."

"Anyone else?"

She gestured to Perkins and Caspar.

He pulled out a small misting bottle. "Close your eyes. Don't inhale."

She obeyed, trying not to breathe as little dots of cold vapor landed on her.

The medic moved quickly to Perkins and Caspar with the spray. The Onlar's bite could be fatal, but other vectors hadn't been fully ruled out. Exposure had to be contained.

Gavin was taking notes, frowning on a number of occasions.

"I think the driver tried to run it over," Jossey said. They all turned to her.

"I heard something loud before the transport showed up," she explained. "I think the creature hung on and was dragged." Tears came suddenly to her eyes, and she took a shuddering breath. "Why – "

She shut her mouth. She refused to cry.

Not in front of Gavin.

"Do you have extra water?" she croaked instead. It was so hot. She felt ill.

The medic handed her a canteen. She drank gratefully.

"Sir?" the medic said. Gavin turned.

"She needs immediate medical attention, sir. Moderate to severe burns, likely concussion. Possible infection from the creature's claws."

Before the commander could say anything, one of the other Patrol agents stepped up, handing him a small reporting stick. "Done, sir."

Tskoulis barely glanced at it. "All clear?"

"Yes, sir."

"Good. Load up. Quickly. Call for a cleanup unit." Tskoulis turned to Caspar. "Where's the body?"

Caspar gestured further up the tunnel. "We left it where it

was. Not sure how far. We – left the driver, too." He looked faintly ashamed. "We needed the stretcher."

"You did what needed to be done." Tskoulis turned and called to the others, "Move out!"

Patrol lined up the transport passengers and began loading them into the vehicle one by one. Jossey automatically began counting them off, just to make sure they weren't missing anyone.

"Don't worry," Tskoulis said. "We're taking it from here."

"It's my job," she said tersely.

"Your job is to heal."

She wanted so badly to close her eyes.

"Are you the one I spoke to?" Caspar asked Tskoulis suddenly. His long silver eyes were watchful. Jossey thought he seemed older again, but she couldn't put her finger on how.

She also realized he was nearly as tall as Gavin.

Tskoulis turned, looking surprised, and glanced at him. "That was dispatch."

"I'm not Patrol anymore, but tell them they need to be a little bit...kinder when essentially sentencing an entire group to death." Caspar's voice was cool.

Jossey started laughing. It wasn't funny. She didn't know why she was laughing. Maybe because she couldn't picture anyone standing up to Gavin. Except Tark.

She kept laughing.

Perkins, Caspar, and Gavin all glanced at her.

Her giggles weakened and trailed off. It was so hot down here.

She reached for her water. She could see her hand fumbling next to it, but she couldn't make contact, couldn't understand why she was seeing double.

As she drifted into unconsciousness, the last thing she heard was their raised voices.

14

Everything was too bright as she came to.

Sounds seemed magnified. She tried to shield her eyes, but her left arm wouldn't move. It seemed tied down. She felt woozy, the world spinning.

Somewhere Jossey heard voices, but couldn't make out the individual words.

Everything was so bright. It hurt.

She closed her eyes. Her pillow was so comfortable, but she wasn't lying down. Why wasn't she lying down?

Well, I'm alive, thank God.

She squinted as she opened her eyes again, and tried to focus. Her head was throbbing, but at least she could sort of see things in the middle distance if she tried.

To her right she noticed a curtain; she could see what she thought were nurses moving back and forth, just the bottoms of their scrubs and their shoes. Shapes. She blinked, trying harder to focus.

Everything was a whirl of sound and light. And smells. Sharp smells, like rubbing alcohol. She felt sick.

Her arm – she realized it was indeed tied down and attached

to an IV. A bag that said something unidentifiable hung from a hook near her bedside. Her left hand was wrapped in white bandaging.

"Nurse?" Her voice cracked, and she realized that her throat was sore.

No one came.

Maybe she would wait a moment. Maybe they were busy with others.

She sank back into her pillow and closed her eyes.

Maybe just for a moment, she thought.

15

———————

It was much dimmer when she awoke again, in an entirely different room. She fuzzily looked around. She guessed it was around eight in the evening, after sunset, because the votive lights around the hospital walls were lit a pretty orange and the dark brown wallpaper was activated.

Her thoughts felt a little clearer. She wondered how long she'd been out.

She heard a noise, and turned carefully.

Gavin was asleep in the chair next to her bed, a bedraggled set of hothouse flowers half falling off his lap. His handsome face looked tired, drawn, as if he'd been there for some time.

Jossey half-smiled. How many women in the City would be beyond thrilled to find *Commander Tskoulis* passed out in their hospital room, flowers in hand, waiting for them to awaken?

She almost laughed at the idea.

It was sweet of him. She just wished he wouldn't be so...so...

She sighed. She hadn't seen him in some time, not counting the tunnel. He was sporting a new scar on his arm, she noticed.

Even unconscious, Gavin was physically intimidating, with enormous arms and shoulders, and deeply tanned from his time up aboveground with Patrol. He wasn't much older than her, but he was more serious by far. Serious, and tall, and reserved, with a knockout smile that he deployed at will.

Mr. Celebrity, she thought, smiling wryly.

But asleep, his face seemed softer. He looked more like the young Gavin, who had once told her not to cry because her scar was a real warrior scar, and then threatened to fight a bully who'd made fun of her.

The kid had immediately backed down – Gavin had towered over him, even in eighth grade. No one had bothered Jossey after that.

The adult Gavin shifted in his sleep, mumbling something, and the flowers dipped dangerously toward the floor.

They were purple, her favorite color.

Like last time.

She squirmed with guilt and looked away, wondering when he would stop trying to save her. He'd always been Tark's friend, not hers. She'd just been the annoying little sister who'd tried to tag along on their tunnel adventuring.

Tark was gone, had been gone for fifteen years. Gavin had other responsibilities, like keeping the City safe. He probably could do without her, promise he'd made to Tark or no.

And his help made her feel guiltier each time, made her dislike herself more. It wasn't that she wasn't grateful, but everything he ever did for her reminded her that Tark was gone because of *her*.

Her idea to go aboveground, she thought. Her fault.

She sighed. No point in being upset. At least Gavin tried.

She turned to face him, rustling the uncomfortable hospital blankets as she tried to move with her left arm still heavily bandaged.

At the slight sound, the young commander jerked awake, mumbling something about Onlar.

He looked around, bleary-eyed, then his dark eyes came to rest on Jossey.

He jolted half out of his chair, barely catching the flowers in time.

"Jossey. You're awake." He rubbed a hand across his face.

Jossey smiled. "How long was I out?"

Gavin's dark eyes were shadowed. He reached over and quickly pressed the nurse call button. "Three days. I didn't know if you were – "

"Three days?!" She struggled to sit up.

He held out the flowers with one arm, jokingly pretended to push her back down with them. She sighed and sank back onto the pillow. He gathered the undamaged half of the bouquet and smiled, holding the flowers out to her.

"Sorry," he said, glancing back at the small pile of petals on the floor and flashing her *that* grin of his. "I didn't realize how tired I was. Best I could do."

Despite herself, she smiled.

She both hated and loved that about him: even when she was angry, even when she was afraid, Gavin Tskoulis could always make her laugh.

Like Tark.

Her smile stilled, and she glanced away from him.

Gavin's smile faded too. "Are you in pain?"

"No – I mean, yes, but – " She sighed, put a hand to her head. "Less than I'd imagined. I think the sleep helped. What did the doctor say?"

He glanced up, toward the corridor window. A nurse was heading toward the room. "Here comes someone."

She looked, then turned back to him. "Gavin, have *you* been here for three days?"

Before he could answer, the door opened.

The nurse came in, wheeling a tray.

Jossey glanced over at it, then closed her eyes and groaned.

Every time. Every time she ended up in the infirmary – and it was quite a lot, considering how relatively safe her job was – she had to drink a row of disgusting medicines, all various colors.

She eyed the tray with apprehension, but happily the nurse wheeled it into the corner and left it there.

Jossey sank back into the pillow, hoping the nurse would forget about it.

"How are you feeling?" the nurse asked, placing her hand on Jossey's forehead.

"Not great," Jossey admitted. "But whatever pain meds you gave me? Amazing." She looked over at her bandaged left hand. "I don't feel a thing."

The nurse laughed and glanced at Gavin. "And you, Commander? Anything I can get for you?"

Gavin flashed her a blinding grin. "Don't worry about me. I'm just here for moral support."

The nurse, who was probably all of fifty, blushed.

Jossey stopped herself from rolling her eyes.

"Your scans are normal," the nurse said to Jossey, her face pink. "But the doctor doesn't recommend you do this again."

Oh thank God. Jossey closed her eyes. She opened them again and looked at the nurse. "How long do I have to stay here?"

"The doctor said a few days, just to rest. And she said no solar crew for two weeks. Limited mental activity. It should give your burn some time to heal as well."

Jossey laughed. "I should fight Onlars more often."

The Patrol commander to her left shot her a look, which she pointedly ignored.

The nurse smiled. "Let us know if you need anything."

She walked over to the tray. Jossey flinched. Gavin looked amused.

"I do have a question, actually." Jossey pointed to her left hand. "How bad is it?"

73

The nurse was wheeling over the tray. "You had moderately severe second-degree burns," she said. "They may take some time to heal."

"Do you think it will likely scar?"

Gavin glanced at her. She avoided his gaze.

The nurse handed her the first of the colored drugs. "Drink."

"Tell me." She took the medicine from the woman, making a face.

"It's too early to say," the nurse said at last. "We've done everything we can. But you did well, Miss Sokol. If you are in pain, let us know." She gestured to the IV.

Jossey frowned and looked at her hand. It had been necessary. She didn't regret it. But if it scarred, too –

She tried to smile. "Can I get a video screen?"

"Not for a while." The nurse smiled apologetically.

Jossey groaned. "Are you serious?"

"You need to rest your brain."

Jossey stared at her.

"And try not to move too much," the nurse went on. "Brain injuries can be – "

Jossey covered her eyes with her arm, waving a hand before the woman could continue. "Please don't talk about that stuff, it makes me sick." She sighed heavily. "What *can* I do?"

"I can get you some books if you'd like. Here, drink this. Are you hungry?" The nurse handed her the second drug.

"Probably not after this," Jossey grumbled, sitting up and downing the stuff. She lay back and covered her eyes again. The reddish one was the worst.

The nurse laughed. "The menu's here on the bedside table." She glanced at the door. "Also, you have visitors."

Jossey uncovered one of her eyes, glanced at Gavin, brow raised.

"Who?" she asked.

"Some of your fellow Engineers. They stopped by about half

an hour ago. I told them you still weren't awake. Should I tell them to come back later?"

Jossey started to shake her head, froze. Minimal movement, she reminded herself.

"No, that's fine, let them in," she said. She was awake enough, she thought. She shot an unhappy glance at the remaining medicine. "Give me a minute to take the rest of these."

"Right away, Miss Sokol."

As the nurse left the room, Jossey sighed, turning to Gavin. "I wish everyone would stop calling me that. It sounds so – ugh. Obnoxious. No one calls *other* people Miss So-and-so." She gulped down the bluish stuff, grimacing. It tasted like paste.

Gavin laughed. "How do you think it feels to be called Commander Tskoulis by your old neighbors?"

Jossey snorted. "As if you actually dislike that, *Commander.*"

He grinned a little.

As she downed the fourth, a cup of greenish sludge, Gavin suddenly said, "Don't worry about it scarring. It's a badge of honor. Who's going to dare make fun of someone who's survived two Onlar attacks?"

She smiled warmly, looked at her bandaged hand. He was always so good to her.

"I guess," she said quietly. "Thanks."

He was a Patrol commander. Scars were a fact of life for him. And he didn't have a huge ugly scar across his face. He didn't have to deal with the stares, the whispers. At least not the negative kind. Not him.

Her expression dropped, and she looked away from him.

"Jossey." His voice was sober.

She looked back at him, pasting a smile on her face.

"About the Onlar," Gavin began, dark eyes serious, "I – "

The door slid open.

· · ·

Three familiar figures stepped into the room.

Perkins and Sally seemed surprised to see the Tiger there, but greeted him briefly, then came over to Jossey's bedside.

Perkins had folded his workman's cap nearly in half in both big hands and was crushing it. He looked worriedly at Jossey. "You feeling any better?" he said, voice gruff.

"I've been better," she joked. He crushed his hat further and made his way to a chair.

Sally smiled nervously at Gavin, who smiled back politely. She turned pink and looked away.

Jossey glanced up to see Caspar standing in the doorway, smiling warmly at her.

She blinked.

His dark hair was loosely tied; his long silver eyes were even more striking than Jossey had remembered. She hadn't seen him in full light before.

He was extraordinarily handsome.

She realized she was staring, and looked quickly at the others, not daring to look at Gavin. "Come in," she said.

Gavin glanced at Jossey and got to his feet.

"Savaş," he said, shaking Caspar's hand.

"Commander." Caspar seemed completely at ease, not typical for people in the vicinity of the Tiger.

Gavin turned and grinned at Jossey. "It turns out your rescuer here was in a rival Patrol unit a long time ago."

She laughed. "Great. Be nice."

Caspar smiled crookedly. "He outranks me so far it's not even funny. I plan to be."

Gavin grinned, but gave him a look that Jossey wasn't sure was entirely a joke.

Caspar sat down by Jossey's bedside, gaze traveling to her bandages, the tray of empty medicine cups. "I see you lived."

Before she could say something sarcastic, his expression changed. "How's your hand?"

She gestured to it. "I feel nothing. These doctors are amazing."

"You did something most Patrol probably wouldn't be brave enough to do," he said. "You should be proud."

Jossey remembered the creature as it dove for her, remembered the searing pain in her hand as she wrapped her hand around the flare. The sensation of the blade in her other hand.

Other things she didn't want to remember.

She shivered. "I hope I never have to do that again," she said in a low voice.

Gavin looked at her. "There you go, you finally got the 'tunnel adventure' you begged me and Tark to take you on back when we were kids. Happy now?"

She made a face at him.

Caspar grinned a little. "Ah, so that's how you know each other."

Jossey raised an eyebrow.

But Gavin just laughed. "Her brother was my best friend. Even back then we tried to keep her out of trouble."

"She's in good hands," Caspar said approvingly.

"'She' is right here," Jossey said sourly.

Caspar's amused eyes traveled over her face. "Indeed."

He'd brought snacks. Jossey suddenly realized how hungry she was. She reached for the box, grabbed a handful of what looked like granola bars. "Thank you. I'm starving."

He grinned and bit into one. "I have more," he said.

The group chatted, Perkins wanting to know about Patrol, which Gavin seemed only too happy to talk about. Jossey yawned and covered her mouth in embarrassment. "Don't go yet," she said. "I'm not tired." But she felt herself drifting.

Then she shot awake as Caspar turned to the rest of the room and said, "I thought you should all know – they've examined the Onlar that attacked us."

Jossey glanced at Gavin, who was suddenly sitting up straight, eyeing Caspar coldly.

She turned back to Caspar, feeling a prickle up her spine as she remembered all too clearly the Onlar's face near her own, the jab of the claws into the ground. Her hands felt icy. "How did you even – "

"I was curious, so I called in a favor with my old unit, the ones who retrieved the body." He popped half a granola bar into his mouth.

A different Patrol unit was technically outside of Gavin's jurisdiction, but from his facial expression Jossey wouldn't have guessed that.

Caspar looked at Gavin. "Don't worry, Commander, they don't share any secure information with civilians. No forensics, nothing like that. I just wanted to know why the thing was trying to kill us." He grinned.

Gavin seemed both perturbed and impressed. She could see his shoulders tense. Caspar seemed unaware of Gavin's discomfort.

Or, Jossey thought, he was ignoring it.

She understood Gavin's perspective, but she wanted to know, too. Needed to know. "What did they say?"

"They think it was a loner. 'Crazed by the desert sun.' That's all he told me." Caspar shrugged. "Better than nothing."

Jossey shivered. "How would a crazed Onlar manage to get past the guards on the upper levels?"

"It's more common than you'd think," Gavin said suddenly, giving Caspar what was, for him, a half-smile. He seemed to have settled on closer to impressed than angry.

"How common?" Perkins asked.

"Once a month, maybe twice. Usually they sneak into the tunnels after nightfall. That's where my unit was when we got the call to come rescue you all."

"I'm so glad you did," Sally said tremulously from where she

78

was seated with her uncle.

Gavin turned, smiling at the pair, and Jossey glanced over, surprised. She'd been under the impression Sally was generally shy.

She tried not to laugh as she realized that Sally appeared to be falling for Commander Tskoulis'...considerable personal appeal, and rather rapidly at that. She failed and turned it into a cough, turning away from Sally's pink face so she could maintain her composure. *Every time*, she thought. *He's not even trying hard.*

Caspar's long silver eyes caught hers. He reminded her a little of an animal she'd seen in one of her father's old picture books. A wolf, Jossey thought. But an amused one.

Gavin frowned, turning back to Jossey. "Do you need water?" he asked.

Jossey smiled sweetly. "I'm fine, thank you, Commander."

Gavin's face flushed. Jossey bit her tongue and tried not to laugh. Caspar looked even more amused now.

But his expression grew serious as he looked back at Gavin. "Commander, I hate to discuss it, but as Jossey said, the attack was out of character. I wonder if Kara– "

Gavin's dark eyes were suddenly no longer friendly. Caspar had crossed a line.

"This had nothing to do with them," the commander said sharply. "It was absolutely an Onlar. The autopsy left no doubt."

Jossey looked at Caspar and shook her head slightly, frowning, as he opened his mouth again. She had learned long ago not to mention Karapartei around Gavin, who took their attacks on Patrol as a personal insult.

Karapartei were worse than Onlar in some ways because they couldn't be physically identified the way the Onlar could. They might be irrational – their claims that Council was covering up the City's decline were ridiculous, thought Jossey. Her *job* was to help keep the City functioning, and as far as she could tell, things were working just fine, had for centuries. But their attacks were all too serious. Gavin had lost a friend a few years back.

Caspar caught Jossey's cue and shut his mouth, but Perkins didn't.

"Karapartei?" He looked back and forth between them. "How? We clearly were attacked by an Onlar."

Jossey looked at Sally, who nudged her uncle unsubtly.

The mood had quickly soured. Gavin was giving Caspar a deadly look. "Speculation isn't helpful," he said. "As I said, the autopsy left no doubt."

Jossey flinched. She looked away, not wanting to think about exactly how the Onlar had died.

Gavin noticed. "You did the right thing," he said quietly to her.

Caspar sobered. "You're right," he said. "I apologize – it's probably not something to relive right now." He looked at the wall. "Where's your viewscreen, Jossey?"

She groaned. "They took it away."

Gavin looked gratified at the change in subject. Sally got to her feet. "I've got some books if you want any!" she said to Jossey.

"Please!"

"Books?" Caspar looked thoughtful.

Then a grin twitched at his mouth. "I...may have just the thing for you."

"And that is?"

He made a quick note on his wrist dial. "Can't tell you."

"Authorized information, I hope," Gavin said.

Jossey looked at him sharply, but he was smiling a little. She felt a surge of warmth toward him.

Perkins passed around bottles of sparkling water he'd brought.

"Let's celebrate," he said gruffly.

16

Jossey blinked as Caspar dumped a pile of books on her bed.

She'd been stuck here for five days now. She'd run out of audiobooks. But she still eyed the pile skeptically.

"The Desert Rider?" she said.

The author's name was Chase E. Spaulding. The cover had what looked like a black-leather-clad man on a...motorized vehicle? In the heat? She scoffed.

Caspar looked very pleased with himself, silver eyes lit with laughter.

"Oh, they're terrible," he said, grinning. "But they're classics."

She turned over the others. *Pirates in Orbit.* Books on aliens and Planet X. "You *read* this stuff?"

Amused eyes glanced at her. Caspar drew himself up, pushed the strands of dark hair away from his face with a grand gesture. "I *beg* your pardon," he said stuffily. He pointed to *The Desert Rider*. "I do believe this is the 250th anniversary edition."

He smiled crookedly at her expression. "I'm impressed it survived that many printings, to be honest, it's that awful. So are they all. But they were all I had."

Jossey was opening her mouth to respond when the door

opened again and Perkins and Sally made their way through, awkwardly carrying a very large box of doughnuts.

Jossey's face lit up. She reached over and dragged the medicine tray over to the bed with her good hand. "Please. Be my guests."

Sally smiled widely and handed her a doughnut. "They were giving free ones out in the Square," she said.

"Didn't they ban chocolate last week?" Jossey asked around a mouthful of the stuff. Something about supply issues. She didn't know what that even meant, since the City's scientists grew it somewhere in a lab.

Perkins held a finger to his lips. "It's fake," he said, smiling. Jossey stopped chewing, thought for a moment, shrugged.

"Tastes fine." If it tasted the same, whatever, she thought.

She gestured to the books. "Look at my treasure trove."

Caspar pretended to be offended. "Those are excellent works of literature," he said, before his laughter betrayed him.

Sally blushed a little again as he glanced at her, and Jossey tried not to laugh. The poor girl. It was already bad enough when Gavin was around.

Speaking of Gavin – "Has anyone seen Gavin?"

Caspar glanced at her. Perkins shrugged. "Not so far today."

Or yesterday, Jossey thought. She knew he had Patrol, but still. With her being in the hospital, she had thought –

She took another doughnut, bit into it. Good. Maybe he finally saw her as a grown-up.

Caspar held one of the books out to her. "Here, Jossey. Please, do us the honors."

She pushed it away. "I only have one working hand. You read."

"Oops, right. Sorry." He looked at the book.

He'd grabbed *The Desert Rider*.

Perkins noticed the cover. "Oh, I had that book as a kid. It was – " He seemed to search for words.

"Amazing, right?" Caspar winked.

Perkins snorted. "If you say so."

Caspar made a show of making himself comfortable in one of the cushioned visitor chairs. He pushed the loose strands of hair out of his eyes and opened the book dramatically to page one.

"The sun beat down on the blinding sands," he intoned. "Dax Draperson stared off into the distance, remembering..."

"Wait – Dax Draperson?" Jossey interrupted. "Are you serious? What kind of a name is – "

"Are you going to let me read?" Caspar said, eyebrows raised.

Jossey held up the doughnut in surrender and took a giant bite of it.

"Dax Draperson was pretty sure they were coming for him," Caspar continued. "The secret agent glanced down at his bike. The gauges were shot, but by his estimate he had fuel enough for five hours, maybe six. The heat was intense. He was beginning to regret that he'd chosen his battle gear..."

"Duh," Jossey muttered. Caspar shot her a look. She mimed zipping her lips.

He went on, remarkably straight-faced, as the writer waxed eloquent about Dax Draperson's super-secret background as a spy.

They were howling with laughter at the terrible writing when Gavin opened the door silently and entered the room.

Caspar stopped short, looked over at him. "Commander. Please, join us."

"Where have you been?" Jossey asked.

"Patrol," Gavin said shortly. He took a seat, gestured for Caspar to go on, grinning a little as he noticed the book in the young Engineer's hands.

Despite his casual expression, Gavin looked like he hadn't slept. Jossey frowned. When he noticed her looking at him, he straightened, giving her a smile.

Caspar was glancing between them. "Shall I go on?" he asked.

"Yes. Please." Gavin smiled. "I've read it before. No back story necessary." For a minute he looked like a kid. "I really hope I haven't missed the motorcycle battle."

"Don't spoil it!" Jossey hissed at him.

Caspar grinned widely. "I thought you didn't like it."

"It's awful, but in a great B-movie kind of way. Don't spoil it." Jossey crossed her arms.

"The things humanity chose to preserve after its near-destruction," Caspar said, grinning even bigger. "Very well, Miss Sokol."

Sally passed Gavin the doughnuts. He took one absently, muttering, "Thank you."

Caspar leaned back in his chair casually.

He glanced at Gavin, one eyebrow raised dramatically. "So, Commander, just to orient you, our protagonist, Dax Draper-son, super-secret-agent extraordinaire, has just found himself trapped in a burning desert cave against an overwhelming ambush..."

He cleared his throat and read.

"Dax reached for his trusty energy modulator. It was top-of-the-line technology. He'd paid dearly for it on that secret mission in Mumbai. That was when he'd met HER – "

Caspar continued on, gleefully narrating as the writing spiraled downward into what could only be described as flaming wreckage.

Gavin looked like he was trying hard not to react, but when Caspar got to the epic motorcycle battle, he lost it.

17

Jossey flinched as the nurse opened the bandages. She forced herself to look the other way. The stronger meds had been wearing off, and now she felt a constant burning. It was manageable, but she took a lot of naps. She just wanted to go back to sleep.

"Good," the nurse said. "This looks very good. Very unlikely to scar."

Jossey peeked at it. She instantly regretted it.

"Are you sure?" It didn't *look* unlikely to scar. And a frightening scar at that. She winced at the thought. Her face alone –

The nurse smiled. "They always look like this at first."

Jossey felt sick. She lay back down. "Do you have any water?"

"I'm sorry," the woman said. She held up her sterile-gloved hands. "It should just be another moment."

The nurse quickly dressed the burn. "I've put some silver nitrate on there. It should make the healing process easier. But it will probably turn your hand purple." She smeared something cool and slimy on Jossey's hand as she spoke.

Jossey opened her eyes, startled, forcing herself not to jerk her hand away. "For how long?!" A scar was bad enough. She didn't want to have to wear gloves for the rest of her life.

The nurse laughed. "I'm sorry, Miss Sokol. I meant temporarily. The oxidation does it. See?" She held up the container in her gloved hands. Jossey could see a shiny silver-white cream.

Jossey lay back against the pillow. "Can I at least walk around?"

"Yes, of course, Miss Sokol. In fact – " She winked. "Your uncle has arranged a small celebration for you this afternoon."

"A celebration?" That wasn't really like Uncle Sokol. "Really?" She looked down at her hospital uniform. "Um. Also. Do you have any normal clothing?"

The nurse washed her hands before handing Jossey a cup of water. "Here you go, my dear. As for an outfit, your mother has brought some things from home."

Jossey's face stilled. "My mother?"

"Why, yes. She dropped them off for you."

"Ah." *Dropped them off. Of course.* "Thank you."

"You're welcome, Miss Sokol."

The nurse left the room. Jossey sat staring at the wall.

Her mother. *Now* she'd come to visit Jossey. Now that they were hosting a celebration. Jossey wondered what remarks she'd hear about the Onlar this time.

Her mother had sunk into a deep depression when Jossey's father had gone off to search for Tark and had returned on one of Patrol's stretchers. Her mother had never recovered, never really left home after that, flinched every time she looked at her remaining child with the large white scar across her eye.

The child who'd been responsible for the disastrous sneaking up above, Jossey thought.

No matter how many times Jossey apologized, no matter how many times Father said he forgave her in the year before he too disappeared, Mother had never let it go. Once, she'd made a

86

remark about Jossey's scar scaring people, how at least it was good for something because other kids who saw it might not sneak off into the tunnels.

Jossey had been eleven.

She blinked, tried to clear her head. She didn't want to think about that. She swallowed the lump in her throat, forced her chin high.

The celebration was being held in the artificially-lit "sunroom" at the end of the hospital. It was a conference and events space, used for special occasions by Council and other VIPs. Jossey had never been in there.

She walked carefully down the hallway, still a little woozy from her concussion and all the bed rest, hoping she looked presentable. She'd put on the dress uniform her mother had brought her.

Bright blue complemented at least one of her eyes, she thought.

As she walked into the room, she noticed it was full of balloons. Balloons and streamers everywhere. And a table of cakes.

It was empty.

She turned, confused, not sure if she was in the right place.

"SURPRISE!" Dozens of people jumped out from behind the small forest of potted plants, shouting, tossing confetti at her. It rained down on her as she looked around.

They were all there – her solar crew, Caspar's, her uncle, some Council members she hadn't met, even her mother. And Gavin, in full Patrol uniform, standing tall and silent next to the Council members.

She beamed.

Sally came up to her. "I know you only have one hand," she said, "so let me open this for you."

87

"Thank you," Jossey said, smiling so hard her face hurt.

Sally tore off the ribbon and opened the box, presenting it gently to Jossey.

On the silky blue cloth lay a shimmering medal.

Jossey gaped at it. It said *FORTIS IN ARDUIS*, the letters catching the light.

Strong in difficulties. One of the City's highest honors to civilians.

She looked around at the crowd, feeling shaky. She'd done nothing special. It had been necessary. Her job. She thought of the driver who hadn't made it.

Sally took the medal and fastened it around Jossey's neck as the room broke into applause.

Jossey was sitting by the food table, helping herself to a slice of amazing lemon cake, exhausted from all the attention, when Caspar came over.

"I guess you won't want to go back to boring old solar crew after this," he said, a wide smile on his face. "Congratulations."

She squirmed. "I really didn't do anything," she said. "It was my job. I was the only one with a weapon. I had to."

"Your job saved dozens of lives," he said seriously. "That's a well-deserved medal. There are many people in Patrol who have done far less than you."

She shoved a bite of cake into her mouth. "This is good. You should try some."

He laughed. "Are you trying to avoid a compliment?"

Jossey flushed. "No," she protested around the cake. She covered her mouth. "Sorry. Seriously, try some."

He shrugged and took a piece. "I suppose you'll try to save me if I choke on this."

She shot him a look.

Suddenly her mother was standing there.

"Congratulations, Jossey." The older woman's eyes were shadowed, as if she hadn't slept much. "That's a beautiful medal. Well-deserved."

Jossey stood up carefully and accepted her mother's hug, standing there stiffly. Her mother backed away after a moment. "I hope you liked the outfit I chose," she said.

"Yes, thank you. It matches my eye." Jossey grinned a little.

Her mother did not smile. Jossey's grin faded.

"How is your hand? Any scarring?" her mother asked.

Jossey flinched. "I don't know yet," she said after a moment. "As long as I can use it, I don't care."

She did care, very much, but her mother didn't need to know that.

"Of course." Her mother smiled, glanced around. "Well, let's hope for the best. Have you seen your uncle?"

With that, her mother was gone.

Jossey watched her go, feeling numb.

Caspar silently handed her another piece of cake. She took it and bit into it angrily.

"She hates that I work aboveground," she muttered to Caspar, face burning, regretting that he'd seen any of that. "She's afraid I won't come back. That's why she's so – "

She wanted that to be the case, at least.

"This is great cake," she finally mumbled. "Thanks."

She glanced up. Her uncle was advancing through the crowd, shadowed by Gavin and two Council members she hadn't met.

She stood up, finishing the last bite quickly. Caspar excused himself.

"Jossey, my dear."

Pyotr Sokol, Minister of Intelligence, her father's brother, stood beaming at her.

She was a bit surprised to see him here, even if he'd been the reason her rescue had been orchestrated. She so rarely saw him, she'd actually half-forgotten what he looked like. He was a fierce loner, living at the edge of the City in a veritable bunker, with only his assistants coming and going.

Sokol's uniform was the same expensive grayish-tan cloth as always. Today, it included a row of medals. He was medium-height, stout, with cropped gray hair and jowls. His eyes were deep-set, a pale grey, faraway.

Grey almost like Caspar's eyes, she thought, but the wrong shape.

And unkind-looking.

She pushed away the thought. He was her uncle, she should be glad to see him, she told herself.

Sokol's smile almost reached his eyes as he took her hands. "Allow me to introduce to you my colleagues from the Council."

He gestured to a tall, thin older man with a hooked nose and very narrow face. "This is Minister Staniek." A middle-aged woman with a long blue dress – "Minister Kellihan. They are my colleagues on the City Security Committee."

Jossey smiled. "A pleasure to meet you," she said to them.

"Thank you for your service to our City," Minister Kellihan said, shaking Jossey's hand. Hers was cool and manicured, her smile bright. Minister Staniek looked mildly pleased, which Jossey guessed was the extent of his warmth.

"And of course you know Commander Tskoulis," Sokol added.

"Yes, of course, Minister." Jossey beamed at Gavin, who was towering behind the group, silently scanning the room with unreadable dark eyes. He spared a moment of warmth as he glanced at her.

"Are you enjoying your party?" Sokol asked.

"Very much, Uncle, thank you." She smiled brilliantly. "I did not expect such a response. I was just d– "

"Doing your job," Sokol said smoothly. "The Commander

informed me. We on the Council, however, felt it was deserving of some public acknowledgment. You have done a great thing for this City. And, of course, I'm very proud of my niece." He smiled.

For a moment, it occurred to Jossey to ask why their first request for Patrol had been denied. But she kept her mouth shut.

After an hour or so, Jossey was exhausted. She smiled apologetically at her uncle, who immediately made excuses for her.

Another round of greetings and goodbyes, and people began making their exits.

Her uncle stayed behind, helping himself to a piece of the lemon cake.

"My dear," he said, "I hope you have had sufficient chance to rest these last few days. I have made sure that your Engineering supervisor is aware of your circumstances. She has agreed to give you an additional two weeks of paid leave."

Jossey's eyes widened. "How – "

She shut her mouth. Of course. Her uncle was on the Council.

She swallowed her pride and hoped her face wasn't too pink. "Thank you, Uncle."

"Of course, my dear." Sokol gestured to Gavin. "Commander Tskoulis is here to escort you back to your room when you are ready."

Tskoulis stood there like a statue.

As Jossey began to clear away her plates, Sokol turned to her and said quietly, "My dear, there is one more matter I want to discuss with you."

"Another matter?"

"Not at this time." He smiled. "Please, my dear, get some rest. And congratulations again on your worthy actions on behalf of our City and its people." He gestured to the remainder of the crowd.

"It was nothing," she muttered.

He squeezed her hands and walked away.

Someone cleared their throat. She glanced up to see Gavin. His smile was grave, not his usual grin.

"Shall we, Miss Sokol?"

She almost laughed, waiting for him to comment on her dress uniform, say something typical, but realized he was very serious. He was on Patrol right now.

"Thank you, Commander," she replied formally.

He walked ahead of her to the door and opened it for her.

18

THE NEXT DAY SHE WAS BACK TO BEING ALONE. THE HOURS seemed to drag, and she was glad when evening came. She was ready to go back to work, she thought.

She was almost ready to go to sleep when there was a knock at her door.

The nurse entered the room, pale as her starched uniform. Jossey frowned and sat up.

"Jossey, my dear." Her uncle smiled and strode into the room without ceremony or announcement. She made to stand, and he gestured for her to stay seated.

He crossed over to her bedside and took her hands.

She smiled up at him. "Uncle Sokol."

The nurse bustled about awkwardly, trying to make the room even more spotless than it already was. "Coffee?" she inquired nervously. "Tea, Minister?"

He waved her away. In his gravelly voice, he said, "No need, thank you. I would like to speak to my niece alone."

"Of course, Minister."

She all but fled the room.

Sokol pulled a chair to Jossey's bedside. "Jossey, dear."

Jossey smiled. "Thank you once again for rescuing us, Uncle. And for yesterday's party."

"But of course. I could not leave my family out in the tunnels for those..."

His fist clenched, and she found herself flinching.

"And for treating my injuries," she went on. "They told me my burns should heal quickly."

He smiled thinly. "That is excellent news, my dear. And your crew members? Are they well? I believe I saw most of them yesterday at the party?"

"Yes, Uncle." She swallowed. "I – "

She wanted again to ask him if they'd really been planning to leave her group in the tunnels overnight. But she couldn't bring herself to continue that sentence. Not with the Minister of Intelligence, uncle or not.

His flat eyes looked into hers inquiringly, and she shivered a little, wondering if he had guessed. He always seemed to know too much. She didn't know how, but he seemed to know things, understand people.

"I – was wondering if you had found out more about the Onlar," she went on hurriedly.

It was true. She didn't understand why one of the creatures from above would so determinedly follow them all the way down into the depths of the earth, not when it had been – she thought – run over and dragged and she didn't know what else.

And to continue after Perkins the way it had.

She shook her head to clear the image of the thing staggering toward Perkins, claws extended, hissing.

"What would They want from us?" she asked.

Sokol's face soured. "If Patrol knew what they 'wanted,' my job would be a lot easier."

"Uncle, I think it held on to our transport and tried to kill Perkins, after – "

He held up a hand, gently. "I know, my dear. Please do not distress yourself. Tskoulis briefed me on the entire incident."

Incident. Like a minor scuffle. She felt her face turning pink. "And?" she said.

"My dear." He smiled thinly again. "At times, the Onlar – they act...irrationally. Even for them. But I appreciate your enthusiasm."

She opened her mouth to respond.

Then, to her surprise, Sokol said, "Enough of them. I am here to discuss your future, Jossey."

Jossey blinked at him. Her future?

"The doctor said I could go back to work," she said carefully. "Isn't that correct? Is my concussion – "

She felt her head. It didn't hurt. She was a little sensitive to light, but she'd done everything the doctor said. They hadn't mentioned anything of concern. Her scans were fine. Was it more severe than she'd thought?

He laughed. "No, my dear, your injuries are not the issue. I am speaking of your career."

"My career?" She sat up further, not sleepy anymore.

"I am here to present you with a suggestion you may wish to consider," the Minister said. "Specifically, I would like you to consider a transfer."

Jossey was taken aback. She just gaped at her uncle for a long moment. "Excuse me?" she finally managed. Engineering was the only thing she'd ever wanted to do. Anything else –

His flat grey eyes grew warm. "My dear niece. Despite – and maybe especially considering – your childhood, you managed to not only take down an Onlar by yourself, but you saved an entire crew of unarmed Citizens with minimal training. You have proven beyond doubt your bravery, and your competence." He smiled. "As if there were any doubt."

She blinked, mouth still agape. She closed it and flushed. Sokol did not praise people easily.

"Thank you," she said shortly. "But a transfer – "

"It has come to my ministry's attention that you would be an excellent transfer candidate for Patrol."

Now Jossey really stared at him. "What?" *Patrol?*

She had recently woken up from three days of unconsciousness, burns on her hand, and a nasty concussion. She'd been forced to face one of her worst fears in a pitch-black tunnel with no preparation and not enough water and dozens of terrified people. And she'd almost fallen into the pit.

She just wanted to stay in this hospital room. Paid vacation sounded great right now. Not fighting.

"Are you seri– " She snapped her mouth shut, remembering who she was speaking to.

Sokol grinned, revealing one crooked tooth, and started laughing.

She watched his face carefully for signs he was joking.

He stopped abruptly. "I am entirely serious, my dear."

"I – what – "

She'd seen Gavin's men. She wasn't tiny, not like Sally, but they were huge. She didn't think she could even take one of them on. The Onlar had been because it had literally fallen on her knife. "I – "

"We are in need of more competent Engineers for the field." He smiled. "I know you are interested in theoretical solar design. I've been keeping an eye on your work with your current team, and have a few classified projects you might be interested in."

He gave her a long look, then added, "I believe you may find it a more...interesting position than your 'tedious and awful' duties aboveground."

Jossey's face went hot. Did he have access to her diary file, too?

He grinned wolfishly, and she knew the answer to that question was probably a yes. She hated Intelligence sometimes.

"It is, of course, up to you," he said.

She looked at him. "What are the projects?" she ventured.

She was indeed very interested in solar design, but her current role was all about maintenance. It was boring, at times. But it was the standard path for an Engineer in the solar plant.

Design was the next level up.

"Security prohibits me from discussing them with you at this time," said her uncle.

She opened her mouth. He continued. "We would also be seeking to transfer Mr. Savaş, who is a specialist in solar efficiency and conversion and should prove quite useful in the field."

Her mind was spinning. Tark would be so excited, was all she could think.

"Does Gavin know about this?" she asked.

Sokol smiled. "He knows about your potential transfer. He can answer any questions you may have."

She didn't trust that first sentence as far as she could throw it. Her uncle might be head of Intelligence, might deal with varying degrees of truthfulness, but clearly he didn't know Gavin very well if he thought the Patrol commander would react well to her joining the most dangerous career path in the City.

Jossey closed her eyes, rubbed her forehead, trying to think of a way to get the Minister to leave so she could process all of this.

"I – Uncle Sokol, I'm sorry, I'm very tired. I don't think I can consider this at the moment. I appreciate the offer. I might consider it if it involved no fighting."

Not likely, she thought.

Indeed, his expression said that was not an option. But he smiled thinly.

"Well. In that case, I must be on my way. I have told the nurse to allow you to rest this evening." He patted her bedside.

"I am so glad to see you have recovered so well, my dear. Do not hurry yourself in deciding. If it would be helpful, the salary – "

He named a figure that made her eyes widen. It was nearly twice what she was making now.

But still. "Uncle Sokol, I'm really not sure – "

"Think about it," he said again.

Abrupt as always, with that he got up and left the room.

Jossey watched him go, almost convinced she had imagined the whole thing. Had he really come here just to offer her a *job*? He'd barely checked on her health.

She smiled grimly. That was Uncle Sokol for you. Always all business.

She had to admit she was curious as to what kinds of projects her uncle was talking about.

"I've been keeping an eye on your work," he had said. She smiled at the thought.

But she couldn't really imagine herself as a fighter. She'd done what she'd done out of necessity, not because she wanted to.

Another thought occurred to her. Her uncle was willing to put her back in the place in the City that terrified her most?

He didn't know, she thought, viciously squashing the tears that threatened. How could he know? After her father had died searching for Tark, after she'd completed school, Jossey had been forced to work to support herself and her mother.

And the only career she wanted would take her aboveground. So she stopped showing fear. Stopped feeling almost altogether. People had praised her bravery, her coping skills. She'd just smiled in thanks.

But now –

In the hospital room, alone, she stared at the ceiling and wept. Father had given her that knife when she recovered from the incident. He'd warned her to always carry it with her. She didn't know how to actually use it, and since she was a civilian, Gavin hadn't been allowed to show her.

She hadn't even purposely stabbed the Onlar. It had just...happened.

She just wanted to be left alone, wanted to go back to her normal boring job. But she knew that Council's offers were often non-refusable.

Maybe she'd join Patrol and fail out, she told herself. It happened all the time.

She felt her scar, felt the rough tissue that ran from her forehead, across her eye, and down her cheek, remembered jerking back just enough that she hadn't lost the eye itself.

She wanted badly to contact Gavin, ask him his thoughts on the matter. But she didn't want to see the look on his face.

He took his vow or whatever to Tark way too seriously sometimes, she thought, and she had her pride. She sighed and turned to the wall.

19

It was cold.

Cold was a relative term, but Wickford was glad he had on his outer layer as he stepped up top into the canyonland with its endless night sky.

He shivered. His safety gauge read seventy degrees. Positively chilly for this time of year.

The Founders, long ago, had written scientific tracts on how, years after the extreme heat had all but baked much of the world, the extra gas in the atmosphere might eventually dissipate. The Earth might cool.

He shrugged it off. Tomorrow would probably be another scorcher.

Wickford turned and eyed the entrance to the old elevator, reaching to make sure his standard-issue knife was still attached to his leg. If he lost his sword, he could at least fight at very close range.

He'd seen enough to know that didn't usually go well.

He glanced at the elevator again, impatiently, waiting for the other Patrol to emerge. He didn't want to get stuck up here with just Pricey. Alistair Price-Ford III, Pricey for short. Obnoxious as they came.

Pricey grinned. "Don't worry, newbie."

Wickford shot him a look. He wasn't worried, he told himself. He'd volunteered for this. Yes, they were as far away from the main City entrances as the service corridors went – Henry had said something about the empty quadrant, unless he'd heard wrong – but the elevator should still be working fine. It was unlikely they'd be trapped, he thought. And if they were, they should have enough water to make it back to the main entrance before sunrise.

He shook his head for even thinking about it. It wasn't a rust bucket anymore, not since the incident years ago. All of the elevators had been upgraded by order of Intelligence, outfitted with Patrol codes to keep people from sneaking up top.

As he had, as a boy, before the Onlar had started invading the tunnels with greater frequency. He wasn't a chicken.

As for "newbie," well, he gritted his teeth. He'd been on tunnel patrols for two years. He was only a "new" recruit when it came to aboveground work. *That's just Pricey*, he told himself. *Henry wants me here. Advocated for me.*

He jumped as the elevator doors opened again and Commander Tskoulis stepped out, armed to the teeth and followed by Henry, second-in-command. Two others followed shortly – the auxiliary medic and the tracker. They were from another unit. Wickford hadn't bothered to learn their names.

Wickford breathed a nearly-inaudible sigh of relief.

Pricey elbowed him. "Toldja."

Wickford said nothing. Pricey might be obnoxious, but he was a better guy to have on your side than against you.

The group saluted Tskoulis. He waved them down, did a quick visual inspection of their equipment, their water rations. Sufficient for a night mission. He smiled grimly, his mouth the only thing visible, his mask obscuring the rest of his features.

"Move out," was all he said.

He brushed past, and Wickford instinctively moved out of the way, getting as usual the unsettling impression of standing next to a wild creature, something barely in control of its power. Tskoulis carried his sword on his back, along with his water rations, and in the moonlight it tilted back and forth as he walked, like a strange antenna. He looked back over his shoulder at them, expression unreadable with the mask, mouth set in a grim line.

The Tiger, the commander was called, after one of the near-mythical giant predators from the distant past.

Tskoulis was certainly built like one. He moved easily for a man of his size. But Wickford had seen how fast he could move, the power he had in his enormous arms, how he could use the sword he carried.

How the commander had pinned another Patrol agent to the tunnel wall with one hand, lifting him nearly off the ground, for insubordination.

Pricey and Henry snapped to attention as Tskoulis waved a hand. Wickford reached again for his water, nervous, hoping he hadn't forgotten anything this time.

The men stepped into line and followed the commander into the darkness.

They lined up along the ridge and crouched, silent shadows, staring down into the valley. They made sure to check that the moon was on the other side of the sky, so they couldn't easily be seen. The elevator felt very far away.

They can see you in the dark. It was true, knew Wickford. But they could try to keep the advantage. Up here, the wind was blasting harshly, warm even at night, and very dry. The only vegetation around was deep in the canyons, where there was water; the ridge was clean of cover, burned during the day, wind-scoured at night.

"Water," Tskoulis murmured. They obediently took a swig from their canisters. It had to be timed, to keep them all sufficiently rationed to make the full loop of whatever mission Council had sent them on this time.

Wickford had only been on one of these aboveground missions before, though he'd fought alongside Tskoulis and Henry down in the tunnels for the past year. Commander Tskoulis never told them much, just gave them brief orders before they moved out.

Usually the aboveground Patrol went through the canyons, driving out any Onlar they could find, or so Henry had explained when Wickford had volunteered for duty. And he'd only done it on a dare, from Henry of course, who'd called him a chicken in the mess hall in front of everyone, saying tunnel duty was for "Patrollets." *Newbies*, Wickford thought sourly.

But fighting Onlar on their home turf was sounding less and less great with every minute that passed, as it dawned on him that they might actually be going *into* the canyons.

The stars might be beautiful, and cool air was always welcome, but he thought that he strongly preferred the tunnels.

That way your enemy was only on one side of you.

He kept his thoughts to himself and off his face. The commander was frighteningly good at noticing any dissent.

Tskoulis raised a hand suddenly, mask shining eerily in the moonlight.

"Quadrant four," he whispered into his com. "Do you copy?"

A faint buzzing that meant "copy."

Tskoulis whispered something into his com.

Then he resumed his study of the valley below.

· · ·

The ridge they were standing on was vertically-edged along the eastern face. Flat sides sloped, notched with half-formed caves, to the valley floor. The wind hissed in the sand.

Below them, the valley spread out in a semi-circle, pocked with holes and rivulets where flash floods had carved their way over the centuries. When it rained here, it poured, Wickford knew. Patrol lost a man or two every year to the deluges.

He glanced at the sky. It was clear.

Beyond the flat valley, the canyon entrances yawned, parallel gashes in the earth. They wound their way toward the horizon.

The Onlar. That's where their caves began. The canyons were pitch-black.

Patrol would be at a huge disadvantage against creatures that could see in the dark.

Wickford shivered, suddenly deeply regretting whatever it was he'd signed up for. Last time had been a routine patrol of the general perimeter of the City's multiple tunnel entrances, far away from any canyons. This time –

He wasn't sure. And he hated that.

Tskoulis was still silent. He appeared to be thinking. Wickford adjusted his water pack, wincing at the sloshing sound. Henry shot him a look.

Then the Tiger glanced at the glowing dial on his wrist, turned it off, and crouched and began to draw in the sand.

Wickford watched closely, but not too closely. Patrol commanders often didn't like their troops to be too inquisitive about their...projects, Wickford called them. Tskoulis was no exception. Wickford just followed orders. It was easier. But he was curious nonetheless.

From what he could see, Tskoulis was drawing a straight line with angles fanning out, a jagged line that might represent one of the numerous canyons in the area, and what looked like a circle off to the right, though what that might be Wickford could not guess.

Tskoulis stood, glanced up at the moon again, raising his thumb and index finger against the horizon, palm flat out, as if calculating something.

Then he crouched again and swept a wide divot in the sand with his hand. It covered half of one of the maybe-canyons. He showed the design to the tracker, who gestured in agreement.

The commander stood, smeared the drawing with his foot, and looked dead ahead into the nearest canyon, tall figure even more frightening against the light of the moon.

They made their way single file down the ridge.

Wickford moved slowly, trailing after the group, trying not to make noise as his feet scraped the gravelly sandstone.

Every so often, Henry would glance back at him. Wickford guessed Pricey was paying attention, was probably thinking how incompetent Wickford was that Henry had to check on him, but he didn't care.

Henry and Wickford had been best friends since sixth grade. Henry had insisted they join Patrol together, even though Wickford was slower, clumsier.

And louder, he thought, wincing.

But he gave Henry a thumbs-up and tried not to trip on the rocks.

"Spread out," Tskoulis said quietly, as they entered one of the pitch-black canyons. "This canyon's unmapped. We need to look for sign."

Sign meant Onlar caves, Onlar tracks.

Henry silently headed to the right, Tskoulis to the left. That left Wickford following Pricey over the stony ground. Every so often Pricey would stop, crouch, touch the ground, move a stone or two. Wickford couldn't tell what the older

Patrol was doing, but he couldn't let *Pricey* of all people know that.

They continued on, silent dark figures moving through the near-blackness.

Wickford found himself watching the sky, the stars, as they disappeared one at a time over the bumpy rim of the canyon. He'd steeled himself long ago to the dark. Yet somehow the half-light scared him more.

But he needed two night missions aboveground to qualify for tunnel duty near the City.

And there was that stupid dare with Henry.

He looked around as he walked, trailing Pricey. The stone here was worn down over centuries, millennia maybe. Wickford didn't know. Hadn't really cared to know about this type of thing when he was in Patrol school.

But now he was curious as to why it was so...lumpy. Like dozens of fingers sticking out of the ground, each so big that twenty men could encircle it. In the sunlight, he knew, the spires were striped, different shades of rock worn down over time.

And the rock at night was almost cold. Beautifully so. He wanted to lean on it, even in this chilly air. No wonder the Onlar lived in caves.

He fell behind a little as they made their slow way down the canyon.

He felt a little better now, safer. His eyes were beginning to adjust, and he could see well enough to tell that this canyon was likely abandoned. It was bone-dry, for one thing, and the steep angle of the sides meant that the sun would probably hit the ground at maximum intensity for more hours during the day than was safe.

He *had* read his safety manuals, he thought proudly, even if he hadn't had much of a chance to go aboveground.

As he drifted over the rocky canyon floor, he looked for sign, which could be anything out of place – a trail over the rocks, a pattern of gravel-fall that looked unnatural. The Onlar didn't leave clear tracks for the most part, but if you knew what to look for...

He glanced up and stopped in his tracks.

The canyon had turned while he'd been wandering, and it now opened onto the glowing path of the Milky Way, in all its stunning shimmering glory. For a moment, Wickford forgot where he was. He'd only heard of it – it hadn't been visible the last time he'd been up above. He gaped.

"With me," Tskoulis' voice drifted back, startling Wickford.

The young Patrol looked up, then behind him, at the nearly-invisible entrance to the canyon.

He suddenly realized how far behind he was, how isolated. Henry was all but invisible up ahead in the darkness, the medic trailing after him.

Tskoulis had taken the tracker with him, and couldn't even be seen.

Even Pricey...

Behind him, Wickford thought he heard a sound. A trickle of rock. A footstep, maybe.

His fascination with the Milky Way vanished, replaced by gut-wrenching terror. The Onlar could be there, right behind him.

Maybe even a group.

And he was alone.

His hands felt like ice. He broke into a run, scrambling over the rocks as he made a beeline for the others.

As he did, he tripped over something and went flying, making a racket as he went down hard, his gear scattering.

The entire group of Patrol turned around.

"It's the newbie," he heard one of them mutter angrily.

He lay there, frozen. He'd lost his canteen, and his knife. He'd heard them both fall somewhere in the darkness. Tskoulis would probably be furious, he thought.

But Wickford didn't care, because he was staring at a skull.

20

WICKFORD LAY THERE FOR A LONG STUNNED MOMENT, GASPING for air.

The skull was small, fragile, half-buried in the sand: empty eye sockets, a thin jaw hanging slightly open like a hinge. The body had been partly dislodged from the earth, or maybe partially covered, Wickford thought, probably by a once-a-year flash flood.

The young recruit could see a frail hand and arm, only bones, protruding from the sand nearby.

As he scrambled to his feet, ignoring the muttering of his comrades, he saw that the skull had a lock of pale hair, still attached to the scalp, he thought where the body had been covered by the sand.

A child, he thought. Maybe twelve.

Wickford yanked off his mask, tears in his eyes, frozen as he stared at the half-buried skeleton.

Pricey stomped over to him, looking furious, opening his mouth as if to berate the young recruit, who barely even looked at him, shaking hand pointing to the ground.

Pricey followed Wickford's horrified gaze and dropped his

pack, letting out an exclamation, the water sloshing as the canister hit the ground.

Out of the dimness, Henry and the medic jogged toward them, footsteps ringing off the canyon walls.

Pricey mutely gestured toward the bones.

The second-in-command stared for a long moment, then took off his pack and dug hurriedly in it.

"Tools," he ordered.

The medic alone looked unfazed, and obediently began to look through his pack.

Sometimes they find only bones.

Wickford was still frozen, staring in horror at what he'd found. He hadn't wanted to believe *this* about the Onlar, despite what else he'd seen.

But not this. He'd always hoped this was just a legend.

He felt sick.

At the commotion, Tskoulis appeared out of the darkness, a looming figure, rage written in the tension of his enormous arms and his clenched jaw.

Wickford looked up, wincing, suddenly realizing just how tall the commander was, how imposing.

Tskoulis' men parted before him as he stalked over to Wickford. Even Pricey fell silent.

Wickford looked up at the commander, terrified, ready to apologize for the noise he'd made, ready to beg him not to throw him off Patrol, but Tskoulis just waved the young recruit into silence, staring down at the small skeleton on the ground.

The men gathered around, ready to carefully excavate, waiting for orders. The medic had an emergency blanket ready.

The air seemed to suddenly go out of Tskoulis' body.

"Stop," he said suddenly, harshly. There was a note to his voice the young recruit had never heard before.

Tskoulis removed his mask with one enormous hand, let his arm drop to his side. His hair was damp underneath, plastered to his head. His expression was fixed, his face appearing completely drained of blood, as he looked down at the small skeleton.

Wickford and the others immediately set aside their tools and backed away from the bones.

The night wind had picked up, ever so slightly, and was stirring the lock of pale hair above the skull's empty eye sockets. Tskoulis' fists clenched. He was crushing his mask, the men noticed.

They stared.

Pricey, usually brash, opened his mouth, and Henry shot him a death glare.

The wind picked up, blowing grains of sand through the small bones of the pathetic arm. It was flung outward, as if its owner had been dropped and left there, discarded, under the desert sky.

"No no no," Tskoulis muttered under his breath.

His broad shoulders drooped as he continued to stare.

"Commander?" Pricey piped up. "What's – "

Henry physically grabbed Pricey, put a gloved hand over his mouth.

Tskoulis didn't seem to hear Pricey, didn't seem to notice his Patrol were even there. The men saw he was shaking, face completely white.

Wickford watched in wonder as the Tiger sank to the ground beside the small skeleton and put his face into his hands.

21

PRICEY LOOKED COMPLETELY SUBDUED AS THEY WRAPPED THE
small skeleton in the emergency blanket and headed back down
the length of the canyon, two men carrying each end of the little
bundle.

No one was looking at Tskoulis. He did not look at any of
them. He stalked ahead, making no attempt to hide the sound of
his steps, going against all Protocol, as if trying purposely to
draw the Onlar out.

Wickford couldn't even process what he'd just witnessed, his
image of the Tiger was so different from the man he'd just seen.
Judging by the other Patrol agents' expressions, neither could
they.

But they all seemed to understand that this moment was not
to be spoken of, ever.

The moon was overhead now, and the light slanted down
through the fingerlike protrusions of the canyon, spreading
strange shadows on the ground.

Wickford walked behind the bundle. He was still shaking
and didn't trust himself not to drop it, and besides, he was
worried that Tskoulis might go ballistic if he did.

He'd never seen the commander look that way before. Angry, yes. Frustrated, yes. But not the way he'd looked just now.

And certainly never –

Something deep within Wickford felt like it was burning as he recalled Tskoulis' reaction. He found himself throwing furious glares at the walls, hoping they would come across a cave, an Onlar. Maybe several of them. He felt a surge of boiling rage. *Child-killers*, he thought. *Cave-dwellers.*

The child – it was too small for an adult, he thought – had probably been just barely older than Wickford's little sister, maybe ten, twelve, if he had to guess. Maybe slightly older. Scrawny. Thin arms.

So thin.

Wickford was glad he was wearing a mask. His eyes were watering.

Male, the medic had said.

And the blond hair. Somehow that had affected Wickford more than anything. That little strip of hair, floating in the night wind. He shivered just thinking about it.

How dare they. A child.

He didn't know of any recent disappearances from the City, although they did happen occasionally. Mostly when kids slipped past Patrol and went tunnel-adventuring. They usually came back, but not always.

He shivered, watching Tskoulis' back as the commander stalked ahead of the group, hands clenching and unclenching. Wickford was again strongly reminded of a wild creature. A desert cat.

Wickford had seen what an Onlar could do with its claws. Maybe had done to this child, he thought. He didn't want to think about it.

He'd also seen what Tskoulis could do with his sword.

The moonlight flooded the earth as they left the canyon.

Henry was carefully holding the corner of the bundle, and as they stepped out of the canyon into the bright light he tripped, catching himself just in time. The little bundle rattled.

Tskoulis jerked around like he'd been struck.

The commander stalked back and grabbed the corner of the bundle from Henry.

Henry stepped back in shock. The rest of them froze.

Tskoulis stood very still for a moment, as if trying to calm himself. Then he gripped the corner of the bundle and pushed it into Henry's hands.

"Here," he said flatly. "Be careful. The family needs to receive the body intact."

With what appeared to be great effort, he added, "I have to run point."

Pricey opened his mouth, seemed to think better of it.

Henry murmured, "Yes, sir."

The elevator glittered faintly in the distance, on the other side of a patch of moonlit open ground easily a hundred yards across. Home base.

Wickford watched in horror as Tskoulis strode out into the moonlight at a furious pace, not even bothering to look around.

Wickford hurried after the group, confused. What was his commander *doing*? Was he insane?

The recruit knew the Onlar traveled in groups on open ground, where they had more room to maneuver. What Tskoulis was doing was beyond stupid.

Wickford didn't want to try to see how well such a small Patrol would fare against a cluster of Them. He doubted the medic even knew how to fight.

He thought he heard noises again behind him, and spun, looking closely at the darkness. Nothing. He kept going, gripping his sword hilt with sweaty hands.

The moonlit ground seemed to go on for miles, and at last he stepped into the shadow of the elevator's rock casing, gasping as much from fear as from the speed. Wickford's senses were on full alert – the night air smelled oddly sweet, something he'd never noticed before. Prickles of fear raced up and down his spine.

Tskoulis punched the button so hard Wickford was worried it would break and trap them up aboveground. He glanced at Pricey, who looked back at him, masked face inscrutable.

As the elevator clunked to the surface and hissed open, Wickford jumped.

Pricey pushed up his mask, pale eyes meeting Wickford's, and Wickford looked at him defiantly, expecting a smirk or a joke about the "newbie" being scared. But Pricey only looked at him solemnly.

The group stepped silently into the elevator and the doors slid shut.

22

GAVIN DIDN'T COME BACK FOR SEVERAL MORE DAYS. THE OTHERS didn't stop by much, either. They had day jobs, Jossey reminded herself.

So did she, if the doctors would ever release her to go do hers.

Her uncle's conversation stuck in her mind. She supposed she didn't have a choice about Patrol, not if the Minister of Intelligence himself had "suggested" her transfer.

To distract herself from both boredom and thinking about anything related to Patrol, she had read and re-read the novels Caspar had brought her, and she was starting to think she should try writing one, just to think about something *interesting*. Chase Spaulding and co. were not exactly the most exciting thriller writers she'd ever seen.

Outside her room, the nurses' scheduling screen flashed on. The light stabbed into Jossey's head, and she flinched, looking away.

No screens. She groaned. It wasn't like there were any good shows on anyway, but she was even willing to watch reality TV at this point.

A nurse opened the door, the hallway screen's light shining through.

Jossey winced and looked away.

"How are you feeling, Miss Sokol?" the nurse asked.

"Honestly – " She gestured to the books. "Do you have anything better?"

The nurse tsked sympathetically. "I'm sorry, we don't, but..."

The door creaked, and both women turned.

Gavin poked his head into the room. "Visitor for Miss Sokol," he said breezily.

"...Commander Tskoulis here is to see you," the nurse finished, blushing. Turning to him, she murmured, "Commander."

She wrote a few hasty scribbles in her notepad, then said something about checking on Jossey in a few hours and hurried out of the room.

Jossey watched her go. "Do you really have to do that to everyone you meet?" she asked. Gavin laughed at her disapproving look and sat down next to her bed.

"It's not on purpose," he said innocently. "I'm just being friendly."

"Uh-huh."

He probably was just being friendly. She'd never seen him express interest toward anyone. Probably didn't know how to, she thought, with all the time he spent fighting Onlar and terrorists and whatever else Patrol did. She half-smiled. Not that she was much better, she thought.

He was wearing his Patrol uniform, and she was surprised as usual at how huge he was even when he sat. But not scary, not to her at least. To her he was just Gavin.

She examined his face. He looked...off. His face was drawn, dark circles under his eyes, but when she looked at him inquisitively he smiled.

"How are you?" he asked. "How's your head?"

She studied his face. "I'm doing okay. What's wrong?"

He winced. "Nothing. Rough week of training. Newbies. They don't know how to be silent up above. We had a couple close calls." Then he grinned. "Enough about me. I'm here to entertain you. I see your book collection is, ah, lacking."

"Enlighten me. I've been reading these 'novels' for the past four hours. I would be willing to listen to quadrant reports at this point."

Jossey tossed the offending books toward her feet. One slid off to the floor.

"Good," she said, glaring at it. "That one was particularly badly written."

He laughed a little, but his attention still seemed elsewhere.

Jossey tilted her head, looked at him more carefully.

"Gavin," she said. "What's wrong?"

He looked up, flinched away from her searching look.

She'd never seen him look this exhausted from just bad training. Newbies flunked out of Patrol all the time. It had to be something else, she thought. To her, fighting with Onlar was terrifying, but to him it was a thrill ride. He and Tark had snuck into the tunnels since the time they were old enough to figure out how, had play-acted Patrol in Tark's living quarters until they were banished for breaking a vase or two.

As far as she knew, Gavin had never wanted to do anything other than join Patrol, protect the City and its people. If he looked this drained...

"What happened?" she asked carefully. He hated when she brought this up, but – "Was it Karapartei?"

She knew the terrorists had been active recently, had been targeting Patrol down in ring 2.

He looked away.

"Can we talk about something else? I told you, I just had a rough training session." He grinned crookedly. "I'm fine. Tell me about Planet X or whatever."

118

"Okay." She glanced at the books ruefully. "You got any better recommendations than these?"

"Sadly, I do not. I mostly read old military stuff anyway, you know that."

Gavin was a regular old stick-in-the-mud when it came to interesting reading habits. "Do you ever relax?" she asked. "Read anything fun?"

He laughed, dark eyes amused. "I'm relaxing now." He gestured to her bandaged limb. "How's your hand?"

Jossey waved the bandage at him. "Pretty nasty looking, but they think it should heal quickly. And I might survive unscarred, or maybe with some battle wounds. Either way I'm practically Patrol." She smiled. "Like you said, now I've had that tunnel adventure you and Tark used to promise to take me on."

His smile vanished.

"Jossey." The word seemed to have slipped out, and he clamped his mouth shut.

She stared at him, unsettled. His eyes were suddenly fixed on hers, full of concern, she thought. Or frustration. As if he wanted desperately to say something. His fists were clenched, his jaw set.

"What?" she ventured.

He looked away, apparently angry. At her or himself, she couldn't tell.

She eyed him, confused. "What did I say?"

He was silent, but she could see that something had deeply upset him.

She'd hit some kind of nerve, she thought. But what, she had no idea.

She mentally went back over what she'd said. She'd only mentioned battle scars? Patrol?

Maybe he really didn't know about what her uncle had just done. "Didn't my uncle tell – "

She faltered. She doubted he would take this well, assuming

he already knew. Uncle Sokol had told her Gavin had been informed that she was to transfer to Patrol. But her uncle might not be telling the truth.

His job, after all, was in Intelligence. Truth was used there as it suited his ends.

Gavin would probably have stormed in here if he'd thought she was about to join Patrol, she thought.

But she'd already started talking. Too late to take the words back now, she thought.

"My uncle," she began again.

Gavin's gaze was stormy, distant, elsewhere, as if he didn't hear her, or was trying not to.

"He's suggested I transfer to Patrol," she said in a rush, not looking at him. "I don't want to, I think it's a terrible idea, but you know how my uncle is, he's Minister of Intelligence, what he says goe– "

"Jossey," Gavin suddenly snapped.

She stopped, startled, and looked wide-eyed at him.

He stood up so fast he almost knocked the chair over. She shrank back involuntarily.

He paced over to the door, paced back, glaring at her.

He wasn't just Gavin anymore. He was Commander Tskoulis. The one feared by practically everyone in Patrol, the one who decimated the Onlar he encountered.

The Tiger.

She'd never seen Gavin actually angry, she thought. Not really.

"Gavin?" she ventured, not understanding this rapid shift. She was frightened by this change in him.

Was he that upset that she had been assigned to Patrol? She wasn't so fragile that she needed a babysitter, she thought angrily.

But even as overprotective as he could be, this was different. It was like he was an entirely different person – like she had struck a raw nerve. He seemed to be under some sort of terrible strain as he stalked back and forth.

He stormed back over to the chair and sat down, hard.

She stared at him, wide-eyed, shrinking back, fully aware for the first time just why people were so terrified of him.

Then she looked at his eyes.

They were bright with – tears?

"Jossey, I'm so sorry." He looked away from her. She stared in confusion. "I'm so sorry," he repeated.

"For wh– "

He was clenching his jaw, eyes bright.

She went on nervously. "Gavin, I don't hate Patrol, what I meant is I'm just not a fighter and I don't think it's a good id– "

He cut her off.

"We found Tark's body," he said.

Jossey gaped at him.

Gavin's eyes were unreadable as he looked at her. The dark shadows underneath were huge.

His face looked half-dead, as if he were letting her see the magnitude of his grief for the first time.

She didn't think he would make something like this up. Not Gavin.

The last time she'd seen him cry, he had been eight and he'd dropped his ice-cream cone. One of the street animals had trotted up and eaten it. Tark had bought him another one.

Tark.

She felt like she couldn't think for a moment.

Then the weight of what he had just said hit her like a physical blow.

She sank back into the pillows, blinking, seeing flashing lights. She couldn't breathe.

Somehow she gasped out, "Gavin – what?"

There was a weight on her chest, a great silence in her head.

Commander Tskoulis, the Tiger, was weeping silently in a chair in front of her. All she could see was the boy he had once been, the boy who had just lost his best friend to the creatures aboveground.

Because of me, she reminded herself.

He looked away from her, eyes red, and put his face in his hands. "I'm sorry," he repeated.

She felt the tears spill over and roll down her face, uncontrollable. She struggled to breathe. "Gavin," she said again, gasping for air. "Gavin, what?" Her throat hurt, an enormous knot fighting her airway for supremacy. She felt her face scrunch into a knot of its own. "What?" she repeated.

He looked at her.

"We found him on Patrol," he said quietly. "We were mapping a canyon and one of my recruits tripped and – "

He gave up speaking.

She stared, tears pouring down her face.

"How do you know it was him?" she finally managed.

He took a shuddering breath, looking at her, some terrible pain in his eyes. "Don't ask me that, Jossey," he said quietly. "Please."

"No, tell me, Gavin. How. How could you be su– "

He looked away, closing his eyes.

"Gavin, TELL ME." Her voice was barely controlled.

Gavin turned back to Jossey. His face was pale. "I don't want to hur– "

"TELL ME." Her teeth were clenched, her burned hand gripping so hard she yelped and released the fist. He glanced at her bandages, concern flashing across his face.

He sat back, raising his hands in surrender.

Jossey looked at him.

Gavin took a deep and shuddering breath.

In a deadened tone, he said carefully, not looking at her, "What do you most remember about Tark?"

"His sense of humor," she said, voice threatening to dissolve into tears again. "His stupid – "she half laughed. "His stupid jokes. Your pranks. Why?"

"No. Physically." Gavin's voice broke.

She blinked. Tark had always been a scrawny boy, tall, but very thin. He'd resembled their father, with pale eyes and even paler hair. The only one in his year.

They'd jokingly called him the Golden Boy.

"His hair," she said in a very small voice.

The weight in her chest was immense.

Gavin didn't meet her gaze.

She began to weep, and shoved her face into the pillow, trying to contain both the sound and her tears.

Gavin jumped to his feet, prying the pillow away from her. "Jossey, I'm sorry, I didn't want to tel– "

"I'm the one who killed him, Gavin," she choked, fumbling for the pillow. "It's my fault. Mine. Why don't you hate me?"

He stared down at her, letting her take the pillow from suddenly-still hands.

"Why don't you hate me?" she repeated, voice breaking. She pressed her face into the pillow again, clutching it to her, soaking it with her tears.

Gavin didn't respond.

As she cried, she heard him leave the room.

23

Jossey tried to make herself presentable in front of the mirror. It had been three days since Gavin had told her they'd found her brother. Every time she'd thought about it, her eyes would well up and she'd retreat to her hospital bed.

Sleep. Sleep had helped a lot.

It was nearly all she had wanted to do. Sometimes the nurse would slip in and leave food for her, but she left it untouched, staring at the tray in the dark, holding onto her pillow as she soaked it with her tears.

Sometimes, the nurse would make her drink water just to keep her hydrated. Jossey was too weak to protest.

Once, Caspar had stopped by, but the nurse had intercepted him in the hallway, and whatever she'd said to him, he'd stood very still for a long moment, and then gone away.

Gavin had come back, once. He'd looked at her coldly, and sat down and told her the story.

She'd listened silently, then finally told him to get out. She hadn't meant to hurt him, but she couldn't hear anymore. Couldn't think anymore.

He hadn't come back.

She wondered what had happened to Tark.

It had been fifteen years.

She lay there in the dark, staring at the uneaten food. All she could picture was the small skull on the ground, the soldier's horrified reaction.

She felt irrationally angry at the young recruit for having discovered the...remains – she could barely bring herself to think the word – by essentially falling on them.

And the Onlar.

She remembered Tark's smug grin as Teacher Peterson had glared at him from the front of the classroom.

"I've heard Patrol only finds bones," Tark had said.

She remembered the gleeful laughter as he and Gavin had fled into the tunnels.

She remembered her pleas for Tark to take her up above-ground to see the moon. How they could go quickly, and Mother and Father probably wouldn't notice.

She thought about the Onlar, and whatever they had done to her brother, and something deep within her shattered.

Now, she stood in front of the mirror, carefully putting her spare uniform together, pinning on the Engineering badge just so. Her uncle had already told her personally that he wanted her to join Patrol, but she wasn't taking any chances. He was not, technically, head of Patrol, after all.

Even if he was effectively in charge anyway.

She had wild thoughts of sneaking up to the surface herself if Patrol said no. She would need a weapon, she thought. She didn't know what the nurse had done with the curved knife she'd brought with her.

She had a moment of terror. What if they'd confiscated it? She'd always wondered just how legal it was.

"Nurse!" Her voice came out high-pitched, frantic. She coughed, smoothed her uniform.

She had to appear rational. Logical.

She tried again, more even-toned this time. "Nurse!"

The nurse opened the door. "Yes, Miss Sokol?"

"Where is my weapon?"

The nurse – Marian, Jossey thought – stepped into the room, hands folded. "Miss, your effects were stored for you."

"I need it. Immediately."

"Of course, Miss Sokol." She disappeared.

Jossey breathed a sigh of relief and turned back to the mirror. She looked awful. Puffy eyes. Sallow skin. But it would have to do. In fact, she reflected, looking awful might actually give her an advantage in this situation.

The more legitimate her desire for revenge seemed, the better.

The nurse returned, carrying Jossey's knife in a scabbard. Jossey took it from her. "Thank you."

She pulled it out of the scabbard, inspecting the blade. It had been cleaned, apparently.

That was good – for the blade. But she was almost disappointed.

"Nurse," she said.

The woman was still waiting there, hands clasped tightly, and for the first time in her life Jossey felt no shame in using her status.

"I need you to make me an appointment with the Minister of Intelligence. For today. And I need you to check me out of the hospital. I need to go home."

The nurse looked stricken. Jossey got the sense the first request was far, far above the woman's station.

"He is my uncle," Jossey said more kindly.

"Yes, Miss Sokol."

The nurse didn't look at her. Jossey felt a little guilty.

"Oh, and nurse? Marian, right?"

The woman turned to her, hands clasped even more firmly than before, so tightly they were pink and white.

"Please get in touch with Commander Tskoulis," Jossey said gently. "I need him to accompany me."

It was about half an hour before there was a knock at Jossey's door. She looked up. She'd strapped on the leg holster and shined the Engineering badge. Her eyes looked reasonably un-puffy.

She smiled faintly as Gavin entered the room, eyes dark with fatigue. He was in full uniform, sans mask. He towered over her and muttered a greeting, not smiling.

Her own smile faded.

"Let's go," he said quietly, not meeting her gaze.

They stepped out into the corridor. Jossey was beyond glad to be leaving behind the hospital room, but she felt as if she were stepping into an unfamiliar world.

The corridor was surprisingly bright – she winced at the light – and the noise was overwhelming. She'd been secluded for quite some time, she realized.

She also realized the staff were staring at her. Furtively, yes, but they were there. She was used to stares, but these were different.

More...fearful. Awed.

Because she had killed an Onlar, she thought.

She was glad Gavin was with her. Especially in his uniform, he parted crowds. She followed in his wake, ignoring the looks, the whispers. So much for patient confidentiality, she thought wryly.

They came to an open reception area, and Jossey was waved through by one of the medical assistants.

"You're all set, Miss Sokol," the man said.

Status did have its perks, she thought.

The City Square was full of life. It was midday, and lunch break. The new doughnut shop had a line out the door. Jossey glanced over at it. The Engineers' visit seemed weeks ago.

Entire clusters of people stopped and stared, whispering, as she crossed the Square with the Tiger. She ignored them, looked determinedly forward. She also ignored her still-bandaged hand, which had begun to throb with the light exercise.

A wound was a wound. She'd probably have to get used to those if she joined Patrol.

Voices rang off the cavern's walls as they crossed the main Square. She looked around, not meeting anyone's eyes, wondering why it was so busy until she saw all the Founders' Day flags being hung from the shop fronts and up the outer sides of the torus-shaped inner tunnel-corridors that ringed the Square. *Circle*, she thought wryly. Like Founders' Day, the word "square" seemed like a traditional holdover from the City's early days, when she knew this place had been basically a cavern, dug from the earth and lit by superefficient solar-powered banks of lights. They'd learned about it in Engineering.

The modern City was a technological wonder, and she marveled at it as usual as they made their way across through the crowds. It was a stack of torus-shaped tunnel-corridors, built around an enclosed center, the remnants of the cavern it had once been. Each level was built as three horizontally-concentric circles: inner for living quarters, mid for navigation, and the outer tunnels, which were carved as far out as necessary into the earth and were off-limits to all but Patrol. Those tunnels spiraled like galaxy arms upward to the surface, and branched out to other places she didn't know, secret passages to nowhere, or nowhere she was supposed to go, anyway.

Somehow the Founding population had built all this in a short period of time, using equipment that was now lost to the dust of history, or at least not taught in Engineering classes.

She'd always wondered, but hadn't known who might tell her.

The Ministry, to which they were heading, was on sublevel 4. She didn't know what was below that, beyond storage and the mechanical rooms. No one seemed to. Not even Gavin. She'd asked.

She looked at him as he forged ahead. He had been dead silent since leaving the hospital room. She had no idea how to react – he'd never ignored her before, not like this. It was her fault, she thought, but still.

The secure elevator system was located next to the City Hall at the far end of the Square. As they approached, Gavin glanced back at her. She looked at him. He looked away.

24

THE GUARD SNAPPED TO ATTENTION WHEN THE PAIR WALKED UP to the elevator, saluting Gavin, and waved them through without so much as a question. Jossey followed, glad she'd asked Gavin to accompany her.

Apparently she was accompanying him, she thought, faintly amused.

The elevator, too, had a guard when they got on. He looked straight ahead as they entered, only quirking an eyebrow when the commander said, "Sublevel 4, Ministry of Intelligence."

Jossey noticed a second door in the elevator, on the opposite wall. She had a vague recollection of it opening onto a secret corridor that ran behind the standard SL-4 ring.

She almost smiled. Tark had loved this type of thing.

Gavin seemed to be thinking the same thing. She glanced sideways at him. He still didn't look at her.

She sighed to herself.

The elevator jumped, and began to descend.

One level. Two. Three.

As they descended, the guard keyed in a code and opened a small panel in the wall. He looked apologetic as he issued them wristbands, activating them with the touch of a button. They both displayed the same sequence of numbers. "For the Ministry's doors," he said. "One-time codes."

Gavin didn't even blink. Clearly he was used to this.

"It's for security, sir, miss," the guard said. "I know who you are."

Jossey took hers without comment. It was thin, made of the plastic material that only the Ministry had access to. It was flexible, and locked onto her wrist immediately when she slipped it on. She didn't know what kind of adhesive they used, but she knew it couldn't be removed without an instrument only security had.

She found it funny that even Commander Tskoulis of Patrol was required to wear a security badge. With a tracker.

In case he went rogue, or something. She didn't know.

She didn't care. She was willing to go through whatever hoops Intelligence required to get to her uncle's office.

The elevator slid open, revealing the second corridor. It was paneled differently than the normal inner and mid tunnels, with blue and green neon lighting strips along the edges, and it was very, very empty. She saw only one guard, pacing up and down.

How depressing, she thought.

She looked in both directions as they exited the elevator. The circle was quite large, the light fading before it curved into oblivion. She followed Gavin silently, half-running to keep up with his stride.

He finally turned to her, looking down at her, face inscrutable.

"If you're going to be on Patrol, you have to keep up," he said flatly.

She stared at him. His eyes were dark. Cold. More like Commander Tskoulis than the Gavin she knew.

She clamped her mouth shut and hurried after him, face burning.

The tunnel curved gently, and they followed the green lights until they came to an unobtrusive door in the outer side. Gavin stepped up to it, keyed in the code on his bracelet. She followed suit.

It hissed open.

They were at the end of a long straight corridor, with another guard at the end. The corridor was chilly.

Seems the Ministry can afford air conditioning, Jossey thought sourly. In a useless outer corridor, no less. Her own living quarters were reasonably cool, but this was freezing. Pleasantly so, but she rubbed her arms as she walked along.

Gavin stopped and waited for her to catch up. She ignored the look he gave her, and stepped up to the door, holding up her wristband for the guard.

The guard looked them over. "Names and business?"

"Jossey Sokol. Engineer. I'm here to see my uncle, Minister Sokol. Gav – *Commander* Tskoulis is accompanying me. On Patrol business."

The guard looked warily at Gavin, then stepped aside. "Enter."

Sokol's office was gorgeous, Jossey had to admit, glancing around as they stepped through the door. He'd somehow managed to procure plants that seemed fine with artificial light, and they were *everywhere*. She made a mental note to ask him for one for her living quarters.

Her uncle was seated at the desk, sipping what appeared to

be some kind of tea. He smiled and stood, coming around his desk and kissing Jossey lightly on both cheeks.

He shook hands with Gavin.

"Sit, please," he said to them.

Jossey sat. She watched his face. His smile never left, but his eyes were as flat as ever.

She wondered how much of that cold look she had inherited. She certainly felt like it right now. She attempted to smile.

"To what do I owe the pleasure?" the Minister said smoothly.

Gavin was silent. Jossey glanced at him, then looked at her uncle. "Uncle Sokol, I'm here to join Patrol, as you've asked."

Gavin looked faintly pained, but remained silent.

Sokol looked between them. "Commander Tskoulis. So nice to see you again. What brings you here?"

Gavin looked at Jossey. "I was requested to accompany your niece," he said formally. "I am here to – support her in her petition to join Patrol."

Jossey glanced at him sharply.

He did not look at her. "She is a highly competent candidate and I would recommend her without hesitation," he said.

Jossey could feel her face turning pink. "Uncle Sokol," she began.

Her uncle silenced her with a wave of his hand. He turned his attention to Gavin.

"Tskoulis, tell me. Is she aware of the latest developments – "

Latest developments. Tark's remains. Jossey tried not to grimace, tried to keep her face neutral.

Gavin said flatly, "She is aware."

Jossey had asked Gavin to accompany her because she wanted him to hear all of this directly from her uncle, not have it filter down to him through whatever chain of command he was in. Out of line, maybe, but she thought he deserved to have some kind of input, especially as a Patrol commander.

133

And, more importantly, maybe if he heard it from her uncle, he'd be more agreeable with fast-tracking her to a surface unit.

She hadn't expected him to actually *agree* with the Minister.

All of this flashed through her mind as the Minister went on. "Very good. And you feel that, given this knowledge, she is in a sufficient state of mind to joi– "

"I do." Gavin's voice was dark.

Jossey looked at him again, stunned.

She'd never heard anyone cut off her uncle. Anyone.

But Sokol seemed more amused than bothered.

"Well, then, Commander. Your professional opinion is well noted."

Sokol turned to Jossey, and his expression became more gentle. She thought she saw a flicker of something in the flatness of his eyes.

"I am deeply sorry to hear about your brother, my dear," he said kindly. "He was my favorite nephew. I am glad we have some closure at last."

He was your only nephew, she thought. But she forced a smile onto her face.

Sokol tapped a couple of things on his desk-screen. Two forms appeared, glowing softly, on the surface. "Shall we, then?"

He beckoned her closer. She approached the desk. She'd never been this close before – last time she'd been here, she had been about six and everything about his office had been intimidating.

Tark had run around touching things until Father had told him to stop, and Uncle Sokol had just laughed. "He can't break anything, Rupert," he had said. Jossey hadn't been so sure.

The desk was beautiful, custom woodwork with an inlaid screen. It was an antique, an heirloom. She felt a slight flicker of jealousy that he'd never taken more of an interest in her life, even after Tark had gone missing and Father had –

She stopped thinking. She'd already lost two family

members to the Onlar. She refused to give the creatures any more of her grief. That was why she was here.

The form glowed softly in front of her. She realized she was supposed to read it.

"Sorry," she murmured, taking a closer look.

It had a standard non-liability clause – *You may lose life and/or limb in pursuit of your Patrol duties, after which time, if any, Patrol pension is set to provide for any remaining family members so long as they are of minority age* – and a selection box.

Which unit do I want to be in?

She glanced at Gavin, who was staring fixedly at the wall, jaw clenched.

"Uncle," she said quietly.

"Yes, my dear?"

Did she want to be in Gavin's unit?

Half of her screamed no. She didn't want to always be Tark's little sister, the one Gavin felt the need to protect. Even if Tark was gone. She felt grateful to him, but –

She'd killed an Onlar. On her own. How much protection did she really need?

And the way Gavin had acted back in the security tunnel – she wasn't sure which Gavin she might be serving under. Her Gavin...or Commander Tskoulis. She gulped.

She nervously glanced at him. He was steadfastly ignoring her.

He doesn't want me to join, she thought. *Well, that's too bad.*

"What is Gavin's – that is, Commander Tskoulis' – unit?" she asked slyly.

Gavin swung around. "Jossey," he hissed.

"You said you'd protect me," she hissed back. "How are you going to do that if you're in a different unit?"

"The Commander oversees all of Patrol Unit 2," Sokol said calmly. "That is ten subunits. To have you serve directly within his subunit is not feasible, I'm afraid, but you have been assigned to one of the other subunits under his command."

"Understood, Minister." The young commander's voice was cold.

Jossey flushed a little as she realized she really, really hadn't understood how the Patrol units worked, sub- or otherwise, and how arrogant her request had probably sounded.

She almost laughed. The Tiger was all but universally feared within Patrol, probably worked with the elite of the elite, she told herself. She could barely wield a knife. She looked away and muttered, "Yes, sir, that's what I was hoping. Thank you."

So that was why Gavin was so upset, she thought. Not only did he not want her to join, he knew it would probably be very difficult for them to work directly together.

Or maybe he *didn't* want to work directly with her, or with her at all, after what she'd said to him, she thought unhappily.

She looked at the screen, refusing to make eye contact with either of them.

"I have already assigned you to a subunit, my dear." Sokol tapped a button. A number appeared: 2-5. She glanced at Gavin. His uniform said 2-1. She looked back at the screen.

Sokol tapped the screen again. "As it happens, and as I mentioned to you in our earlier conversation, there is at least one other individual assigned to your subunit with whom you are familiar."

A photo appeared on the desk.

Caspar.

She blinked. She hadn't seen Caspar in days. Hadn't seen any of them. She had a faint memory of a sly grin and amused silver eyes.

Sokol was speaking. She looked up.

"In fact, I believe he is due for an appointment with me shortly. Standard intake procedure. Why don't you wait just a moment? After you sign, of course." He gestured to the desk.

She glanced at her uncle. It seemed odd that she had made a special appointment with him, with almost no warning time, and yet he had an appointment with Caspar directly after hers.

He smiled smoothly at her confused expression. "Naturally, my dear, it only made sense to process everything at once. I'm a busy man."

She wondered how quickly his assistants had had to get THAT set up.

The sheet glowed up at her. She glanced through it.

Life and limb.

Sounds like an adventure.

She didn't look at Gavin, and signed.

25

"Suit up!"

The call blared down the hallway. Jossey groaned and rolled over, fumbling for her alarm clock, realized there was none.

She stared at the ceiling, at the bunk above her. She remembered now – with three hours of warning, at 9:00 PM, they'd gone through her living quarters, quickly packed up anything she might need into a standard-issue duffel, and taken her down to sublevel 1, where Patrol apparently lived. She'd managed to grab a few small items of personal value before they'd sealed her quarters and shut off any energy inputs.

At least her uncle had given her an extra week of reprieve for her hand to heal sufficiently before Patrol came to take her on. Her concussion was anyone's guess.

She wasn't sure why they were so particular, why they insisted on packing her bags themselves, but the crisply-dressed agent had told her it was for security. Amazingly, she'd been allowed to keep her knife. But no outside reading material.

Karapartei, she thought. *Idea-sharing. Recruiting.*

"Suit up!" The call came again, blaring over a loudspeaker. She rolled out of bed. She'd been assigned to a room with two women – Maja and Olivia. Maja was already awake and fully suited – tall, strong, athletic.

And unfriendly so far.

Jossey hadn't met Olivia yet – the woman had already been asleep when Jossey had come in after lights-out. She'd just been told their names, said hello briefly to Maja, who'd let her in, and been told to report to the mess hall at 6:00 sharp.

She glanced at her wrist. 5:40.

Not much earlier than solar crew, she thought. She got up, grabbing for her things. Maja was already by the door. Olivia was in the bathroom. Jossey said good morning to the tall woman. Maja stared openly at her face, at the scar running across Jossey's eye, and barely smiled.

Okay then. Jossey half-smiled, trying not to care. She wasn't here to make friends, she told herself.

They joined a flood of recruits in the hallway and trooped down a set of stairs to an open area. She tried to cover her yawns as she shuffled into a food line behind one of the male recruits. He turned around, started to say hello, then seemed to recognize her and simply stared, open-mouthed.

Great.

Maja didn't scoot over when Jossey went to go sit at their table. The tall woman eyed her with distaste.

Jossey stared at her for a long moment, noting Olivia's apologetic smile, then shrugged and walked to an empty table. Food was food.

She sat down and tasted the nasty-looking stuff on her plate, looking around curiously. Most of the tables were full of men; a few women sat in clusters here and there. She didn't recognize anyone; she'd gone straight into Engineering school after the first two years of secondary school, and that had been a decade ago.

She thought one of the bigger men on the far end *might* look like Eddie, the kid who'd blown up his science fair experiment in sixth grade, if she squinted hard enough.

"May I sit?"

She looked up, startled, to see Caspar smiling down at her.

She smiled. "Good morning. It's been a while."

"Yes, it has. Your roommates aren't here?"

"The tall one – doesn't seem fond of me." She glanced over her shoulder. Indeed, Maja was giving her a death-glare from across the way.

He followed her gaze. "Wow. You make friends quickly."

Jossey poked at the slop on her plate and sighed. "I literally have done nothing to her. I came in after lights-out, I guess? The other one seems nice enough."

Caspar shrugged, taking a giant bite. *He* seemed to enjoy the food, she thought sourly.

Somehow the Patrol uniform, plus the half-ponytail, made him look even more handsome. She blinked the thought away, annoyed at herself. She didn't have time to think those things. Besides, with her scar, why would he ever –

She stopped thinking, took another bite of food.

At least he didn't seem to flaunt it. Gavin seemed to revel in the effect he had on people, she thought, half-smiling to herself.

Caspar looked at her. "What?"

"Nothing." She smeared some of the...bean paste?...on her bread. "How do you stand this stuff?"

"We ate a lot worse back when I was an apprentice." He grinned, silver eyes dancing. "I think it was fully artificial. Your roommate's staring at you again."

She didn't turn around. "It's probably my scar. I think some people are bothered by it. Not my problem."

He snorted. "Probably the fact that you don't have to prove yourself to the boys. They already know who you are. I guess your commander friend told the entire unit about the security...incident. He was, um, most displeased."

140

She could imagine. Caspar went on. *"My* roommates wouldn't stop asking me about what happened in the tunnels, how you fought the Onlar."

Jossey was horrified. "What do you– "

"FIVE MINUTES," a familiar voice bellowed, cutting her off.

Jossey whipped around. Gavin was standing there, in full uniform, hands behind his back.

Only it wasn't Gavin here. She reminded herself she couldn't call him that. Commander Tskoulis. Tskoulis for short. Or just Commander.

She glanced down at her own uniform, where the badge said 2-5.

She looked back up at Gavin for a long moment. He was scanning the room.

His gaze passed right over her without apparent recognition. She wilted.

Caspar tapped her plate with his fork, and she realized he'd been watching her. She quickly looked away from his gaze.

"Better hurry," was all he said.

"I know." She stuffed another forkful of maybe-beans into her mouth, trying not to breathe.

Maja and Olivia hurried down the hallway ahead of her, bags slung over their shoulders. Jossey was glad she'd at least noticed the bags before going to the mess hall. She pulled hers up higher on her back, hoping her old leg injury wouldn't ache today.

The training area was a wide-open space, she guessed somewhere between sublevels 1 and 2. It was a giant square. Sets of weights and other mysterious-looking piles of equipment were scattered around the perimeter. A series of red rubbery mats was laid out on the ground.

Jossey followed the group over to the mats. Olivia split off and joined a different subunit. The Patrol troops stood in clusters, whispering, as Commander Tskoulis walked to the front of the room and turned to them.

He didn't need to shout, didn't need to say a word. They all went dead silent, standing up straighter, as if by instinct. There was an undercurrent of something in the air – excitement. Fear.

He seemed even taller in full uniform.

"Good morning, troops," he said.

His voice was like gravel. Powerful. Not the friendly, joking Gavin she knew.

"Good morning, SIR!"

Jossey looked around, awed at the response. He'd never used *this* version of himself on her.

Tskoulis glanced wordlessly at a group of tall men dressed in dark-blue uniforms. They immediately stepped up next to him, stood in a line, shoulders squared.

"In brief. For the new members among us, welcome to Patrol," he went on. "These are the members of my subunit, 2-1. You report to them." He looked around the room, eyes piercing. "I want no reports about you *from* them. Do you understand me?"

"Sir!"

The room shouted, Jossey along with them.

For just a split second, Tskoulis' eyes passed over her, and she saw a tiny flicker of – something. Then he looked away.

"That is all. You may begin this week with basic training. Remember, failure is an option here. Just not one you probably want." He grinned a little, glanced at his men. "Carry on."

With that, Tskoulis strode out of the training room, taking a couple of his men with him, and she saw everyone else visibly relax. She let out a breath she didn't realize she'd been holding.

"Wow," she muttered to Caspar as she watched the commander go.

He looked down at her, a mocking smile on his face. "Don't tell me you too are overawed by the Tiger."

"I am no such thing." She made a face, feeling herself turning pink at the suggestion.

The mocking smile hovered around his mouth as he opened it.

"Recruits!"

She and Caspar fell silent as one of the subunit leaders strode over to their group.

"Three paces apart. Now." He looked at them coldly. "I want absolute silence on this training floor."

Jossey snapped to attention and stepped away from Caspar. She found herself next to Maja, who looked coldly at her. She tried to smile.

The man stood in front of them, hands behind his back. "My name is Sergeant Henry. I work directly with Commander Tskoulis. When I am not on duty with him, you are under my command."

"Yes, sir." They stood straighter.

Henry was tall, dark hair, green eyes. He had a warm smile, like Gavin, and an air that clearly said he would not appreciate incompetence. Jossey tried her best to look as awake as possible, regretting that she'd only had one cup of what passed for "coffee" in the mess.

He asked for their names. It was Jossey, Maja, Caspar, and three others — Thompson, "Elisedd, Ellis for short," and Wickford.

Thompson was the recruit who had stared at Jossey in line. He kept glancing at her. Ellis looked less than enthused to be there. Wickford looked at ease, but with an air of faint awkwardness, as if he knew he were prone to tripping over his own feet.

Wickford. The name sounded vaguely familiar, but Jossey couldn't place it.

Henry glanced from face to face. "This is training day," he said. "We train every morning, and one full day a week. The rest of the time, auxiliary Engineers work directly with your respective teams on whatever the commander orders."

They watched him silently.

"Now," he said. "Let's begin."

Now? thought Jossey. He seemed serious. She fidgeted.

"Any injuries?" He glanced at Jossey, at the bandage still on her hand.

"My burn is okay." It probably wasn't, but she didn't care. But her head was another story. She needed that fully intact. She pointed to it with her bandaged hand. "Concussion, a couple of weeks ago."

"Very well." He smiled warmly, and she guessed that he, too, knew how she'd gotten her injuries. "Try not to go for Sokol's head until she's healed," he said to the rest of them. "But don't forget. There are no safeguards in the tunnels."

Jossey murmured, "Yes, sir."

She could see Maja looking at her out of the corner of her eye. *What is your problem,* she thought.

Henry gestured to the bags on their backs. "Let's start with basic self-defense."

26

THEY PULLED OPEN THE BAGS.

The equipment bags contained folding poles, what looked like boxing gloves, and pads for the chest and head. Jossey slipped hers on, apprehensive.

"First let's see where you all are in terms of skill," Henry said. "Pair up. Warm up."

Jossey lined up opposite Maja. The tall woman cracked her knuckles. Jossey eyed her and stretched her own arms.

Caspar's words sounded in her head. "You don't have to prove yourself to the boys," he'd said. Or something like that. She needed more coffee to process what he'd meant. A lot more, she suspected.

She glanced over at him. He was opposite Thompson, who kept craning his neck to turn around and glance at her. Caspar seemed amused by this. She turned back to Maja.

"Sokol, is it?" Maja said.

"That's right." Jossey glanced at her uniform. It said ZLOTNIK.

I guess we're on last-name terms, she thought.

"I hear you killed an Onlar."

"I did." Jossey didn't smile.

"Is that why you're here? You enjoy fighting?" Maja smiled. "Because I do."

It's too early for this, Jossey thought. *I've done nothing wrong.*

Ellis looked bored. "Zlotnik, be nice."

The tall woman made a face at him, cracked her knuckles again. "Speak for yourself, Ellis. A newbie's a newbie. Gotta learn the Patrol way."

Ellis shrugged. "Yeah, well, she's not a hundred percent a newbie."

Thompson was grinning at Jossey. She felt her face burning.

Zlotnik groaned, throwing a glance Thompson's way. "You too?"

I hate you, Gavin.

"All right, enough." Henry cut through their conversation. "Let's go. Hands up."

Jossey found herself staring into Zlotnik's eyes. The tall woman seemed to be enjoying this, trying to intimidate her.

Jossey remembered the Onlar, its burning green eyes, its inhuman hissing. She held up her hands, balled them into fists.

She was down on the mat before she realized what had happened. Zlotnik looked almost disappointed.

Jossey didn't look at any of them, especially Caspar. Her face was hot with embarrassment.

"Get up," Henry snapped. "Again."

She was down a moment later, chest throbbing where Zlotnik had hit her, hard.

They gave her a break. She sat and watched Thompson and Caspar square off. Henry was watching closely.

Thompson wasn't bad, she thought. He was clearly experi-

146

enced in hand-to-hand combat. As far as Jossey knew, Caspar had last fought as an apprentice Patrol, but he seemed to be enjoying himself, as if he'd been away from the training floor for far too long.

Thompson lunged forward and Caspar stepped aside casually, as if he'd been waiting. Under his red helmet, Jossey could see his long silver eyes narrowed as he watched Thompson.

Thompson did not seem to have been expecting this, and staggered as he tried to back up, regain his footing. Caspar threw a punch that barely missed him.

They circled each other. Ellis perked up a little.

Caspar didn't seem to be afraid of being hit. He just seemed to be taking his time in a strange way. Jossey frowned.

Finally, Thompson landed what looked like a direct hit. As he did, Caspar shoved Thompson's striking arm to the side and threw his weight into a solid punch to Thompson's jaw.

Thompson staggered back, clutching his face. Jossey blinked. Something about the movement had seemed off to her.

In general, something about the fluid way Caspar moved was ringing a bell in her head somewhere.

Henry said, "All right. Stand down."

"I have a good idea of where you all are now." The sergeant stood there quietly. Jossey got to her feet. They all lined up.

Jossey was quite all right with staying far away from the mats for now.

The sergeant seemed to be thinking. He turned to Caspar. "You were in Patrol how long ago?"

"Thirteen years, sir."

Henry raised an eyebrow. Thompson was sporting a rapidly-swelling bruise on his face. He was breathing hard. Caspar, on the other hand, looked completely untouched. And relaxed, despite the last several minutes. As if he were playing a game of shuttlepong.

"Not as efficient of a hit as I'd like," said Henry, smiling. "There's room for improvement. But still impressive, considering." He looked carefully at Caspar. "Excellent reflexes. Are you sure it was that long ago?"

"Yes, sir. Well, I was on call-up for three years after that. But yes, sir, that's correct." Caspar grinned and clapped Thompson on the shoulder. "You have a nasty right hook. I did what I had to."

Jossey gave Thompson a thumbs-up. He turned pink.

Zlotnik huffed and looked away.

The room went silent. Tskoulis had just entered.

Henry went and spoke with him. Jossey pulled off the helmet and gloves and held them loosely, watching. The other sergeants had gone over as well. The commander seemed to be telling them about something.

"Where'd you learn to fight?"

Jossey jumped. Thompson was smiling at her.

"Me? I didn't," she said. "Didn't you see me just now?"

He looked dumbfounded for a moment. "Then how'd you – "

"The Onlar – " She glanced at Caspar, who was looking at Thompson with an odd expression on his face. "It just kind of – happened. I wasn't really thinking," she said truthfully. She assumed they all knew the details.

"Instinctive fighting. Nice," Thompson said, facial expression dead serious.

In the background, Caspar bit his knuckle as if to keep from laughing.

Jossey felt flustered, felt the need to stop Thompson from continuing. Whatever Zlotnik was angry about, it seemed to have to do with this, she thought. And indeed, Zlotnik looked annoyed. But the woman kept her mouth shut. Henry was heading back across the floor to them.

"At ease," Henry said. He did not fill them in.

He pointed to the pads. "Back on."

Jossey watched Zlotnik as they lined up again. Henry took them through a series of basic self-defense moves. To her credit, Zlotnik performed them as ordered, nothing sneaky.

They took a break. Jossey's arms were aching. And her chest. She was grateful for the pads. She sat, took a big swig of water from her canteen.

Thompson and Ellis sat apart from the rest, talking in low tones about something. Caspar wandered off and refilled his canteen. *He* seemed just fine, Jossey noticed. Like he could do this all day.

Maybe he was one of those gym people, she thought. Some of the other Patrol definitely looked like it. Then she almost laughed. Most of the Engineers she knew spent their free time napping. Caspar might be tall, muscular, but didn't look the type to get obsessed with protein stats and leg day and whatever else.

He looked like – well, like he'd been the type of kid who read *The Desert Rider* and thought it was worth saving for twenty-plus years. A goof. Like Gavin. And Tark. At the thought, she allowed herself a smile.

Zlotnik sat as far from Jossey as possible, tying her boot laces.

"How long have you been on Patrol?" Jossey asked her.

Zlotnik grunted. "Two years." She yanked the laces out of her boots. "I hate these."

Jossey got the hint. She focused on stretching.

"Up," said Henry, much sooner than Jossey had hoped. "Break's over."

27

JOSSEY FLOPPED ONTO HER BED. IT WAS JUST AFTER DINNER, BUT she couldn't move. She thought about turning off the light, but it was so far away.

At least tomorrow should be a normal day, she thought.

They'd been working for six hours, with a lunch break. Gavin hadn't been kidding before about keeping up, she thought. She thought she had done all right, considering her lack of fighting experience. No one had laughed at her, at least.

Well, almost no one.

Gav – Tskoulis, she told herself – had stopped by and watched them, making the rounds of all the units. She'd managed to get in a couple of good hits over the day, but that round she'd gotten hit pretty solidly by Zlotnik.

She'd gone down hard, lain gasping for breath on the mat while Zlotnik stood over her.

Tskoulis hadn't so much as looked at her. It had been Caspar who'd asked if she was okay, had grabbed her water.

She was, physically.

She had watched Tskoulis walk away, her chest aching.

. . .

She woke up in the dark.

She'd fallen asleep, hadn't realized it. It must be late, she thought. She rolled over a little, tried to see the time, but froze when she heard Olivia and Zlotnik whispering.

"You've got to calm down," Olivia was saying. "You can't compromise unit integrity. You know that."

Jossey stared at the bunk above her. That was Zlotnik's. Olivia's was across the room.

"I can't stand it, Olivia. She's been – stupid Thompson won't shut up about her. After she left at dinner – I know he gets a crush on every female recruit, but this time it's like – " She hissed. "Sokol this, Sokol that. It's ridiculous. She can't even fight."

Olivia was quiet, said cautiously, "She killed an Onlar. That's not exactly typical of a new recruit. So even if she's not great at fighting, there must be a reason that – "

Zlotnik snorted.

Jossey wanted to close her ears, stop from hearing any more.

Zlotnik went on. "I watched her today. I went easy on her. She has *no* skill, Olivia. None. She got here because her uncle is Minister. You remember how I started? I *earned* my spot. I started from nothing. She's just a pampered Council kid. And now they're fawning all over her. For what? An Onlar falling on her knife?" She made an unpleasant sound. "An accident?"

Jossey felt her face burning. *I was fighting fair*, she thought furiously. *I was following Henry's instructions. Sticking to the training.*

The training, she thought. Something occurred to her – the ease with which Caspar had learned it. Something was buzzing in the back of her mind.

"Shh," Olivia said. "She can probably hear you."

"She's asleep. Out like a light. I checked."

"Well, still. We shouldn't be – "

Zlotnik huffed. "She'll probably make a mistake, and be out

in a day like that one kid. Wickford. The clumsy one in my unit. You know the one with reddish hair? He was on night mission up aboveground for what, twice? Then he got demoted." She snorted. "I'm not sure how he didn't get thrown out of Patrol. Endangered the mission. Tskoulis was MAD, from what Ellis told me."

Olivia was silent for a long time. "Maja, you should get some sleep," she finally said. "Ignore Thompson. Don't take it personally. Let the commander sort it out. If Sokol's not competent, he's the one to deal with it."

Jossey bit her lip to stop from screaming at them.

She waited until they were quiet, then rolled over and stared into the darkness for a long time.

28

As she lay there, nearly asleep at last, a memory floated to the surface.

A half-remembered movement. The way Caspar had taken the knife from Liam back in the tunnel, right before Patrol had shown up to rescue them.

She'd been half-delirious with heat and her burn and her concussion, but part of her had noted the fluidity of the action, the casual ease with which he'd reached for it as if he'd been holding one for years.

The way he'd wielded the stretcher pole when she was scrabbling for the flare. Not awkwardly, like Liam had, but like he could do real damage with it up close.

The way he'd automatically wiped the Onlar's blood on his uniform.

Habit, he'd said.

Her eyes opened. That's what she'd found odd about the way he'd moved when he'd hit Thompson.

That's what Henry had been frowning about, as if he weren't sure what he'd just seen, she thought. Caspar had pulled that punch.

29

JOSSEY FELT HALF-DEAD THE NEXT DAY. SHE STAGGERED INTO THE mess hall.

Caspar looked mildly concerned as she ate her food automatically. She mumbled hello to him around a mouthful of fake eggs and kept eating.

"Good morning," Thompson said brightly, plunking himself down across from her. Jossey looked up at him foggily over her cup of disgusting coffee.

He pushed the bowl of sugar toward her. "Need some?"

She smiled and said, "I'm fine, thanks." He looked disappointed.

No need to give Zlotnik any more ammunition.

Caspar leaned over and said quietly, "You might want to have some more of that coffee. We have more training scheduled today, according to Ellis. At least this morning. And I doubt Henry is going to go easy on us."

Jossey absently took the coffee and poured more into her mug.

She flinched as Zlotnik sat down. Caspar looked up.

"Good morning," Zlotnik said, smiling at the others. Caspar responded in kind, silver eyes cool, as Jossey mumbled a reply.

He turned to Ellis and began discussing something training-related that Jossey tuned out. He did not offer Zlotnik coffee.

They lined up in pairs again. At least today was supposed to be a short session, thought Jossey. She looked warily at Zlotnik.

"Let's try to incorporate what you learned yesterday," Henry said. "Sokol, Zlotnik, let's start with you. Ready?"

Almost as soon as Henry opened his mouth, Zlotnik had moved sideways and flipped Jossey to the mat.

Jossey didn't move for a long moment, looking up at Zlotnik, trying not to smile.

She'd been right.

She'd lain awake long after Zlotnik and Olivia's conversation, thinking about it, thinking about how Zlotnik fought. Thinking about how the others fought.

Zlotnik was swift and brutal, but she had a flaw: she was *too* straightforward. She went for the obvious weaknesses, Jossey had noticed. So far it had been Jossey's sense of balance. She hadn't yet learned to stand strong enough to not be moved if struck yesterday. Now she had, and Zlotnik had attacked her sense of balance sideways.

Jossey was an Engineer. To her, Zlotnik's logic was sound, useful even. To demolish a building, you went for the stress points.

And Jossey had an obvious stress point. One that Henry hadn't forbidden.

The caffeine was starting to hit her system.

Fine, she thought. *I thought we were fighting fair. But let's do it your way.*

There are no safeguards in the tunnels, the sergeant had said.

She stood up, slightly wobbly, ignoring the pain in her bad leg. She'd slept on it wrong, on purpose.

Zlotnik noticed. She glanced at Jossey's injured leg, just barely, and smiled a little.

Jossey stood still, watching her carefully, noticing the direction of her gaze.

How pathetic, she thought.

"Go," said Henry.

"You got this, Sokol," Thompson said in the background, unnecessarily. Jossey could practically hear Zlotnik gritting her teeth.

She tuned Thompson out. Zlotnik's eyes stared into hers, as if trying to intimidate her again.

They were green. Like the Onlar.

Zlotnik feinted for a moment, then went low with her left arm, sweeping toward Jossey's long-ago-injured leg, just as Jossey had guessed.

At the last second Zlotnik added her right arm, straight out, palm forward, toward Jossey's face.

Don't go for Sokol's head, Henry had said.

Zlotnik was fast, brutal. But the Onlar had been faster.

Jossey dodged inward, stepping directly into Zlotnik's grasp, moving her head sideways to avoid the blow. The taller woman, surprised, overbalanced, her strike going to the left of Jossey's head.

As Jossey had seen Tark do once with Gavin, she put her weight on her bad leg and swung her elbow forward, hard, into Zlotnik's face.

They had those padded helmets on, but the tall woman still went down, gasping, holding her nose. Jossey jumped out of reach and stood back, breathing hard, trying to ignore the burning in her bad leg. She didn't think she could do that again, hoped she wouldn't need to. But it had been worth it.

The others were silent. Thompson's mouth was hanging open.

Jossey stood back, held out a hand. The other woman pushed it aside, lay there, holding her face. Her eyes were streaming.

"I don't recommend you do that with an Onlar," Henry said wryly, coming over and standing beside Jossey. "But not bad."

Caspar and Wickford looked impressed. Even Ellis seemed more awake now.

Zlotnik finally removed her hand from her face. Her nose was swollen, but not bleeding. She glared at Thompson. "You can shut your mouth now. It wasn't that impressive."

He reddened, stepped back a little.

Zlotnik's green eyes bored into Jossey's.

"I see you've learned something from yesterday," was all she said.

30

LUNCH WAS VERY AWKWARD. ZLOTNIK DIDN'T LOOK AT HER, speaking entirely to Caspar when she had to ask Jossey to pass some dish or other. Her nose looked pretty bad.

Jossey hoped Henry had seen the whole thing. From the short conversation he had had with Zlotnik on the other side of the mess hall while the others had waited in line, she guessed he had.

Jossey was relieved when a Patrol functionary wearing a badge that said RICHARDS came to get her and Caspar for Engineering auxiliary training. She didn't look at the group as she followed Caspar out of the mess.

They headed for the conference room on the second sublevel.

She stretched as she walked. Something cracked. Caspar laughed. "You okay?"

"No." But she grinned. "I got her a couple times."

Caspar's expression changed. "She really has it in for you. Maybe you shouldn't have done what you just did."

He actually looked worried. She smiled a little.

"I know." She sighed. "I just wanted to show her that I don't plan to just let her walk all over me. I don't know why Gav-Tskoulis had to tell everyone what happened. Isn't that like – a security issue?"

Caspar laughed, but it wasn't warm.

"What did you mean before about not having to prove myself to the boys?" she asked.

He looked at her oddly, but closed his mouth. A guard was coming their way.

"Unit 2-5?" the woman asked.

"Yes," Caspar said.

"Very good. Come with me." She escorted them into the conference room. Minister Sokol was seated at the head of the table.

"Jossey, my dear. Mr. Savaş. What a pleasure." He stood and greeted them.

They received glossy red folders, marked CLASSIFIED – PATROL. They didn't touch them, waiting for instructions.

"Welcome," her uncle said, "to the Patrol auxiliary service. Please, let's begin."

31

JOSSEY CROSSED THE ROOM, DROPPING HER EQUIPMENT BAG, AND sank onto her bed. Zlotnik looked at her coldly and disappeared into the bathroom.

It was the end of the first week. She'd put up with this for days, had hoped knocking Zlotnik down at training would have broken through some wall, but that had not been the case, it seemed. She was tired and just wanted to sleep.

Olivia entered the room, dragging her bag. She looked exhausted too, but gave Jossey a smile. At least she was friendly enough, Jossey thought, smiling back.

"How was training?" Olivia asked.

Jossey shrugged. "I survived. Things hurt. It's kind of fun, actually." She gestured to the bathroom. "But – "

Olivia glanced in that direction, smiled sympathetically. "Don't worry," she said quietly. "She hated me too at first."

The door opened, and Zlotnik stepped out. "I can hear you."

Olivia busied herself with unpacking her equipment bag.

Jossey sat up on her bed, sighed.

Enough was enough. She was here to avenge her brother.

Her parents. Her own scars. Not fight some stupid popularity contest.

She looked directly at Zlotnik. "What's your problem?" she asked bluntly.

Zlotnik sneered at her, and Jossey got the feeling she'd been waiting for this for a while.

The tall woman took her time putting her equipment away. Then she turned to Jossey, a smile on her face.

"If you must know...Patrol is all about respect, darling. You have to earn it. Just because you're a Council kid, just because you managed to get one good hit in...just because you killed one Onlar...by accident..." Zlotnik's voice trailed off contemptuously.

Olivia didn't look at them.

Jossey felt her face burning with fury. "You think you know what happened in that tunnel?" she began.

She was sick and tired of people assuming things about her, staring at her, whispering about her scar, her brother, her family name.

She stood up, not caring who might hear.

If Zlotnik got in trouble, so much the better.

She looked Zlotnik dead in the eye. Her voice was deadly cold. "Don't forget, I knocked *you* down. With almost no training. After you went for my face. Which Sergeant Henry *specifically* told you not to do."

Jossey went on, raising her voice. "People forget. I get that. And it's instinctive to go for the head. But my scarred leg? The injured one, from the *first* Onlar attack I survived. You saw I was having trouble with it. Don't think I didn't notice you look at it right before you attacked." She grinned, not kindly. "Someone smaller, someone injured."

Olivia was staring at the two of them. "You did what?!"

"Olivia," Zlotnik hissed. She looked – different. Smaller.

Jossey smiled coldly. "It's why I dodged the way I did. I didn't really think you'd actually do it...but you did. What was that again about earning respect?"

The others were both silent now.

"I don't like to fight," Jossey said slowly. "I hate it. I avoid it. And I'm not here to earn anyone's respect, or be some kind of star or something. You're clearly a great fighter. I have nothing at all against you. I'd like to learn from you, even."

She touched her scar, lightly. "I saw you looking at this the first day. Trust me, I know how it looks. The Onlar took my brother from me, and my father, when I was ten, and They almost killed me twice. I'm here to learn how to destroy Them."

Zlotnik opened her mouth. Jossey held up a hand. She could feel the ice in her eyes as she glared at the tall woman.

"You can apologize, or not," Jossey said. "But don't get in my way."

* * *

The next morning, Zlotnik sat down next to Jossey at the table. Jossey ignored her, pouring herself a cup of coffee and greeting Caspar as he sat on her other side.

Caspar kept glancing past her. Jossey looked at him, confused, until he tilted his head slightly, as if telling her to turn around.

Zlotnik wasn't looking at her. She was holding the sugar bowl, seemed to be waiting for Jossey to take it. "Hurry up," she grumbled.

32

THEY LINED UP ON THE TRAINING FLOOR. HENRY LOOKED MORE serious than usual, as if he hadn't slept much.

"At ease," he said. "Today is beginning weapons training."

Jossey glanced at Caspar, startled. So quickly? It had only been a week.

He smiled a little at her, but his eyes were narrowed as he turned back to Henry. "Sir?"

"Founders' Day. We need to be ready for duty. There've been threats from Karapartei again." He looked at them. "And then, after that, the tunnels. Security exercises."

Founders' Day. Jossey had forgotten. Every year, the Council held a celebration of their long-ago founding, gave speeches, all that. It was fun for children, a big day off work for adults. She always enjoyed it.

Karapartei – she frowned. She'd heard whispers of supply disruptions, talk of potential unrest. Council had been silent, except to assure citizens that all was well. Apparently it wasn't.

She'd been fairly insulated from it all in her government solar crew job, but even she had heard the rumors: a discovery of tunnels used by the Karapartei to shuttle supplies. An elaborate system, people had said, extending to the surface. She'd immediately dismissed it as ridiculous. No one but Council – no one but the Engineering arm of the government – had access to the kind of mining equipment necessary to make such tunnels.

And no one would be stupid enough, or traitorous enough, Jossey thought, to give that kind of access to the Onlar.

Henry was talking again.

"You have two main weapons before we advance to sword training," he said. "The baton, and the pole. Both can be used in crowd-control situations." He gestured to their bags. "Equipment."

They pulled out the batons.

Henry demonstrated how to unscrew them so they telescoped into a longer pole, then secured his at that length. The pole was flexible, but strong. He pointed to Caspar. "Bring yours up here."

Caspar disassembled the pole, walked over to Henry. He stood easily before the sergeant.

"All right, people. Let's learn some basic moves."

Jossey quickly found she was not a natural with the pole. She kept sneaking glances at Caspar, wondering how he seemed to be.

Henry seemed to notice as well. He immediately stepped up his training with Caspar, pushing him back, forcing him to defend. Caspar seemed a little rusty, but held his ground, silver eyes narrowed.

"Still remember this from Patrol?"

"Yes sir." Caspar grinned. "If I recall I had to practice this a lot."

Henry smiled, suddenly flipped the pole, hit Caspar sideways in the knee. Lightly, but his point was made. "Never lose your focus."

"Sir."

Jossey frowned. Something still didn't seem right. Like the other day. But he did seem to be trying hard, not letting Henry get past him.

He wasn't pulling any punches here, as far as she could tell.

She shook her head, turned her focus back to Zlotnik.

Zlotnik was looking at her steadily. "Ready to go, Sokol?"

There was no hatred in the tall woman's eyes. Jossey blinked, held up the pole. "Yes. Show me," she said.

* * *

They were in auxiliary Engineering class again. Jossey pulled out the red folder marked CLASSIFIED. Across from her, Caspar did the same.

Minister Sokol was personally overseeing this session as well. *Odd*, thought Jossey. She realized she wasn't sure what he did all day, but she doubted it had to do with training Patrol Engineers.

"Jossey, would you do the honors."

He was so formal around her. So unlike his brother, her father. She smiled and opened the folder.

Her smile vanished. She stared for a long moment, fascinated. Maps upon maps, of the aboveground, and of what looked like a strange sideways drawing of the tunnels system. She didn't have a chance to study them, because her uncle was speaking again.

"As you know, Caspar is an expert in solar efficiency. I believe your role, Jossey, was to monitor systemwide capacity fluctuations and maximize load, am I correct?"

"Yes, Unc-that is, Minister." Her job had been to keep everything running at maximum capacity, to power the City evenly and make sure the civilian water supplies kept flowing. She'd never gotten to work with the Engineers who dealt with the underground river; that was a different branch. Yet still relevant, she thought.

"Minister?" She raised her hand. Sokol smiled. "May I ask a question about system capacity?" she asked.

"Please."

"The underground river – why don't we use that for hydropower? It seems – "

The amount of cubic feet that poured through the caverns under the surface would power the City with no need for sunlight at all, she thought. It had been something she'd wondered about in Engineering school, but had never gotten a satisfactory answer on.

Caspar glanced at her sideways.

Sokol's eyes did not change, but his expression was pleased. "Resourceful as always." He tapped the map before her, which showed the basic cross-section plan of the City. "However, as you can see, the underground river is needed for our agricultural farms down in the sublevels. The condenser farms alone would be insufficient for the City's water needs when agriculture is accounted for. Happily, we have plenty of sunlight available to generate our electricity."

"Hmm." She went back to the maps. "Thank you. I've been wondering."

"However," he said. "You and Caspar are both experts in energy efficiency and variability. As you have noticed" – he glanced at them both – "we are facing significant security issues with regard to our ability to protect our infrastructure, which especially includes solar. As we are not able to divert our single reliable water supply" – he glanced at Caspar, who was sitting up, paying close attention – "we need to design a better solar grid system." He stood and walked to the front of the room. "I have not yet approached Engineering with this. I wanted to begin with people who work on the ground in security situations, yet also have Engineering backgrounds.

Hence, I have chosen the pair of you to assist me with this project. "

Jossey lit up. This was exactly her kind of thing. She'd been waiting for years to be able to work on something more interesting than the old grids they had aboveground. She felt like a kid. "Yes, sir!"

She could feel her face glowing.

She looked across the table at Caspar, a huge smile on her face, not bothering to hide her excitement. "Caspar, this is – "

She stopped dead at the expression on his face.

Caspar seemed frozen, unable to look away from her, as if he'd glanced up and now couldn't move.

His long silver eyes looked almost frightened.

She felt the glow in her cheeks heating even further, and tried to make herself look away.

Suddenly he blinked and smiled coolly, turning immediately to the Minister.

"Thank you, sir. I assume we would be able to consult with security experts?"

"Of course. However," Sokol said, "again, do keep in mind that this information is classified. Karapartei would likely be very interested in such a project, if you understand me."

Jossey looked up sharply, Caspar's strange expression fading from her mind. "Karapartei? What use would they have for such a system?"

"I am not at liberty to share at this time, Jossey," Sokol said quietly.

He stood. "And now, I must go. I suggest you study these maps at your leisure. They may be of use in your upcoming Patrol missions. I hope to hear some baseline ideas with regard to this project at our next meeting. And, of course, I hope I need not remind you, yet again, that these sessions are entirely classified. This information must not leave this room."

They stood. "Yes, sir."

He left the room. The silent guard hovered outside the door, just the back of her head visible through the glass.

"I guess in case we decide to make a run for it with these maps," Jossey joked nervously.

Caspar smiled wryly. He seemed very focused on the maps, she thought. Too focused, as if trying not to look at her.

She looked at her own hands. His expression – his eyes –

Her scar must look strange when she smiled like that, she thought. Frightening. Maybe hideous. She looked at the maps, trying to block out the negative thoughts.

She'd thought it had looked pretty cool as a kid. She'd even been excited about it when Gavin had told her it was a real warrior scar.

But now –

She frowned again, looking determinedly at her folder, and pulled out a map at random, looked at it curiously. It looked like someone had drawn a bunch of noodles and then erased half of them. "What is this?"

Caspar looked at it. "Not sure. You okay? You look mad."

"Huh?" She looked up at him. He was watching her.

"Nothing." She shook her head, annoyed at herself. "Just concentrating."

She tried to smile.

33

FOUNDERS' DAY WAS ALWAYS NOISY, JOSSEY THOUGHT.

She was very uncomfortable in the tiny seat. The Patrol vehicle was driving slowly through the throng, letting off a few agents at a time. She'd been matched with Zlotnik and Caspar to help keep order.

The smell of fried dough and other Founders' Day special foods wafted through the air. She smiled, remembering how she'd attended with her family as a child, sitting on Father's shoulders, watching Tark dart away through the crowd with Gavin and his other friends. Even as a kid he'd been rowdy.

She looked around apprehensively. Henry had gone over the procedure should anything happen. Batons only, and only to restrain, not to injure. Jossey almost laughed. She was pretty sure she'd only injure herself, if anyone.

Caspar glanced over, face half-invisible behind his mask. "You all set?"

"Not really."

He grinned. "Let's go."

She sighed. "Can we skip this? I just want to get back to

tunnel security training." She hadn't signed on to be private security for Council.

Zlotnik lightly elbowed her. "That's a no. Gotta earn your way into the real battles, Sokol."

But she smiled a little.

Jossey followed her out of the vehicle. They were in riot gear, but the crowds seemed peaceful. Up ahead, she could see a tall figure – Gavin. He was standing next to one of the Ministers. She imagined Karapartei, if they were here, wouldn't even think of going anywhere near *him*.

She stood still, watching people walk nervously past her. She tried to look less threatening. Zlotnik just held her baton at the ready, eyes up, not seeming to care a whit what people thought.

The Council members were all seated on a long decorative stage at the front of the large crowd. Someone was testing a very squeaky audio system.

SCREE. The microphone squawked. Jossey saw a little kid ahead of her jump.

The child looked like her, holding hands with a boy with flaxen hair. She blinked, looked away, forcing back the sudden tears. Now was NOT the time, she told herself angrily.

The Council President, Phillip Macaulay, stepped up to the microphone.

"Citizens!"

His voice rang out around the Square, up and down the walls of the enclosed cavern. The crowd applauded and whistled.

Jossey looked out across the crowd. This mask was remarkably useful, she thought. It enhanced her vision, blocked out glare.

It was the same speech every year, the same thing about freedom and security. Jossey looked around, searching for odd patterns of movement. She shifted uncomfortably – her boots were brand-new and too tight and not helping her concentrate.

She was tall, but standing next to Caspar, she realized how much taller he was. His broad shoulders looked much wider in armor, the black-dyed plates shining dully in the artificial lighting. His dark hair had been tied halfway back and gleamed beneath his mask.

She hoped she looked half as intimidating in her armor.

Now the Minister of Agriculture was up on the stand. She never remembered his name – there were several Council members, and she knew nothing about agriculture, other than that they had somehow run out of chocolate.

She tried not to yawn as the Agriculture Minister began by telling the story of the first underground food labs – hydroponic, whatever that meant – established by the pioneering Founders, a group of intrepid survivors from the burning surface world who had brought their technological know-how down with them...

She tuned him out, keeping an eye on the crowds. The system was an engineering marvel, yes, but she had zero interest in economics and supply chains. She was fine with fake eggs.

There was a protester, at the front, yelling something about food prices and lies. Something about the system. Jossey couldn't quite hear him. But she saw Tskoulis mutter something into his com, and a couple of blank-faced Patrol pulled the protester to the side.

She didn't give him a second glance. There was always at least one. The Minister continued.

At least there was only one, she thought. That seemed good.

The kid in front of her looked equally bored, tugging on the boy's hand. Jossey smiled.

The Minister finished his speech, to loud applause.

The applause continued for a very long time. She frowned.

Jossey realized it wasn't applause as the stage disappeared in a tremendous explosion and a cloud of blinding white smoke.

She was running toward the stage even before she consciously heard Henry's voice shouting at them to move. Her uncle was up there.

Gavin was up there.

Caspar overtook her within three strides. "Jossey!" he yelled. "Wait! Slow down!"

"It's Karapartei!" she yelled at him. "We have to – "

The smoke hit her in the face, and she stopped, coughing, gasping for breath. Was it poison? She choked, turning away. She had to get through.

The screaming crowd sprinted every which way, shoving her to the side and separating her from Caspar. She could hear him, but she couldn't see him.

She tore off her mask, coughing.

Through the mayhem and dimness she could see what she thought was Gavin, or one of his sergeants, locked in combat with a tall dark figure.

Splintered pieces of the stage had fallen everywhere. Bits of the banners were floating through the air like ash. She thought she could see blood, and tried to look away.

"Jossey!"

Caspar. She turned, looked for him. The stuff was burning her eyes.

"Jossey, stop!"

She turned again, waving away the smoke, and found herself face to face with another figure in black.

. . .

The figure was tall, she thought. Male. At least as big as the men on Patrol, maybe bigger. This wasn't like sparring with Zlotnik. He looked easily twice as strong.

She looked up at him in terror as he pulled a knife out of his robes.

"Patrol scum," he hissed, dark eyes locked on her, glittering.

Her hands fumbled for her baton, numb and shaking. It fell, telescoped on its own, the pole rolling on the ground.

The Karapartei glanced at her fallen pole, at her shaking hands. He lifted the knife. Long, straight, with a serrated edge. She stared at it, terrified.

The man advanced toward her through the fog.

"Jossey!" Caspar's voice seemed so far away.

She probably wouldn't be able to stop a knife with her elbow, she thought. She desperately reached for the pole, keeping her eyes on the man.

As her hands closed on one end, the Karapartei stomped on the other, kicked it away from her so hard it bent. She yelped and let go as the shockwave hit her hands.

Behind his wrappings, the Karapartei seemed to be grinning as he lifted the knife.

Then Caspar appeared.

He was like a different person as he stalked out of the mist, bearing down on the Karapartei. He, too, was no longer wearing his Patrol mask, and carried it in one clenched fist. There was a darkness about him, the darkness Jossey had sensed before in the tunnel. She instinctively shrank back.

The masked Karapartei's face, or what she could see of it, suddenly went white. He stared at Caspar, eyes full of terror.

Caspar's silver eyes were burning with fury. He stepped in front of Jossey. To her surprise, he was armed with more than just a baton.

In his hand was a curved blade. She had no idea where it had come from.

The two armed men stared at each other. The Karapartei took a step backward.

"Patrol! To me!" The voice rang through the smoke and screams.

Henry. Jossey whipped around, couldn't see anything. Caspar turned his head too, for half a second.

Half a second too long.

The Karapartei turned and fled into the smoke.

Jossey was shaking with terror. And rage.

It had been worse than the Onlar. She wasn't armed. Not really. And it had been in the middle of a brightly-lit open space. On Founders' Day. With children around.

"Are you okay?" Caspar's eyes were warmer now. Concerned. He glanced at her. "Did he harm you?"

"No." Angry tears were spilling over. She wiped at them furiously. "What do they want?" What could be worth attacking a festival? Children?

"Later. Not here. Put your mask back on." Caspar handed it to her. She realized she'd dropped it. He looked at her seriously. "Are you sure you're all right?"

She tried to smile. "I'm okay. Thank you."

"Good. Let's go."

She began to follow him through the crowd, before she realized that her pole was still back where she'd left it.

"Wait!"

She ran back. The pole had been smashed at the end where the Karapartei had stomped on it. *Metal boots?* she thought. She looked at it miserably. It was bent as well. A total loss.

She picked it up, tried to fit it back in as a baton.

Caspar caught up with her. "Jossey – "

She turned to show him the damage. As she did, a voice barked out of the mist, "Sokol!"

174

Tskoulis was striding toward them.

Jossey flinched. She tried to jam the baton together, realized it didn't fit. She didn't want Gavin to see how badly she'd failed on her first real mission.

Caspar stood at attention. Jossey gave up her efforts, saluted the commander.

He took off his mask. It looked like he had been fighting, hard. He was sweating. There was blood on his uniform.

She looked away.

"Report," was all he said.

She showed him the broken pole. "There was a – " She faltered.

He took it from her hands, examined it. "Are you injured?" he asked.

"A Karapartei attacked while she was trying to come to the Minister's aid," Caspar interjected.

"Are you injured?" Gavin repeated, harshly. He looked at Caspar for a long moment, then turned back to Jossey, examining her.

"No," she said. "I'm sorry about the baton."

"It can be replaced," he said, voice cool. "Now, Savaş. An attack, you said?"

"Yes, sir." Caspar's voice was cool as well. "I saw she was in danger, and – "

"He saved me," Jossey said quietly.

Gavin glanced at her, then at Caspar. A shadow seemed to pass over his face. "Good work," he finally said. "And the terrorist?"

"Escaped."

Tskoulis' jaw set, but he said nothing, other than, "Report to your subunit. The Ministers have been secured. Intelligence units are on their way." He handed Jossey back her baton. "Discard this. And Sokol, permission to carry that knife of yours. Get Henry to show you how to use it."

"Yes, sir," they both said.

As they turned and walked away, Jossey glanced back at Gavin.

Tskoulis, not Gavin, she reminded herself.

He was watching them go.

34

"I WANT YOU ALL TO UNDERSTAND WHAT WE ARE DEALING WITH." Henry strode in front of the group, hands behind his back, looking at them carefully.

They'd had the day off from training while Henry and the others went over some things with Tskoulis. Henry had called them all for an emergency meeting after dinner.

"Intelligence's report came back, and the news is very bad," he said. "I hate to inform you that we are required to suspend our surface missions for the time being."

Jossey's head jerked up. "What?"

Beside her, Zlotnik hissed, "Be quiet." Jossey shot her a dirty look. Henry continued as if he had not heard them.

"This new development, however, directly affects our surface missions," he said. "It has come to our attention that the Karapartei have discovered the Old Sector and are using it for their own ends."

There was an audible gasp from Zlotnik and Ellis, who had been with the unit the longest. Wickford looked concerned, if slightly uncomprehending.

Jossey had no idea what they were talking about. What was the Old Sector? Some part of the outer tunnels?

Henry had seated them before a projector screen. He tapped a button, and a very familiar image appeared.

Jossey frowned as she recognized what she'd taken to calling the noodle map. It really did look, she thought, like someone had drawn a bunch of noodles connecting to what might represent an outer tunnel, or maybe an outer cavern, one of the unexplored natural great spaces underground.

"The Karapartei," Henry explained, "are using the Sector to transport and store materiel. That is, supplies for military purposes."

Jossey felt stupid. What was the Old Sector? As far as she knew, there were just the City tunnels. Zlotnik seemed to know. Even Thompson seemed to have more of a clue than she did.

"As you may recall, our unit lost several members some years ago during a routine mission in the Old Sector. The Onlar had been using it as a hiding area. A den, so to speak. We happened across twenty of them, and only two of us survived." He glanced across the room at one of the other sergeants. "We have long had reason to believe that They continue to use it, hence it had been blocked off for the last decade. Or so we thought."

He pointed to an area where a large amount of the noodles appeared to overlap right next to what Jossey realized was indeed one of the outer tunnels.

"This new usage by Karapartei could represent a significant and survival-threatening security breach for the entire population of the City."

It took a moment before the magnitude of what Henry was saying washed over Jossey. She stared at him in petrified horror. "So you're saying that Karapartei could accidentally let entire groups of Onlar into the City?"

Henry looked sober. "Exactly."

Her chest was burning. She realized she was clutching the briefing papers in her hands.

She was quite happy to leave the surface missions alone if the Onlar were within range of the City. And the Karapartei. She hadn't forgotten the look on the man's face. *Traitor*, she thought. *Coward.*

She looked at Henry, waiting for further instruction. Preferably immediate instruction.

His voice was dark as he spoke next. "Prepare yourselves. Get enough sleep. Tomorrow we need to begin real weapons training."

35

JOSSEY WAS UP AT DAWN.

She felt itchy. Like she needed to run. Do something. She headed to the mess hall.

The others were there too. She said hello to them, sat, fidgeted, drinking her coffee. She stared at the table in front of her, wondered when they were going to get out into the tunnels.

Caspar and Ellis sat down across from her. She mumbled something and downed her coffee, reached for the pot again.

"Whoa there. Don't want to be too caffeinated." Ellis smirked. "Not if we're playing with real swords today."

Caspar glanced at him. Ellis jerked a thumb over his shoulder. "Thompson nearly took off my ear from too much caffeine last time."

Thompson slouched his way into the mess hall. He looked barely functional. He perked up when he saw Jossey.

She sighed under her breath and scooted over, making room for him at the table, hoping for once that Zlotnik would show up and rescue her from his endless questions.

Caspar seemed amused. She ignored all of them and poured a second cup.

"Excited about today?" Thompson asked, as if right on cue.

She took a giant gulp of her coffee, turned, and smiled at him. "Very," she said.

Before he could say any more, the mess cafe line's metal sliding door opened with a clank-clank-clank.

They jumped up as one, made a beeline for the eggs.

Ellis always took more than his fair share. Jossey darted her hand in, grabbed the spatula before he could scoop out half her portion.

He looked affronted.

"Ladies first," Caspar said. She grinned at him over Ellis' protests.

She handed Thompson, who had squashed in next to her, the spatula. He took it with a gleeful look in Ellis' direction.

They ate their breakfast, Ellis moaning about the morning's small portions.

"You eat plenty of protein," Caspar joked, prodding him in one giant bicep. "Don't worry. Henry'll probably go easy on us today."

Ellis grumbled and took another bite.

Zlotnik joined them, yawning loudly. "Ready for weapons day, children?"

Jossey was ready. She shoveled eggs into her mouth, mumbling good morning.

They lined up. To Jossey's disappointment, Henry handed them each a stout stick.

It was the size of a sword, sure, but it was just wood.

What are we supposed to do with this? she thought.

Henry called up Ellis to the front. He demonstrated how to properly hold the "sword." It immediately made Jossey's wrist sore. She ignored the pain. The actual swords were heavier, she guessed.

"Now," said Henry. "Attack me, Ellis."

Ellis immediately sliced downward, only to be caught by Henry's backhand. Henry shoved Ellis' "sword" sideways and down, pushing it along his own stick, then lunged forward and slammed Ellis in the chest with his shoulder and elbow.

Ellis stepped back, grinning. He seemed unsurprised, as if he'd done this before. But he winced a little as he touched his chest.

"Fighting is not only done with a blade," Henry said. "Understood?"

"Yes, sir!"

"Your turn." Henry gestured to Caspar.

Jossey felt far from ready to do any type of fighting by the time the day was over. Her wrists were killing her and she hadn't so much as touched Zlotnik with her stick-sword. It hadn't been for lack of trying, either.

Zlotnik had been remarkably patient with her. Jossey decided she just wasn't good at anticipating the blade. Or blocking it in a certain way. To remember three or four different forms – it was too much for her brain to handle at once.

She'd never been very good at sequences of movement, she thought. But when she *didn't* think...

She was like this in Engineering too, she realized. She'd always gotten in trouble in school for not following the manual. The solutions just seemed apparent to her. Small details would click in her mind, a full picture unfolding, and when she would try to explain how she'd gotten to that solution, she couldn't. It just made sense to her.

Maybe fighting was like that, she thought.

She hoped.

She sat, rubbing her wrists, as the others wandered off to get lunch.

Henry sat down next to her. "How's it going?"

She winced. "Not great. I'm sorry. I really want to be good at this. Need to be."

Henry picked up a piece of something, idly twirled it between his fingers. "What's the problem?"

"I – can't remember all the moves. I can't think through them all when someone is coming at me. It's too much thought to decide what to do. So I just flail."

"I see. I've noticed."

She flushed. But no use being embarrassed. She couldn't let this stop her.

Caspar had gone and filled his water canteen. He came back, stopped, stood there. "Going to lunch?"

"Hold on." She turned back to Henry. "I can keep practicing."

Caspar took a drink of his water, looked at her.

Then he glanced up, stood straighter, saluted. The others turned. Jossey looked up.

It was Tskoulis.

He strode over to the group. He was wearing his full uniform, no mask. He was not smiling.

"Anything the matter?" he asked.

Jossey got to her feet too and saluted, feeling ridiculous. But she was Patrol now. "No, sir. Just trying to improve my sword skills."

She thought she saw something twitch at the corner of his mouth.

But all he said was, "Those are a prerequisite to go into the tunnels, Sokol."

She stared. "What?"

Henry was standing next to Tskoulis. "The commander is right. The tunnels are every agent for themselves if anything goes wrong. You have to be able to fight."

Is Gavin purposely trying to keep me out of the tunnels? Jossey looked at Tskoulis, then looked away. "I'm willing to practice extra, sir."

Tskoulis looked down at her, face unreadable. "I expect it, Sokol."

She flushed.

Caspar took another drink of water, then closed it slowly and looked at the commander.

"I can help her," he said carefully.

Tskoulis' expression was cool as he looked Caspar in the eye. "And how," he said, "are your skills with the sword, recruit?"

Caspar grinned lopsidedly. "I remember more than I'd realized."

"He's correct, sir." Henry spoke up. "I think today was enough of a refresher course. He remembers everything Patrol taught him, it seems. Gave me a bruise." He looked proud.

Jossey had seen it, knew they weren't joking. While Caspar had seemed a little rusty with the pole, the way he'd moved with the stick-sword...Even Henry had seemed impressed, had asked him to demonstrate a couple of things for the group.

She had no idea how Caspar remembered things a decade later, but his skill was undeniable.

Not like me, she thought sourly.

Caspar took another drink of water, wiped his sleeve across his mouth.

Tskoulis' eyes narrowed. "Let's see."

Jossey's own eyes widened. She looked at Henry, then at Tskoulis, then at Caspar.

"Yes, sir." Caspar set down the water.

Tskoulis stalked over to the equipment stand, grabbed two training sticks, tossed one to Caspar.

Caspar reached out and plucked it out of the air, and for a second Jossey saw yet another flicker of...something. Something fluid. Like he'd been using a weapon his whole life.

The two men lined up across the mat, facing each other. Henry seemed apprehensive all of a sudden.

Gavin's face was still unreadable.

"Begin," was all he said.

They circled each other. Caspar's face seemed to change, no longer grinning, no longer amused. His long silver eyes narrowed, as if reading Gavin's expression. Jossey had never seen him so focused.

Gavin suddenly sliced through the air with his sword.

But Caspar wasn't there. He'd stepped aside as the blow was falling.

Jossey stared. It was like he'd guessed Gavin's plan through the tensing of the commander's body, almost before Gavin actually followed through with the full swing.

Caspar countered the blow lightly, facing off with Gavin again. As if toying with him.

Gavin actually grinned. "Well done."

But then he flipped his wrists, and in a single move he brought the stick-sword to Caspar's neck.

Caspar seemed strangely calm with the stick held to his neck. He grinned in turn. "I told you I remembered something from Patrol."

"Indeed." Tskoulis lowered the stick. "How to dodge." He smiled a little. Caspar accepted the insult gamely, lowering his as well.

For a moment, Jossey felt as if she were looking at Gavin and Tark again, laughing after they fought.

They shook hands. Tskoulis glanced over at Jossey. "If you can teach her how to dodge like that, I accept your offer."

Jossey was too elated to be annoyed. She was fast, she knew.

She could probably stay out of range. Enough to formulate a plan. And that might be all she needed.

"But," Tskoulis went on, "If our Minister's niece gets hurt..." He looked at Caspar closely. "Do I make myself clear?"

"Sir." Caspar's gaze was even.

Jossey's elation faded as quickly as it had come, replaced by burning frustration. Minister's niece this, Minister's niece that...

She spoke up, eyes fierce. "My uncle was the one who assigned me to Patrol. Don't worry about me."

"You have an assignment, Sokol. Security-related. One you're not allowed to fail. Stay out of trouble." Gavin's face was unreadable again.

He tossed the stick to Henry. "Here. I have to meet with Dalton. Make sure they're ready for tunnel duty by Friday. We need to move out."

He walked out of the room.

36

Jossey stayed behind in the training room. Olivia and one of her friends were there, lifting weights across the way.

Caspar stood there, holding a pair of sticks. He tossed one to her, squared off across from her.

"Ready?" His long silver eyes were focused.

"Yes."

He charged at her with no warning. She swung the stick at him, caught him on the shoulder. He calmly struck it away and put the stick to her throat.

"Again," he said.

"Again."

It had been an hour. She sat down, frustrated, red and breathing hard, downing an entire canteen in a few gulps. He sat down next to her, looking half-amused, toying with the stick.

"You still want to try?"

"Yes." She glared at him. "How do you do it?"

"Do what?"

"Know how to dodge." She looked closely at him. "In fact, how do you remember so much from ten-plus years ago?"

He shrugged. "Muscle memory. And I like working out, I guess."

Jossey opened her mouth to say something, and then stopped. He wasn't even breathing hard.

She looked hard at him. "Caspar. Really?"

Something flashed over his face, and then he looked closely at her.

"Close your eyes," he said.

"What?"

"Do it."

She obeyed, feeling silly. His voice continued.

"What do you remember about the Onlar?"

"What do you mean?" She opened half an eye.

"Eyes closed."

"Ugh, fine. What do you mean?"

He tapped something on the ground, the stick, maybe. "When it turned on you, and we thought you were de— anyway. How did you know to dodge?"

She thought. She remembered it turning toward her, the motion of its claws. She'd blocked out everything but the gleam as it sliced toward her.

"I don't know. I just sensed it," she said slowly. "It was like I could feel it coming toward me faster than I could see it. I just moved. "

"Exactly."

She opened her eyes. He was staring seriously at her.

"Your mind seems to process everything faster when you're afraid, when you're highly focused," he said. "It's like how you blink before you consciously see something coming at your eye. You have to read your enemy, act accordingly." He glanced down at the stick. "I was good at that."

Habit, she remembered he'd said, as he'd wiped the knife on his uniform.

She remembered focusing on Zlotnik's motions, not on the woman's eyes. The tension in her arms before she went for Jossey's feet. The way she'd seemed to prepare to move, more than the way she'd actually moved.

"It's hard to change mid-motion," Caspar said. "Especially with a heavy weapon. You have to anticipate the motion and get out of the way. Understand?"

"Understood." She was frowning. But it made sense.

He stood. "Again."

He came at her. She watched him carefully, as he raised the sword.

To the left and down, she guessed. His shoulder looked too high for anything else.

She dodged. He hit her in the leg, and she bit her lip to keep from crying out. That was probably going to leave a bruise. But she smiled. She'd almost made it.

"Better," he said.

* * *

As Jossey drifted off to sleep that night, thinking about what he had taught her, she remembered something. Caspar, when Gavin had put the stick to his throat.

It had been a flicker, but she'd seen it. That's what had been bothering her all day. She was surprised Henry hadn't seemed to notice.

Caspar had tensed as if to move away. But he'd stayed.

37

Friday's alarm went off. Jossey shot out of bed, raced to the bathroom, and was out of the room before the others stumbled to their equipment bags.

She was determined to prove herself to Henry, to the commander. She had to go into those tunnels.

"Whoa, whoa." Thompson was already in the mess hall. She tried not to groan. He looked shyly at her. "Want some coffee? You're up early."

She sat down. "Yes. I need to be able to focus."

Henry had told them they'd face an exam of sorts, make sure they were up to par for the tunnels.

He wordlessly shoved the coffee pot toward her. "Here, have some sugar."

"Thanks."

She downed the coffee as he fidgeted. She finally glanced at him. "What?"

He went red.

"How'd you get your scar?" he blurted out. "It looks – "

She self-consciously reached up and touched it. "Awful, I know."

Thompson shook his head. "No, it's – "

The door to the mess opened, and Caspar and Ellis came in. Wickford was not far behind. Zlotnik and Olivia trailed behind them, looking half-awake. Thompson clamped his mouth shut.

Did he almost say my scar looked cool? Jossey stirred her coffee, not willing to believe it. *Nah*, she thought. *Intimidating, maybe.*

She smiled at the group. "Ellis, you ready to fight for your, uh, portion today?"

Ellis looked sourly at her. "So that was your plan."

"You realize you always take more than you're supposed to?"

"I'm a big guy. I need extra protein."

She made a face at him. "Whatever."

They got in line. This time they let Ellis go third, behind Jossey and Zlotnik. He complained, but good-naturedly.

They were eating and talking when Henry entered the room. "Recruits!" he said.

They stopped talking, looked over at him.

"Training room. Now."

Ellis looked at the remainder of his eggs.

"Now," repeated Henry.

Ellis glanced at Henry, grabbed the plate, tipped it into his mouth, and stood up, grumbling.

Jossey stood nervously, watching Henry as he paced back and forth in front of them. She was half expecting him to yank her out of line and pair her with Thompson.

But all he said was, "Suit up."

They gaped at him.

"No exam?" Wickford asked disbelievingly.

"No exam. Change of plans. There's been a breach. We need to go into the tunnels. Get ready."

. . .

Jossey followed Zlotnik to the equipment locker. She'd never put on a real Patrol uniform, not the ones they used for the tunnel missions.

Her heart was beating quickly. She'd been looking forward to this, but the urgency in Henry's voice, the look on his face –

What kind of breach? Had the Onlar entered the City tunnels?

She strapped on her sword with shaking hands. Her knife was there in her leg holster. She slipped the mask on over her head.

She looked at Zlotnik, who looked tall and terrifying in her Patrol mask.

A siren was blaring somewhere. The lights were flashing in their corridor. She grabbed water, added it to her pack.

Just in case.

They met in front of the mess hall, almost unrecognizable in full uniform. She met Caspar's reassuring gaze. She tried to smile. The caffeine was pumping in her veins.

"Move out," said Henry.

At the end of a long series of tunnels, Henry held up a hand.

"Lights," he said. "Be silent. Follow Protocol. Stick with your partner. Whatever you do, do not break Protocol." He slid his hand over a panel in the wall. A narrow door that Jossey hadn't noticed slid open. Beyond it was blackness.

Jossey looked back for Zlotnik, who gave her a thumbs-up. She turned back around, squared her shoulders.

Then she followed Caspar and the other Patrol agents into the dark.

38

It was dark, very dark, and dusty.

In the faint red light from her safety lamp, she saw that she was in a passage no wider than a single man. She could see no end to it.

What is this place? she thought, straining to see.

The City tunnels were uniform, round, carved smoothly out of the rock. This tunnel – she ran her hand along the wall, feeling the bumps in the stone. It felt...carved. By hand.

But that was impossible, thought Jossey. The Founders had dug directly into the earth, using the best mining equipment available at the time, after they'd found a suitable open cavern underground.

She coughed, covered her mouth, as she inhaled dust. She winced as Henry turned around and gave her a warning look. "Sorry," she mouthed.

They could barely fit in the tunnel. She was glad she didn't mind small spaces, because if she had to turn around quickly with all her equipment, she didn't think she could.

She kept moving, and stumbled on something.

Zlotnik grabbed her, pulled her upright.

She looked down, could see nothing in the darkness. *A stair? Who would have carved –*

Zlotnik prodded her in the back. She kept walking.

Then the tunnel opened up.

They were in a small cavern. Henry had lit his safety light, and the red glow illuminated a large space, big enough for some twenty people. Maybe fifty, now that her eyes were beginning to adjust.

The cavern had columns. The columns were clearly not natural.

Jossey gaped. What was this place?

The Patrol agents seemed to be in some kind of storage chamber. The walls were lined with benches, and there were holes in the walls above them, again looking hand-carved.

Jossey had never heard of this place, not in all her years as an Engineer.

The noodle map came to mind. She recalled Henry's words: the Old Sector.

What Old Sector?

She wanted to ask, but she knew they had to be dead silent. She contented herself with looking around, trying not to breathe in the dust.

Henry waved his hand. They fanned out. Jossey didn't know exactly what they were looking for. He'd mentioned a breach.

He must be really agitated, she thought, *to give us next to no instructions.* She wondered suddenly just how much danger they were in.

Zlotnik seemed to know what to do. She was searching the floor. All Jossey saw was a layer of dust.

Then she realized. Sign. They were looking for Onlar sign.

. . .

"Clear," Zlotnik whispered at last, holding up a hand.

Henry beckoned for them to follow him.

"Weapons out," he said in a low voice. They headed for the far side of the chamber.

"I hope you've brought your water," Henry said. He gestured to a staircase.

It led up into the dark.

Jossey nervously reached for her knife as she climbed.

Zlotnik climbed slowly and steadily behind her. The tunnel had widened slightly, and somewhere Jossey could hear the dripping of water. It sounded as if it were coming from far below them. Other than that, and the footsteps of her comrades, it was completely silent. The soft glow of Henry's safety light was just sufficient to see the rough-hewn curves of the walls as they vanished overhead into darkness.

She wondered if there were bats here.

She silently started counting the stairs. *Twenty. Twenty-five.* They were remarkably flat and even, considering that they appeared to have been hand-carved.

Thirty. Thirty-five.

There was cool air up ahead. She could barely see, but it looked like a greater darkness beyond.

She had to cover her mouth to keep from gasping as they stepped into an enormous carved hall.

The room they'd come from had been some kind of chamber, she thought, maybe storage, maybe living. This looked like a meeting space of some kind.

"Lights," Henry said softly. "Fan out."

She turned up her light. It was attached to the front of her uniform, not like the string versions they'd used on solar crew. It illuminated the ten or so feet in front of her.

She followed Caspar and Zlotnik ahead into the dimness. The chamber was long; on her left, she could see what looked like an arch carved into the rock. She walked over and looked. Another set of stairs disappeared up into the darkness. She moved closer, curious.

What is this place?

"Jossey," hissed Caspar. She turned and quickly followed after him.

"Don't wander off," he said quietly.

"Sorry," she muttered.

The walls were pitted, like they'd been dug out using stones or metal tools. She stood facing one of them, reaching out a hand to touch the surface, awestruck at the sheer scale of the place.

"Stop gaping, Sokol. Look for sign," Henry said irritably.

"Yes, sir." She turned her attention to the ground.

It was dusty, and she could see the dust lift from the earth as they walked. She saw nothing that would indicate any creatures had recently been here, but it was hard to tell.

Zlotnik had gone to the right, Caspar to the left. Jossey saw something in the faint glow of their lights – a hole. On the wall next to it she saw something else, something she hoped she was not seeing correctly.

She went quickly to Caspar's side, careful not to make noise as she walked.

"Caspar – "

"I see it." His expression was grim.

On the wall, there were smears of what looked like blood. They were several feet off the ground, as if the Onlar – or maybe a member of Karapartei – had gripped the doorway before sliding into the darkness.

"Go get Henry," he said. "Quickly. And silently."

She obeyed, racing across the chamber floor.

"Sir," she said. "We've found something."

Henry whipped around.

"Follow me," he said to the others.

They descended another set of stairs. This time they turned off their lights and put on their masks, activated them. It wasn't great, but it helped – Jossey could see their figures as they crept down into the blackness.

This time the stairs felt smoother, less even. She frowned, feeling them through her Patrol boots as she set each foot carefully in front of the other.

There were grooves in the stone. Identical grooves.

As if the steps had been worn over the centuries by hundreds of feet.

She shook her head, feeling strangely cold. *Focus*, she told herself.

They exited the narrow staircase into another chamber. Jossey looked around. It was long, too, but Henry strode confidently into the space, as if he'd been here before.

They followed him, scanning the room. It appeared to be empty. The far end looked like it had once extended further, but a cave-in seemed to have blocked off the rest. Somewhere she could hear more water dripping, feel a slight breeze. She shivered.

As Jossey turned to scan the doorway behind her, turning on her safety light at Henry's orders, she saw something: a massive stone disc, flat, with a hole in the center. It was taller than Caspar, at least three feet thick.

It sat motionless, ready to be rolled across the doorway. By whom, she had no idea. If that moved, she thought, they might never get out of here.

She turned back to tell Henry, but he was too far ahead. She gritted her teeth and plunged after the group.

Down another staircase, and another. It curved as they descended. Jossey was losing all sense of direction as they moved deeper into the earth.

At least there was only one exit per room so far, she thought, but she wasn't sure she would recognize the original chamber.

If she got back up to it, she thought.

Caspar glanced back at her, gave her a half-smile. She was glad he probably couldn't see the worry on her face. She gave him a thumbs-up and kept going.

The water was louder now. Jossey could hear the sound of her own breathing. She was glad for the extra layer of Patrol battle uniform – it was almost cold here.

The pitch of the staircase lessened, until she was walking on nearly-flat ground.

They stepped into the largest chamber they'd yet seen. Columns extended across the length of it; wings disappeared into darkness on the left and right. From the center Jossey could feel air moving.

They fanned out again. Jossey walked closer to the source of the sound. She could hear water too – dripping...and splashing?

"Caspar," she said in a low tone. "Look."

She walked closer. There was something in the center of the room. She squinted, trying to make it out.

She took another step and gasped as the toes of her boots almost disappeared over the edge of a hole.

She stumbled back, breathing quickly. "Stop," she said to Caspar.

She hadn't seen it – how had she not seen it?

Jossey crouched down, moved the light so it shone more directly on the hole and the object behind it.

"Is that a well?" Caspar hovered beside her.

"I think so."

On the other side of the maybe-well was what looked like a thin block of stone. It had a groove on the top where, she guessed, centuries of heavy buckets had been placed.

"Did the Founders use this place?" she asked Caspar under her breath.

"I have no idea," he answered, frowning. "I didn't even know this existed."

She shined her light into the well.

"Look!" she said. "I think there are handholds."

Indeed, there were holes that looked carved in the side of the well shaft. She could hear water sloshing below.

Henry came over, taking off his mask. Jossey did as well. She could see better now – the reddish light had helped her adjust. Besides, she preferred to see people's expressions.

"No sign," Henry said. "This is the farthest down I know. Not sure where the creature could have gone."

"Or Karapartei," Jossey added.

"Or Karapartei. Into the upper levels, possibly." He waved the others over. "All clear?"

"Yes, sir." Wickford saluted. "We've found nothing."

"Good. Let's go. We can check the upper tunnels next."

As they turned and exited the large chamber, Jossey felt something move. The ground.

Something shaking.

Above them. Dust fell from the chamber's ceiling.

She felt herself pale as she remembered the giant stone door.

"Henry," she said. "Henry!"

He turned and met her eyes. He seemed to be thinking the same thing.

"Lights on," he said. "Run!"

199

. . .

They scrambled up the staircase. Jossey's heart was pounding in her ears. One chamber. Two chambers.

She tripped and barely caught herself. Zlotnik grabbed her arm.

Three chambers. Jossey couldn't breathe with the heavy dust. Her bad leg was burning. They ran out into the long open space.

The door was shut.

39

JOSSEY STOOD, BREATHING HEAVILY, LOOKING AROUND THE ROOM. She saw nothing. Her heart was pounding, the whoosh-whoosh of fear drowning out whatever Henry was saying. She looked at him, trying to make out the words.

It had been a trap, she thought. Whatever was waiting for them had lured them down into the deeper levels, and locked them in.

She looked around frantically. Still nothing.

Where are you? she thought.

"Stay close!" Henry said. He unsheathed his sword, flipped his mask down.

Jossey's hands went to her sword, shaking. She clapped her mask back on as well.

She inched around the room, standing close to Caspar.

Still nothing. No sound. Just their footsteps and her breath.

Near the cave-in in the corner, there was something in the darkness. Something out of place.

She inched closer. An alcove, maybe. Old storage containers.

She peered more closely, and froze.

. . .

The Onlar sat still in the darkness, a huddled figure with broad shoulders and claws that gleamed in the muted red light. Then, as she watched in horror, its eyes lit up, an uncanny green glow.

Something like a guttural roar came out of its throat, its gaze locked on her, as it burst out of its hiding place.

She shrieked. Caspar whirled, unsheathing his sword.

"Get down!" he shouted. Around her, she could hear similar roars, the sound of swords against claws as more appeared out of the darkness, Henry's shouts to attack, someone's screams.

Then her thoughts seemed to slow as Caspar moved, silver eyes locked on the Onlar.

There was no more rustiness about him as he stepped forward. In what seemed like a single fluid motion, he shoved aside the creature's claws with his plated arm and stabbed the Onlar cleanly through the center of its chest. Jossey barely had time to blink.

He stepped back. The Onlar crumpled to the stone, claws slicing at him, its glowing eyes fading as its head hit the ground.

The precision, the speed – Jossey's mouth was hanging open.

All around her she heard more fighting, and looked to see that several more Onlar had emerged from somewhere. They seemed to be all over.

She felt dizzy, frozen, not sure what to do. Across the room, Thompson and Ellis were fighting a single Onlar; Wickford was barely holding his own against another. Henry was nowhere to be seen.

Zlotnik was backed into a corner, taking on one of them with her sword. She kicked it in the chest and it staggered backward, then sliced out with its giant claws. She took a direct hit to the face and went down, bleeding heavily.

Jossey screamed, "Zlotnik!" She started in Zlotnik's direction, but stopped dead as five more Onlar emerged from the darkness.

Patrol was completely surrounded. She had no idea what to do.

"Jossey, go! Run!" It was Caspar. "Go get backup!" He was fighting another Onlar.

She realized with a jolt that she almost didn't recognize this Caspar.

The way he moved, the way he had dispatched the first Onlar with such brutal efficiency – she felt almost certain now that whatever he'd been doing for the last ten years, it hadn't been just Engineering.

She had never seen anyone move like him. Not even Gavin.

She watched, still frozen, as he sidestepped the thing's claws, stepped forward and elbowed it in the face. His knife was in his hand. She flinched as he yanked it across the creature's throat.

Blood sprayed everywhere, across his face, his uniform.

He wiped it with his arm, looked directly at her. "Go!"

She fled.

Behind her, she could hear Thompson's voice, Wickford, the enraged sounds of the creatures.

She tried the stone door, but only for a second. It must weigh several hundred pounds at least. The creatures must be tremendously strong, she thought.

What else?

She remembered the cave-in. She remembered feeling air when they'd first stepped into this chamber. Air, and the sound of water. Maybe –

Jossey sprinted, trying not to trip on rocks or the bodies of the Onlar. She thought she saw one of theirs on the ground, and didn't allow herself to look. An injured Onlar swiped at her legs with its claws as she stepped past it, and she jumped out of the way.

She kept going, frantically searching the walls.

And then she saw it.

A crack, in between the caved-in rock and the wall. Another well shaft, she thought. Just wide enough for her to squeeze through.

Not wide enough for her equipment bag. She looked at it, looked at the hole. Looked behind her. None of the Onlar seemed to have noticed her yet.

If she left the bag here, they might come looking for her. But if she tried to take it with her –

She grabbed one of her water bottles, slung it on a long equipment-holding chain with shaking hands, and tossed the whole thing over her head. Then she squeezed herself through the crack.

40

THE WELL SHAFT WAS SLIMY. COOL AIR FLOWED UP AND DOWN, and she shivered in the darkness. All she could see was the red spot in front of her face, illuminating the bumpy surface. She clung to the handholds and leaned back as far as she dared, surveying the shaft above her.

It extended up, up, into blackness. Below her – far below – she could hear water.

One step wrong and she would probably fall to her death.

She closed her eyes. *It's like the rail,* she told herself. *One movement at a time. One handhold at a time. Don't think about it.*

She took a step up, put her foot solidly into the handholds. They were deep enough for her whole foot. *Good,* she thought.

One more.

Two more.

Ten more.

Keep going, she told herself.

There was a noise below her, a scrabbling, and she froze in terror, what seemed like every nerve in her body firing at once. Reaching up carefully, she turned off the light, listened hard in the pitch darkness.

She heard something scrabbling again, stones moving. She heard some of them hitting the sides of the shaft as they fell. It was a very long time before she heard them splash.

She heard a grunt, then breathing. An Onlar, she thought.

Jossey closed her eyes and prayed it wouldn't notice her.

She imagined she could see the creature's blazing eyes sweeping over the shaft, seeing her suspended there helplessly. She pressed herself as closely as she could to the wall.

Then the sound slowly receded, and she heard nothing.

She let out a long breath and pressed her forehead to the cool, wet stone. *Thank God.*

Above her she could feel a shift in the air. She kept climbing with renewed vigor.

Get help, Caspar had said. Get backup.

She had no idea how, didn't know if she remembered the access code to the City tunnels, wasn't even sure where the tunnels were relative to her, but she had to try.

She could feel the air shifting direction now.

Her foot slipped suddenly and shot out of the hole. She grabbed for the wall as her leg dangled, gasping, trying not to cry, trying not to reveal her location. Her water bottle banged against the shaft's wall, and she let it clank, unable to move, hoping the Onlar wouldn't hear it and come to investigate.

After a very long moment, during which she could hear nothing, she put her foot carefully back into the hole and reached one shaking hand above her for the next handhold.

There was none.

Jossey felt tears of pain and frustration come to her eyes as she stared into the endless blackness above her. The air was rushing now, and she was freezing. There was nowhere left to climb, not that she could tell.

Not without turning on her light and maybe alerting the Onlar to her presence.

Claws, or death in a well. She didn't know which she preferred less.

She felt around above her. Maybe – wait! There was one more handhold. It was thinner than the others. It was also almost too high for her to reach. Maybe if she jumped –

Jump for it, and probably miss, she thought. Especially if it was mossy.

She needed light. She hadn't heard anything for a while. She could hear the sounds of the battle below, but that was it. The well shaft was well concealed from the rest of whatever these tunnels were. She hoped she was concealed enough to risk it.

There was nothing for it. Gritting her teeth, she turned on her light again.

She looked up, to her left, where the strongest air current seemed to be coming from, blinking at the light.

There was indeed one last handhold – because she'd reached the top of the shaft.

It was closer than she'd thought. She blinked away tears of relief – she needed to be able to see, now more than ever.

The hold was uneven on purpose, it seemed, in order to help someone in and out of the shaft. She'd been reaching for what she now thought was a random crack in the wall.

She reached up, swung herself over the edge, and squeezed through the opening into a chamber.

She lay there for a long moment, holding her hand over her light, breathing carefully, trying not to make a sound. All her nerves were on full alert. Maybe there were more of Them up here.

She switched off her light and pulled her mask down over her eyes. At least that way she could see movement more clearly.

Jossey got to her feet. She could see she was in a long low chamber, with columns. It looked familiar, but she couldn't be sure – these rooms all looked the same, she thought.

In the distance, on the right, she spotted a familiar arch, and grinned triumphantly. Just to be sure, she turned and went to the hole in the wall.

The blood was still there.

Her friends had been just below, down the staircase, behind that giant stone door. It would probably take three men to move the stone, she thought. She had to get backup. If she just went across this way and through that tunnel at the end, it should lead her back to –

Behind her, she heard a low hiss.

41

JOSSEY TURNED, VERY SLOWLY.

The Onlar standing there was huge, much bigger than the others she'd seen. It had stepped out of the archway, she guessed.

It unsheathed its giant claws and stood there, eyes burning in the blackness. She tried to remain calm.

Focus, Caspar had told her. *Observe. Don't calculate. Get a sense of its movement.*

She put her hand on the hilt of her knife.

The Onlar lurched toward her. It had something wrong with it, she realized. An old injury that had healed badly, it looked like.

Like hers.

Its green eyes flared. She looked into them, and suddenly felt calm.

You took my brother, she thought. *My father.*

It hissed, and charged.

She dodged, barely missed by its claws. She kicked out with her steel-toed boots, hard, hitting it solidly in the leg. The creature howled and tipped sideways, catching itself.

She ran.

Her water sloshed as she fled, the chain clinking, and she had a sudden idea.

She darted up the staircase in the arch, ignoring the pain in her leg and praying there were no more Onlar at the top. The chamber at the top had more columns. She hid behind one of them, quickly unlinking the water bottle from the chain.

As the creature's footsteps came thudding up the steps after her, she threaded the chain through a hole in her curved knife's pommel.

She'd seen a weapon like this in the training room. She hadn't tried it, of course – she doubted she'd be able to until she'd proven herself on an aboveground mission, but she didn't have time now to wonder if she could use it.

The chain wasn't very long – maybe six feet – but it might just keep her out of the reach of the thing's claws if she got in a good shot.

She froze as the creature entered the room, panting. She'd been right about its bad leg, she thought. Much worse than hers. More recent, maybe. Her metal toe probably hadn't helped much.

Normally she would hide, wait for help. She didn't think she could take this one on, wasn't even sure one of the more experienced Patrol could. But they were trapped down below. And, she hoped, alive.

She had to save them. Had to save herself. She waited until the creature was in what sounded like the right spot.

She said another silent prayer, knowing the next thing she did might easily be her last.

Then she stepped out from behind the column, and swung the chain as hard as she could.

. . .

She watched the curved knife move as if in slow motion, could feel the tension in her arms, prepared herself to dodge if the blade swung back at her. Wondered if she would ever see her mother again. Her City.

The knife swung cleanly through the air and sliced the creature directly across the top of its shoulder, continuing straight into its upper chest, beneath its arm.

She gaped as the Onlar made a terrible sound and dropped to the ground. She had had almost zero expectation this would actually work.

The creature made a pained sound this time and tried to get to its feet. She jumped in terror and pulled on the chain. The curved blade came out, along with the Onlar's blood. Lots of it. She had hit an artery, she thought.

The creature moaned, then fell back, trying feebly to press against the wound. She heard a strange noise from its throat that she couldn't identify.

Jossey sank to a crouch on the floor, shivering, frozen in place. She didn't know what the Onlar wanted, or why it was trying to kill her, and she knew its kind had taken her family from her, but she suddenly felt horrified at the thought of letting it die this way.

But neither could she move to help it. She was completely frozen, wanting to cover her eyes, wanting to run. It continued to bleed.

"I'm sorry," she managed. "I'm sorry." She began to weep, tears pouring down her face.

"You took my family," she shouted at it. "You took Tark, you took my father...why? Why?"

The creature tried to raise its claws. She buried her face in her hands, no longer wanting revenge, wanting desperately to erase this moment from her mind.

When she looked up again, the Onlar no longer appeared to be breathing.

. . .

She inched forward and inspected the Onlar, almost expecting it to open its eyes and lash out at her with its claws, part of her wondering if she deserved it.

It was less grimy and matted-looking than the one in the shuttle tunnel had been, but it had the same long hair around its face, the same enormous forearms, the same giant claws. Its face was sunk down onto its chest and she couldn't see much of it. But its eyes –

She frowned suddenly, looked more closely. The green almost-flames of its eyes – they were still flaring. Dim, but flaring.

If it was dead…

Protocol was not to touch the bodies, to leave them for Forensics. It was an ironclad rule, one of the first things Henry had told them about tunnel duty. Something about disease. Henry hadn't really explained, had apparently been in too much of a rush to train them. He'd just said not to touch the bodies.

Right now Jossey didn't care. She already had the Onlar's blood all over her anyway.

She dug through the pockets of her new Patrol uniform, found the medical examination gloves Zlotnik had showed her. They were supposed to be used in case of injury. She hadn't expected to use them on this trip.

She steeled herself, crouching beside the body, then reached over carefully through the hair and touched the creature's face.

She jerked her hand back, almost screamed.

It was metal. The face was metal. Painted like skin with greenish-brown scales. Surrounded by the strange fur, it made the Onlar look like some alien creature.

Feeling queasy, Jossey reached in among the matted hair and found the edges of the metal plate. She tried not to think about what she was touching.

With a creaking sound, she pried off what she'd thought was the creature's face.

The face underneath was a man's, the eyes glassy in death.

42

Jossey dropped what she was holding and choked back a sob.

The Onlar's eyes, clouded and frozen in a stare that unnerved her, were blue like her father's had been. The skin was deeply tanned, so much so that it was almost leathery. She reached trembling fingers out toward his claws.

An arm sheath, bound around a tanned forearm.

The inside of the mask was an intricate contraption, some kind of greenish goggles she had never seen before. She touched a button. The light faded. She jumped.

With trembling fingers, Jossey touched one of the claws.

Metal. It was metal. Of course it was metal, she thought angrily. Hot tears were pouring down her face now.

She looked back at the Onlar's – the man's – features. Like her father. But the eyes were longer, a little like Caspar's.

She felt like her head was going to explode.

She touched the man's neck, carefully felt for a heartbeat. There was none. He was no longer breathing.

She'd killed him. Horribly.

"I didn't know," she whispered to herself. "I didn't – how – "

She reached down again for the claws, turned over the contraption gently. His palms were leathery too. She bit her lip, hard, tears running over again. Why was this man –

Was this one of the Karapartei? Dressed as an Onlar? That would make sense, she thought frantically.

But it didn't make sense. There was no reason for the Karapartei to pretend to be the creatures from above, unless they were trying to force more security measures? But that would just give more power to the government they were opposing, she thought. And where would they get this equipment?

Her head was spinning.

She was about to turn over the man's hand and let him lie there when she noticed something on his finger.

Jossey lifted the claws again with her gloved hands. It was a ring of some kind.

She carefully slid the ring off the man's finger, and looked at it, squinting in the dimness.

Then she heard herself gasp sharply as it came into focus.

It was Tark's.

Tark's silver ring. The Sokol family crest. He'd been wearing it the night he disappeared. Father had just given it to him, said it was a family tradition. Tark had been so excited, she remembered.

She'd never asked Gavin if they'd found it on the body. She realized she'd forgotten all about it until just now.

She stared at it, then at the Onlar, then back at the ring. How was this possible? Had this man been the one to kill Tark?

She heard shouts in the distance. Her name.

Jossey suddenly felt an overpowering urge to hide this from them. All of it. The Onlar's real face, the ring –

"Jossey!"

She whispered "I'm sorry" again to the Onlar. Then she carefully placed the mask back onto his face and stepped back.

With a rasping sound, the mask sealed itself.

43

CASPAR CAME RUNNING UP THE STAIRS INTO THE CHAMBER, followed by Zlotnik and Thompson. They must have been able to move the stone, Jossey thought, half-heartedly looking in their direction.

The agents stopped dead.

Jossey had seated herself by the column, knife in hand, not particularly caring if any more Onlar showed up. She was shivering, tears flowing freely down her face.

They took in the scene – the weeping young woman and the dead Onlar on the floor, blood everywhere. Zlotnik gaped. Thompson looked sick.

Only Caspar kept calm. He made his way over to her, eyes traveling over the chain, the knife. He crouched down in front of her. "Jossey, are you hurt?"

She shook her head. Her tears wouldn't stop.

"Are you sure?" He frowned, looked closely at her. "The creature? It didn't hurt you?"

She closed her eyes, hot tears pouring down her face. "I killed – I killed it," she choked out, stammering.

Zlotnik had gone to check. "Dead," she confirmed. Her face

was thickly bandaged; she looked pale, but upright. "Room's clear."

Jossey wiped viciously at her eyes. She choked, tears spilling over again.

"Let's go," Caspar said quietly.

He looked over at Zlotnik, jerked his head in Jossey's direction. The tall woman came over and helped Jossey to her feet. Jossey attempted to shrug her off, wobbling toward the exit, still clutching her knife, the chain trailing after her.

Zlotnik stopped her, carefully took the knife, and unhooked the chain, leaving it on the floor. Jossey took the knife silently and sheathed it. Her roommate wrapped a supporting arm around her waist.

Down in the lower chamber, Ellis was standing over an unconscious Henry. Wickford was seated nearby, panting, putting pressure on an injured left arm. The Onlar – Jossey didn't look at them.

Ellis looked up wearily at them. "He's still out," he said. "We need to get back to base."

Caspar glanced over. "Thompson."

He and Thompson lifted Henry and carried him up the stairs. Jossey and Zlotnik went first into the small tunnel through which they'd entered the Old Sector. Wickford and Ellis followed the group, swords at the ready.

They reached the end of the tunnel and Zlotnik keyed in the City access code.

44

THE BRIGHT LIGHTS OF THE CITY TUNNEL WERE IMMEDIATE AND blinding. Jossey covered her eyes.

Caspar immediately turned on his com. "Medic!" he shouted into it. "Patrol Unit 2, base. We're on our way. Priority one. One unconscious, two injured." He glanced at Zlotnik. "You doing okay?"

She smiled grimly through the bandages. "I've been better."

"Good. Let's go."

They hurried through the tunnels. Jossey looked back at Henry. He had been hit in the head, it appeared, and he was breathing shallowly. Wickford looked pale. She glanced at Thompson, who seemed afraid to meet her eyes.

She looked ahead again.

The medic team met them at the entrance to the Patrol base, pushed them in the direction of the chemical baths, where they walked through a kind of mist. The Quarantinatron, Zlotnik had jokingly called it.

Henry was whisked away immediately into another room. They followed, and were stopped at the door by the head doctor, who smiled kindly but firmly and directed them toward the training room. Zlotnik and Wickford were taken away by one of the nurses.

"She's probably going to look like me," Jossey muttered.

Caspar smiled a little. "She's proud of that type of thing, I'd guess."

"Equipment," Ellis said shortly. He gestured to the cleaning station.

"Right." Caspar glanced down at his weapons. "Thanks."

Jossey mechanically followed after the men.

As they cleaned their blades, she tried not to think about what hers had just done.

Caspar was looking closely at her as she cleaned. She glanced up at him. "What?"

"How did you come up with the chain idea?" he asked. "That was brilliant."

She bristled, forced back the tears that arose. She took a very deep breath. "I don't want to talk about it."

"Sorry."

"And you – "

She glanced over toward Thompson and Ellis. They had seated themselves far away. She saw Thompson look at her, then look away quickly as if seeing something that frightened him. Her face flushed, and she turned back to Caspar. "How did you learn to fight like that?" she hissed.

Caspar suddenly stiffened. "Like what?"

"Like – " She gestured. "What you did when the Onlar attacked me. And the second one, with the knife. I've only seen Gavin move like that. How – I thought you were rusty, I thought you didn't remember that much."

"Jossey."

His tone was a warning.

She looked at him sharply, feeling something cold and prickly creep up her spine, little stabs of fear.

"It was instinct," he said slowly, looking straight into her eyes. "Nothing more. Whatever you saw, it was instinct."

"Instinct." She looked down at her knife, turning it over.

She'd never been afraid of Caspar, just as she'd never been afraid of Gavin, but suddenly she wondered if maybe she should be.

"Yes," he said carefully, silver eyes unreadable. "And adrenaline."

Adrenaline, she thought.

She hadn't imagined it, she was almost sure. Just like she was nearly certain she hadn't imagined the way he had taken the knife from Liam in the tunnel, or the way he'd pulled that punch with Thompson.

Or the way he'd stood there and allowed Tskoulis to beat him on the training floor.

The questions were burning in her mind. But something in Caspar's tone was warning her not to say anything more.

She closed her mouth, went back to cleaning her blade, not looking at him.

Caspar watched her for another long uncomfortable moment, appeared satisfied. He set his cleaned sword aside, reached for his knife.

Jossey jumped as a voice shouted, "Patrol! On your feet!"

They leapt to their feet and turned to find Tskoulis standing there, glowering at them. Jossey stood as straight as she could, tipping a little on her bad leg, fully aware of the blood all over her uniform. On all of theirs. She winced.

"Ellis, full report, now," Tskoulis said darkly. He took in the state of their uniforms. "Anyone injured?"

He looked straight at Jossey. She looked straight back at him, unflinching.

"Sir, we were attacked," Ellis said. He counted off the injuries on his hand. "Henry is unconscious. Zlotnik got clawed in the face. Wickford took a hit to the arm. They're in with the medical staff."

Tskoulis gestured to them. "And the rest of you?"

"We're unhurt, sir. There were at least ten of the Onlar, maybe more. They – " Ellis paused a moment. "They trapped us in one of the chambers using those stone doors."

"Explain." Tskoulis looked deadly serious.

Ellis detailed how they had been apparently lured down into the lower chamber, then attacked when they had tried to return to the upper levels. When he explained that Jossey had gone for help, Tskoulis turned unreadable eyes on her. "You climbed up the air shaft? Alone?"

"Yes, sir," she said, squirming.

"Quick thinking, Sokol. Good work."

"It was his idea." She pointed to Caspar.

"The air shaft wasn't my idea," Caspar said quietly. "I just told her to go for help."

Gavin looked strangely gratified. "Noted, agent."

He turned back to Jossey. "And you managed to get to the City?"

"No, sir," she said. "I – "

She stopped talking, felt her heart rate increase. She forced the memory down viciously. She couldn't think about that right now.

She took a deep breath and continued. "There was...one of Them in the chamber when I got there. I – "

She couldn't speak, gestured instead to her stained uniform. "I killed it," she managed at last.

Tskoulis' jaw was clenched. She felt very small. Why did he look so angry? What had she done wrong?

"And then you rescued the rest of them, or got backup?" he said finally.

"No, sir," she said, feeling even smaller. Caspar had tasked her with just one thing. She'd tried. "They fought off the rest, I guess, and then moved the stone themselves while I was fighting the Onlar."

He appeared to be thinking. "Understood," he said at last. "You did well, all of you. Anything else to report?"

Jossey thought of the ring she had hidden in her uniform pocket. She wanted badly to tell Gavin about it, but if he thought she had failed – or worse, broken Protocol on her very first mission –

If she said anything more about the Onlar, even to tell Tskoulis about Tark's ring, she could be thrown off Patrol.

And besides, he probably wouldn't believe her if she told him the Onlar were human. She doubted Gavin Tskoulis had ever broken Protocol to discover what she had just discovered. Gavin was probably as straight-laced as Patrol came.

She shook her head silently, trying not to meet Tskoulis' gaze. She was determined to figure out why that Onlar – that man, she reminded herself – had had Tark's ring.

And that meant keeping silent so she could keep going into the tunnels.

In the bunk above Jossey's, Zlotnik was out cold, the sedative the medic had given her working so well that Jossey was a little worried.

Jossey lay in her bunk. Her mind was going too fast to even think about sleeping, even though her body was all but screaming at her to rest.

She turned her thoughts back to the Onlar. She couldn't stop coming back to the face beneath the mask.

It was so hard to think of them as human. Again, she wondered if it could have been an agent of Karapartei, dressed as one of the Onlar. But it didn't make sense to her. How would they have gotten the equipment necessary?

And where would they have gotten Tark's ring?

Her thoughts swirled. Henry had said there had been a breach – that Karapartei was using the Old Sector tunnels to move supplies, or something like that. But that didn't make sense to her either. Karapartei ultimately just wanted a different government, as far as she'd gathered. Their intent was not, it seemed, to harm the City's population. They'd specifically targeted the Ministers on that stage, not the audience.

Why would they risk something so dangerous as letting the Onlar into the City's tunnels?

And why would they risk having their agents in the same tunnels as the Onlar?

Unless, her mind said, *they were already trained to fight them...*

She sat bolt upright, frowning into the darkness.

The only people who had access to combat training were Patrol. And only Patrol knew the access codes to get into the tunnels. How would Karapartei have gotten those? Unless...

Her thoughts were whirling. The man she'd been attacked by on Founders' Day – he'd kicked her pole and bent it. That was only possible with steel-toed boots. Only Patrol wore steel-toed boots.

The thought hit her like a blow.

Were Karapartei members of Patrol? A splinter faction?

Her head was killing her. It was 3:00 AM. She had to be up at 5:00. Her muscles were screaming at her. But this was something she should tell Tskoulis, she thought. Or her uncle.

As she closed her eyes and tried to force herself to relax, the face behind the mask drifted before her yet again. She let herself look at it – the long eyes, so like Caspar's.

The leathery skin from, she guessed, decades of sunlight.

She needed to get back into those tunnels.

45

THE NEXT DAY, JOSSEY FELT LIKE SHE HAD BEEN KICKED IN THE chest.

Everything hurt. Her arms and back were burning, probably from her climb up the shaft, and her bad leg was making itself felt even more than normal. Her head was just generally in pain.

Water. She needed water. Lots of it.

She pulled the pillow over her head and groaned when she heard the call in the corridor.

"Can I pretend I'm in a coma?" she muttered. Olivia laughed sympathetically and shook her head.

"Gotta report to duty, soldier."

"Ugh." She lifted the pillow from her face and glanced at Olivia. "Is Zlotnik alive?"

An answering groan came from the top bunk.

"I think that's a yes." Olivia smiled and went into the bathroom, shutting the door.

Jossey clawed her way out of bed and stood unsteadily, looking up at Zlotnik's bunk. "Are you okay?"

Zlotnik half-smiled at her, face still heavily bandaged.

"They say I'll probably have a scar like yours," she said drowsily. "I'm sorry I stared before."

Jossey looked away. "It's okay. I'm used to it." She cracked a half-grin. "It might be useful for intimidating people, if that's any consolation."

Zlotnik stared at the ceiling for a long moment. "I'm sorry," she said quietly. "I didn't think much of you when we first met. That wasn't fair of me. Council kid or not, you're resourceful, and I admire that. You don't use your family's name. I see why you were picked for Patrol."

Jossey looked at her in silence. "Thank you," she finally said. "I'm sorry I elbowed you in the face."

Zlotnik smiled crookedly, wincing a little. "Like I said, resourceful." She sat up on one elbow. "And you tried to come to my aid back in the tunnels."

"Yes. Before Caspar sent me to get help."

Zlotnik looked thoughtful. "That was the right thing he did. I get the feeling that Tskoulis would have our badges, and maybe worse, if anything happened to you."

Jossey flushed. "What do you mean?"

The woman shrugged. "It's just a feeling. Seems your uncle, the Minister, has a tight rein on Tskoulis where it comes to you. Understandably so. Don't worry so much, Council kid." She winked.

Jossey let out a breath she didn't realize she'd been holding. "Oh. Yeah, he's – overprotective." She purposely didn't say who.

"Come on, ladies, rise and shine."

They both stared daggers at Olivia as she breezed out of the bathroom. She grinned at them. "You want breakfast, yes?"

They glanced at each other and raised their eyebrows, then started laughing.

. . .

Ellis, for once, was gentlemanly and allowed the women to get their protein first. Thompson still seemed a little afraid to look at Jossey. She sighed and ignored him, pouring her customary cup of coffee.

Caspar sat down, looking fairly well-rested.

She caught her reflection in one of the spoons and almost jumped. She looked a mess, giant dark circles under her eyes and the expression of someone who'd just dropped their keycard in the elevator shaft. No wonder Thompson was trying not to look at her.

Caspar raised an eyebrow. "You all right, Sokol?"

Sokol. Maybe he hadn't forgotten the strange tension yesterday.

She shook her head and downed the second coffee, glaring at him. "How are you so...functional?"

He shrugged. "I was exhausted. Went to sleep right away."

The rest of them looked reasonably well-slept, she realized. Just not her. *Great.*

She went back over and took an extra helping of eggs. To her surprise, Ellis didn't say a word.

Thompson, still avoiding her gaze, got into an enthusiastic discussion with Caspar about yesterday's battle. He, at least, seemed to treat it as a sport. Jossey sourly nursed her second coffee, wishing Zlotnik would come up with something else to talk about. Wickford was no help, following the men's conversation breathlessly.

Jossey glanced at Ellis. He shrugged and went back to his eggs, looking faintly amused.

6:00 came and went.

6:10.

6:12. Unthinkable by Patrol's standards.

No Henry. No one came to get them.

They looked at one another uncomfortably, finishing their fake eggs in silence.

Finally one of the lower-level flunkies, as Ellis called them, wandered into the mess hall.

"Unit 2-5, report to training," he said.

They got up.

The training floor was nearly empty. Tskoulis was standing there, arms folded.

They filed into the room and stood before him.

"At ease," he said. Jossey found herself wishing he would smile more. It felt strange to be scared of him.

He did not seem in a smiling mood, however. "I regret to inform you that Sergeant Henry is on indefinite medical leave."

They glanced at each other. Wickford looked stricken. He opened his mouth, but a look from Tskoulis silenced him.

"The doctors say he should recover with sufficient rest," the commander went on. "However, I have no more members of my unit to spare."

He looked pointedly at Wickford, who wilted.

Something Zlotnik had said a while back floated through Jossey's mind as she wondered what Wickford had done. He looked miserable.

"Wickford. The clumsy one. He was on a night mission...then he got demoted."

She smiled sympathetically at him.

Tskoulis was talking again. She snapped back to attention.

"Due to the urgency of the current situation, and our lack of available leadership," Tskoulis said, "I am now in command of Patrol Unit 2-5."

Jossey had no idea how to feel. She looked at him, stricken.

Caspar was one thing. He seemed to take care of her, sort of

– make sure she didn't get lost, that type of thing. But Ga-Tskoulis?

She felt fairly certain that if he were to take them on a mission in the tunnels, she'd be stuck as far from combat as possible.

The whole thing between him and Tark had been a joke, once. They'd been best friends, inseparable. Jossey had been the annoying little sister that Tark would defend with his life.

Literally, she thought, forcing the lump in her throat away.

And when Jossey's father had disappeared into the desert, when they'd found him – Gavin had come up to her at her father's funeral, holding a crushed purple flower. His face was pale with crying.

"Tark and me were best friends, we promised," he said, chin trembling. "And that means I have to be there for you too, 'specially since your dad..." He trailed off, holding the smashed blossom out to her with one clenched fist. "Here." He shoved it toward her.

She took the flower and started bawling. He started crying, too, helpless silent tears, a child in the midst of a sea of adults.

She ran away and refused to speak to him for the rest of the funeral. She didn't want him there, because that meant that Tark had really left her, that her father was really gone. That she was to blame.

She'd hoped Gavin would forget his promise, and leave her alone in her misery. But he hadn't.

She'd spent the next decade, and more, trying to get him to stop caring what happened to her.

It was her fault, after all. Why couldn't he see that?

"Jossey. *Jossey.*"

Jossey blinked, confused. The child Gavin in her memory morphed into the modern-day Gavin.

The modern-day Gavin did not look pleased.

"Sokol. Wake up." His arms were crossed, dark eyes boring into hers. "Tell me what I just said."

She flushed wildly, glancing around at the others in terror. They were staring at her. "I'm sorry, sir," she mumbled. "I didn't sleep very well."

Tskoulis sighed heavily. "Twenty push-ups."

"What?"

"You heard me. Now."

Her arms felt like they were about to fall off. But she gritted her teeth and dropped to the floor.

"Paying attention can mean the difference between life or death," Tskoulis said to them. "Before, you had the luxury of time and training. Now we may have neither. The Onlar are dangerously close to a breach. We need to be in top condition, do you understand me?"

"Yes sir!"

Jossey shouted it at the floor. Her arms felt like rubber. But she refused to let Tskoulis see any weakness, now more than ever.

Not now that she had somewhere to be.

She slumped halfway over the table at lunch, groaning. She heard Tskoulis laugh a little, and looked to her left.

He was *sitting* with them, she thought, horrified.

"Sokol, do I need to call you a medic?"

He was *enjoying* this.

She sat up straight and gave him a death-glare. His handsome face was amused, dark eyes dancing.

She turned away in disgust. *So much for protecting me.* "No, sir."

Caspar was watching their interaction silently as he ate his lunch. Finally, he said, "Jossey, the Minister wants us to resume our Engineering class right after lunch."

She smiled at him. "I remember. I've been working hard. When I'm not...working out." She gave Tskoulis a sidelong glance.

Gavin looked even more amused. She stuffed a spring roll in her mouth and determinedly looked away from him.

"This is for your own good, Sokol," he said at last, giving her the Tskoulis grin and shoveling down some kind of strange protein-y dish.

She wanted very badly to say something snide, but decided she didn't want another set of push-ups.

I liked you better before, Gavin, she thought darkly, but gave him a sweet smile.

He seemed to get the message, though. His grin faded, and he went back to eating his food.

Caspar seemed absorbed by the material in front of him. He finished eating quickly, sharp silver eyes flickering over the pages. It was some kind of solar engineering text, Jossey noticed.

"What's that?" she asked.

"Material for today," he said. It looked advanced. She leaned closer, hoping she remembered this stuff from school. "Is that–"

"Yep." He grinned. "Entirely theoretical, but – "

Her face lighting up, she forgot about Tskoulis, forgot about the rest of them. "Let me see that."

She pulled the text across the table, studying it.

This was some next-level tech. She got to *work* on this?

She was beaming when she handed it back to Caspar. She turned to Gavin. "Sir, may we– "

Tskoulis had a strange expression on his face.

She fell silent, looking at him inquisitively. "Sir?"

He blinked. "Yes. Go. Excused."

He got up quickly. "Break's over. The rest of you, to training. Now."

46

JOSSEY RETREATED TO THE SMALL CONFERENCE ROOM THAT SHE
and Caspar had converted into a library for their Engineering
project.

Caspar disappeared, saying something about extra coffee.
She let herself into the room and opened the folder marked
CLASSIFIED.

Maps tumbled out. She carefully arranged them on the table.

If she was going to create a functioning smart grid, she
needed to know how to defend it.

A smart grid was theoretically designed to continue functioning even if disrupted at one or more points. Her goal was to
make it as hard as possible to disrupt it at all.

She chose the oldest-looking map and laid it flat next to an
official Patrol map, which had diagrams of the canyons with
Onlar caves, traveling routes, water supplies. The older map had
handwriting she could barely read.

It looked like it was from the time of the Founders. She was
amazed it didn't fall apart in her hands.

Something on it caught her eye, and she frowned, looking
more closely.

The older map had the City on it, in the center. To the south were mountains; to the northeast, the Onlar canyons began.

Jossey knew that the City was located in the middle of a plain, in an area the Founders had deemed suitable after the decades of war and famine had left the entire region all but unusable. Aboveground, that was. Underground, they could use their technology, the best available, to carve out a small wonder of engineering in the volcanic rock: a hollow multi-ringed, multi-level tunnel-based city for many thousands of people. The scale of the project had been enormous, almost unthinkable.

Yet on the maps, to Jossey's surprise, the City's plain was relatively small. Even the Onlar's canyons didn't take up much space.

She looked more carefully. What else could possibly be relevant out there? It was a wasteland.

There, on the old map, was the City, and the words Old Sector to the south. She calculated in her head. Quadrant 3 in City terms. That made sense. That's where they'd headed into the dusty tunnel system and encountered the Onlar.

Suddenly she frowned. The handwriting was barely legible, but there was unmistakably a number there.

The map said Old Sector *1*.

She traced a finger to the north of the City. *Old Sector 2.* Toward the Onlar canyons to the northeast. A second Old Sector. She'd always understood the Founders' City to be a one-time project. Two Old Sectors? How had she never heard of these?

She looked more carefully at the rest of the old map. It looked like those decorative ones her mother had collected, from the time before the heat: fanciful scribbles, waves, implausible coastlines, with little whimsical sayings like "here be dragons." Things written in a language her mother had called Latin.

At first glance, Jossey had assumed the mountains at the bottom of the old map were the same thing.

But now she wondered.

She'd never thought much about the land around them, other than what she could see from the solar farm's control box on her solar crew runs. Survival had dictated staying below-ground as much as possible.

She remembered evenings up above, waiting for the solar crew shuttle: an endless plain of rough, lumpy tan volcanic stone, sliced by the beginnings of canyons; purplish low mountains in the distance; a pink haze in the greyish evening air.

She knew, generally speaking, that to the south were more flat plains, and in the far southern distance there were mountains. Ancient volcanoes, they'd learned in school. She'd never really cared. Hot, dusty plains meant near-certain death if you were up there too long in the sunlight.

There was a label on the mountains, or, rather, just to the north of them. *Ilara.*

She'd never heard of it.

Patrol's job was to protect the City from the Onlar, and from internal unrest. Part of that job was to map everything.

She put one finger on the old map to hold her place, then looked at the Patrol map next to it.

The Patrol map, she noticed, had a circle, a kind of ring, around the City. A dotted line. It encompassed the City and both Old Sectors.

Jossey glanced outside the circle.

Ilara wasn't on there.

She blinked, looked again, wanting to rub her eyes. There was nothing. Just more canyons. The Patrol map was topographical. It showed water features, defensible positions, that type of thing.

Nothing to indicate that the region had had a name.

Jossey looked back at the old map. *Ilara* sounded to her like something in the Old Language. It sounded a lot like the world *Onlar*. Maybe –

There was a tap at the door, and she jumped.

She looked up. Caspar was there, grinning at her through the window. He held up his hands. They were full.

She got up and opened the door for him. He breezed into the room and set a pile of doughnuts before her.

"Agent Sokol, I bring baked goods to help fuel our project," he said, smirking.

"I've barely started," she admitted.

"What are you looking at?" Long silver eyes glanced at the table.

She followed his gaze. "Defensible positions for the smart grid," she said.

He walked over and looked down at the side-by-side maps. "Interesting. Find anything useful?"

Jossey noted how casual he looked as he bit into a doughnut, leaning on the table with one hand. She frowned the tiniest bit. How did he switch back and forth from terrifying to this?

He raised an eyebrow at her. "Did I do something?"

Jossey flushed, realized he had caught her watching him. She shook her head. "Just trying to think if I *have* found anything useful. Not much, I guess." She shrugged. "I realized I hadn't given much thought to the land around here until today."

She came around the table and stood next to him, feeling very short, not a feeling she appreciated. He handed her another doughnut. She bit into it and traced a finger over the map.

"Here are the solar farms," she said thoughtfully around a mouthful of doughnut. "And here – "

She stopped. The Patrol map had the elevator on it.

She sat down, shaking. She hadn't expected to see it, hadn't expected it to hit so hard.

"Jossey?"

She avoided eye contact, hating herself for looking like this in front of him. *Again.* She was never this emotional around Gavin, she thought bitterly. She looked at the map and froze again.

The elevator, a little x on the map that said Service Exit, sat there in black and white, next to a small field of condenser pods. *Farm #3.*

It was all she could see.

"Jossey, what's wrong?" Caspar's voice was concerned.

"That – " She forced her shaking hand to be still. As calmly as she could, she placed a finger on the map. "That elevator – "

"How do you know it's an elevator?" Caspar frowned suddenly. "It just says – "

Jossey laughed bitterly, cutting him off.

She gestured to her scar. "Because that's where I got this. That's where I lost my brother."

Caspar was silent for a long time. He retreated to the other end of the table, seeming lost in thought.

She let him go, poring over the maps again, eating her third doughnut, not caring that she'd probably feel terrible tomorrow.

The Patrol map was useful, even without the labels. The central plain was relatively flat; rivers began to the west of the Onlar lands, due north of the City.

She had even worked out the approximate source of the underground river that ran through the City; it had been diverted, maybe near the time of the Founders. She wondered if it was the same water that fed the wells of the Old Sector.

She traced the northwestern rivers. Despite the heat-induced flooding and droughts that seemed to hit every other year, she thought, the rivers here to the north should be more than adequate to feed the City's agricultural labs. Maybe the Old Sector could even be used to add additional growth labs.

"I need to take a look at one of the hydroponic labs," she muttered to herself.

Caspar perked up. "What?"

She glanced at him. "I need to know how much water each needs in order to function. I have an idea – what if we were to use the Old Sector's wells as a water source for City needs, or divert that river system for agricultural needs?"

He looked warily at her. "We'd likely have to get rid of any Onlar in there. And Karapartei probably wouldn't give up their new tunnel access without a fight."

Jossey frowned. "So let's fight them. What's their problem, anyway? The City functions just fine. Karapartei seems to think there's some kind of dire threat to resources or something."

He was silent. She looked quizzically at him, but he said nothing other than, "It's not a bad idea, but your uncle seems pretty strict on staying within our own lanes."

"What do you mean?"

"I mean," he said carefully, "that we should probably focus on the solar grid."

She grinned a little. "Are you afraid of my uncle?"

His face got very serious. "Yes. And you should be too. He's Head of Intelligence, uncle or not."

Jossey gave him a funny look. She shrugged and went back to the maps.

Two hours later, she'd mapped a rudimentary smart-grid system, using the topographical map and consulting Caspar on some of the more technical aspects of the grid itself. The distribution switches would extend in an apparently random scatter across the landscape to prevent systematic takedown of the system; the solar panels themselves would be sealed behind electric fences. Power would be stored in giant batteries located near the main City entrances, heavily guarded.

Short of tossing a boulder directly on the panels, she thought bitterly, the network should be safe.

Caspar looked impressed. About fifteen minutes before she'd finished, her uncle had appeared silently, watching her work. She'd ignored him and kept going.

Now Sokol sat down across from them and looked through the plans, looking more and more pleased with each page.

"Wonderful, my dear, wonderful," he kept saying.

He finished reading and looked at Caspar. "You agree this is technically sound?"

Caspar smiled. "I do. It's excellent work." He gave Jossey a look. "Your talents were clearly wasted on that solar crew."

She flushed. "Don't say that."

The Minister glanced down at his wrist, then looked back at the plans. "How long would it take to develop and test a proto-type, Jossey?"

She thought. "I'd need – " She calculated in her head. Ten foldable panels was the minimum for an efficient netwide distribution. She needed to fit at least three switches per section.

She looked at Caspar. "Ten sections and thirty switches?"

He glanced at the map, where she'd marked little red x's. One was close to the elevator. The x's formed a ring around the City, all easily accessible and defensible.

"We'd have to install them at night, when it's cool enough," he warned. "Are you up for that?"

"Yes."

She was. She couldn't wait.

"Very good." Sokol clapped his hands, once. "Then this meeting is adjourned. I have just sent in an order for an Engi-neering crew." He smiled at Jossey. "You may recall some of its members."

She brightened. "Perkins? Sally?"

"Indeed."

She beamed again. "Thank you," she said earnestly. She'd missed them.

Then something occurred to her. "Uncle?"

"Yes, my dear." He had gotten up, was putting on his cloak.

"Uncle Sokol," she said, "what's Ilara?"

Sokol turned back to her. "What do you mean?"

Jossey pulled out the old map, pointed to it. "This region. It doesn't appear on any further maps."

Sokol looked down at it. Then he smiled. "Ah. One of the names of the region. I don't know the meaning. Maybe the Founders were at one time interested in putting the City there."

"Ah." It made sense. "And the Old Sectors?"

"Long ago, the population here built their own tunnel system. It was the inspiration for the City, from what I understand." He donned his cloak. "I fear I must leave you now."

"Goodbye, Minister," Caspar said deferentially as the older man left the room, the door sliding shut behind him.

Jossey looked at him. "What?"

He gave her an innocent look. "What?"

"You were watching me the whole time I was talking to him."

Caspar pretended to be wounded. "I was just curious. The name Ilara sounds interesting. Mysterious. Disappearing off the maps and all. You get to do the fun stuff. I just do the calculations."

She made a face at him. "Whatever."

He picked up the plans she'd drawn up. "Your uncle said he'd put in the request for the parts. He ordered a team." He grinned at her. "That means we're free."

. . .

They left the conference room, Jossey grinning ear-to-ear as the realization hit her that she was in charge of a *smart-grid project.* Well, she and Caspar.

He followed behind, having snagged the last of the doughnuts.

They had an hour before dinner. They had no responsibilities.

Jossey had forgotten what it was like to have free time. She was giddy over the project, over the pent-up emotion of the last several days. She felt like sprinting through the Patrol corridors.

So she did.

Caspar started laughing as she took off running. "Where are you going?" he yelled after her.

She turned her head and yelled, "I don't know!"

Their uniforms were loose and designed for ease of motion. Running felt, literally, like a breeze. She sprinted around the curve in the tunnel, losing sight of Caspar. His amused shout to wait faded as she kept going.

She turned a corner as the tunnel branched, and nearly plowed into Tskoulis, who was wandering, looking lost in thought.

She barely caught herself in time, inches from smashing right into him. He had held up his hands as if to block her fall, and she all but leaped back, burning with embarrassment.

They stared at each other, Jossey flushed with running and embarrassment, Gavin's dark eyes warm and slightly confused as he looked down at her. For a moment his face broke into a brilliant smile.

"Jossey? Why are you running?"

"Gavin," she gasped out, burning with shame. "I mean." She coughed. "Commander. I apologize."

Of all people, she had to run into *him.* But she hadn't seen him smile in so long, not a real smile. She hadn't realized how much she'd missed it.

She stood up straighter, tried to appear presentable. "Sir. I'm sorry," she said again.

He still looked confused, the Tskoulis grin gone but a smile tugging at his lips, his handsome face flushed. He didn't seem to have processed her words.

She blinked at him. Since when had Tskoulis –

"Sorry," she said again, "I was just – "

"Jossey! Wait!" Caspar came running around the corner after her, the laughter in his voice dying as he spotted Tskoulis.

The Patrol commander instantly stiffened, stepped away from Jossey. Caspar snapped to attention.

Jossey could feel something in the air between the two men. It wasn't anything good.

She brushed off her uniform and stood with her hands behind her back, trying to appear professional.

"Sorry, sir," she said again, more clearly. "I didn't see you."

He barely looked at her. The warmth in his eyes was gone, replaced by a kind of veiled anger. He was staring at Caspar.

Just as she'd sensed a darkness in Caspar before, now she sensed it emanating from Gavin. She suddenly felt very small beside the two of them.

"Sir?" she ventured.

"What," he said to Caspar, "are you doing sprinting through the tunnels? Is there an emergency, recruit?"

Caspar's eyes were cold, but all he said was, "No, sir. No emergency." Jossey stared at him as he went on. "We just got out of class. I wasn't thinking. I apologize."

What is he doing?

She opened her mouth to say something, but his silver eyes flickered to hers, and she fell silent.

She couldn't understand why the commander looked so angry all of a sudden. She was the one who had nearly bowled him over, not Caspar.

He seemed to be angry a lot around her recently, she realized. He was staring at Caspar now like he wanted to slug him.

Caspar looked back at him evenly.

For running in the corridors. She didn't understand.

At last, Tskoulis said, "Don't let it happen again."

"Sir." Caspar stepped aside as the Tiger pushed past them and continued on his way.

When he was out of sight, Jossey whispered to Caspar, "What's he so angry about? He seemed so happy a moment ago. I know we were acting like kids, but I mean come on, we deserved it. "

Caspar's mouth twisted. Long silver eyes glanced sideways at her.

"He's not called the Tiger for nothing," was all he said.

47

DURING TRAINING THE NEXT DAY, ONE OF THE PATROL FLUNKIES darted in, a pile of papers half-falling from his arms. He spoke breathlessly to Tskoulis, then darted back out. Jossey glanced over at the young man, curious, but Tskoulis gave her a look and she went back to the weights machine she was using.

His training was effective, she admitted to herself, even if it was painful and she had various half-murderous thoughts directed his way while she was doing it. She could now handle a sword much more easily than before, even if she preferred the knife.

Tskoulis had paired her with Thompson, who now seemed terrified of her and clammed up whenever she approached. But he was an excellent sparring partner, and a good teacher, she had to say. She just wished he would make eye contact.

It's not like she was the only person in this group to ever kill an Onlar, she thought.

Zlotnik's face had started to heal, and she was otherwise back in action, but the doctors had been right – she sported a double line of raised scars, directly across her face. They'd barely missed her eyes, which were both at least still green.

It looked like a child had painted red streaks across her forehead and across her nose and one of her cheeks.

"Cool scar," Jossey had said sympathetically when Zlotnik had returned for training a few days after the disastrous mission. Zlotnik had just half-smiled.

It *was* cool, though, Jossey thought. Zlotnik was tall with striking green eyes and a proud tilt to her head. Everything looked cool on her.

Jossey tried not to think about how her own scar looked.

The weights clanked as she returned them to the rack. She grabbed her stuff and went over to fill her water canteen. Caspar was there, drinking deeply from his. He started to greet her, but glanced over her shoulder and instead smiled tightly and stepped away.

"Sokol." It was Tskoulis.

Jossey turned around, bound haircloth swinging down her back. "Sir."

"Your equipment has arrived." He gestured to a pair of flunkies who were bringing in boxes in the back of the room. There was a twinkle in his eye, an almost-smile.

"Thank you sir!" she said, beaming. "Can I – "

"Yes. Go."

She jogged across the room, inspecting the equipment.

Wonderful. Ten pallets of foldable mobile-installable solar panels, and a crate of distribution switches and relays. This could easily be assembled over the course of a night, if they had enough personnel. It was an ideal size for a test grid.

She flashed Caspar a thumbs-up across the room, noting he had remained at the water cooler. *Whatever*, she thought.

Then she jogged back and picked up the weights again.

She was halfway through the set when she heard Tskoulis' voice ring out. "At ease."

The group stopped, the only sound their breathing as they recovered.

Tskoulis walked among them, hands behind his back. "At ease," he said, smiling a little. "Good work."

It was high praise.

"Sokol, to me," Tskoulis said. "Savaş."

Jossey and Caspar stepped up next to him. Tskoulis waved his arm toward the pallets. "Minister Sokol has ordered that we assist our auxiliary Engineers here with a high-priority project." He looked hard at Unit 2-5. "The classification level is Top Secret. A breach of Top Secret clearance is considered treason. Do I make myself clear?"

A ripple of fear ran through the room.

"Yes sir!"

"Good." He looked at Jossey. "Explain."

She cleared her throat. "Minister Sokol has requested that we put together and test a – a solar grid." She didn't know how much information her uncle would be all right with her sharing, and decided to err on the side of caution. "No training is necessary – I have a specially-commissioned Engineering crew to help me. Our mission as Patrol is to successfully put together the grid aboveground. This needs to be completed in a single night, with a second wiring mission to follow. Commander Tskoulis has the details." She smiled, glanced at Tskoulis. "If there are any Engineering questions, please come to me directly, but the assembly process is very self-explanatory."

Tskoulis added, "The crew is scheduled to arrive tomorrow evening to transport everything up to the surface, then convene after dinner. Due to the size of the operation, my unit, 2-1, plans to join us."

The agents glanced at each other. 2-1 was the elite of the elite, other than Patrol Unit 1, which none of them had ever seen, and weren't really sure existed.

Jossey was convinced, from conversations she'd had with Gavin, that Unit 1 was just a label that Patrol put out there to intimidate people. Like the old Delta Unit and such from the classics she'd read. But 2-1 was very real.

"Dismissed," Tskoulis said. "Take a break. Ten minutes."

They chatted as they walked over and refilled their canteens or stretched. Jossey cooled off, then wandered over to refill hers.

Wickford and Ellis were standing by the water, talking. They ignored her.

"I doubt they hate you, calm down man, but you know it's your own fault you aren't in 2-1 anymore," Ellis was saying quietly as Jossey unscrewed her canteen.

Her ears perked up, but she told herself not to eavesdrop. It wasn't her business.

The water poured at first, then dripped slower and slower, and then stopped.

She glared at the machine and reached up, jiggling the knob on the cooler to unstick it. *Every time.*

"Henry put me on that mission," Wickford said, a mournful note to his voice. "Pricey seems to think I'm a total doofus. But yeah, it's my fault. I shouldn't have run."

"Why was Tskoulis *so* pissed, though?" Ellis.

Jossey shook the machine, hearing despite herself. The water began to flow normally. *Technology*, she thought.

Wickford sounded far away, almost relieved to be speaking the words.

"I'm not sure it was anything *I* did," he said. "I mean, the noise, yeah. But he was – you know we found bones, right? A kid. I pretty much fell on them. You should have SEEN the look on – "

Jossey's water canteen fell from her hands.

The men both stopped talking and stared at her. She started and grabbed for the canteen, water sloshing everywhere.

"You okay, Sokol?" Ellis asked, an eyebrow raised.

"I'm fine." She looked anywhere but at them.

She managed to grab the canteen and twist the lid on tightly, leaving a puddle a foot wide on the floor.

Wickford. It had been him. He'd found Tark. Had all but fallen on Tark, she thought.

"Is something wrong?" Wickford. Clumsy, sweet Wickford.

She couldn't look at him.

She hurried away across the training floor, hating that she had to feel. Hating that she felt anything right now. She wanted to fight something. Punch something.

An Onlar, preferably.

"Whoa, whoa, Sokol, where do you think you're going?" Caspar. He was smiling.

"Move," she said.

His eyebrows shot up, but he stepped aside. She stormed toward the corridor.

"Sokol!"

It was Tskoulis. She kept going. She didn't think she could face him right now. Especially not him.

People stared.

"*Sokol.*" The voice was not amused.

She stopped, took a deep breath. Turned around.

Tskoulis was staring at her, expression equal parts concerned and dark. She looked pleadingly at him.

He looked back for a very long moment.

"Dismissed for dinner," he announced at last, his tone abrupt.

It was early. The others looked at him, confusion written on their faces.

"You're excused," he said. "Lots to do tonight and tomorrow. Prepare yourselves."

There were a few whoops, an overenthusiastic *clunk* as

someone set a weights set down too hard. Tskoulis shot a look at the offender.

Jossey didn't wait, didn't meet his eyes. She stormed out into the corridor.

48

She showed up for dinner, but barely looked at anyone.

Zlotnik finally set her food down in front of Jossey and sat across from her, looking her straight in the eyes. "What's the problem?" she demanded.

Jossey shook her head. "I'm sorry. I've been – there's been a lot going on." She looked away. "I'm doing my best," she added. No one looked convinced.

What she wanted to say was that she was *feeling* for the first time in years, had been feeling since she'd saved the transport, and it was horrible, and she just wanted to fight instead.

But she couldn't say that in front of a table of Patrol.

She stabbed at her salad and ignored the raised eyebrows.

"I'm nervous about the project," she finally said. It was sort of true.

"Get a grip, Sokol," Zlotnik said, not unkindly. "If it's as important as you say, you need to be on top of your game tomorrow. You especially."

"I know." Jossey tried to smile. "Thanks."

Ellis soberly reached over and deposited an extra piece of meat on her plate. "Here."

Ellis giving up protein was like – she didn't even know. Unprecedented. She gave him a real smile, then tucked into it, trying to avoid eye contact.

Wickford followed suit, passing the salt in her direction, looking confused when she glanced away from him quickly.

Caspar had been observing them all silently. He spoke up around a mouthful of food. "Besides, I'm also in charge," he said, reaching for the dish of vegetables. "Don't worry, Sokol, I know how to install a distributor switch."

Jossey gave him a grateful smile. He was good at covering for her, she had to say. She went back to her meal.

Tskoulis wasn't there, she noticed. He'd taken to eating with them, but he hadn't come over this time. She looked over and saw him sitting with a group of tall silent men.

Unit 2-1, she guessed. They were enormous. She glanced at Wickford, wondered how he'd ended up with them on that night mission. But only for a moment. It was too painful to think about.

Uncomfortable. It was *uncomfortable*, she told herself.

49

Mission day arrived.

Jossey had gone over everything at least five times when Caspar made her go to the mess for lunch and took her books away from her, handing them to Zlotnik for safekeeping. Jossey grudgingly admitted that she didn't need to go over everything *again*. She was the designer, after all.

Yet, when they were called into the training room after dinner, Jossey felt the sharp stabs of anxiety and wished there were more time to prepare.

A group of familiar faces was there.

When the crew saw Jossey, many of them broke into applause. She beamed at them. She desperately wanted to hug Sally and some others she saw among her crew, but she stayed still, waving instead.

Tskoulis smiled a little and introduced them. "Solar Crew A," he said. "Brought together specifically for this mission. Crew A, we are Patrol units 2-1 and 2-5, here to escort you."

Jossey saw Perkins grinning in the background. Sally was pink as usual as Tskoulis looked over the group, inspecting their equipment. Jossey almost laughed at Sally's expression. Maybe

Sally would like him less if *she* had to do twenty pushups for zoning out.

But, Jossey had to admit, it had been effective.

I promised to protect you, Gavin had told her many times.

She snorted inwardly. She was not willing to extend Gavin's protection to weight training, no matter how strong or prepared it made her.

She brushed the thought aside and focused. Gavin was giving the group a surprisingly accurate technical rundown of the process, from deployment aboveground to the actual installation. He'd done his homework, thought Jossey, feeling a little miffed that he hadn't consulted her.

But she felt calmer listening to all of it, more sure of what needed to be done. She just hoped they wouldn't spend much time near *that* elevator.

At the end of Tskoulis' speech, he turned to the Patrol subunits. "Suit up," he said. "Departure in ET twenty minutes."

So quickly? Jossey was startled.

It's just a grid, she told herself. *Simple concept, simple execution.*

But she'd never gone aboveground at night. Not since...

She shook her head again to clear it. *Focus*, she told herself.

Everyone was disappearing from the training room, likely heading to their rooms to get ready. She saw Caspar leave with Ellis and Thompson, saw Wickford amble after them, flinched a little as she watched him stumble slightly over his big feet.

She picked up her equipment and was turning to leave when a voice sounded close behind her.

"Jossey, we need to talk."

50

She turned around. Tskoulis was standing there, an unreadable look in his eyes.

"Of course, sir," she said.

"Not here." He gestured. "Come with me."

Jossey followed him, hoping he wasn't still angry with her for earlier. She was having real trouble with this feelings thing. It was painful and strange and –

He was leading her out into the corridor. She eyed him warily. "Yes, sir?"

Tskoulis led her toward the bend, just within sight but far enough that they were probably well out of earshot of anyone walking by. She realized again how small she felt next to him. Up close, he was huge, intimidating.

But his eyes were dark. Troubled. He looked at her face for a long moment. "Jossey."

"Yes, sir?"

"I – " He ran a hand through his hair. "I need to know. Are you all right?"

Jossey blinked. "What's this about, Gavin?" she asked carefully. "That is, Comm– "

"Call me Gavin, Commander, whichever," he said irritably, cutting her off. There was a harsh tone to his voice, like something held back. "Right now I'm talking to you as Gavin to Jossey, understand? I need to know if you're all right before I send you up there on this project. At night, especially. You know that's when They hunt."

Jossey shivered a little. "Yes, I'm all right. Just tired. Why?"

"You've been – " He stopped, as if searching for words. "Really strange lately."

"Me?" She smiled a little. "Maybe because now I have to call you Commander Tskoulis and salute and..."

She trailed off.

He was staring intently at her, the same look in his eyes as he'd had just before he'd told her they'd found Tark.

As if he needed to speak, desperately, but could not.

"Jossey."

He kept saying her name.

"What, Gavin?"

Tskoulis opened his mouth, closed it, flushed. He looked almost flustered, as if he couldn't quite say the words. "I – " He looked away, then at her. At last he said, "Be careful tonight."

That's it? She frowned. "Aren't you coming with us?"

"I have a meeting with someone. Top priority. You should have plenty of support with my men from 2-1. But – " He stopped again, looked directly at her. "Promise me."

"Promise you what?" He was the one acting strange, not her, she thought.

He made as if to speak, then clamped his mouth shut. Footsteps were approaching.

It was one of his people from 2-1. The man saluted.

"Report, Pricey," Gavin said.

"The units are ready, sir." Pricey was tall, blue eyes, sardonic smile on an arrogant-looking face.

"Excellent. Prepare for departure." The Patrol commander glanced at Jossey. "Sokol should be ready shortly."

Pricey saluted again, turned around and strode away.

Gavin turned to Jossey again, looking urgently into her eyes. "Promise me."

"I – " Then she smiled. "Don't worry, Gavin, my uncle probably won't throw you off Patrol if anything happens to me."

He flushed, looked even more frustrated. "Do you really think that's – "

"Commander!"

Tskoulis muttered something angrily under his breath. He tore his gaze away from Jossey, glared at the recruit who was approaching quickly.

Jossey followed his gaze. It was one of the flunkies she'd seen earlier.

The recruit withered under the Tiger's glare. Tskoulis was a good ten inches taller than him.

"Sir," the young man half-squeaked. "The solar crew needs night masks."

Tskoulis sighed explosively. "Very good. Pass them out."

He turned back to Jossey. "I have to go. Don't make me come find you, Sokol."

She wanted to laugh, but the look in his eyes was deadly serious.

She'd never seen him look quite so...earnest.

She gave him a tiny smile. "Don't worry so much about me, Gavin," she said. "You've prepared me well."

"That was the plan," he muttered. She blinked, not sure if she'd misheard.

He turned to the flunky. "Let's go, recruit." The young man snapped to attention and hurried after him, toward the solar crew.

Jossey watched him go, his words repeating in her head.

51

THEY SUITED UP. JOSSEY WAS CALM AS SHE FASTENED THE ARMOR over a flowing uniform that allowed the outfit to breathe, allowed her to move quickly and efficiently while staying cool in the desert heat.

She put on her arm-plates and bent to tie plates across her shins. She set the heavy chest-and-shoulders piece over her head and tied her headcloth tightly, draping an extra piece in case of dust storms.

She sheathed her weapons and attached the mask to her headcovering.

Zlotnik was doing the same thing. She stood in the gloom of the changing area, seeming to tower in the darkness. Jossey smiled at her.

"We match," Zlotnik said, grinning. She pointed to her scar.

Jossey looked away. "I was worried about that."

"Why?" Zlotnik smiled. "Don't you know how awesome yours makes you look?"

"What do you mean?" Jossey touched her scar. It was white, ridged. It sliced directly across her eye. The surgeons had barely saved her vision, and only because the tips of the Onlar's claws had touched her, flicked across her face, not actually dug in. "This thing? It makes me look awful."

Zlotnik snorted. "That is *clearly* what Thompson thinks."

Jossey flushed wildly. "You said – " She clamped her mouth shut. Zlotnik didn't need to know that she'd overheard their conversation. Besides, whatever interest Thompson had had in the new girl, that seemed completely and utterly dead.

But Zlotnik didn't appear to have noticed Jossey's half-sentence. She was tying her headcloth, looking in the mirror at the scar.

"And someone else," she added, glancing sideways at Jossey and grinning a little.

Jossey stared at her. What was she talking about?

Before she could ask, their watches beeped, loudly. Time to go.

They grabbed their bags, checked each other's weapons and armor, jogged down the hallway. The others met them in the training room.

Solar Crew A was outfitted with Patrol masks. They looked both excited and uncomfortable. But mostly excited.

Tskoulis wasn't there. Instead, Pricey stood there, hands behind his back.

"You've been briefed," Pricey said laconically. "2-1, you run point. 2-5, other than Sokol and Savaş, you follow up the rear. Solar Crew, in the middle. We divide up into two groups at the surface. Sokol, your group is responsible for the switches and relays; Savaş, yours installs the actual panels."

He looked at them, as if to make sure they were paying attention. They were all dead silent, eyes trained on him. "Once one group finishes, radio and rendezvous with the other. We should have approximately ten hours of darkness, maybe a little more. No light. Use your masks. Let's make this count."

Pricey clapped his hands. "Move out."

They shuffled down the hallway as a group. Jossey found herself next to Caspar. He lifted his mask. "You ready?"

"I guess so," she said. She left hers on so he wouldn't see the burning in her face.

Or maybe Zlotnik hadn't been talking about Caspar.

Jossey almost laughed at the thought. Not likely with her scar, no matter what Zlotnik thought, she told herself. She felt ashamed for even thinking it.

She turned and gave Caspar a thumbs-up. "Yeah, I'm ready. Let's do this."

The elevator doors slid shut, and with a jolt the car began to make its way to the surface.

The entire group went suddenly silent. They'd been sent up in clusters. This one was her, Caspar, and Zlotnik, and a few people from the solar crew. Some of them were new. Liam was there, and Sally, and a woman she didn't recognize.

Sally smiled widely at Jossey. She smiled back. The young woman seemed less afraid than Jossey had expected. Maybe the whole tunnel incident had been good for her. She seemed remarkably calm.

The elevator clanked its way upward. Jossey shivered inwardly with every noise, every jerk in the line.

Caspar and Zlotnik put their hands on their swords. They motioned for the crew to stay back. Jossey drew her knife.

The doors slid open.

52

THE ABOVEGROUND WAS SILENT, GRAY WITH A FAINT HAZE THAT hovered above the canyons, and almost chilly in the dimness. It was just after 9:00 PM. The sun had been down for a couple of hours, and she could see a few stars scattered across the sky, half-visible through the haze.

She was glad she was wearing her slightly warmer combat uniform as she stepped out of the elevator and stood silently, waiting for Pricey's command.

He'd gone up in the first car and had cleared the area along with a couple of men from 2-1. Now he stood eyeing the entrances to the canyons.

There were so many, thought Jossey. So many places for the Onlar to hide.

She switched on her mask.

She'd studied the maps extensively. She knew the area almost as well as the back of her hand. But in the dimness, it was still a little confusing. She pulled out her copy of the map and double-checked.

That one first. The entrance yawned to her right.

She turned and watched the next group emerge from the elevator.

Once everyone had ascended to the surface, she split them into their groups. Hers was smaller: Pricey, Liam, a man from 2-1 called Tarrington, and Zlotnik. A skeleton crew, just enough to install the switches and move quickly through the canyons. Caspar's group was responsible for the actual panels. He was taking most of 2-5 with him, along with the rest of the solar crew.

They all knew the plan. No time to brief now.

"We should have about ten hours," she said. "Radio for help. Follow Savaş's instructions." She gestured to Caspar.

"Each station should take about an hour," she added. "Take turns with the pallets. Don't tire yourselves out. This is delicate work."

"Ma'am." They saluted.

"Prepare to move." She took a step and gestured to Pricey, who was subbing for Tskoulis. "Commander."

The groups scattered to their respective solar panels. The equipment was heavy – at least a hundred and fifty pounds per pallet, plus the wooden base, she estimated. More like two hundred. They should be able to drag them for the most part on the excess sand left by canyon flooding, but they'd added snap-down wheels just in case.

Tskoulis had accounted for the travel time in his calculations. She had not, she thought, embarrassed.

She watched the group hurrying about, hoping she hadn't forgotten anything else.

Caspar came up to her as she stood there.

"Everything all set?" he said quietly.

"Yes," she said, watching Liam manhandle one of the panels. It had slid precariously toward the corner of the pallet during transit. She hoped this wouldn't happen while they were moving.

260

Had she added enough excess tie-down rope? She calculated in her head. There should be enough for two accidents. She wondered if there was anything else she hadn't accounted for. *Water, check. Weapons, check. Medical supplies, check.*

"Jossey." Caspar's tone was urgent, low, bringing her sharply back to the present.

She looked at him.

His silver eyes were troubled as he glanced around. As if he could hear something she couldn't.

"What is it?"

"I know it's more efficient travel-wise, but I don't like that the group is split. Do you have your radio?"

She looked over at Pricey and the other 2-1 Patrol. They were barking orders, seemingly unconcerned.

"Why are you bringing this up now?" she hissed. "Why not in the meeting?"

"It seemed more efficient at the time. But something seems wrong." He put a foot on one of the boulders, retied his boots, glanced sideways up at her, strands of hair falling over his face. His silver eyes were luminous in the darkness. "I don't hear anything. No night creatures."

She went silent, listened. He was right. No sound. The haze over the canyons suddenly seemed heavy, oppressive. A shiver went through her.

"It's probably just because we're out here," she said, unconvinced.

He looked at her soberly. "Maybe." Then he smiled a little. "Maybe it's just too cold. This haze. Maybe that's what seems off."

"Move out!" Pricey's voice floated across the desert sands.

Caspar's smile faded. He looked at her intently.

"Report in when you can. And Jossey, if – *if* – anything happens, I want you to get on that radio. Call me. Anything. Do you understand?" His tone was urgent.

She looked at him, at the long silver eyes trained on hers. He was afraid, she thought.

She'd seen him fight, seen him kill an Onlar in seconds, and *he* was afraid.

She reached for her radio, made very sure it was attached to her hip belt.

"Understood," she said.

53

Her small group started off into the night. The stars were brilliant overhead, the slight haze in the sky fading, as they ventured into the foothills that led up into the deeper canyons.

Pricey walked in front, Jossey behind him.

They'd slung the bundles of distribution switches and relay cables on their backs. They also had a pallet of tools and backup equipment.

The pallet wasn't that heavy, as equipment went, but the best way to transport it was to drag it with rope. She offered to take a turn with pulling her group's equipment pallet, but Pricey looked at her, then at Tarrington's huge arms, and just smiled.

She glared at him.

"Don't take it personally, Sokol. You're needed to run point," Pricey said, grinning.

She conceded defeat and looked around her as they hiked.

The landscape aboveground never ceased to amaze her. The canyons at the beginning looked like solid sand piles, before fracturing into stacks of what looked like huge building blocks. At night they looked truly frightening, unfamiliar and looming out of the darkness.

The wind whistled through the towers of stone, and she strained to hear anything out of the ordinary. Nothing but the breathing of the group and the sound of equipment being dragged. She hoped it wasn't loud enough to alert the Onlar to the group.

She kept an eye out for sign as they went.

She'd chosen this canyon for the first station for a good reason. On the Patrol map, she'd seen a blue x and asked Caspar what it meant.

"Floods," he'd said. "I think. Ask Tskoulis."

Tskoulis hadn't been around, so she'd double-checked with Ellis. He'd told her that some of the canyons were prone to violent flash floods during the storm season, and burning sunlight with little useful cover the rest of the time; the Onlar rarely used them. Additionally, the floods deposited plenty of river sand and other debris, making it less than ideal for any group to move quickly. Not an easily defensible position.

Armed with this information, Jossey had decided on using three of the flood-prone canyons as installation sites. On the uneven canyon walls, the equipment should be relatively hidden and hard for the Onlar to reach, she thought. Especially if the solar crew installed them high above the flood line.

As she had several times before, she checked the sky, feeling uneasy about the haze. It was usually dry during this time of year, one reason her uncle had approved a quick turnaround on the installation. If it wasn't dry –

She took off her gloves and quickly felt the air. The humidity was low, so low her hands felt stiff in the ultra-dry air. Good. She hadn't seen any clouds in the night sky up near the staging point either. Unlikely for it to rain, she thought.

She hoped, because it was very clear that this canyon was especially prone to flooding.

It was full of deposited sand and other items – branches and rocks and whatever else. In some places the sand was nearly two feet deep. She could see a faint line along the canyon wall, about fifteen feet off the ground, where the water had apparently scoured the volcanic rock during one of its violent episodes.

Just right to hide some distribution switches.

The sand shifted under their feet as they walked. Jossey could feel her leg muscles burning.

"Everyone all right?" she whispered, glancing back. They all gave her thumbs-up.

The mask was helping, but she almost didn't need it. Her eyes were adjusting quickly.

She checked for Onlar sign as she went. Unsurprisingly, she saw none. Ellis had been right – the Onlar wouldn't be likely to use this canyon to travel, not where they were in danger of flooding or being chased down by Patrol agents able to move more quickly in the sand.

She peered ahead into the dimness. They should be there soon, she hoped.

There was a scrabbling sound up ahead, and the group froze. The agents' hands shot to their swords.

A desert jackrabbit raced across the sand, followed by some small rodent. Jossey sighed, almost laughing with relief, and beckoned the group forward.

Another two twists of the canyon, and she saw it.

Using surveillance photos of the canyons that her uncle had given her, she'd selected a ledge that was workable but difficult to reach, and would not likely be detected by Onlar traveling below.

She looked appraisingly at the ledge, flexed her arms. Good thing she'd been lifting those weights, she thought grimly.

Pricey called a halt and beckoned to the group.

They set down their equipment and gathered around. In a low voice, he ordered Zlotnik and Tarrington to set a perimeter, then pointed to Jossey and Liam. "You two, with me," he said. "Let's go."

The canyon was dead silent. No night creatures, Jossey thought. She remembered Caspar's warning, and checked the radio. No blinking red light. The other group was probably okay so far, then.

Good.

Liam dragged the pallet to the base of the rock. He selected some tools and slung them into his equipment bag.

The switches were coiled in bundles. They worked on a wired relay system; once the switches were installed, there was a second mission scheduled to go up aboveground and thread the wires through. That could be accomplished by Patrol; the crew's expertise was only needed for the first stage, as Jossey had explained to her uncle.

Pricey and Liam made sure the switches were secure, then started climbing.

Jossey followed after them. Liam should be able to do the install, she knew, but she was in charge. She had to make sure there was no issue before they moved on to the next, or the mission could fail.

She wondered how Caspar's group was doing. Still no blinking red light.

The night breeze hit her as she ascended to nearly the top of the ridge and climbed out onto the thin ledge with Liam and Pricey. She looked around. She was quite high up – thirty feet or more – and realized she still wasn't comfortable with heights, not when she could see the bottom of the drop. She felt dizzy, and clung to the side of the canyon for a moment, remembering the rail in the tunnel and her almost-fall.

"Sokol." Pricey's voice was close beside her.

She snapped out of it. "Sorry." No time to be afraid. There were much worse things to be afraid of.

Pricey handed her the switch bundle. She glanced at Liam and started to unwrap it.

He worked quickly, taking a handheld pickaxe and chipping into the rock. It was loud, and she flinched, but she saw no motion below in the canyon, other than the glint of weapons as Zlotnik and Tarrington shifted from foot to foot.

Jossey was glad Liam was so strong – the job was done quickly, and he began using a cordless drill to burrow into the rock in a parallel line behind the hole he'd made. From here, they could use the City's drilling equipment to thread a wire under the surface.

She'd done it many times; it should be simple for Patrol once she showed them how.

Liam installed the distribution switch, threading the relays through the small tunnels he'd drilled in the rock.

She handed him the second bundle, and he attached the connectors to each end of the pre-attached relays. Done.

She checked the serial number on the switch. E-2250-1. She wrote it down on the map. Excellent.

Her watch said forty minutes had elapsed. They were ahead of schedule. Her plan was to finish the switches as quickly as they could, then head back and assist with the solar panels while there was still plenty of darkness. The ten hours applied more to the solar panel group, for which dawn shouldn't be an issue; Jossey's group couldn't afford for there to be any light in the canyons or on the way back, not if they wanted their switches to stay hidden.

They climbed down from the ridge. Still no movement in the canyon.

She glanced again at her watch, then waved them deeper in.

They had two switches left and were deep into the final canyon when she had the feeling they were being followed.

She looked around, unsure where the feeling was coming from. Everything looked the same.

There was no movement, nothing specific she could point to.

But the feeling persisted, slow prickles climbing up her spine. She set down the switches and gestured to Pricey.

He came over silently and crouched beside her.

"Something seems – " she began.

He glanced around, holding up a hand to cut her off. "We're being trailed," he said flatly. "I've been keeping an eye on them."

Jossey's face felt pale. Beside her, Liam's shoulders stiffened.

"You were planning to tell me this when?" she hissed.

Pricey put a finger to his lips. "You and the crewman need to finish. Leave the Onlar to us."

Jossey fumbled for the radio. "Shouldn't we – "

"Not yet." He seemed to be holding his gestures close, as if for her eyes only. He picked up a random tool and handed it to her, as if helping her with the installation. "The other group needs to finish their mission as well." His voice was deadly, calm. "It's a small group of Onlar, three at most."

She turned to him. "Then we need to take them out. We can't allow them to see what we're doing."

"Exactly. Let's finish the last switch. Don't alert them to the fact that we know. Then – " He put his hand on his sword.

"All right." She turned to Liam. "Hand me the switch. Act normal."

He handed her the switch.

They had probably two hours until dawn. Cutting it close – but an hour in the early sunlight on the way back should be manageable, she thought. She'd been aboveground much longer than that. They just needed to stay hydrated.

Zlotnik and Tarrington were keeping a close watch on the canyon. Pricey had gone down and joined them.

Jossey and Liam attached the last set of connectors and brushed the canyon dust off their hands, replacing their gloves.

She still couldn't see the Onlar, but every so often she could hear the trickle of rocks, the shifting of sand. She guessed they were lying in wait, probably for the group to exit the canyon bogged down with equipment.

That seemed to be Pricey's assumption too. He was loading the excess equipment onto the pallet while Zlotnik and Tarrington stood watch.

Jossey was nearly at the top of the canyon. She could see across to the next canyon's ridges.

She took a step up to see better.

To her horror, the ridges weren't the only thing she could see.

She scrambled back down to Liam and whispered as loud as she dared, "Pricey!"

He turned, looked up at her. She pointed to the top of the canyon wall and held up both hands. Eight fingers.

Eight Onlar, heading toward their canyon, walking across the top of the parallel ridge.

She had no idea if the Onlar knew her group was there, or how. But they were headed this way, and moving fast.

"Move," she hissed to Liam.

He packed up the equipment quickly. They climbed down, Liam going first, Jossey following up the rear with a tool bag slung over her shoulder.

They were halfway down when the small group of Onlar stepped out of the canyon.

* * *

The Onlar had what looked like glowing green eyes, their claws extended.

Goggles, Jossey reminded herself. *Not eyes. They're human.*

Zlotnik and Tarrington drew their swords.

Pricey drew his too. A knife had appeared in his other hand.

Jossey suddenly understood why he'd been named commander in Tskoulis' absence. Despite his sardonic, laid-back style, he stood facing the Onlar, a feral grin on his face. As if he alone could take them on. He certainly looked like he wanted to.

He turned to Jossey and jerked his masked face upward, toward the ridgetop.

Check, he mouthed.

"Go," she said to Liam. He hurried down, slapping his mask down over his face, hand going to the knife they'd given him. She scrambled back up onto the ledge.

She looked across the canyon, to the ridge.

The figures had disappeared. She couldn't see them anywhere. She looked frantically down at Pricey, signaling "zero" with her hand.

She had no idea where they'd gone. Maybe it had been a hunting party, unrelated to her group or the Onlar trailing them.

But she doubted it.

Pricey looked at her for a long moment, then signaled for her to come back down.

She made sure her bag was secure, weapon reachable. She turned to look up for a handhold.

Then she jerked backward as an Onlar's head and shoulders appeared over the top of the ridge.

. . .

The Onlar hissed through its metal mask and reached down over the ridge, brutally fast. She scrambled sideways as it swept the air with its claws, inches from her face.

She shrieked, "Pricey! More above!" She didn't turn to see his response. She was too busy trying to stay out of claws' reach.

She drew her knife. She couldn't reach her sword from here, not on this narrow ledge.

The Onlar climbed down, started inching toward her along the ledge.

Below her, she could hear her team's voices, shouting, as the three Onlar on the ground attacked.

"Liam!" she cried. He wasn't armed, not like them. At least up here –

The Onlar was precariously balanced on the ledge. It hissed again and moved toward her. She pressed her back along the ledge.

The Onlar looked down at the distributor switch. It reached into the hole and grabbed hold of the equipment.

"No!" Jossey shouted at it.

The Onlar stood up, slashed at her again. She leaped back, catching its razor-sharp claws on her shin-plate. They scored the metal, and she gasped, realizing she was really trapped. Her knife – she didn't have a chain. Not this time.

Below her, she saw that Liam was climbing back up the ridge, moving fast.

She might have one chance. She had to keep it occupied.

"I know what you are!" she hissed at the creature.

It looked up at her, a blank mask, glowing green where its eyes should be.

"I took something from you," she taunted. "Just like you took something from me."

She realized its gaze was fixed on her uniform. She glanced down.

Engineer, her badge said.

She heard a low hiss, maybe a word, from its mouth.

Liam was very close.

She stared at the creature. It dropped the connectors and took a step toward her. She backed up, hit the wall again.

There was nowhere to move.

"Sokol!" Zlotnik's frantic voice sounded from the canyon. "Sokol, get down from there!"

"I'm trying!" Jossey shouted back, looking the Onlar dead in the face, willing herself not to betray Liam as he reached above the ledge line and raised his knife.

The blond giant jammed the blade into the Onlar's ankle and twisted it. The Onlar made a terrible sound and turned on him, overbalancing and toppling off the ledge, clawing at his face.

The pair fell, grappling, and Jossey sprinted to the other end of the ledge, trying to make her way down.

She was halfway down when a group of Onlar streamed into the canyon, coming from both sides.

* * *

They poured out of the darkness.

Jossey stared in horror. They must have signaled each other somehow. But how?

She remembered the goggles she'd taken for eyes. Maybe coms weren't out of the question.

It was a trap, she thought. Her group had been trailed, and others had been called, and now they were trapped.

Zlotnik and Tarrington were immediately overwhelmed.

As Jossey watched, four Onlar moved in and separated Zlotnik from Tarrington.

The big man shouted her name and fought his way toward

her. Pricey, across the canyon, was locked in combat with a fifth and sixth. A seventh approached him from behind.

"Pricey!" Jossey screamed.

He whipped around, saw the Onlar. The knife in his hand was there one second, in the Onlar's throat the next. The attacker dropped to the ground. Pricey grabbed the knife, moved on to the next Onlar.

There was a howl of pain, and Jossey saw that Tarrington had been stabbed in the thigh, below the armor. He fell, Zlotnik screeching his name. She lashed out at the Onlar around her like a wild creature, fighting her way toward him.

Jossey realized suddenly that they might not make it.

She reached frantically for her radio, hands shaking. She fumbled for the button.

"Caspar!" she shouted into it. "Caspar!"

A hiss of static. They were out of range, she realized. Too far into the canyon. Or maybe his group was out of range.

"Caspar! If you can hear me, we need help! Emergency! Third canyon!"

She turned to see Zlotnik go down under the claws of an Onlar. She choked, turning away.

"Caspar!" she shouted again.

There was a slight crackle, then a very faint voice on the other end. "Jossey?"

"Caspar? Caspar! We need help!"

Some of the Onlar turned toward her.

Two broke away from Zlotnik and headed across the sandy canyon floor toward Jossey, claws unsheathed.

Pricey threw his knife. It caught one of the Onlar squarely in the back, sending it to the ground.

The other kept coming.

"Caspar!" Jossey kept shouting. "We need backup!"

Beside her, Liam lost his battle with the Onlar.

She backed up toward the ledge.

She was always running away, she thought. But she had no choice. It was stupid to run into a fight with more than one of Them at a time.

And she needed to get radio signal. Had to finish the mission.

Maybe at the top of the ridge.

She turned back and started to climb.

The Onlar who had attacked her stepped over Liam's body. It stalked toward her, limping, still coming despite the bloody wound Liam had left in its leg.

It looked over its shoulder and waved to the others.

Pricey was still fighting. Jossey saw him take a slice across the top of his sword arm. He grimaced and grabbed the Onlar by the forearm, twisting it backward so hard the other howled.

He kicked the Onlar square in the chest, sending it to the ground, then speared it with his sword.

"Go!" he shouted at her, turning to the others. "Go! Call the others!"

He might be okay, Jossey thought. But she might not.

Her attacker was getting closer. Jossey hoped it wouldn't be able to climb.

She scrambled up to the ledge and up onto the ridge.

* * *

The land was vast, ridges as far as the eye could see. They were empty. The moon was beginning to rise, a faded golden-orange crescent, through the haze on the horizon.

"Caspar!" she shouted again into the radio as she started to run.

274

This time there was a crackle of static, and then Caspar's voice. "Jossey? What's happening?"

"Caspar, we've been attacked," she gasped out, almost crying with relief. "Where are you?"

"How many?" His voice was controlled, urgent.

"Ten. Eleven. More. I don't know. Liam is dead. Zlotnik went down. The others – "

She slowed and turned to look. She suddenly went silent as an Onlar appeared over the ridge.

"Jossey?"

She stepped backward.

"Caspar?" she said in a small voice. "How close are you?"

Two Onlar. Three. Their goggles flared a brilliant green in the night.

She made a small sound.

"Jossey!" Caspar's voice was not calm anymore. "Jossey, talk to me!"

Jossey turned and broke into a sprint.

The Onlar were injured, or maybe tired from fighting, and she was faster anyway, as she raced across the landscape. Just her and the moonlight, and the endless whitish ridges on both sides, toward a flat, desolate horizon. Like flying. The ridge was uneven, but wide enough, and her boots barely made a sound.

Not so with the Onlar — she could hear their footsteps pounding behind her.

She risked a glance behind her. They were coming up fast. She let out a half-gasp and focused on the ground ahead of her. Keep running. Keep running.

They fanned out. She turned, ran faster. She didn't know where to go, just away.

There was nowhere to go. She couldn't breathe. Her injured leg couldn't handle the strain.

Caspar's voice still sounded over the radio. She raised it to her lips.

"Caspar," she gasped out. "I'm on the ridge, they're – "

Something struck her between the shoulder blades.

A rock, she thought.

She fell, gasping in pain, scrambled forward on hands and knees, still trying to get away.

"Jossey!" Caspar's voice was frantic.

She turned and looked up at the three of them, shrieked, scrambled backward, fell, tried once more to get up. "No! Please! Don't!" she screamed.

"Jossey!"

One of them dropped to her level, put claws to her throat. She went silent and stared up at the Onlar, terrified.

And then Caspar's voice was stilled as one of Them stepped on the radio, crushing it.

54

GAVIN FINISHED UP HIS MEETING WITH HIS SUPERIOR, THEN stepped outside of the man's office, finally turning up the volume on his radio. It had been crackling faintly all night, but he knew that truly high-priority news would ordinarily be brought by hand, by a messenger, so he'd left the volume on the lowest setting. He was not happy that Dalton had scheduled their annual meeting for tonight, but it couldn't be avoided. And Pricey was more than competent to handle a mission like this.

Although he didn't want to admit it to himself, he'd been on edge all night. The grid project had been much too hastily implemented for his comfort. Especially with the increasing Onlar attacks in the last year or so.

He preferred to have more than a week to set in motion such a delicate operation. More like a month.

But the Minister had insisted.

Gavin didn't know what the rush was, but what Sokol wanted and what Sokol explained to Patrol leadership were often two different things.

It was a matter of grave importance, City-security-linked,

one of Council's top priorities, Sokol had explained, and Gavin's job was to provide that security, not to ask questions.

No matter who was involved.

Now, frowning at the amount of blinking his radio was doing, he turned up the volume.

The radio waves were swimming with messages. Some of it was flunky chatter, faintly audible. But some of it –

"Base unit! Base unit! Calling all backup units!" The voice was familiar. "This is Caspar Savaş from Unit 2-5. Calling all backup units."

Savaş. Jossey's Engineering partner, the one Gavin couldn't stand. He frowned, turned the volume all the way up.

Caspar sounded like he was trying very hard to be calm. "One unit down, attacked. We need immediate backup. Do you copy?"

Gavin hit the button.

"This is Tskoulis." His voice was icy. "Come in, Savaş."

"Commander," Caspar shouted. His voice was tinny, fractured, as if he were almost out of range. "Sokol called. Her unit's been attacked, several down. Third canyon. She's no longer responding." Static. Then his voice again. "Radio – went dead. We're en route from Entrance 12. Do you copy?"

Tskoulis was very still, the radio gripped tightly in his fist. He stared at the small black box.

No longer responding.

Caspar's voice continued on the other end, rising in volume and what Tskoulis thought might be fury. "Come in, Commander. Requesting immediate backup. Do you copy?"

"Copy," Gavin Tskoulis said.

Tskoulis stormed down the corridor to Sokol's Ministry office. The guard took one look at his face and didn't even try to stop him.

Sokol glanced up at the intrusion.

Tskoulis towered above him. The smaller man gestured to a chair. "Commander. What can I do for you? Please, sit."

"I prefer to stand," Tskoulis said, voice icy. "Permission to launch a retrieval team. 2-5 has been attacked."

Sokol stood up from his desk, looking flustered for the first time in Gavin's memory.

"Of course, Commander. Bring me back my niece. All Patrol's resources are at your disposal."

"All resources, sir?"

Sokol smiled, somewhat nastily. "All."

55

THE MORNING LIGHT WAS STARTING TO DAWN. PRICEY GROANED and opened his eyes, looking up at the branches of a half-dead tree above him. A bird was sitting in its branches, twittering loudly.

He wiped his face. His hand came away wet with blood.

He had no idea where he was.

Then he rolled over.

There were Onlar everywhere, scattered on the ground. He vaguely recalled fighting with one of them, getting hit hard in the temple, going down. They must have left him for dead, he thought.

With the blood on his face, he'd probably looked it.

He got to his feet, groaning, reaching for his water canteen. It was gone.

The closest Onlar lay on the sand, strangely-mottled face half-exposed, its greenish scales shimmering in the early morning light.

Leave the bodies of the creatures for Forensics, was the Protocol. Don't touch them. Maintain a safe distance. If you get saliva on you, wash it off immediately.

He'd imagined all sorts of terrible things behind their strange masks. Three eyes, giant fangs, like the strange skulls of animals they found occasionally in the sand. Warped features. He didn't know, but he *did* know of a few agents who had broken this particular Protocol, got too close, touched the masks. Not in person, but he'd heard stories.

They'd never been seen again. Their chambers had been cordoned off, wrapped in plastic, fumigated.

Pricey looked grimly at the Onlar. That mask could stay on.

He staggered to his feet, the bird still chirping away in the branches. He glared up at it. At least something seemed happy this morning, he thought.

He was three hours' walk from the nearest tunnel, probably already dehydrated. He didn't feel like chirping.

He stumbled forward and saw Zlotnik.

She was lying half-buried in sand that had apparently drifted during the night. Her knife was still in her hand, buried up to the hilt in an Onlar's chest.

Pricey ignored the searing pain in his arm and limped over to her.

"Zlotnik!" he shouted.

He dropped to her side. She was still breathing, if barely.

"Zlotnik." He crouched next to her face. "Can you hear me?"

A faint sound came from her mouth.

"Stay awake." He grabbed her water bottle.

Hers was empty. He looked around. This was one of the flood canyons. Ironically, it was bone-dry, but for a muddy trickle near the base of the opposite wall, below the ledge where Jossey and Liam had installed the equipment.

Speaking of –

Pricey didn't need to examine Liam to know he was dead. He closed the man's eyes gently.

Liam's water canteen was full. Pricey took it, feeling faintly guilty, and carried it back over to Zlotnik.

One of the Onlar started to move. Pricey spun, grabbed a knife he saw lying on the ground.

The Onlar rolled over and away, and Pricey saw Tarrington sit up from underneath, gasping.

"Pricey," the huge man coughed. His face was deathly pale.

Pricey jogged to his side, handed him the water. "Drink."

"Thanks, man." He drank, slowly. "Backup?" He coughed again. There was blood. He lay back and groaned.

"You're bleeding," Pricey said.

Tarrington's thigh. The Onlar had clawed it pretty deeply, Pricey saw. "It missed the artery," he said grimly. "But you've lost a lot of blood."

Tarrington half-laughed. "I think that one's body kept enough pressure on it," he said, pointing to the Onlar he'd rolled off of him. He groaned in pain. "I need a tourniquet. Did you call for backup?" Sweat beaded on his forehead. He lay down, looking up at the sky. "Nice morning."

Pricey smiled a little. "Sokol tried to." He looked up at the ledge, realizing she wasn't there.

"Sokol!" he shouted.

No answer. The only sound was the whistling desert wind.

"Sokol! Answer me!" He tried again, louder. Nothing.

Zlotnik groaned faintly.

Pricey stared up at the cliff. She could be anywhere. She could be dead. And the radio –

He looked down at his injured shoulder. If he tried to climb now, he might aggravate it, maybe end up like the other two. But he could see no choice other than that or trek back three hours in the sun, which, given his state, would be almost certain death.

He had to try.

He started toward the ledge. Tarrington dragged himself over to Zlotnik. "Don't go to sleep, Zlotnik," Pricey heard the big man say.

Pricey examined the ledge. There was a pretty clear path up to it, dug deeper by Jossey and Liam as they'd run up and down last night, but the top lip of the canyon wall presented a challenge. He'd have to wait until it was a little lighter out to try, unless he wanted to fall and probably break his neck. The ledge was a good thirty feet up, if not more.

He climbed halfway up and was examining it again when he heard rumbling coming from up the canyon.

Pricey staggered back down the hill and was hunting around for his sword when there were shouts.

He turned.

Three of Patrol's mobile open-air land vehicles rumbled into the canyon. It was the Tiger and the Engineer who'd been in charge of the other group. Caspar something. The second was full of Patrol agents, the third of medics. An entire search party.

The first vehicle swerved to a stop, dust cloud billowing, and Tskoulis jumped out, followed by Caspar.

Pricey saluted. "Commander."

Tskoulis put a hand on his shoulder, then looked around at the carnage. Zlotnik, on the ground. Tarrington, trying to give her water.

Liam's body.

"Where's Sokol?" His voice was quiet, dangerous. His whole body seemed tense.

Pricey stood up straighter, not looking his commander in the eye. "She went for help, Commander. Up over that wall. She didn't – " He faltered.

Tskoulis turned and sprinted for the wall.

Caspar was right behind him.

. . .

283

They pulled themselves over the lip and stood staring into the morning sun.

The ridges were a blinding white. And empty as far as the eye could see.

Gavin's face was drained of blood as he looked around. Caspar stood silently behind him, eyeing the ground.

"This way," the Engineer said curtly.

They took off, across the sandy stone.

"Three," shouted Caspar as they ran. "At least one wounded." He pointed to the drops of blood on the ground.

Tskoulis glanced sideways at him, kept going.

They stopped dead when they saw the radio, broken into pieces on the sandy ridge. There was no sign of the Onlar or Jossey.

Tskoulis shouted, "Jossey!" He ripped off his mask, stood squinting across the blinding empty landscape, as if trying to see something, anything.

Caspar was staring at the radio, at the bits of metal. His hands were balled into fists.

Tskoulis shouted again, once more. Caspar was silent, long silver eyes locked on the heat waves beginning to shimmer in the distance.

For a moment, the two men looked at each other, then at the horizon.

56

Gavin stormed back to the vehicle. He snapped at Pricey to hurry up and jumped into the driver's seat.

With a vehicle, they could cover the canyons. But the ridges needed to be explored on foot. They might have half a day with the sun beating down overhead.

And they had wounded to attend to. That left just him and Caspar, and a couple of his agents.

"Take them back to the City," he ordered, gesturing to the wounded and to Liam. "You, with me," he said to Caspar.

The second vehicle followed them down the canyon.

They had most likely pulled her down into one of the canyons with them, Gavin thought. No blood, other than from the wounded Onlar. That was good.

He wasn't sure how Caspar'd been able to track them, but right now he didn't care.

He didn't want to think about what They did with their prisoners. He still couldn't get the image of Tark's small skeleton out of his mind. And he'd tried.

The thought of finding Jossey in a canyon –

He gripped the wheel hard. Caspar glanced sideways at him.

"What are you looking at?" Tskoulis' voice was dark.

Caspar didn't answer. His silver eyes were focused, thoughtful, as they bounced over the rocky ground.

"They probably took her up one of the rivers," he said at last. "Less tracks for us to follow."

Tskoulis considered it. It was a good point. They were headed toward one of the larger ones, he knew. Its runoff flooded this canyon on a regular basis. It would make sense for the Onlar to try to disguise their passage that way, and stay cool besides.

He maneuvered carefully around a log, then put his foot down on the accelerator.

"What was the last thing she said?" He glanced at Caspar. "On the radio? You said she called in?"

Caspar went very still. He looked away.

"Well?" Tskoulis kept his eyes on the canyon floor ahead of them. He didn't like how silent Caspar had suddenly become.

"It wasn't to me," Caspar said finally, voice strained, still looking away from him. "She was screaming."

57

Tskoulis and Caspar reached the river. The sun was already burning the earth. They downed the contents of their canteens and refilled them in the river, then started up the left bank.

Nothing. Absolutely nothing. There was no sign that anyone or anything had been here recently. The water was crystal-clear. No muddied water to indicate displaced rocks.

"I don't think they're here," Caspar said at last. They'd been out there for an hour, had traced the side canyons. Silence. Wind. He wiped the sweat from his forehead, splashed water on his face.

Gavin knew these canyons like the back of his hand. He didn't want to admit that Caspar was probably right, but there was nowhere to go. The caves were few and far between along the river, and they were all south-facing ones that didn't provide enough shelter during the day from the baking sunlight. Already it was dangerously hot.

"We need to go back," he said at last.

Caspar refilled his canteen again, let the filter do its work, then drank slowly. "They've gone somewhere, most likely," he said, wiping his mouth. "Otherwise we'd probably have found her body."

Tskoulis gave him a sharp look that said he'd crossed a line.

Caspar didn't flinch. "I want to find her too, Commander. Maybe more than you."

Tskoulis laughed shortly. "Do you."

"I'm responsible." Caspar's eyes were cool. "I helped design this mission."

"Trust me, you don't want me to hold you responsible for this." He looked at Caspar for just a moment too long. Most people would start shifting uncomfortably at this point. "Do you understand?"

"Yes, sir." Caspar just gave him an infuriating smile. They were nearly toe-to-toe. Caspar was almost as tall as he was.

Tskoulis turned away, very strongly wanting to slug the man for insubordination and for just generally being irritating.

But he needed him to search, as much as he hated to admit it.

I'm doing this for you, Jossey, he thought grimly.

"Patrol!" he shouted. "Head back."

58

Jossey awoke slowly. Her head was killing her. All she could see was a dull flickering in the background. The air was chilly; the ground was colder.

She groaned and tried to look around.

She was in a dark space, on what felt like stone. A tunnel?

But they didn't allow fires in the tunnels. Only in the living spaces.

She realized her hands were tied. She shifted her weight experimentally. Her feet were free, but barely.

She froze as she heard voices, everything coming back to her in an instant. The Onlar. They'd taken her. Where, she had no idea. At least they hadn't killed her, thank God.

There was even a blanket under her head, she realized.

How courteous, she thought sardonically. The monsters of the canyons, providing a lady with a pillow.

She looked at the ceiling, where the flickering light showed divots that might be natural. A cavern?

The voices continued. She could smell food cooking close by. She craned her neck, trying not to move too quickly.

Her head did not feel good, but her stomach was quickly overruling it. Her mouth watered.

Three men were seated to her right, around a small fire. They were cooking something that smelled like meat. She turned a little further, trying to make out what they were cooking. A spit, some kind of small animal. Maybe a bird. They were wrapped in cloaks. She noticed one's arm was heavily bandaged. Blood was seeping through.

At her movement, one of them looked over.

She froze and stared despite herself. He was young, quite handsome, not monstrous at all. He had strangely-shaped eyes, much like the first Onlar she'd seen. Not like the eyes of most of the people in the City. A scar ran down his face, but it suited him.

He stared back at her, what looked like burning hatred in his eyes. She flinched.

One of his companions said something to him in what she thought might be the Old Language. The accent was strange, rounded.

She knew it had been spoken by the people who had lived here before the famines and war, before the Founders had incorporated the local population into the City. Most of the people in the City spoke it a little. Her nanny had used it with her until she was three or so. She wasn't conversant, but she could understand well enough.

She thought the Onlar might have said *"Ona da biraz ver,"* give her some. She had to focus to understand them.

The young man muttered something, then got up and took a piece of the meat off the spit. He walked over and crouched beside her.

"Sit up," the young Onlar said, voice heavily accented. She blinked, surprised. It was still strange to hear any words from them, let alone English.

She obeyed. He held a knife to her throat and untied her

hands. She winced as the circulation began to return.

"Eat," he said. "We have a long journey."

"Thank you," she ventured in English. She couldn't remember how to say it in the Old Language, wasn't even sure that's what they were speaking.

He did not smile, just handed her the food.

Jossey took a bite. It was delicious. She tried not to cram it into her mouth, but evidently failed, judging by the looks on the men's faces.

They laughed a little, and tossed her a canteen of water. She caught it with half-numb hands.

"Drink," they said in the Old Language.

She obeyed, trying to keep her face neutral. They might be feeding her, but to what end she had no idea. She was alive, but she was fairly sure Zlotnik and the others were not. She wondered which of these men had killed them.

"Altan." The oldest-looking of the three, a large man with bright blue eyes, looked at the young Onlar and jerked his head toward the supply bag.

The young Onlar got up again, grumbling a little.

He pulled out what looked like a cloak. He tossed it to her. "Wear it," he said.

She silently put on the cloak. It was too big, and smelled musty. She tried not to gag.

He tied her hands again.

"Where are we going?" she asked. The men were silent.

She sat back down, staring at the fire, remembering the crushed radio. Her friends. Liam.

It all seemed much worse now that she knew the Onlar were human.

She had no idea what they wanted. Or why she was alive.

She sat stone-faced, refusing to be afraid, refusing to cry. She'd cried enough these last few weeks. And after she'd seen

291

what these men had done to her group, she was having trouble believing she'd ever pitied that first Onlar.

The fire was burning low as they finished their food. She listened to their low conversation, meanings of words slowly floating back to her. At least she could understand reasonably well, she thought. Even if she had no idea how to speak with them.

From what she was able to piece together, they'd gone underground somewhere. Something about an animal. Or maybe she'd misheard. At one point, the oldest unwrapped his wounded arm and put some kind of cream on it. Altan helped him re-wrap it and stared at her as he did so, face inscrutable.

She stared back.

59

WHEREVER THEY WERE, THESE TUNNELS WERE DEEP underground, thought Jossey. They'd been walking for hours, days it felt like, and she could barely feel her legs anymore. Her boots weren't made for this type of long-distance hiking. On top of that, they were forcing her to carry some of their equipment.

She had no idea what direction they were going, what time it was. On occasion she saw faint pools of light coming from mysterious chambers to her left and right, felt fresh air descending from somewhere above.

A well shaft? Was this part of Old Sector 1?

They carried what looked like a glowing lamp, but she couldn't figure out what was powering it. It wasn't electricity. Neither was it exactly a torch. It seemed instead to shimmer, liquid gold, pushing back the shadows in the tunnels. She watched it, mesmerized, as they walked.

The third Onlar, with green eyes, looked back at her. He had what looked like a giant knife scar across his face, slashing from one brow to the opposite cheek. It was much worse than hers, and bright red in the lamplight. She wondered which Patrol agent had given him that.

He muttered something to the leader, who looked at her and laughed. Jossey stopped looking at the lamp, face heating.

They were clearly barbarians, she thought. They built fires in their tunnels. No electricity. What did they know about technology? She could stare all she wanted.

She stumbled forward as she stepped on a bit of uneven ground, and Altan yanked sharply on her rope. She cried out as the rope burned her wrists.

The man with blue eyes said something uncomplimentary sounding, something sharp, and she felt herself burning with hatred.

But Altan flushed and let the rope go slack. She realized they'd been talking to him.

She hadn't figured out all their names, but they were definitely not what she'd been expecting. The one with blue eyes, the injured one, seemed to be in charge; the other two referred to him as "Sir." He was maybe her father's age when Father had disappeared, maybe a little older. Then there was Altan.

The third, whom she'd decided to label Scarface, seemed perpetually unsmiling, narrow mouth twisted cruelly.

The Onlar wore cloaks on their journey, and she soon understood why. It was almost cold down here. She wasn't used to it, and was grateful for the musty piece of cloth Altan had given her. She found herself shivering.

They began to descend further into the earth.

The tunnel was fairly narrow here. She looked nervously at the ceiling, wondering how long it had been since this section had been used. Cave-ins weren't uncommon down below; Gavin's father had lost an arm in a mining accident, she knew, and those tunnels had been dug using the best equipment available, at the height of the technological revolution of the early 2200s CE.

These looked like they'd been hacked out of the earth in the thirteenth century. Using trowels.

"Where are we?" she asked for the third time in probably an hour.

They ignored her, again. She lurched after them, trying not to overbalance the giant bag they'd strapped to her, trying not to give Altan an excuse to pull on the rope again.

She realized she still had her wrist gauge on. They'd stripped her of weapons, but for whatever reason they'd left that alone. Probably had no use for it, she thought. She tried to glance at it without alerting Altan.

1:00 PM. Past noon. She estimated she'd been taken around 4:00 AM. She'd been gone for nine hours.

"Water," she gasped out. She couldn't move any further. It was nearly two in the afternoon.

They stopped and looked at her. Finally the leader gestured to Scarface, who stepped over and held the canteen to her lips. She drank greedily, feeling the cold seep through her, gulping it down.

Scarface yanked it away from her. "*Yeter,*" he said sharply. *Enough.*

She knew that word. Definitely the Old Language. The accent was a little strange, but she could understand.

She stood straight, took her time wiping her mouth on her uniform sleeve, ignoring their looks. She at least wanted to keep her dignity. Even if her legs failed her.

They had reached an open chamber. The leader called for a halt. Jossey sank to the ground, her ankles burning.

After some discussion, they took her boots and allowed her to go relieve herself in a small side chamber that had been apparently designed for that purpose. They'd been here before, she guessed. Altan stood guard at a reasonable distance.

She hobbled back and retrieved her boots, glaring at them all.

The leader looked at Jossey, blue eyes luminous in the light from the strange lamp.

"Let's go," he said in accented English. "Do not worry, Engineer. You are valuable." He smiled.

Altan's glare said otherwise.

Jossey looked away.

She imagined Patrol was scouring the canyons, looking for her. She wondered if Pricey and the others had survived.

Poor Liam, she thought. He'd died trying to save her, save them all, so she could get up on the ridge and call for help.

She wondered if they'd found the radio. She wondered if Gavin –

Gavin.

She wondered if he was searching for her, whether he'd give up eventually if he found no trace. She had no idea where they were, didn't even know that there were tunnels in the vicinity of those canyons. And they'd been walking for at least half a day, in what direction she didn't know.

She'd studied the Patrol maps, the old maps, everything her uncle had given her. Wherever they were, she was pretty sure it wasn't on any of them. That meant Gavin would probably have no idea either.

But she also knew Gavin Tskoulis. When he made a promise, he kept it to the best of his ability.

She smiled a little. He'd vowed to protect her. Her smile fell as she thought how he must be feeling now.

She suddenly pitied the Onlar.

And Caspar. His voice on the radio, frantic, as she called for help. He must think she was dead, she thought. He'd heard her shrieking for them to stop.

That must have been the last thing he'd heard.

As far as Patrol knew, the Onlar were wild creatures that dragged off their prey into the caves. Not humans.

Tears pricked at her eyes.

"Valuable," the leader had said. Whatever that meant.

The tunnel had widened after the chamber. Now five men could fit abreast. She saw what looked like very old ruts, parallel lines, in the tunnel floor. As if a wagon had traveled up and down at one point.

Once again, she wondered how old this place was. Or *where* it was.

The tunnel up ahead split into two, one traveling up, the other down. The right fork led toward the surface, she thought. There must be another air shaft nearby – she could see faint daylight spilling into the tunnel.

The left traveled down into a murky darkness.

The Onlar stopped, conferred. Maybe, she thought, if we take the right, I can escape when we get close to the surface.

They took the left.

60

PATROL THAT NIGHT WAS SOBER. IT HAD BEEN NEARLY TWENTY-four hours, and they hadn't found any further sign of Jossey, or the Onlar. No one talked much at dinner. Wickford and Thompson looked particularly upset. Zlotnik was recovering slowly in the hospital. Tarrington was very badly off – he'd lost a great deal of blood, and the surgeons told Pricey that he'd likely been close to death. At least Henry was slowly on the mend, they'd heard.

Pricey was wounded, too, but not so badly that he had to stay overnight. He was discharged and told to go home and rest.

He wandered into the mess hall to get something to eat. It was empty except for one table.

Tskoulis was sitting there, hunched over his plate, mechanically eating something that looked disgusting. Soy protein, maybe. His face looked dark with sunburn. His hair spilled over into his eyes. He didn't seem to notice.

The Tiger barely looked up when Pricey sat down with his plate.

"Mind if I join you?"

Tskoulis waved a hand and continued eating. Pricey carefully set his bandaged right arm on the table, wincing. He took a bite. It wasn't terrible. Better than it looked.

They sat in silence for a long time. Tskoulis wasn't talkative at the best of times. Pricey was thinking back over the events of the night.

"I should have gone with them," Tskoulis suddenly said.

Pricey took a bite of food, not quite looking at his commander. Tskoulis had put him in charge of the mission, he knew. It was his responsibility. That's why he'd sought out the commander. Might as well get this over now, so they could focus on the search.

He swallowed, looked up at the Tiger.

"You had to do that meeting," he said. "Protocol. Couldn't be broken. We were well prepared. You had no choice if your superior wanted a meeting. I take full blame for – "

Tskoulis slammed his fist onto the table, making the plates jump. "I had a choice," he said furiously.

Pricey sat up straight, looked into Tskoulis' eyes, immediately regretted it.

Instinctively, he started to back away, started to get to his feet.

He'd only seen Tskoulis this angry once before. When they'd found the child's remains.

"Sit down, Pricey," the Tiger growled. "At ease."

Pricey sank back down to the mess stool automatically, wanting to flee despite his years of experience on Patrol, remembering all the stories he'd heard about the Tiger. He'd personally witnessed several of the events.

Even seated, Tskoulis towered over him.

"You did well out there. But I was given a choice," Tskoulis said again, more quietly. "And I made the wrong one."

Pricey sat back, eyebrows raised, not expecting that response.

He'd seen Tskoulis demote men, punish them, for much less incompetence. Wickford, for instance.

Pricey's mission had failed, even if by events completely outside of his control. He was the one who had to answer to Tskoulis, to Patrol, for that failure.

He wondered if Tskoulis had misheard him. It had been a long day.

"I understand if you're not happy with me, sir," he said, trying again. "I take full responsibility."

Tskoulis' face took on a shadow as he continued to eat, not looking at his subordinate, and it dawned on Pricey that the commander's anger wasn't directed at him. Tskoulis blamed himself for something, Pricey thought. What, he didn't know. People died on Patrol all the time. Sub-commanders were assigned for missions. He'd never seen Tskoulis take a mission so personally.

Pricey wanted to ask, considered Tskoulis one of his few real friends on Patrol outside the training arena and the tunnels, but he knew better.

He chewed his food thoughtfully.

"Maybe Sokol's alive," he said at last. He didn't really believe it, but Tskoulis seemed to need to.

Tskoulis took another bite. Based on the way the man was crushing the spoon in his hand, Pricey almost pitied the Onlar.

61

GAVIN HAD FINALLY FORCED HIMSELF TO SLEEP AROUND DAWN. HE woke up a few hours later, went to the mess hall, drank a double coffee, then went to the Patrol office. Pricey was waiting for him.

Gavin greeted him, then went to the table and tapped the screen. A map appeared.

He zoomed in to the location of the City. A dotted line indicated where the OS1 and OS2 were.

"We've searched the canyons," he said, sweeping a line across to the north and northeast. "Nothing. The old mine entrances were heavily sealed."

"Did you check the southern caves?" Pricey asked.

Tskoulis gave him a look. Pricey shut his mouth.

The commander zoomed in further. "There is one more place we want to try. There are several parallel canyons running to the east and west of where we searched. They'd have to have climbed over ridges to get there, and I have no idea why they'd–"

He cut himself off and stared at the map. "The canyons are deeper here, near Gurime," he said.

That was the entrance to the Onlar's world. The deepest ones were beyond a ruin called Asmalih. There were abandoned Onlar caves there, but the water sources had long since dried up, and they'd moved north, toward Avanos, the river he'd searched with Caspar. It was quite a hike.

In the burning sun, with a prisoner and an injured Onlar, it seemed unlikely. But he had to try.

He wrapped up the briefing, and told Pricey to get ready to move out. Pricey saluted and headed down the corridor toward the training area. Tskoulis was transferring information to a paper chart.

As the room emptied and he rolled the chart into a scroll, he heard a familiar voice saying his name.

He looked up to see Minister Sokol.

Sokol looked like he hadn't slept.

Join the club, thought Gavin grimly.

"My boy," Sokol said in greeting. Gavin almost laughed. No one else in the City would dare call the Tiger that.

"Minister."

"I trust you have made arrangements for the search party?"

"Yes, I have." Gavin gestured to the scroll. "My agents are gathering supplies now."

Sokol put his hand on the tall man's shoulder. "I am sorry you have had to go through this, my boy. I know how much my niece means to you. To us both."

Gavin's jaw clenched. He didn't respond.

Sokol looked him in the eye. "I would like to speak with you before you leave for the search. It is of great importance. Jossey's life – "

Gavin looked sharply at him. "Sir?"

"Not here, Commander. Please come by my office."

"Yes, sir."

Gavin finished rolling the map, watching the man go.

For the first time, he wondered if Jossey had been kidnapped for a reason.

Maybe they hadn't been Onlar? Their movements had been too coordinated for the creatures. In his experience, they usually attacked in small groups, tracking Patrol and coming from behind. Not a pincer movement with decoys. These ones had seemed...trained.

And the trap they'd pulled down in the tunnels? Ellis had explained how the bloody print had lured the Patrol agents down into the lower chamber, and the Onlar had locked them in by rolling the stone. Very sophisticated behavior for Onlar, Gavin thought.

Maybe Karapartei? He wouldn't put it past them to ambush a Patrol mission.

But dressed as Onlar? He shook his head. That made no sense. After the Onlar's bodies were cleared by Forensics, their wrappings were destroyed, boiled in the same chemical that Patrol had to walk through a misted version of after missions. There was no way for Karapartei to get Onlar uniforms, not even an approximation of them.

He strode down the corridors, glaring at the flunkies who made the mistake of getting in his way.

A few turns later, and he found himself in front of the corridor to the Ministry.

Sokol was seated at his desk. He greeted Gavin with a smile and waved him into a seat.

Gavin sat.

Sokol gave the guard a look. The man turned around and left the room, sliding the reinforced steel door shut behind him.

"You wanted to see me, sir?"

"Yes, yes." Sokol clasped his hands on the table in front of him. "Where to begin."

Gavin watched him silently.

Sokol said, "Patrol has stumbled into a matter of City security that must be dealt with swiftly and deftly, if you understand me. This is why I have called you here."

"Sir?"

Sokol looked exhausted, Gavin saw now. Truly exhausted. And he was examining Gavin as if trying to make a decision.

The Minister pursed his lips together at last.

He cleared his throat. "As you know, our solar grid project is a matter of highest security. It is imperative that the grid remain...under the radar, so to speak, while it is being constructed, so as not to attract the attention of...certain factions that might desire to bring further mayhem to an already-fragile system."

Gavin looked at Sokol, not sure either of them was fully awake. He knew all this. Why was Sokol telling him these things? What did this have to do with the Onlar?

"However," Sokol continued, "we now have a problem. As you know, one of our own – my dear niece – has gone missing. Not only is it personally a problem for me, but she is in possession of a great deal of very valuable information."

Gavin wasn't following. Had Sokol finally started going senile? She hadn't been taken by Karapartei. She'd been taken by Onlar. He had no idea why the creatures hadn't killed her on the spot.

He was deathly afraid they'd find what was left of her, like –

He clenched his fists under the table, willing himself to stop thinking. He had no idea how Sokol was so calm right now.

The older man's unnerving gaze fell on him. Gavin focused his gaze back on the Minister.

"Before we continue this conversation," Sokol went on slowly, "I need you to fully understand that you have fallen into a matter of *most* delicate City security. This involves top-level Intelligence clearance, which even your supervisor, Dalton, does not have. However, given that you are already in charge of this mission, Commander, and I feel that you are best suited among Patrol's agents to lead such, I am content to leave you in charge." He paused, looked at Gavin. "If you would prefer not to continue, speak now, and I can arrange to have someone else sent out after Jossey."

Gavin stood up so fast he almost knocked over the chair.

"Not on your life," he said.

Sokol eyed him for an uncomfortably long moment, flat eyes unreadable.

Then he said, "Good."

He smiled. "Sit down, Commander. As I said, this is a matter of vital City security, and one that must never leave this office, or I think I need not explain the penalty for treason. Do you understand?"

Gavin stared at him. "Go on," he said slowly.

"Now then," Sokol said. "Commander, before you go after my niece, there is something you should know."

"What do you mean, interrogated? By those creatures?" Gavin frowned. "How is that possible?"

Sokol sighed. "This City operates as it does because certain information is...partitioned. The less the Citizenry understands about certain aspects of their lives, the more order we can keep, do you understand me?"

His flat gaze met Gavin's. "This is a very fragile artificial ecosystem we have created underground. It requires constant maintenance. Part of that maintenance includes the flow of information."

Gavin frowned. "Like the reported versus actual number of Onlar attacks."

It was common knowledge among Patrol that the numbers were vastly deflated to keep the public calm. Part of the job. He'd never worried about it. Technically they *were* reporting attacks, just not all of them.

"Precisely." Sokol tapped his desk. "The problem in this particular instance is that the Onlar are...shall we say...more intelligent than Patrol has typically viewed them."

Gavin sat very still. "What?"

"The Protocol is there for a reason," Sokol said carefully. "It is ironclad. Those who break it, disappear."

"The disease," Gavin said.

"It is...imperative that the population of the City be kept separate from the Onlar. Our survival depends on it."

"I don't understand."

Sokol smiled a little. "No one does, not at first." He pointed to something on his desk. "Shall we?"

62

GAVIN SLOWED AS SOON AS HE EXITED THE MINISTRY CORRIDORS. His mind was reeling.

The Onlar were ordinary humans. Like him.

He'd known they were human, had always been taught they were the warped descendants of the survivors of nuclear war in nearby India, before the time of the Founders. When the Founders had come here to build their city, a giant under-ground bunker system to ride out the collapse of civilizations, they'd encountered both the local population and its monstrous enemies, whom the locals had simply called "Them": *Onları.*

That local population, absorbed into the City, was the reason some of the elders today spoke the Old Language. That was how people like Caspar had such unusual last names, not standard City surnames like Foster and Davidson and Sokol. Beck. O'Leary. Gavin's own name was from a local family, as far as he knew.

But the Onlar –

He'd fought them for years, had figured out at some point that they wore masks, even if he'd never quite figured out how they communicated using hisses and grunts. But he'd never actually broken Protocol to check what was *behind* those masks. Those who had...

They'd vanished. Never seen again. The disease, it had been said. It killed quickly.

Maybe there was indeed a disease. Or maybe they were...removed, as a matter of security.

Gavin's fists clenched. But Sokol had told him that some things were necessary to keep order. Had thanked him for his service, saying leadership required difficult decisions.

He thought as he walked. So many things made more sense now.

There was no mutant population. There were no inherited enemies, no age-old conflict. The Onlar had been ordinary locals, Sokol had told him, who had rebelled back when their population was absorbed into the Founders' new City.

They'd seen the Founders as invaders, had tried to overthrow the new government, had bombed the tunnels. They'd been driven out, into the heat and havoc of the aboveground. Locked out, to preserve the City's population.

And they'd been fighting with the City ever since. Not the type of group it made sense to try to make peace with. Especially not with Karapartei trying to cause trouble internally in the last several years.

Sokol had also shared that things were extra shaky right now. There were electricity shortages, and, due to those, food supply issues with the hydroponic labs when the grow lights wouldn't work. The City's population was nearing critical mass. Council was looking into expansion options. They couldn't afford unrest, Sokol said, not if they wanted to survive.

With Karapartei in operation, and other groups before them, it could be fatal to the City's fragile order were people to start to sympathize with the Onlar.

It was a brutal calculus: there were only so many resources, as Sokol had pointed out. And the Onlar had been surviving aboveground for long enough, it was clear they had plenty for themselves, wherever it came from.

Gavin was surprised Sokol had told him as much as he had, considering how sensitive the information was. He knew plenty of people who agreed with Karapartei's line that resources should be more widely distributed, even if they didn't say so publicly. If they knew that there was an entire population walled off from the cool of the underground tunnels, left out in the burning heat to fend for themselves...

Gavin set his jaw and continued on. The whole situation seemed wrong, but he was so far below Council in terms of rank that almost all he could do was try to defend the City given the tools available to him.

And Gavin Tskoulis was a loyal soldier. Whatever Council was up to, it *had* carried this City through numerous crises, coup attempts, disease outbreaks. For several hundred years, it had helped keep society functioning.

This latest crisis was why Sokol was creating the upgraded power grid. Not just to update the system. To keep the City from collapsing altogether. And now the City's enemies had apparently taken Jossey, with her detailed knowledge of how the system worked.

She was tough, Gavin knew, but she'd probably break easily under interrogation.

The young commander clenched his fists, willing himself not to punch the corridor wall.

He strode to the Patrol door and typed in his code.

63

JOSSEY AWOKE WITH HER FACE PRESSED AGAINST THE COLD STONE floor and her neck aching. She groaned. She'd slipped off her pillow in the middle of the night. She wrapped herself in the blanket and sat up, shivering. Her rope was still attached to her wrists, but her captors had added some length to it so she could move about.

Altan and the others were already awake. She looked at them bleary-eyed, at the meal they were cooking over a fire. She was starving, she realized.

She shuffled over to the fire, still wrapped in her blanket.

Altan and Scarface glanced at her, looking bored, and kept eating. The leader muttered something to them and shoveled some into a metal bowl.

She took it in shivering hands and muttered "Thank you" before wolfing it down.

If she was so far underground that she was freezing, Jossey thought, she didn't know how Gavin would even know where to begin looking for her. She had no sense of direction down here. As far as she knew, they could have doubled back, could still be directly underneath the canyons.

"Where are we going?" she tried once more.

The leader smiled a little. "You are valuable," he said again, and kept eating his meal.

She gritted her teeth with frustration. "Is this the Old Sector?" she asked angrily.

They glanced at each other. She realized they seemed to have no idea what she meant. Maybe they didn't know the words.

Altan got to his feet, yawned, and pulled on her rope. Jossey staggered upward, glaring at him.

They put out the fire and began to strap their equipment on their backs.

She had to escape, she decided. They were taking her ever deeper into the earth. She didn't know what "valuable" meant and she didn't want to know.

But there was nowhere to run. Even if she did get away, she might easily get lost down here. Right now they were in a single tunnel, but every so often, additional tunnels branched off the main line and led into inky darkness. They'd taken at least two of the branches previously, maybe three. She couldn't remember.

She shivered again and pulled her blanket closer, glaring at Altan as he approached with her equipment bag. He smiled mockingly. "What's the matter, Engineer?"

Jossey took the bag without comment. He looked almost disappointed. When he turned around, she smiled.

They started walking. She glanced around at the other unusual things about this tunnel – the niches in the wall, the small marks every so often that she thought might be distance markers.

Such a strange place, she thought.

But she was glad it was strange. At least if she tried to figure out the secrets of this place, it might take her mind off where she was going.

64

———

Tskoulis exited the tunnel, blinking at the bright sunlight.

It was already burning hot, at nine in the morning. He double-checked his water supply.

After his meeting with the Minister, he'd wasted no time putting together a team of his top agents and headed out through one of the service tunnels, to the exit under the ruin called Uchisar.

Behind him, Pricey and some of his agents climbed out of the tunnel and into the dusty air. They were about an hour's hike from Asmalih.

"Let's get going," Tskoulis said grimly.

"Sir."

They started off into the dust.

They hiked up into the foothills of the old city of Uchisar, surrounded by cave-pocked giant rock spires. Below them, the plain stretched away into the distance, a small mountain standing up out of the horizon, very far to the west. Ruins of houses were scattered everywhere. At the very top of Uchisar's hill was an enormous fortress, one of several. The Onlar used this as a hiding place even during the day, Gavin knew.

This area could be very dangerous at night.

They followed an old footpath up into one of the fortresses. It was quite a hike – by the time they made it up to the fortress, they'd been forced to stop for water not once, as planned, but twice.

They stood at the summit, gasping.

To the north and east were canyons, most running parallel to one another, like gouges in the earth. The clouds marched overhead to a flat horizon. Here and there still-standing homes gave a strange air of domesticity to the landscape.

The commander looked at his map, then out at the horizon.

"There." He pointed to the long pair of ridges to the northeast. "That first one." It was an hour and a half walk, give or take.

They started down the hill.

The landscape was vast, the stone everywhere a sandy brown color and pocked with holes. Where the houses ended, homes cut in the rock began. Gavin didn't like coming here even during the day. The canyons were all right – dangerous, but contained. Being up here, with all the hundreds of possible hiding places in the old abandoned forts and houses, was like walking into a snake's pit.

At least it was out on an exposed rock face, he thought, so it was less likely for the Onlar to be here when it was bright out.

Asmalih was across a couple of canyons. Or, Tskoulis knew, there was an old road that ran up to the north, through Gurime, and down again to Asmalih. It was faster, but more exposed.

He'd used vehicles in the canyon before, but the roads to Gurime had had rockslides in the recent past. He'd have to make sure the roads were clear before they could get through.

He raised his wrist to his mouth. "Come in, Base."

The com crackled. "Base here, Commander."

"Ready the vehicles. ETA twenty-five minutes."

"Sir."

He clicked off the com.

Pricey walked next to him, surveying the landscape. "I don't like it," the agent said. "Why bother to take her this far? Don't they usually kill prisoners right away?"

Tskoulis glared at him. "Pricey."

Pricey stepped back. "Sorry, sir."

Pricey had no idea of the real situation, of course. But the commander still didn't want to even think about the possibility. Interrogation was preferable to death.

As they descended, the main road to Gurime came into view, meandering in an S-curve and behind a rock formation. It was clear.

They reached the road, and Tskoulis examined it. The rockslide had eroded the edge of the roadway significantly, but it looked navigable. He clicked on the com again.

"Base, come in."

"Copy, sir."

"Confirm vehicles." He gave the location.

"Yes, sir."

The landscape changed again as they made their way slowly in their vehicles, two strong, searching for sign along the way. Below the road, to the right, the stone towers had become a strange forest of spikes. The barren lands, Patrol called them. Very little shelter and hard to navigate. The only thing down there, in Tskoulis' experience, was scrub grass.

As he drove, he remembered the night they'd found Tark. Or what was left of him. Tskoulis winced. If the Onlar were ordinary humans, sane and intelligent, why would they bother to take a child?

The same reasons the City would, he thought. *Revenge. Opportunity.*

What does that say about us? he wondered.

But still – a child.

Tark was gone, he thought, but Jossey – he could bring *her* back. Could make that right.

She'd asked why he didn't hate her for Tark's death. He'd left so she didn't see his face.

Tark's disappearance was Gavin's fault.

Not hers. It had never been hers. And it didn't matter anyway, he thought, because he –

He drove faster, jaw clenched.

They reached Gurime, and drove in silence between the long squat houses, no longer carved from rock but built homes, desolate and falling apart under the burning sun. A thin balcony threaded its way delicately along the edge of one.

A viewing patio, once upon a time, when there were people here.

Between Gurime and Asmalih was a vast plain. The plateau loomed in the distance.

The road was blocked outside of Gurime. Old military equipment lay abandoned, scorched tanks and craters where someone had fought a battle. Tskoulis edged his vehicle around.

Another few minutes, and then they were in Asmalih.

It wasn't the ruins of the town Tskoulis was looking for. It was an old road just beyond.

This area had once been a huge tourist destination, if Tskoulis remembered his history correctly. People would take hot air balloons up to watch the sunset. There was a name for it, but he couldn't recall at the moment. He just knew it as Gurime.

He almost laughed at the irony. Sunset-watchers. Now the solar crews fled underground as the sun was approaching the western horizon.

He squinted through the dust. Up ahead, the road forked. On the left, breaking away from the main highway, there should be an even smaller road. This was the extent of the mapping they'd done in this area. The road he was searching for led up into a steep canyon. There had once been a place for tourists to stop, but the sign was long faded. They called it the Campsite.

There was the fork.

He took a sharp left.

65

THEY GOT OUT OF THE VEHICLES AND SMELLED SOMETHING SHARP in the air. Ashy. Patrol continued on foot, past the ruins of the Campsite and up into the wilds.

The land here was particularly alien, Gavin thought, as they crossed the threshold into the wilderness and into a giant stone bowl. The soil looked like chalk, and the stone formations no longer had any pattern to them that he could tell.

Everything was brown and white, dead trees and ground so parched it had cracked many times over. Pathways that might have been man-made or might have been natural, he couldn't tell, wound upward toward an enormous jagged rock face pocked with holes. Below the road to the left was what looked like a once-farm: a small plain leading to nowhere, to the edge of the bowl.

There was no out, no escape, except forward into the shadowed canyon. He shuddered a little.

They drank another ration of water. Some of his men looked nervous. He waved them onward. No time to worry now. The sun was more dangerous than anything out here.

He hoped.

They reached the top of the rock formation and checked the caves for Onlar. Nothing.

It was now almost eleven. Clouds had come in from the south, and the sun wasn't as boiling as usual, but they rested in the shade for some time before they continued on. Noon to three was mandatory resting period. They had an hour to search.

It was dead silent up here, other than the wind whistling through the caves. They made an eerie sound, a sort of moaning, if you listened long enough. Tskoulis tried to block it out, concentrate on what they were doing.

They carefully edged around the side of the formation and stood against the north wall. They could see directly down the canyon, which wound its way toward the ridge in the distance, slices of whitish stone overlapping on both sides until it opened up in the far distance to a wide river, its water a gleaming band. He didn't think it was the same river they'd checked, but it was hard to tell.

Much too far for the Onlar have hiked there, he thought. Especially with a prisoner.

But maybe not. Maybe they'd taken her north, then along the river, then back down one of these canyons. Maybe they had a hiding place here. There were plenty of old caves with sufficient shade and some kind of water source, from what he could see.

He'd never been this far to the northeast. It had always been considered too dangerous for Patrol.

Looking at the length and twisting of the canyon and the steepness of both sides, he realized he needed to make a decision. If they went into this canyon, they might not be able to return before dark.

He beckoned to Pricey.

In a low voice, he explained the situation. Pricey looked thoughtful for a long moment.

"We've already cleared this formation," he said at last. "It's high ground. If we get back up here before dark, we can probably keep watch here."

"And if not?"

Pricey smiled crookedly and shrugged. "What's a few more Onlar?"

As they descended into the canyon, Tskoulis quickly realized the probable reason this canyon had never been mapped.

He had never seen such a dangerous place.

Everything was close in, the walls towering above them on all sides, some of the bases appearing to be eroded so badly that they looked ready to fall. The atmosphere was one of decay. A few skinny trees had managed to survive here and there, leafless branches hitting Patrol in the faces as they tried to navigate through the narrow clearing. It was almost entirely shaded here, to the point that Tskoulis glanced back just to make sure they weren't being followed.

This would make a good daytime hideout for the Onlar, he thought.

The path they'd just walked wound out of sight. Up ahead, it was hard to see where it even went, disappearing behind an enormous cliff.

Pricey alone looked calm. The other agents seemed jumpy. Tskoulis didn't blame them.

From here, the canyon got markedly narrower. There was room for maybe two men at a time. Gavin reached for his sword.

They edged through a narrow pass, enormous white rocks looming against a now-blue sky, and made their way out single file into a brush-filled clearing.

Despite the potential danger of such a landscape, Tskoulis had the strong sense that they were alone. Deeply alone.

It was a beautiful place, now that they were out of the strange ashy zone. The trees were greener here, the brush slightly thicker, as if there were water somewhere.

He hadn't seen so much green in some time.

They went around another bend and stood staring at the landscape before them.

It was a meadow. A lush green meadow in the midst of burning canyons.

Small bluish flowers dotted the ground. The trees here were still fairly leafless – it was October, after all – but there was *life* here. And where there was life, there must be water, Tskoulis thought.

He motioned to his men. They fanned out.

Where there was water –

Tskoulis scoured the ground. Nothing that he could see. But when he reached the far edge of the meadow, he could see plants growing at the base of rocks where there was no obvious water source. Around the bases of the plants he could see dark brown dirt. He touched it. It was damp.

A spring, he thought. Or seeping groundwater.

The only water sources he knew around here were the Avanos River and some of the smaller canyon ones. This water source appeared to be underground. And if it was underground...

"Search for tunnels," he said abruptly.

Tskoulis' men looked at him. "Tunnels?" Pricey asked. "This far out?"

It was unlikely, but not impossible. If the Onlar had managed to take her this far, and she wasn't in one of the caves, then a tunnel was the next likely scenario. Maybe they'd hidden her underground somewhere. He knew the Old Sector had been built long before by the local population; it was possible there was a local tunnel network in this area too. There were enough aboveground homes carved into the stone.

If there was an underground river or stream, that made the likelihood of caverns much higher.

He grinned.

"Commander, it's almost noon. We need shade," Pricey said.

Tskoulis glanced at his wrist gauge. Indeed. He looked up at the rock formation.

One good thing about this strange landscape was that there was almost always somewhere to hide from the sun. Any cave would need to be north-facing, although in a canyon it was less important.

He looked back to where they'd come into the meadow. There were some large caves up on one of the walls. They looked easy enough to access with climbing equipment. He was motioning to Pricey to check them out when his gaze fell on something.

He held up a hand.

There was a hole in the cliff.

It was small, but it seemed out of place, as if it weren't natural or had been made bigger by human hands. Nearby, the cliff face was covered in vegetation.

Water. Lots of it. Probably a cavern.

He wordlessly motioned for his men to follow him. As they neared the foot of the cliff, they saw something.

The grass looked squashed down.

It could have been from an animal, but Tskoulis didn't think so. It looked as if someone had tried to push the grass back upright.

And on the grass, just far enough off the trail that the traveler might have thought they were safe –

He reached down, pulled up a rust-colored piece of grass.

"Blood," he said.

66

PRICEY EXAMINED THE GRASS. "LOOKS OLD," HE SAID. "MAYBE A day or two." He grinned, handed it back to Tskoulis. "They must have been in a hurry. Maybe the injury re-opened."

Tskoulis crouched beside Pricey. Now that he looked more closely at the ground, he could see a faint depression in the dust beneath. There probably wasn't enough wind down here to blow it away, he thought.

Thick footprints. As if the traveler had been heavy.

Or as if they had been carrying something heavy.

He looked up sharply at the cliff face. The hole was too high up. But maybe to the side...

"Spread out," he ordered. "Look for sign."

They walked in a line toward the cliff face.

He saw more blood at about the same time Pricey did.

Pricey pumped a fist into the air.

Tskoulis examined it. It seemed like the other, but there was more of it. Droplets, in a line, as if the wound had been reopened without the Onlar noticing. They were a few feet apart, as if the Onlar had been walking at a good pace. Or maybe running.

Tskoulis' jaw tightened.

The blood disappeared shortly after that, but Tskoulis didn't need it anymore. The traveler's direction had been clear.

He pointed to a dark spot at the base of the cliff.

"There," he said.

They climbed carefully down into a small cave, weapons at the ready.

It was empty.

For a moment, Tskoulis felt the rage of defeat boil up inside.

He looked around, forcing his face into a neutral expression. The others were still climbing into the cave. It was quite large – they were able to stand, all six of them.

But it was empty. And there was no exit but the one they'd just used.

67

HE CLENCHED HIS FISTS, WILLING HIMSELF NOT TO SHOW EMOTION on his face.

Pricey stepped forward. "What now, Commander?"

Sometimes Tskoulis really wished Pricey would just stay quiet.

The other Patrol watched the commander warily. He examined the floor, looking for sign. There were what might be footprints, but it was hard to tell. The Onlar seemed to have been aware that they needed to cover their tracks. Except for the blood out there. Maybe they'd been attacked and had to run? Maybe they simply hadn't noticed? He doubted it, if they were as crafty as Sokol had let on.

Or maybe there'd been a struggle. Maybe Jossey had tried to escape.

Or maybe this was a trap.

He motioned to two of his men. "Guard the entrance."

They moved silently to the cave entrance and peered out into the meadow.

· · ·

Tskoulis looked around the cavern once more, holding up his light. The whole thing made no sense, he thought. Where would they have gone? Maybe they were hiding in here?

It looked like an ordinary cave, but there was something strange about the back wall. A shadow that shouldn't be there, he thought. A thin line with no obvious source.

He walked up to it. As he shone the light in that direction, the shadow seemed to move.

He moved the light back and forth. A thin strip of shadow widened and narrowed.

Tskoulis grinned.

He walked closer, watching the motion of the shadow, shaking his head in admiration. If this was what he thought it was…

He reached the shadow, and looked to the left into sudden blackness.

Truly amazing.

He was looking at a partition. An optical illusion. The tunnel curved sideways behind a partition wall. It was just wide enough for a large man to squeeze through. If you looked at it dead on, it looked like there was nothing at the back of the cave.

"With me," he whispered to Pricey, who followed him, staring in amazement.

"Stay here," he said to the other four. They saluted.

Tskoulis and Pricey inched forward into the dark.

68

———

THE TUNNEL IMMEDIATELY MOVED BACK TO THE RIGHT AROUND A second thick wall and straightened, heading directly into the earth and slightly downward as they passed the partition. Amazing, thought Tskoulis. Light was unlikely to pass through to the cave on the other side.

This was definitely not natural, or it had been heavily modified from a natural cavern system, he thought. He could see what looked like chisel-marks on the rock walls on either side of them, and the ceiling.

The sound of water was louder now.

He glanced at his wrist gauge. 12:30. They could spend the shade hours down here exploring, then head back to base. If, of course, this was the right place to explore.

He imagined Jossey would be down here somewhere, further down the tunnel. Maybe there was a chamber here somewhere, like in the Old Sector. Maybe several.

He inched forward, red light illuminating the flat tunnel floor, the strangely-rounded walls. Pricey was right behind him.

. . .

It was some time before Tskoulis realized something was wrong.

"Where do you think this goes?" whispered Pricey.

They had been traveling for around twenty minutes, Tskoulis realized, glancing at his wrist gauge. 12:52. There was no chamber. Nothing. Just a tunnel. Tskoulis frowned, turning up his safety light.

It vanished into dimness ahead of him.

"I have no idea," he muttered.

He knew the population once upon a time had made houses out of the strange rock formations here. Was it possible that they had made a system of tunnels too? Not just underground cities like the Old Sector, but tunnels connecting them?

He'd never heard of such a thing. Much of the Old Sector had collapsed in the bombings of the early wars; it was sealed off both to prevent Onlar intrusion and to protect the Citizens. He'd snuck into one of the less-well-protected tunnels back as a kid, and had promptly gotten lost with Tark for two terrifying hours.

They'd never tried again, never told anyone where they'd gone.

Tskoulis glanced at Pricey. "Let's go a little further," he said.

The water was even louder. Maybe an underground stream, like the one in the Old Sector. The tunnel felt colder. He removed his glove and touched the wall. It was slimy.

They continued into the dimness.

After what felt like hours, the tunnel suddenly opened up into a larger space. Tskoulis couldn't see much, but he could hear their footsteps reverberating.

"Lights off," he hissed to Pricey.

There were only two of them. They couldn't afford to be

attacked, not here. Not that he really thought any Onlar would be down here. There'd been no sign in the cave.

But still. Jossey had gone *somewhere*.

The masks alone didn't do much, but he was able to at least see movement without the aid of the safety light. He stood frozen for a long time, looking around, waiting for something to move in the blackness. Sound seemed amplified – he could hear Pricey's breathing, the drip-drip of water somewhere. The darkness was near-absolute, even with the masks.

And it stank. Lots of tunnel bats lived here, Tskoulis thought.

There was no movement in the cavern that he could see.

Eventually, satisfied, he turned on his light.

They were in a fairly large open space; the ceiling disappeared into blackness, and he thought he could hear bats somewhere far above. Across the cavern, in the dimness, he could see several holes – probably tunnel entrances, spaced far apart. Which one they might have taken, he had no idea.

It looked like this had been some kind of waystation. How strange, he thought. A very old waystation. Not something constructed recently by the Onlar.

He and Pricey made their way across the ground, watching for erosion, stepping carefully over piles of bat guano. It was everywhere. He tried not to breathe. Pricey was covering his nose.

They reached the other side. Three tunnels. One appeared to have collapsed. The other two –

Nothing suggested either of them had been used recently. Except –

Tskoulis frowned. There was something carved into the wall of the tunnel on the right. He held up the light.

A word, he thought.

"Can you read that?" Pricey asked. Tskoulis examined it more closely.

ΝΕΒΣΕΚΗΙΡ. It was carved deeply into the stone.

He had no idea what language it was, or if it was even a word.

Like most of the City, he could speak a little of the Old Language, and they'd learned about it in school, mostly in history class, although he'd never understood why until his conversation with Sokol. Even before he'd known who the Onlar really were, it had been helpful on various Patrol raids, where ruins could be mapped according to their original names.

But any other languages of the region – and he knew there'd once been many – he had no clue about.

He thought it might be Greek, but he wasn't sure.

"Mean anything to you?" he asked Pricey, who shook his head.

Either way, this particular tunnel seemed to lead somewhere important, since it had been marked.

"This is likely where they took her," Tskoulis said. He shined his light down into the darkness. Once again, it vanished into dimness. "Wherever this goes, I don't think it's very close."

Pricey seemed deep in thought, eyeing the word on the tunnel wall. "I've seen this somewhere before," he said.

Tskoulis pulled out a pad of paper he always kept in his equipment pouch. He carefully wrote down the word. Maybe Sokol would know.

"Let's head back," he said shortly. "Keep trying to remember. It's nearly 1:30. If we're right, this might be a much longer expedition than planned. We'd need to get more supplies and more men."

Pricey suddenly turned to him. "Why is this so important, Tskoulis?" he asked bluntly. "She's one lost person. People go missing. It happens."

The commander looked at him, hoping his gaze was unreadable. "You know this was a direct order from Minister Sokol."

"Yeah, but – "

"Don't ask questions, Pricey. Sometimes you really need to learn to keep your mouth shut."

He put the pad of paper away and turned to go.

Pricey said behind him, "Are you sure this is just about the Minister?"

Tskoulis didn't respond.

They were heading back across the cavern when there was a sound in the tunnel. Tskoulis and Pricey reached for their swords.

Running footsteps. A red light, bouncing up and down.

One of their men burst into the cavern. "Sir!" he gasped out. "Sir!"

"What is it, Stanton?" Tskoulis grabbed the man's shoulders, steadying him.

"Sir," Stanton struggled to catch his breath. "Sir, we've been attacked."

"Onlar? How many? Anyone down?"

"No, sir." He stood, doubled over. "We're all right. But Commander, sir – " He coughed. Tskoulis could see blood on his hand, his arm.

Stanton said, "Sir, it was a wolf."

There were wolves in this region, Tskoulis knew, but he'd only seen one, a long time ago.

"Did you kill it?" he asked.

"Yes, sir." Stanton had recovered somewhat, was drinking water carefully. "It came out of nowhere. The two guards at the entrance saw it coming. It must have smelled us."

He still looked terrified. "It had blood all over its face."

Tskoulis sheathed his sword. "We have to go back. Now."

The blood on the ground. It was possible the Onlar had been attacked by the creature first.

If that was the case –

He turned his light to full illumination and broke into a sprint.

The other three Patrol agents were standing somberly around the scrawny creature when Tskoulis and the others burst out of the tunnel.

The wolf was pitiful in death. It wasn't very big – Tskoulis had imagined them much larger. Its ribs were visible. Blood was all over its snout, as Stanton had said. It lay on its side.

"It jumped through the opening at us," one of the agents told Tskoulis. "We barely reacted fast enough."

Tskoulis examined the wolf carefully. Its face was covered in blood and – fur?

Rabbit fur, he thought. Little bits of greyish white fluff stuck to the nose.

He started laughing with relief. His men looked at him strangely. He ignored them.

Pricey started laughing as well.

"The poor creature looks like it was starving," Tskoulis said at last to his men. "I guess it missed our targets and went for a rabbit or two instead. So far, we may still have a chance of finding Agent Sokol alive."

"The blood?" Pricey asked.

"Outside? Probably our Onlar targets. The footprints. But I think whoever left those footprints saw our poor friend here and ran. Didn't bother to come back to cover their tracks, happily for us."

He was grinning ear to ear.

"Did you find anything in the tunnel, sir?" one of the entrance agents asked.

332

Tskoulis sobered and glanced at Pricey. "Maybe. We need to head back to base at this point. This may be a more...involved operation than anticipated."

Another spoke up. "Sir. What should we do with this animal?"

"Dispose of the body properly. Clean the blood. If the Onlar do use this cave regularly, better if they don't guess we've been here." Tskoulis smiled grimly. "Then let's rest before we head back to base."

69

THEY REACHED THE HATCH TO THE SERVICE TUNNEL AS THE SUN was starting to sink toward the horizon. Tskoulis gazed across the landscape. The plateau now seemed very distant, like another world. He wondered where the tunnel went, whether Jossey was underground still.

He felt in his equipment pouch, made sure he still had the paper with the writing on it. *Good.*

He counted off his men, then descended into the City's outer tunnel.

They took a waiting Patrol transport the six or so miles to the Patrol base. It whirred almost silently through the service tunnels, the lights flashing overhead as they flew through the underground. Gavin sat back and thought. His men were silent as well. It had been a long day.

But Gavin had no interest in resting, not now.

He idly traced the logo on the seat ahead of him, a star, and thought about the word he'd seen in the tunnel.

N. E. B. They were all English letters. And then there was

that odd jagged one, like a sideways M. He'd seen it somewhere before. A math textbook? Science?

The commander turned around. "Stanton. Weren't you a math student before Patrol?"

"Yes, sir." Stanton looked puzzled at being asked.

"What is this symbol? Do you recognize it?" He drew the jagged symbol in the air.

"That's sigma, sir."

At Tskoulis' raised eyebrow, Stanton continued. "It means the sum of something, sir."

Tskoulis frowned. "Is it a letter? Or just a symbol?"

"Yes, sir, both. It's a Greek letter." Stanton looked even more puzzled now.

"Thank you."

Pricey was watching the exchange, but caught Tskoulis' eye, and for once kept his mouth shut.

Tskoulis turned back to the windows and watched the lights flashing past, wishing the shuttle would move faster.

The shuttle began to slow as they reached the main ring of outer tunnels. Tskoulis sat up, looked out the window.

Henry was there.

Tskoulis broke into a smile.

As soon as the shuttle stopped, he hopped out, grabbed Henry and pulled him into a firm hug. "Glad to have you back, you big doof."

Henry clapped him on the back, wincing a little. "Glad to be back, Commander." He pulled back, looked seriously at Tskoulis. "Anything?"

"Maybe." Tskoulis glanced at his men. "I need to talk with Minister Sokol. Are you up and about now?"

"Mostly." Henry grimaced. "I got hit pretty bad. Probably won't be going on any real missions anytime soon. But you should be proud of 2-5. They've been training hard since Jossey disappeared."

Tskoulis looked at him, smiled. "Let's go. You can tell me on the way."

He dismissed the others, told them to clean up and report for a debriefing in an hour. Then he turned back to his second-in-command.

They walked down the corridor, Henry limping slightly.

"2-5's very keen to go out and search for her, I have to warn you," Henry said. "You might have a tough time telling them this is a restricted operation."

Tskoulis smiled a little. "I see you've been briefed by the Minister?"

"Yes, sir. All he told me was that all personnel decisions were yours." Henry's gaze was shuttered.

"Correct, sergeant. And you told them what?"

"Nothing, sir. I told them you were the right one to brief them."

"Good work." As they neared the training room, Tskoulis heard the babble of voices. He clapped Henry on the shoulder. "Go. Let them know I should be briefing them tomorrow morning. I have to report to the Minister."

"Yes, sir."

Sokol was in his office, as Tskoulis had thought he might be. He stood up immediately when Tskoulis entered, face drawn, and Tskoulis saw him deflate a little even before the commander opened his mouth.

"You haven't found her," he said flatly.

"No, sir. But sir – "

Sokol looked up at him with those disconcertingly flat eyes.

"Sir, we may have found *something*. Permission to come forward."

"Granted, Commander."

Tskoulis strode forward to the desk. He pulled out the paper and showed it to the Minister. "Does this mean anything to you, Minister?"

Minister Sokol put on his glasses and looked at the handwriting:

N E B Σ E K H I P

"I believe that fourth letter is Greek," Tskoulis said, "but I have no idea what – "

Sokol had a strange look on his face. "Where did you find this?" He glanced up at Tskoulis.

Tskoulis described the canyon, the cave with the hidden tunnel inside, the strange cavern with multiple tunnels leading to it. Sokol watched him silently.

When the commander finished, Sokol burst out laughing.

Tskoulis blinked, confused. "Sir?"

Sokol seemed to be finding something hysterically funny. "I'm sorry, my boy," he said between giggles. "It's just – oh, it's *true*. It's true. I hadn't thought – "

He composed himself at last and tapped something on his desk, entering a series of characters into the system. "My boy, I believe you are familiar with the Old Sectors?"

"Of course, sir."

Sokol zoomed out on the map. "And the canyons of the Onlar to the northeast?"

"Yes, sir."

Sokol looked positively gleeful. He rubbed his hands together as he stared at the map.

"If you are correct, Tskoulis, you may have just discovered how the Onlar have been evading us so successfully for so many years."

. . .

Tskoulis was almost certain he'd misheard. "Excuse me, sir?"

Sokol pointed to the map. "You say you were here? And Jossey disappeared here, correct?"

"Yes, sir."

The Minister took a stylus and drew a line from the canyon they'd just searched, directly through Gurime and back through Uchisar. He continued until the line ended directly in the middle of Old Sector 2.

"As you know, Tskoulis, there is quite an extensive network of underground dwellings here. And there was, once, a large city aboveground as well."

"Yes, sir."

"You may have just found a tunnel reaching directly from the OS2 into the Onlar heartland."

"Sir?" Tskoulis frowned. OS2 was emptied. Completely. They'd cleared it out many years before. "You don't think some of the Onlar are living in OS2?"

"Maybe, maybe not, Commander. But do you know what OS2 was called at the time of the Founders?"

"I'm afraid I do not, sir."

"Let me see that note." Sokol picked up the paper. "These are Greek letters. The sigma is an S. The rho" – he pointed to the P – "is an R. This is the Old Language written in a Greek script. It was common among some of the old Christians who lived in this region long before the Founders arrived."

Tskoulis silently wondered how the Minister knew all this, but he did not comment. It was Intelligence's job to know, he supposed. "Go on, sir."

Sokol wrote something on the pad and stood back triumphantly. "What you found, Commander, appears to have been a sign pointing to the city of Nevşehir."

He pointed a fat finger to the ruins over Old Sector 2.

"This," he said, "was Nevşehir."

70

Tskoulis was floored. "That's almost eight miles," he said, stunned. "Are you saying there may be eight-mile tunnels solely to connect the – "

"Yes, that's exactly what I'm saying." Sokol pointed to the map again. "Our City was built on the approximate location of another of the underground cities of the region, which is why you have some of those strange half-tunnels that go nowhere, extending out of our outer tunnels."

Tskoulis had seen them. Tark had pointed them out on their tunnel adventures. The boys had figured they were mining mistakes.

"And we did know of a couple of these longer tunnels between our City and the Old Sectors," Sokol continued. "But my predecessors did an extensive mapping job of the Sectors. To our knowledge, there were no additional tunnels." He smiled widely. "You, Commander, may have just opened up an entire new underground world to us. Truly excellent work."

"Happy to be of service, sir."

Sokol glanced at him. "Who else knows about this?"

"Pricey, sir. That's it."

"Is Pricey trustworthy?"

"I'd trust him with my life, sir."

"Is he silent?" Sokol's eyes were cold.

"I wouldn't describe him as such, sir, but in the cases that matter, yes."

"You understand that this may be a matter of highest security, like the rest of this mission?"

"Yes, sir, I understand that." Tskoulis looked at him carefully. "Would you...prefer I take Pricey with me?"

Sokol took a seat and carefully arranged a small stack of papers on his desk.

"No, that's not necessary. However, please do be sure to impress upon him the...highly classified nature of what was discovered. Even among your best men. I think I need not remind you of the price of disclosure."

"Sir, understood, sir."

Tskoulis glanced at the map on the desk, feeling suddenly uncomfortable. But he'd agreed to keep certain things quiet, he told himself. Leadership meant responsibility.

Much more responsibility than he'd realized.

"I need some time to prepare for this mission, sir."

"Yes, of course, Commander. At this point, if they have taken her any reasonable distance, it is likely to be an extraction mission rather than a rescue. For that, I am authorizing you to use Unit 1, and from here on only that unit."

"Thank you, sir." Tskoulis got to his feet. *Unit 1.* "With permission, sir, I'd like to begin preparing. Ideally we can leave tomorrow once the sun is past its peak, and reach the tunnel entrance by sunset."

Sokol stood as well.

"Very good. Tell Henry that he and Pricey are now in charge of continuing the solar panel mission. The wiring must continue. We need that operational within the next week or two." Sokol looked worried. "I'd like to have it tested by the end of the year. If we have another Karapartei incident and the power gets cut again – "

Tskoulis saluted. "Understood, sir." He turned to go.

"And Commander."

Tskoulis turned to look at him. Sokol's expression seemed far away.

"I believe I said *all* resources would be at your disposal," he said.

"Yes, sir?"

The Minister looked hesitant. Finally he said, "Come and find me when your plan is finalized, Commander. Do you have an approximate timeframe?"

"I can probably complete it by around eleven tomorrow morning, sir."

"Good. Come see me then." He went back to arranging the papers.

"Yes, sir." Gavin saluted and strode swiftly out of the office.

71

IT WAS LATE EVENING WHEN JOSSEY AND THE ONLAR EXITED THE maze of tunnels onto still-burning sands. They'd been traveling for two days. Jossey was exhausted, half-stumbling over the rocks as she staggered forward on swollen feet. Altan had actually taken pity on her and taken the bundle from her back.

The stars were overhead, and Jossey could hear voices in the distance. She squinted, eyes puffy with all the travel in the dark. Everything was blue in the twilight, and she realized she'd never seen the desert like this. There was an enormous mountain to the south, faintly visible in the dimness.

She kept staggering forward.

Altan half-heartedly jerked on her rope as they approached what seemed to be a celebration. A bonfire was lit, and sparks flew upward into the evening desert sky. Jossey could smell meat cooking, and hear what sounded like dozens of voices speaking in the Old Language, talking loudly, joking, arguing. Here and there, she caught a word she recognized.

There were three figures on the dais beyond the bonfire. She could hear laughter, see the glint of what might be jewelry. Or weapons.

As her captors dragged her into the firelight, the voices suddenly hushed.

Jossey stared wide-eyed around her. Everywhere were Onlar, dozens, maybe even hundreds, but they were – people. She still couldn't comprehend it. The women were dressed in long loose gowns, their hair-wraps braided with strands of multicolored ribbon. The men wore loose material under armor, just as Patrol did, but better suited to the desert heat. Some wore hoods. Some of their faces were covered, showing only their eyes.

They all stared. She felt a chill.

A small child ran up to Jossey. He stared up into her face, and she realized with a start that he had the same strange eyes as Caspar. Only his were a brilliant green.

"Canavar!" he shrieked. "Canavar!"

Canavar meant monster, Jossey suddenly remembered.

One of the women grabbed him, yanked him back from Jossey. "Patrol," she spat, pronouncing it Paa-trol.

A second child hurled a stone. It was small but sharp, and struck Jossey in the shoulder, hard. She willed herself not to make a sound.

Had they brought her all this way just to kill her now?

She turned slowly and glared at the child, suddenly glad she had the awful scar over her eye. The child whimpered and ran.

Laughter from the dais at the front of the group. A tall figure stood up, clapping slowly, and stepped into the firelight.

He was at least six foot four, muscular, like Gavin, and he walked toward her with assurance. He wore armor too, but his was clearly different from the others' – a chest-and-shoulder plate and arm guards with silver decorations that spoke of high rank.

He, too, wore a draped hood and face guard, though his had silver trim. His outfit suggested he was either a general or, maybe, their leader.

"Bayim," said her captor. *Sir.*

The tall man clapped Jossey's captor on the shoulder, motioning to the Onlar's bandaged arm, then said something quietly.

Jossey's lead captor looked uncomfortable, but said what Jossey thought was *"I don't know, sir. We took her and ran."*

The tall man did not ask further. Instead, he gestured to Jossey. Jossey's captor grabbed her rope, pulled on it, hard. She fell to the ground, grimaced, trying not to make any noise.

The tall man moved toward her, stopped a few feet away. She didn't acknowledge him, staring fixedly to the side, ignoring the blood now seeping from her knee.

Whatever he wanted from her, she'd given Them enough.

"Look up," hissed her lead captor. "Pay respect."

The newcomer murmured something to him. The older man saluted and backed off. The entire crowd waited, dead silent. The only sound was the crackling of the bonfire.

The newcomer took the rope and jerked Jossey to her feet.

"Your name," he said, in English. "Don't make me ask again."

Jossey's head shot up suddenly at the voice.

Behind the cover, the man's eyes were silver. As they met hers, they widened in shock.

His face went white.

"Tark?" she whispered.

The man didn't move, looked completely frozen, blood gone out of his face. His stunned silver eyes ranged over her face, her scar.

All she could see was those eyes. But she knew.

"Tark," she said, disbelievingly, barely a whisper, eyes streaming. She choked. "Tark, it's me." Tears streaked down her dusty face.

He started to reach out, seemingly unconsciously, then jerked his hand back.

He reached up and removed the silvered cloth, and she was staring into her brother's face.

72

THE CROWD SHIFTED, STARING AT THE PAIR, MUTTERING.

"Where are our men, Bey?" one woman called out. "I only see three."

Tark spoke quickly, without turning. Whatever he said, the Onlar seemed pacified. He did not seem able to tear his eyes away from Jossey. He half reached out again.

Jossey was half-listening, still staring at his face.

His face was so strange, she thought. So familiar, yet unfamiliar. She'd only seen him as a boy. He looked a little like their father. She could see it in the shape of his chin.

It was a long moment before she realized that one of the other figures from the dais had come forward into the firelight. An older woman, white hair unbound, jewel-encrusted hands clenched around thick robes.

"*Son?*" the Onlar said in their language, voice not quite quavering. In a few years, maybe. She looked from him to Jossey and back.

Son? Jossey looked sharply from him to the woman.

Tark turned to the woman and dropped his hand suddenly, as if remembering where he was. His face was still pale.

346

The woman stared at Jossey, eyes narrowed, as if recognizing her. Then her features suddenly contorted in rage. She shrieked at Jossey, something about "my son," and drew a knife from her robes.

There was instant mayhem. Tark turned and grabbed the woman, shouting, *"Hayır, anne!"* Jossey stumbled, falling backward, eyes wide as the woman sliced the air where Jossey's face had been. Tark was shouting orders, the woman screaming.

"Tark!" A young woman's voice, crying his name.

One of Jossey's captors yanked her back, dragging her to the ground. She hit hard, but for once she did not protest. She sat shivering on the desert floor, hands bent awkwardly before her, looking up at them all, terrified. Altan hovered, a knife in his hands, ready to protect her, she thought. Or kill her.

Jossey saw a flash of motion, the glitter of ornaments in the firelight, as a third figure came running from the dais.

Tark had taken the older woman by the shoulders, forced her to look into his eyes. He said something low to her. He kissed her forehead as she shivered, her pale green eyes darting wildly to Jossey and back to him.

"Anne," he said. *Mother.* *"Anne Aysun'la git."*

Jossey understood that much: "Mother, go with Aysun."

Aysun appeared to be the young woman who had come running. She was around Jossey's age, with lovely dark eyes and delicate features. She wore silver threads in her hair wrapping, and her dress, too, suggested rank.

She was staring down at Jossey the way one might look at a snake.

The young woman took the older one by the arm, pulled her away gently. *"Gel, annem,"* she said. *Come on.*

She looked over her shoulder at Jossey, dark eyes full of hatred.

Jossey looked around her, choking as she breathed in dust,

still struggling to sit straight. The other Onlar were still silent, looking almost frightened.

The little boy who had thrown a rock had his mouth hanging open.

Tark gazed after Aysun and the old woman. Then he turned abruptly to the rest of the people standing around. He pointed to Jossey. "We have her!" he said loudly.

They seemed to have been waiting for this. The crowd erupted into cheers. Another child threw a stone, and Jossey dodged it, just barely.

Tark held up a hand. A man immediately grabbed the boy's arm. The child howled with protest and tried to twist away.

Tark gestured to the bonfire. "*Buyrun,*" he said. "Enjoy yourselves." He looked at the man coldly. "And the prisoner is mine."

The man saluted and looked away.

They understand English, Jossey thought. Somehow this surprised her even more than the rest.

People began circulating with dishes. Jossey realized she'd been brought to a celebratory feast, or so it looked. For her capture, she guessed.

Tark was approaching. She looked up at him.

Without looking at her, without even seeming to notice she was there, Tark picked up her rope, handed it to the lead captor.

Then he said coldly, "Erkan, take her."

Tark replaced his face cover and strode away, not looking back.

Jossey still had dried tears on her face. She stared after him, feeling suddenly very cold.

What was he doing? Did he not recognize her after all? Was he just leaving her here?

She wanted to shout his name, sprint after him, but the leader, Erkan, was tightly holding her rope.

She clamped her mouth shut, tears streaming down her face.

They could drag her wherever they wanted. She didn't care. Not anymore.

Altan walked ahead of them up an incline. Jossey could see the beginnings of stars. But all she could think about was Tark's face, the shock in his eyes. His coldness just now.

It had been the woman he called "mother" who had almost killed her so long ago, she thought. She remembered the voice.

In fact, she thought, she would probably never forget that voice. That shriek, almost a wail, the endless sound in the desert night, before the claws had flicked out and scarred Jossey's young face.

Before Jossey had been left for dead in the burning sand.

She didn't know what was happening, why Tark was here, why he was dressed like royalty. She numbly followed her Onlar captors.

They were walking along a wall now. The landscape looked similar to her home. There were holes here and there in the rock, like small living quarters.

They unceremoniously pushed her through one of the doorways. She protested.

"Quiet, Patrol dog," Altan spat.

He threw a bundled cloak and a full canteen in after her. "Wait for our bey," he said.

Then he grinned a little. "I'm waiting too."

Bey. Leader. Tark was their leader.

She sat down on the stone floor. She could see the stars through the doorway.

She curled up into the cloak and cried.

73

JOSSEY AWAKENED TO THE MURMURS OF HER GUARDS. IT WAS WELL after midnight, based on her half-functioning wrist gauge.

The bonfire was a faint orange glow in the distance. She could see stars glimmering in the sky beyond. The air was almost chilly.

Outside her cell, Altan and Erkan were conversing. Scarface was asleep against a rock. She thought briefly about escape, but even if she could get out of this place, she couldn't run with no boots, which they'd confiscated again. They'd probably track her down immediately. She had enough water to last maybe a few hours in the sun.

And there was the small problem that she had no idea where she was.

They'd traveled for more than two days, she knew. It had been underground, in what direction she didn't know. When they'd come up aboveground, they'd been facing south, but she couldn't swear that the tunnel hadn't curved in all the time they'd spent traveling it.

Her faint memory of the maps didn't help her, because there weren't many underground tunnels listed on them, and, more importantly, she didn't know *where* they'd gone underground. She'd been unconscious at the time.

After that awful Altan kicked me in the head, she thought bitterly.

As far as she knew, she could be south of the mountains the old map had labeled Ilara. Or beyond the salt lake to the far northwest. She had no clue. Wherever they were, they were apparently far enough from the City that the Onlar felt comfortable having a large open-air bonfire. Fires were visible for miles, she guessed.

She put her face in her hands.

There was a step outside her cell, and what sounded like the guards shifting.

Jossey's head shot up. A tall figure was standing there, dark against the sky. Tark?

"Buyrun, Beyim," one of the guards said. *Welcome, Bey.*

Tark greeted them, then entered the cell. "Leave us," he said to the guards.

They saluted and wandered off, laughing, toward the bonfire.

Tark stood there in the dimness and looked at her for a long moment. His entire body seemed frozen.

She sat there, unsure whether to go to him or shrink back. His behavior earlier – she couldn't tell if he even remembered who she was.

He took a step forward. She recoiled, staring up at him, eyes enormous.

Then Tark gently lifted her to her feet and pulled her into his arms.

She felt pain boiling up inside. Fifteen years of hope. Fear. Anger. She wanted to push him away, stop feeling.

Instead, she clung to her older brother, weeping.

Tark held her close. She could feel his shoulders shaking. He kissed her on the top of her head and pulled her even closer.

She sobbed into his shoulder.

He finally pulled away and looked at her, holding her face in his hands. He touched her scar carefully. In the faint light his eyes were as luminous as she remembered.

"I thought you died," he said very quietly.

Jossey laughed shakily, gripping his hands in her own. "Your – mother – she didn't quite finish me off." She gestured to her scar.

His face contorted. "She thought you were dying, thought you probably wouldn't survive the trip back here. But – " He went silent.

"You're really tall," she mumbled after a moment, tears still streaming down her face. "You were so skinny."

Tark held her at arm's length. "And you're strong." His voice became flat as he glanced down at her ruined uniform. "You're Patrol."

"Yes," she said.

Something flickered in his eyes. "Why?"

"What do you mean?"

He stopped talking. The guards' voices sounded in the distance. They seemed to be heading back toward the cell.

He muttered something under his breath, said quietly, urgently, "Jossey, you're in great danger here. These people – my people. They don't know – "

"Your people?" she repeated.

He ignored her, continued. "We've been trying to capture one of the Engineers for months. We lost several men. You're a prize, do you understand? A prize to interrogate, to use against the City."

"Why?" She frowned. "Why an Engineer?"

"I can't explain right now. But they think I'm interrogating you. You need to remain silent, do you understand me? Pretend you understand none of our language. Don't speak to them. You can ask for water and food. That's it." He gripped her shoulders, looked into her eyes, speaking urgently. "They *can't* know who you are to me, do you understand me?"

She opened her mouth. He looked earnestly at her. "Please, Jossey. I thought you were dead. Until tonight I thought you were dead."

"And I thought – " She shut her mouth. The guards were getting louder. They sounded like they were almost within earshot.

"Tark," she said in a small voice.

He looked at her.

"Why did you stay with them? Why didn't you try to escape?" It was a whisper.

Why did you leave me?

He looked pained for a long moment, then said, "I have to go."

Before he left, he turned and raised a finger to his lips.

Then he stepped out and greeted his guards.

"*She's weak,*" he said in the Old Language. "*Keep her in ------. Keep her safe, but don't let her run.*"

Jossey understood half of it. It was enough that she retreated to the corner of her cell, and pulled her blanket around her.

74

JOSSEY PICKED AT THE SMALL BREAKFAST HER GUARDS HAD SET before her. Tark's words about silence were reverberating in her mind.

She was happy to ignore her captors, listen in when she could. But why did it matter if they realized who she was? His "mother" clearly already knew. Or seemed like she did, at least.

Jossey looked around, seeing the morning light filtering into the cell, and realized she'd never been aboveground, exposed like this to the heat, for longer than the allowed six hours, most of which had been in a temperature-controlled environment.

But she was in a cell on the side of some kind of ridge, and it was autumn. Maybe she would be safe here? The Onlar had clearly survived aboveground for long enough with no real shelter.

Assuming they wanted her to survive, that was.

Scarface and Altan were lounging by the entrance to her cell, alternately snoozing and tossing rocks. They seemed to have some kind of game going, though she couldn't figure out the rules.

Scarface sauntered over to her cage and peered in. "Ah, you're awake," he said in English.

Stay silent, she told herself. She just looked at him.

He grinned nastily. "What happened to your face, Patrol dog?" He turned to Altan. "Bir canavara benziyor."

She looks like a monster.

Altan laughed.

It was only because Tark had begged her not to react, and because she didn't fancy another boot to the head, that she was able to keep the emotion off her face.

The Onlar thought she looked like a monster.

She stuffed a piece of bread into her mouth and chewed, looking coolly at him, resisting the urge to pull her hood further down over her face.

He wasn't exactly beautiful either, she thought. Every part of her wanted to respond with "What happened to yours?" She kept her mouth shut, but Scarface could clearly see her response in her eyes. He huffed angrily, turning to Altan.

There was a commotion in the direction of the encampment, and Altan perked up, dropping his rock to the ground. He glanced at Scarface. *"Stay here."*

Scarface grumbled, but did as he was told.

Altan disappeared from Jossey's sight. She stood up, approached the doorway, tried to peek around the edge. Scarface drew his sword, which she'd discovered they carried around the camp, rather than use claws. She shrank back, but he just grinned and began to draw circles in the dust, one leg propped up on a rock.

"Scared, dog?"

She pretended not to understand.

"Water," she croaked.

He flung a canteen in her general direction. It missed the cell doorway and dropped to the ground just outside, where she dared not reach for it.

She glared at him. She really hoped it had been Gavin who had given him that scar.

Speaking of Gavin –

Jossey wondered where he was now. Whether he'd be out searching for her in the daytime heat. Or maybe he'd try at night. She hoped the fires were close enough for him to see.

Based on where the sky had been darkest, and the direction they'd exited the tunnel, they'd headed roughly southwest for some time. But she didn't know if that had been their general direction. Time and space were less clear underground.

At least in the City, the quadrants and various sectors were all labeled so you couldn't really get lost.

Not so in the underground noodle city, she thought bitterly.

She almost laughed at the stupid nickname. She didn't know what else to call it, because no one would tell her. And no one might find her out here. This was the third morning she'd been gone. Maybe they assumed she was dead.

She felt anxiety rising in her chest. She might never see them again. Sally. Perkins. Her uncle. Her unit.

She'd only been with 2-5 a few weeks, and it felt like a lifetime. Wickford's awkward smile. Zlotnik's anger, her annoyed sigh whenever Jossey stumbled. Thompson's inane bumbling, turning red whenever Jossey so much as spoke. Ellis fighting with Thompson over the eggs.

Caspar.

And Gavin.

She inhaled sharply. Part of her wanted the commotion to be Commander Tskoulis, storming out of the tunnel with an entire Patrol unit, here to take her back home.

She closed her eyes. He could be as overprotective as he wanted, she thought. He was welcome to.

And Caspar. His silver eyes, focused on the Onlar in front of him as he moved with brutal precision.

I could even be of some use, she thought, if I got my hands on a weapon.

Suddenly a thought occurred to her.

Maybe she could use her wrist gauge somehow. She wouldn't be surprised if it could somehow send signals. It was coordinated to sunset time, after all, which changed daily. It must be getting a signal from *somewhere*. She was surprised they'd left it on her.

She began to fiddle with the strap. She was an Engineer, after all, she told herself.

Scarface perked up at the motion. She glanced at him. He watched her for a long moment with bored green eyes, then went back to drawing circles in the sand.

She shrank back into the shadows, where he couldn't easily see. It was a reasonable movement; if he wasn't going to give her water, she might as well retreat into the shade. Nothing suspicious. Indeed, Scarface glanced at her, then down again.

The wrist gauge was flickering. It hadn't been charged in some time, she realized. She had no idea how the signal worked, but if she could just get it off –

Her hands were still tied, but more loosely now. Now she just had a foot-long piece of rope connecting her wrists. The Onlar seemed to have thought that removing her boots was enough to keep her from running.

They were right, she thought.

But the loosened rope gave her the ability to reach her gauge.

The strap was stuck, she'd worn it so long. She gripped it with her teeth and pulled on it carefully. It was an over-under design, old-fashioned, and the fabric was stiff from having been left on for so long. She pulled at it, trying not to tear it.

It peeled slowly away from the main band.

She grinned and worked away at the small metal pin with her other hand. It came undone and she flipped it over.

She needed something to pry it open. Something thin.

She looked around.

The bowl? It was metal, steel, it looked like. Probably much too strong to shave off a piece.

Either way, she needed wire to boost any kind of signal. She had no idea where these gauges even were monitored, or if they were monitored. But she had to try.

She decided to use the metal pin on the strap.

She was determinedly fiddling away at the back panel when the light in the cell dimmed.

"What are you doing?" Scarface asked, looming in the doorway. He took two steps and grabbed the wrist gauge from her.

"No! No!" she shrieked at him as he threw it to the ground.

As They had with the radio, he crushed it beneath his boot.

Jossey was cold with anger. She said nothing, just sat against the cave wall and stared at Scarface, wrapping herself in the blanket again. It was hot now, but she didn't care. It was like a barrier that she could hold between them.

He stared back at her.

"Where are you going?" he asked her mockingly. "Away?" He gestured to her bare feet. "On those?"

She gritted her teeth and did not respond.

"You want to know where we were going, and now you don't talk." Scarface grinned. "Well. Welcome to Ilara."

Her eyes widened at the name. He frowned at the movement. "You know it?"

She shook her head, hoping Tark wouldn't be angry.

Scarface arched an eyebrow. "I knew you were valuable."

Jossey clenched her fists under her blanket.

Before Scarface could say anything else, footsteps sounded outside.

It was Altan. His face was dark with emotion.

"They've brought the ----" he said quietly in their language to Scarface, who whipped around. Jossey frowned, not recognizing the word.

"All," Altan choked. He sat down hard, hands trembling. The sword fell from Scarface's grasp and clattered on the stone.

Jossey looked back and forth between them, only half understanding, feeling she was missing something vitally important. All what?

Then Scarface looked up, straight at her. She'd never seen so much hatred in someone's eyes.

He got to his feet, slowly, and picked up his sword.

75

"KÖPEK," SCARFACE SAID. *DOG.* "YOU KILLED MY FRIENDS. MY men. My uncle."

Jossey inched away, further into the cell. He stepped inside.

"Why we deserved this?" Scarface shouted at Jossey.

"*Yazar!*" Altan had scrambled to his feet. "*Yazar, stop!*"

She pressed herself against the back of the cell, wishing she had anything to defend herself. A rock. Anything.

"Please," she whispered.

"Always. Always you, Patrol dogs," Scarface shouted. "You kill our men. You kill my mother." In two steps he was towering over her, voice rough, bellowing in her face.

She covered her head with her arms, unable to move, weeping, expecting a blade at any moment.

"Yazar!" Altan dragged Scarface back outside. "Yeter! Yeter, Yazar! Ne yapiyorsun?" He pushed Scarface backward, grabbing his arms. "*Our bey has forbidden it! This is our ------, Yazar!*"

Scarface – Yazar – backed down, went limp. He sank to the ground, face in his hands.

"*Ali,*" he said quietly. "*I saw him die.*"

"We must not harm the prisoner," Altan repeated in English,

still grasping Scarface's arms tightly. He glared at Jossey. She curled into the corner, feeling very small, wondering if Tark would be able to protect her if these people suddenly decided she was not worth saving.

Footsteps approached rapidly. The two men turned. Altan released the other's arms.

"*Get up.*" It was Erkan. He stepped into the cell, tossing a rope to Altan. "*Put this on her.*"

Erkan looked at Jossey. His eyes were reddened.

To Jossey, he said, "Come see what your people have done."

She walked slowly out into the sunlight, wrists bound, aware of how terrible she looked, how she must smell, after three days of travel and lack of sleep. Erkan yanked on her rope, and she stumbled after him.

She flinched at the brightness and the heat as they walked out onto an open plain. The sand felt like an oven on her bare soles.

The Onlar did not seem to mind the heat. They were arrayed in two lines, surrounding a line of bodies on pallets. The bodies had been thickly covered, but flies were beginning to hover. The pallets were surrounded by what looked like family members, breathing through their face-covers, some sinking to the ground beside their loved ones.

There were so many women, Jossey realized. And children.

Of course there were.

One young woman was being held up by two others. Beside her, a young child was sitting on the ground, staring straight ahead, thumb in his mouth.

When Jossey stepped out onto the burning plain, they all turned and fell silent, except some of the old women who were chanting in a language Jossey had never heard.

Tark was standing at the head of the line, next to the woman named Aysun. A baby, maybe a year old, was on her hip, looking around with dark curious eyes.

When the mourning woman saw Jossey, she shrieked and grabbed a knife from her dress, running toward the prisoner.

Altan stepped directly into the woman's path, sword in hand. She screamed at him and tried to dart past. He stood firm, joined by Scarface.

Jossey stood stock-still, unable to move, staring across the dusty earth at her brother.

Tark murmured something to Aysun, who handed him the baby.

His son, Jossey thought with a pang.

Aysun made her way over to the young woman, touched her shoulders gently. The woman jumped and half swung around with the weapon.

Aysun moved swiftly, relieving her of the knife, then put her arms around the young mother, who burst into tears.

Aysun pulled the mother off to the side with her, holding her tightly, murmuring in her ear and glaring daggers at Jossey. She beckoned to the little boy on the ground.

He toddled over to his mother, who scooped him up and pressed her lips to his small forehead, still weeping.

Aysun returned to Tark's side and took the child. He said something quietly to her.

Then Tark strode over, armor glinting in the sunlight.

In the burning sunlight, he still wore his face-cover, his dark hood. Jossey looked up at him, frightened. He was her brother, she told herself. But he was also their leader. He had a responsibility to them.

"You are in great danger here," he'd told her. How much he could protect her now, she didn't know.

She looked at him, expressionless.

"This is what your people have done," Tark said coldly to her. He gestured to the pallets, gave her a long look with narrowed eyes. She flinched.

Then he turned to the Onlar, hands spread.

"My people!" he shouted. "My men have brought you a prisoner, an Engineer, from the Colony, as I promised, praise God."

He spoke in English. So she could know exactly what they wanted to do to her, she assumed.

"My father-in-law, Diros Bey, lost his life in this cause," Tark went on.

There was some muttering among the Onlar.

"We stand here under the sun with our dead so that we may remember what the Colonizers have done to us, what the Founders promised us, what they have taken from us." He looked among them. "You have chosen me as your bey. I have vowed to bring the Colony to justice, if God so wills."

He pointed to Jossey. "This woman is the key to that justice."

She had no idea what justice he meant.

The Onlar had been attacking the City for years, with no apparent provocation. They had stolen children, killed those Citizens they caught outside the tunnels after dark. Some of the solar engineers had gone missing even during the daytime, their bodies recovered weeks later.

Why are you doing this, Tark? she thought.

The sun was starting to get to her. She was grateful for the dry climate, and she had on her protective Patrol uniform, but she was feeling faint. She hadn't had enough water, she realized.

A tall man in what looked like his forties came forward, saluted Tark.

"Bey, I would like to speak," he said in lightly-accented English.

"Speak, Kudret." Tark's eyes were narrowed. He removed his face cover.

The man called Kudret smiled unpleasantly. His face was

craggy; his entire body was rocklike, giant fingers interlaced as he stood before Tark. He saluted.

"We are grateful," he said, "that our noble bey has brought us this Engineer." He gestured to Jossey. "However, I do not understand how you plan to use her against the Colony. I imagine she would not volunteer to help us destroy her home."

Tark's eyes were cold.

"If she does not help us," he said, "the penalty is death."

Jossey stared at him, stricken. She felt even more faint in the heat.

"Water," she croaked to Altan, who stood beside her. He ignored her.

Kudret applauded slowly.

"Güzel, Beyim. Have you forgotten one thing?"

"What is that?" Tark said coldly.

"She can die, or she can live. But if she is released back to her people, she can tell them where we are."

"I am aware of that, Kudret."

Kudret's dark eyes glittered. "Unless she asked for safety here. Of course, it is unlikely that we could accept a...Colonist to live among us." He smiled unpleasantly. "With certain exceptions, of course, Bey. Your noble mother-in-law's request was, of course, a very different situation. But this woman? No, I think this we could not accept. What think you?" he shouted to the crowd, some of whom were translating for the rest, a low constant murmur.

They roared in assent.

He smiled, turned to Tark. "You have heard the people. What is the value of this woman, then? Why would she help us if she knows either way may mean death?"

Tark stepped up to the man, nearly face-to-face with him.

"Are you questioning the decision of Diros Bey, Kudret?" His voice was like ice.

Altan put his hand on his sword.

Kudret looked calmly at him. "No, of course not, Bey. I am just – looking practically at this situation. Besides" – he smiled nastily – "Diros Bey is no longer here. There may have been...conditions of which he knew that you do not. I mean no disrespect, of course." He took a step back, saluted.

"That may be." Tark did not smile. "But our former bey had his reasons, as you may understand. I am continuing to carry out his plan."

Kudret turned halfway toward the people, raised his voice.

"You have still not answered my question as to why the woman would help us," he said. "I assume the people would want to know. They have suffered greatly."

Tark glanced at Jossey. She still felt ill, but stood as straight as she could.

"Her city is failing," Tark said shortly. "It is in her interest."

Jossey stared. What was he talking about?

Kudret suddenly looked sour.

"You know as well as I do, Kudret." Tark smiled coldly. "I believe you were at our meeting with the Colony's ambassador at Avanos."

Avanos? The river to the north? What ambassador? Jossey's head was spinning.

Tark turned to Jossey. "Your City – what we call the Colony – is unable to sustain itself agriculturally, Engineer. There are too many of you. You are running out of food. You need our help. Your City is aware of this."

Jossey remembered the protester at the Agriculture Minister's speech. But their help? What did he mean?

She licked dry lips, opened her mouth to speak.

Tark met her gaze and shook his head, just a fraction.

"At one point one of your Council members reached out to us to try to negotiate a...new order," Tark said. His smile stilled. "Sadly, he...disappeared. It seems your Council has made their position clear on the matter."

What matter? She felt even more faint.

Kudret spoke up again, directly to Jossey this time. Tark gave him a hard look. He ignored it and continued. "Your captors have told us of the project your people were working on. Why, I wonder, would your Colony be upgrading its solar grid system?" Kudret looked closely at her.

Jossey just looked back at him, startled. How –

He laughed at the expression on her face. "You think we don't have our own scientists? Our own engineers? You poor, poor girl. What an education you must have had."

Tark spoke up. "That's enough, Kudret."

Kudret backed down, smiling unkindly at Jossey as he went back to his place.

Tark looked at him for a long moment, then turned to the people. "Let us bury our dead."

Then he looked at Jossey. "Give the prisoner some water. Let us not forget who we are."

They took her back to her cell.

She sat on the stone floor. Altan handed her a canteen of water. She drank it greedily.

"Thank you," she muttered to him. He yanked it out of her hand.

She didn't bother to look at him, kept staring at the dust instead.

"Her city is failing."

What was he talking about? She knew that there had been

366

some supply disruptions in the last couple of years. They hadn't had some things in a long time.

She rarely saw the ag workers, as their schedules were quite different, didn't really know any of them, but everyone admired what they did. It was vital work, quite literally. It was considered a great honor to be chosen to work in the agricultural sector; there was a special exam every year.

Something was bothering her, some connection her mind was trying to make.

Why would that man have mentioned the solar upgrade?

Her uncle had said that the solar disruptions due to Onlar activity was a security issue.

She knew there were occasional power outages. One had lasted two days. Two days in blackness, with only LED lanterns scattered everywhere to keep the darkness away. They'd even had to pump water by hand. The only thing that hadn't failed was the locks on the upper gates, which the Founders had wisely thought to make manual ones.

For the first time, it occurred to Jossey that the outages could affect the food labs, the grow lights.

If the Onlar wanted to take out the City, she thought, all they had to do was disrupt the solar panels enough to keep the grow lights off, kill the plants. Starve the people.

She looked up at her captors, horrified. That man Kudret – was that his goal? Not Tark's, she thought. Not her brother. Not his people, no matter how much of an Onlar he might be now.

She hoped.

And what did he mean about needing their help? What could the Onlar possibly do, other than not cut the electricity?

She had no idea. She just wanted to sleep.

It had been almost an hour when Altan appeared in the doorway of her cell. He tossed her her Patrol boots.

"Get up," he said to her. "We are leaving."

She scrambled to her feet. "What? Where?"

"The heat," he said. "We need to go into the canyon."

Jossey followed Altan out of her cell. He silently handed her another canteen of water. She thanked him. He still didn't look at her.

She wanted to ask him what Tark had been talking about, but she knew she shouldn't say anything. Whatever Tark was doing, he was the only person she could trust here, she thought.

Scarface and Erkan joined them, and they walked back toward the desert plain.

The entire camp was moving. She thought there must be at least three hundred people in the daylight.

"This is just a few of us," Altan hissed to her. She believed it.

They were streaming in a line toward what she could see in the daylight was a shallow gorge in the earth. It was very wide.

It was filled with trees.

76

THEY WALKED DOWN AMONG THE TREES, WHERE A STREAM WAS flowing. She looked around in amazement, remembering her father's description of the lone tree aboveground. Across the gorge, she could see what looked to be the ruins of some long-ago city.

The group began to follow the stream. As they went, she turned around to see where they'd exited the tunnel.

They'd come out of the side of a cliff. An enormous plateau rose to the north, so big it was difficult to comprehend the scale. She gaped.

Assuming she was right, the mountain she'd seen and this cliff meant she was very far to the south of the City.

The City had been dug down into a plain. Whenever Jossey had gone aboveground, every direction but the northeast had been flat, with faintly visible mountains in the distance. Even if she went very far to the south, she suspected she wouldn't be able to see Ilara until she was nearly on top of it. With the Onlar activity concentrated to the northeast canyons near Gurime, no wonder the City had never apparently searched for the Onlar all the way down here.

The canyon walls grew higher as they walked. Soon, the shadows began to cut the heat enough that she was able to remove the extra piece of white cloth that Altan had given to her to drape over her head. She glanced at him sideways as she wrapped it around her shoulders.

She looked for Tark in the crowd. He was there, at the front, with his small family. The little boy was too small to walk, barely more than an infant, and was being carried on Tark's shoulders.

He was a beautiful child. Her eyes stung as she wondered if she would ever be allowed to meet him.

It had been several miles, and Jossey was starting to feel the heat again despite the extra shade, when the canyon opened up into a massive gorge and she understood why the Onlar had chosen to come here.

The stream had become a river. It flowed swiftly, white in places where it jumped over rocks, and all around it was so much green she didn't know where to look. Even in late autumn, trees bent toward the water, and the boulders were covered by moss. She stared in amazement.

Altan turned to her, and grinned. "Welcome," he said, "to *our* land."

"It's..." She didn't know what words would be most appropriate. She'd never seen a place so beautiful, didn't know they existed anymore. "It's magnificent," she finally said.

He looked confused at the term. She had forgotten he did not speak English fluently. "Amazing," she said. "Wonderful. I don't know how to say it. *Güzel.*"

He understood that. He smiled widely at her.

Then, as if remembering, he looked away and jerked on the rope, but lightly.

77

THEY MADE CAMP AMONG THE TREES, AND IT OCCURRED TO Jossey for the first time that the Onlar might not in fact live underground, not entirely. At least not during the cooler seasons.

They had her sit under one of the trees, and busied themselves putting together shelters. She looked around her, fascinated. Her whole life had been spent underground, as had her parents' and their parents' and their parents' and so on, back several centuries to the time of the Founders. The idea of living aboveground was unthinkable for people.

Or so she'd been told.

Those who worked outside had been carefully trained how to interact aboveground – monitoring their water intake, checking the humidity, which was thankfully quite low in this region. Checking for heat exhaustion. They weren't allowed to travel beyond the short perimeter established around the solar plants, or the condensers, both due to heat and the threat of Onlar attacks. But the people here seemed unconcerned about the sun. They had water right here, she thought. And plenty of shade. It was late fall, according to the old calendar, but there were still enough leaves on the trees to keep everyone comfortably cool.

And, she supposed, there were probably tunnels near here if it got too warm.

She looked at the walls of the canyon. She could see holes carved into the rock. One set of them looked more precisely designed than the rest. A house?

"What is that?" she asked Altan, who turned irritably to her. He was on guard duty but had also been tasked with wrapping bundles of poles for the shelters. He did not look happy.

"Ruins," he said shortly. Then he said something she didn't understand.

"Ah," she said, pretending to understand. He made a sound and turned back to his work.

78

GAVIN SAT ALONE IN THE MESS HALL, MINDLESSLY SHOVELING down a giant pile of eggs and what passed for hash browns. He had a stack of maps in front of him, spread out all over the table.

He'd stayed up very late the night before working through the logistics. They couldn't afford to fail. Not this time.

He poured himself a third cup of coffee.

Unit 1 should be here after he briefed 2-5. He was not looking forward to telling his agents what he had to tell them. But it had to be done.

2-5 fell silent as he walked into the training area. Pricey had gotten there before him and evidently been questioned already, from the determinedly closed-mouth look on his face.

Tskoulis smiled. When it mattered, Pricey could be quiet.

"Agents," the commander said.

"SIR." They all snapped to attention, eyes on him. He glanced at them and saw that Zlotnik was still missing. Thompson and Ellis were there, along with Wickford and Caspar.

No Jossey trying to be serious while saluting him.

"I've heard you've been training hard with Henry," he began.

"Yes, sir," they murmured.

"That's excellent news. Good work." He paused, gauging. "Despite our efforts yesterday, as you may have guessed, we were unable to locate Agent Sokol."

He saw Caspar's jaw clench. Wickford looked stricken.

"However," the commander added, "we may have a lead. For security reasons I am unable to disclose this lead" – he glanced at Pricey – "but I wanted to keep you informed as to our ongoing investigation."

Tskoulis put his hands behind his back. Now to deliver the other bad news.

"As you may have been made aware," he said, "whether or not Agent Sokol is here, we are to continue with the wiring segment of the project the Minister has assigned us to complete. This is again of the highest order of security, and is on an extremely tight timeframe. It is scheduled to take place tomorrow night, under the command of Pricey. Technical supervision is the responsibility of Agent Savaş. Be ready to deploy at seven PM sharp."

Pricey looked gratified.

Caspar did not.

He looked furious.

"You're planning on leaving us here while you search for her, aren't you," he said flatly.

Tskoulis looked stone-faced at him. "That is what I have been ordered, Savaş. This operation is of the utmost – "

"Delicacy, I know," Caspar interrupted. "It's a security issue. I understand, *sir*. But there are other Patrol units that could–"

"Savaş. Stand down." Tskoulis turned toward him, took a step forward. "Don't think I don't punish insubordination."

Caspar's silver eyes grew very cold as he looked Tskoulis straight in the face.

A long moment, in which the others stared at both Caspar and Tskoulis.

Then Caspar stood straight.

"Understood, sir," was all he said.

* * *

Tskoulis stalked back to the mess hall, Pricey right behind him.

He was fuming, but he didn't want to think about Savaş right now. He had a mission to plan.

Four masked agents were there, waiting for him. They did not go by names, he knew. Not Unit 1. Instead, they went by letters: Alpha, Gamma, Rho, Phi. This was to protect their identities in case of exposure.

Pricey closed the mess doors. Tskoulis locked them from the inside.

Tskoulis greeted them. "Thank you for coming," he added. "Let's get started."

* * *

They arranged themselves around the long table and Tskoulis laid out the maps.

"I assume you've been filled in on whom we are trying to extract," he said.

"Yes, sir," they said.

Tskoulis gave them a grim smile.

He did not plan to explain what, specifically, Jossey was being held for, or why her interrogation was so dangerous. Sokol had instructed him only to use Unit 1 as an extraction team. He had, however, been given the green light to tell them about the new tunnels.

"We're here," he said. He drew a line with his finger to the old camping area in Asmalih. "This is approximately where we found a tunnel that may lead to the OS2."

"That far?" Alpha asked.

"We have reason to believe this is part of a much larger undiscovered tunnel network." Tskoulis explained to them what he'd told Sokol, about the sign that seemed to indicate that the tunnel in Asmalih ran all the way to Nevşehir. That if They had taken Jossey, that meant she could be anywhere within the vast Old Sectors, or even beyond.

"How long has Agent Sokol been missing?" Rho asked.

"This is the third day," Tskoulis said.

He knew from previous kidnappings that after four days, the likelihood of finding someone alive dropped to nearly zero. He pushed the thought out of his head and returned to the map.

"What we need to do is do a walk-through of the tunnel, see where it leads. This may take more than one day, and depending on how long the tunnel is, we may need to prepare to spend a night underground. Maybe two."

"You think she's been taken that far?" Phi asked.

"Maybe. Maybe not. The OS1 is big enough to hold thousands of people," Tskoulis said. "The OS2, Nevşehir, has been semi-destroyed, from what I've seen, but we've never fully mapped either of them. It's very likely she's been taken deep underground, rather than laterally far or aboveground." He glanced at them. "Which of you are trackers?"

Gamma raised his hand.

"Good." Tskoulis turned to Alpha. "I've requested four days' worth of supplies for five men. We can add extra if you think that's feasible."

"Make it for seven men," Alpha said. "Sokol assigned us an extra couple of trackers, said they should be helpful since we only have one at the moment. No offense, Gamma."

Gamma grinned. "None taken."

Tskoulis usually hated it when superiors did this. But in this case he was grateful. He was a little annoyed Sokol hadn't told him, but considering this was all being planned literally overnight, and to Sokol's exacting standards, he was more than okay with it.

"Where are they?" he asked.

"En route from quadrant 1, last time I checked." Alpha glanced at his wrist gauge. "Sokol said to expect significant tardiness. They're being pulled off some kind of field duty. Want me to tell your man outside?"

"Go ahead. If they aren't here soon, just have them meet at three with the rest of us." No point holding up the meeting. He still had to meet with Sokol and go update the supply order.

Alpha saluted, went outside to speak with Pricey. Tskoulis turned back to the maps. "Now, about the Old Sectors," he said. He pointed to the Uchisar area. "This is where we exited. Our service tunnel runs almost directly parallel to one of the major entrances to the old underground city. However, I doubt that the tunnel we discovered feeds into, or near, that one. It seems to me that if a secret tunnel network among these underground cities exists, it would not be easily discovered from any of them. Or, if it did, it would be able to be blocked off from any of them. You have seen the stone doors in Old Sector 1."

"We have, sir."

"They function to seal off that city from the interior. My assumption is that the tunnels connecting the cities would be far down, maybe below the seventh or eighth level, and maybe only accessible at a single point in each city, maybe two. I believe Patrol has in the past gone through and numbered the floors of OS2, is that correct?"

"That's correct, sir," said Rho. "As far down as we could go. I have a catalog of the codes we've put together for that sector."

"Excellent. That should give us a quick visual location,

assuming of course that the tunnel we found actually goes to OS2."

"And with all due respect, if it doesn't, sir?" Gamma asked.

Tskoulis looked grim. "Then let's hope those two extra trackers are worth their salt."

79

TSKOULIS FOLDED THE MAPS. HE TOLD ALPHA AND THE OTHERS to reconvene at 3:00 PM and be ready to head out.

"If anything major changes in the meantime, radio me," Tskoulis said. "Frequency 1120."

"Yes, sir."

They headed out into the corridor.

Tskoulis waited a few moments, thinking, hoping he'd left nothing out. He needed to present the plan to Sokol, contact Logistics.

Batteries. He needed batteries. And oxygen. If they were going to be exploring unknown tunnels for any length of time –

He made a note, then left, heading for Sokol's office.

He wondered where Jossey was now. Whether she was aboveground somewhere, dehydrated, burning in the overwhelming sunlight. Whether they'd interrogated her and left her to die. Or maybe –

He pushed the horrible images out of his mind, angry for even thinking about it. He couldn't allow himself to think like that, not if he wanted to remain focused, think clearly.

He glared at the floor as he walked toward the Ministry. A flunky straightened as they saw him and skittered past like a terrified mouse.

80

"You had wanted to meet with me, sir?" Tskoulis stood in Sokol's doorway.

"Yes, yes, come in, my boy."

Tskoulis walked forward to the oversized desk. The office was barely lit, as if Sokol had just gotten there.

A bright light shone glaringly down on his desk, where the Minister was standing going through a large stack of papers, taking sheets out at intervals and laying them in a grid. He was wearing his glasses, looking oddly studious.

As Tskoulis walked over, Sokol took them off and straightened, facing the Patrol leader.

"Are you prepared for the mission, Commander? Were you able to convince 2-5 to work on the wiring?" he asked.

"Yes to both, sir. I have the plans with me." Tskoulis replied. He didn't bother to bring up Savaş's insubordination. That was to be expected, he thought with annoyance. "2-5 should be leaving tomorrow night to complete the southern panels. The northern half should be completed the following evening."

"Excellent. And you've met with Unit 1 to discuss the mission?"

"Yes sir. I'm planning to order additional supplies for the trackers you've added."

"Wonderful, my boy." Sokol smiled.

Tskoulis glanced at the Minister. "I think we're fully prepared, sir. Is there anything you'd like to go over?"

Sokol smiled flatly. "Something like that. If you recall, I said to you yesterday that *all* resources would be at your disposal."

"You did, sir." Tskoulis frowned, "I'm afraid I don't follow. Was there something else?"

"Indeed, Commander." He stacked the papers carefully before looking up at Tskoulis. "As you know, this mission is critically important to City security. I believe it is...only proper that you make use of the City's full complement of resources."

He put his hands behind his back, looked evenly at the commander.

"I would like you to take with you Delta," he said.

* * *

Tskoulis was so taken aback, he almost laughed in the Minister's face.

"Delta, sir?" he managed.

Delta Unit was a legend, the commander thought. For the second time, he wondered if Sokol was fully in his right mind.

Sokol smiled. "As I said, Tskoulis, this is a critically sensitive mission. You presumably understand what Delta...does."

Tskoulis had some idea. Delta were sent out on only the most sensitive of clandestine missions. He'd only known they even existed due to a conversation he'd had once with his superior.

He privately didn't think they were real.

He glanced at Sokol, who was watching him calmly, a hint of amusement in his flat eyes.

"You recall the...incident with Councilman Shaw some years ago?" Sokol said.

Tskoulis did. On the eve of an election, Shaw had been found dead in his apartment. Heart attack, according to the autopsy.

So had all five of his personal guards.

Security footage had shown nothing. There had been possible signs of a struggle: quick and brutal ends, questionable defensive wounds that could have been otherwise sustained, like when one of the guards had apparently fallen through a glass coffee table and landed just right on a sharp bookend that had been sitting there.

Cardiac arrest, times two, but with inconclusive toxicology reports.

Tskoulis couldn't remember the rest of the details. What he did remember was that it was like they had just...died.

Puzzled investigators had finally just blamed it on an over-abundance of carbon monoxide in the man's living quarters.

But there had been whispers within Patrol.

Tskoulis frowned, then glanced up. Sokol was speaking.

"Shaw's...alliances were of concern," Sokol said. "Specifically, Karapartei."

Tskoulis stared at the Minister. "Shaw?" he repeated, incredulous. Shaw had been the cleanest of the Council politicians, per public opinion, by far. Almost prudish by political standards.

"Yes. And with the Onlar, as you now understand them."

The commander watched Sokol warily. The disease. Now this. What more might he have to learn before he got Jossey back and returned to normal life?

He wondered if he even could after this.

"How did those guards die?" he finally asked, not sure he wanted to know the answer.

Sokol smiled. "That," he said, "is exactly why I want you to take one of my finest resources with you."

The Minister had been leaning against the desk; now he stood and beckoned to the darkened corner.

Tskoulis suddenly realized there was someone else in the room.

Sokol said, "Commander Tskoulis, I'd like you to meet Delta."

A tall figure stepped out of the darkness.

For once in his life, Gavin Tskoulis was speechless.

* * *

Caspar smiled coolly at him. "Hello, Tskoulis."

He strapped on one arm plate and glove, then the other, taking his time, glancing up at the commander, grinning a little. His hair was half pulled back as usual; strands framed his face. Long silver eyes glinted with amusement.

He looked like a pirate from one of those old adventure classics, Gavin thought, a little sourly. No wonder Jossey –

The commander cleared his throat, shoving aside the thought. Caspar looked up at him, looking amused.

Delta. Intelligence's whispered-about, officially-disavowed elite unit. Caspar Savaş was their leader.

Of all people.

"Couldn't get rid of me that easily," Caspar said languidly.

Tskoulis stood there, eyeing him, things suddenly clicking into place.

He remembered how Henry had reported to him that Caspar had re-learned things impressively fast, had frightening reflexes. How Henry suspected that Caspar was holding back, but couldn't put his finger on anything in particular.

How Tskoulis himself had called Caspar out on the training floor, making sure the man's sword skills were up to par before letting him train Jossey for the tunnels. How Caspar had seemed strangely calm when Tskoulis had brought a sword to the man's throat.

At the time Tskoulis had chalked it up to surprise.

Savaş probably hadn't flinched, Tskoulis thought now, groaning inwardly, because he didn't want them all to know just how easily he could dodge.

"I see you have met before," Sokol said, a wide smile on his face.

"Yes, sir," Tskoulis muttered.

"It may please you to know that Mr. Savaş was placed in my niece's solar crew unit recently for her safety during working hours."

Tskoulis bristled. "Why?" he asked, wincing internally as he realized how he sounded.

Sokol smiled. "We had received intelligence that the Onlar were looking to capture some of our own in order to undermine our security. Naturally, the solar crew leaders would be a top choice."

"So you sent your most elite agent to protect your niece?" Tskoulis asked flatly.

No wonder Jossey was so angry about status and favoritism. This reeked of it. Tskoulis stared daggers at Caspar.

"Jossey had...been working on some projects for some time that she did not inform her superior about," Sokol said. "Projects that Intelligence found of great interest from a security standpoint. This is not an act of nepotism, although I appreciate how it may appear."

"That 'theoretical solar stuff' you two kept talking about," Tskoulis said to Caspar.

Caspar smiled. Tskoulis did not.

"Well, now that the two of you are working together, let me explain how this needs to go," Sokol said.

The commander glared at Caspar. "You're still one of my agents," he said.

"I'm not, but you're free to believe that," Caspar said calmly. "For the sake of unit integrity, I'm willing to pretend."

"You're an Intelligence agent. Isn't that what you do?"

He saw Caspar flinch, just a little.

But he didn't trust even that. He didn't trust Savaş as far as he could throw him. Which, he thought darkly, he'd really like to try.

"Delta is one of your trackers," Sokol explained. "He is, obviously, unknown to the members of Unit 1. You may refer to him as Tracker, in the same manner as you refer to your colleagues. They need no further identification, nor does he. Do I make myself clear?"

Tskoulis' arms were folded. "Understood, sir. And the other tracker?"

"The other tracker has been otherwise engaged, despite my efforts."

"I see, sir."

"Very good, Commander."

Sokol turned to Caspar, who was currently putting on a mask like the ones Unit 1 had. "Your orders are clear?"

Caspar was adjusting the mask. "Yes, sir."

Tskoulis turned to him. "And what are those orders?" The Tiger's voice was dangerous.

"His orders are not your concern, Tskoulis." Sokol snapped. "Your concern is retrieving my niece, and, should that tunnel system prove to be as we think, mapping it to the best of your ability."

Tskoulis stared down the Minister. "Sir, with all due respect—"

"They are not your concern," Sokol repeated firmly.

For the first time, something terrible occurred to Tskoulis.

If Jossey had indeed been interrogated, had given information to the Onlar, would she become another Councilman Shaw?

Even if she was a Sokol?

The question burned inside him. But if he said anything, he might jeopardize his spot on the mission.

He looked silently at Caspar for a moment, considering. Caspar wasn't looking at either of them, seemed focused on the mask.

If those were indeed Caspar's orders –

Tskoulis kept his face neutral.

"I understand, Minister," he said at last, coldly. "Permission to head out."

81

Eventually Jossey had taken a nap. They didn't seem to need her for anything, and Altan seemed more than happy to just let her sleep, tied soundly to one of the trees. She drifted off, listening to the sound of the water and the chatter of voices.

It was evening when she awoke. Confused, she sat up, immediately restricted by the thick rope around her middle. Then she remembered that in the late fall, the sun set much earlier. They'd always had to cut their shifts – and their pay – short on those days, unless you were brave enough to stay for the latest shuttle bus. She hadn't been.

The Onlar's fires had been lit, and the sparks flew up, joining hundreds of stars above the canyon walls. She looked up. Above what she thought was the eastern canyon wall, she could see what looked like a thick band of stardust, winding overhead. She stared openmouthed at its beauty. She'd never seen stars like this. Not since the night Tark had been taken.

Altan was sitting with Yazar and Erkan by the fire. She let them be, hoping they wouldn't notice she was awake. She wanted a moment to just sit and think. And observe.

The Onlar were clustered around what looked like family fires. She could see Tark with his wife and son, and the old woman he called "Anne." "*Mother.*" Jossey wondered again what had happened.

No matter what Tark said, Jossey didn't believe that it had been simply a case of Jossey "not surviving the journey." The woman had only wanted one of them, she thought.

She watched Tark's smiling face in the firelight. His little boy was beginning to walk, she saw, trying to toddle toward his father. The child had dark eyes like his mother. Again, Jossey's eyes stung, and she turned her head so she wouldn't look at them again.

Altan and Scarface looked over. That was fast, she thought. She sighed, expecting them to tell her to get up, to relocate to another cage of some sort.

But, to her surprise, they walked over with a bowl of food. Real food.

She thanked them, averting her gaze, and tried her best to eat politely.

"Our Bey wants to speak with you," Scarface said. "After dinner."

Jossey looked up. "Your Bey?"

"Yes." He looked almost disappointed. "Don't worry, Patrol. He said speak, not interrogate. Come with us when you have finished."

She went back to her food. Whatever this was, she'd never tasted anything like it in the City.

She finished her food, and waited for them, but they took their time eating, laughing and telling jokes around the fire. Jossey watched them, feeling slightly envious.

She couldn't remember the last time Mother had sat with her, just enjoyed their time together. Or even her cousins.

She looked up at the stars, regretting that she hadn't braved the final night shuttle more often.

Finally, the men finished their food. They got up, wiping their hands, and shuffled over to her.

"Let's go, Patrol," Scarface said. He untied her and pulled her upright, not ungently. Maybe Tark had said something to him, she thought.

The Onlar looked at them as they marched her out of the campsite, some of them jeering. The children were quiet, seeming to know something was going on. She still remembered the little boy who had referred to her as a monster.

She looked over at Tark's fire. He was gone.

The three captors took her further down the canyon. As the lights faded in the distance, she began to feel uneasy. Were they really taking her to speak with Tark?

The stars were even more luminous now. She had to watch where she placed her feet; there were fallen branches here, and the ground was spongy by the river. Altan and Scarface did not slow down, and she found herself stumbling over stones and trying not to aggravate her bad leg.

At last they came to the edge of the river, and stood waiting, Jossey's rope still in Scarface's hands. They were dead silent, the river and the night wind the only sounds she could hear.

She wondered to her horror if they were going to just push her in and leave her.

But a figure stepped out of the darkness.

"Bey," the three said, saluting.

"Let's go," Tark said quietly. He had a bag over one shoulder.

"Go where?" Jossey asked him, hoping she wouldn't be in trouble simply for speaking to him.

His gaze was inscrutable. "To see why I have brought you here, Engineer."

82

THE STARS HAD RISEN ABOVE THE EDGE OF THE CANYON, AND THE river glistened before them.

Tark handed Jossey and his men packs filled with water, and they crossed the river carefully. It was shallower than she'd thought, but she still felt her bad leg give way more than once as she misjudged the rocks. She yelped and grabbed for Tark's arm as she started to fall, but he pulled away. The others gave her suspicious looks.

She flushed and stepped more carefully.

Her eyes were beginning to adjust. She could hear the sound of night birds. It was unfamiliar and eerie, reverberating off the canyon walls.

She shuddered.

They reached the other side of the river, and Tark made sure she did not slip down the muddy bank.

"You're injured, Engineer," he said, sounding unconcerned. "Can you climb?"

"It happened a long time ago. I can climb." She gave him a significant look. He looked away.

To his men, he said, "Let's take the easier way."

The canyon was steep, but they'd left the most vertical part behind them. Here the sides were more like layered hills, triangles jutting out in sections. The climb was difficult, but it was more of a scramble upward. There were plenty of useful handholds along the way.

Jossey was grateful for Gavin's endless training. At least her arms didn't feel like they were going to fall off. Her bad leg was another story, but now was not the time.

Erkan's arm was still recovering, and he climbed even more slowly than Jossey. But unlike Jossey, he showed absolutely nothing on his face. She watched him, impressed.

They crept up over the edge of the canyon.

"Where – "

Tark silenced her with a look.

He turned to his men. "Are they ready?"

Are what ready?

"Yes, Bey," said Erkan.

"Good."

Erkan asked something in the Old Language that Jossey didn't quite catch. He glanced at Jossey.

In reply, Tark held up something that looked like a wrist gauge.

Erkan smiled. "Anladım, Bey." *Understood, sir.*

"Go on ahead."

Erkan saluted and jogged off.

There was what looked like the remains of a road to their immediate right, following the edge of the gorge. Tark jerked his head in that direction. Erkan was already far ahead of them. Jossey and the others followed Tark, single file.

"Have you ever driven a vehicle, Engineer?" Tark asked offhandedly.

"A couple of times, yes." She'd used those little electric Patrol bikes that they let the crew leaders use when they had to make emergency repairs. "Why?"

He grinned crookedly. "Good. These are...well, try not to fall."

"What?"

She glanced at him. He looked strangely amused.

She had a sudden memory of one of those career-day fairs in the City Square, where Patrol brought some of their electric vehicles and took the kids on rides. Tark and Gavin had waited about eight turns each.

She'd ridden just once.

She'd fallen off.

Her cheeks burned. He actually remembered that? She turned away so he wouldn't see her expression. In some ways he was still very much the old Tark, she thought, trying not to smile.

Maybe ten minutes later, they stepped onto what looked like it had once been a highway. The asphalt was old and crumbling underfoot. Tark took a sharp turn to the right, headed toward the ruins of an old village.

The houses all had orange-red roofs – those that were still standing, anyway. Some looked like they'd been heavily bombed in the early wars. The others had just crumbled due to the weather, she supposed. A few near the edge of the city were still relatively intact.

"This was the village of Ilara," Tark said somberly. He gestured toward one of the houses. "And these – are what our military left us."

Erkan had come out of one of the houses. Five motorcycles, painted a matte black, were sitting there. Unlike the metal antennas on the rooftops, they did not gleam in the faint light. It was like they'd been painted specifically to blend into the darkness.

She stared. "Where – "

"Kudret had a point," Tark said, almost spitting the man's name. "Your education was...lacking, Engineer."

He gestured to the bikes. "Ladies first."

She went forward and carefully sat on one of the bikes. It was electric, she saw. Like the Patrol bikes, but this one was both clearly older and clearly better designed. Tark handed her a helmet, showed her how to turn on the bike, how to steer, how to accelerate, how to brake. "Take a few turns," he said.

Glancing at his men, he said, "And just in case you get any ideas – "

He tapped a code into his wrist gauge. Her bike's screen went instantly dark, the engine silent.

"I don't recommend you try to run," he said.

Jossey shivered. For a moment she forgot he was her brother.

And maybe he'd forgotten she was his sister.

"Yes, understood," she said.

"Good. Take it for a test drive."

She saluted, not sure what else to do and feeling silly, but he reminded her so much of Tskoulis at that moment that the movement was almost automatic. She ignored the strange looks Tark's men were giving her and turned on the bike, feeling the slight hum of the engine, marveling at the near-silence. What a beautiful machine. She wondered how they generated the electricity to charge it, but glancing up at the roof of the house, she saw a modified solar panel.

"How far is too far?" she asked.

"Go with Altan," Tark said.

Altan saluted and hopped on the bike next to hers.

She stood astride the bike and looked at her brother through the helmet. "Why don't you use these all the time?" she asked.

Tark grinned. "That, Engineer, is not your business."

Jossey flipped down the visor. She carefully nosed the bike away from the Onlar and twisted the throttle.

The bike shot forward. She jumped and stomped on the

brake. The machine lurched to a stop. She continued forward, knocking the wind out of herself. She sat, gasping.

"Wow," was all she said.

They stood silently, watching her. She tried again, more carefully this time.

The bike smoothly pulled away.

The air rushing past cut all sound, but she realized she had a com as she heard Tark's voice in her ear. "Careful when you turn," he said sharply. She jumped.

"Got it," she said.

Altan was right behind her, far enough that if she wiped out he should have time to adjust.

She got to the end of the road and made a wide turn, then, realizing it was easier to balance than she'd thought, made a couple more.

This was *fun*.

She made one more sweeping turn, sped up as she approached Tark and the others, hit the brakes. She skidded to a stop, grinning ear to ear.

Tark was smiling a little. He turned to his men. "Good enough. Let's go."

To her, he said, "These things have a range of about a hundred miles. We can get there and back, probably twice over, but let's not take any chances. We *must not* be seen. Even you, Engineer. If you're seen, you're probably dead, do you understand me?"

Seen by what? Or who? Jossey wondered.

"Okay," she finally said.

"Ready?"

She wasn't. But she flipped the visor down and turned on the bike.

. . .

They tore across the landscape, nearly silent, as if on wings. The wind rushed past Jossey's helmet. She could hear nothing, see nothing but the landscape flying past and Tark's bike a few lengths ahead of hers. She concentrated on keeping her bike steady. Forty miles per hour. Forty-five. If she turned too quickly –

Tark glanced over his shoulder at her, and she wanted to give him a thumbs-up, but was terrified to take her hands off the handlebars. Instead, she waited until she heard his familiar voice in her helmet – how strange it was, still, to hear his voice!

"You all set?" he asked.

"Fine," she said shortly, eyes on the road ahead.

They banked a little to the left, crossing over into the fields. To the right were the beginnings of hills, rugged under the starlight. Then another bank to the right, and they headed almost straight north.

Tark gestured to the left. She could see a fork in the highway up ahead.

Here and there were scattered bits of metal that might have once been vehicles, the old fossil-fuel type. Some lay rusted in the ditches. She'd heard from Gavin there were military vehicles abandoned near Gurime, where the Onlar's canyons began to the northeast of the City. People had fled the region however they could once the wars had begun.

She'd always wondered why the Founders had chosen to come here, when everyone else was running away.

They took the left fork. Tark slowed his bike, waved for her to do so.

"Be prepared to stop and dismount," he said into her com.

"Altan, Yazar, weapons," he added. "Erkan, be prepared to clear the area if needed."

She heard nothing further, but assumed they had responded.

Tark held up a hand. They all slowed, Jossey carefully easing off the accelerator before applying the brake. She winced as the bike jerkily slowed down. Tark seemed to be pretending not to notice.

They pulled slowly into a ruined village square. Jossey knew there were small towns in the region, but she hadn't realized just how many. She looked around, fascinated. Empty buildings, windows cracked and signs destroyed, towered over her, electric poles downed, the wires snapped and fraying in the weeds. She guessed this place had once had around a thousand people.

They parked the bikes in the shadow of one of the alleyways, and the Onlar pulled forearm sheaths out of the storage compartments. They strapped them on silently.

They took the coms out of the helmets and placed them in their ears. Jossey followed suit.

Tark looked at her silently for a long moment. "Stay behind me," he said at last. "Don't try to run."

Jossey almost laughed. "Where would I run?" she asked.

Tark gave her a crooked smile.

The highway to the east was strange, grayish, under the starlight. They took it on foot. Almost immediately they left the road and fanned out into the field. When Jossey began to ask what they were doing, Tark muttered into her com, "This is so they can't see us coming up the road."

Who? Jossey thought.

There was a ridge to their left. Tark led them toward it.

Jossey was glad she had water, and that it was late autumn, as they began to climb. She was not prepared for this, she thought. She had no idea where Tark was taking her, and she'd just been walking for two days.

There was a hint of amusement in her brother's voice as he said, "Only a few miles, Engineer."

She huffed and kept going.

Wherever they were going, this did not seem like the most efficient way to get there. But maybe, Jossey thought, that was the point.

Below them, to the right, she could see the glint of roof antennas in another ruined village. To her surprise, she could see lights in some of the houses.

She pointed them out to the others. Tark's expression was grim.

"Yes, there are people there," he said quietly.

"But – " She gaped. "How?"

"Keep silent from here," he said. "Sound carries."

She clamped her mouth shut. If the Onlar were afraid of whatever was out there...

And she had no weapon. They'd made sure of that.

She kept climbing.

After what felt like several hours, she looked up to see an enormous bulk rising out of the ground.

Tark started climbing. She looked in dismay at it.

He turned, beckoned to her. She glanced at him, at his men's metal claws. If it were just Tark, she'd protest, probably whine if she were being honest, make him let her rest for a few minutes. But –

She set her jaw and climbed.

The stone was lumpy, uneven. It took every ounce of her strength to traverse some spots on her bad leg. She refused to make a scene, let them know she was in any pain. She drank another of her water canteens, and continued.

The path was hard to see in the starlight, and more than once she barely caught herself. The men looked impatient, and she scrambled to keep up with Tark.

They reached the top at last, and she turned around to see

how far they'd come. From up here, she realized with wonder, she could see for miles. There was the village with its few out-of-place lights, a village that otherwise had probably not been inhabited in centuries. And the way they were heading –

One of the Onlar prodded her, lightly, with a claw, and she jumped.

It was Altan. Of course, she thought sourly. He jerked his head, as if to say "Turn around."

She turned slowly. There was a strange glow on the horizon.

She followed Tark, feet dragging a little, up to the top of the ridge. Whatever it was they wanted her to see, had dragged her for miles at night across strange ground to see, she wasn't sure *she* wanted to know.

Then Tark dropped to the ground and tugged on her sleeve. "Get down," he hissed.

She complied, and looked, her mouth dropping open as she saw what was on the plain before her.

83

SHE'D NEVER SEEN ANYTHING LIKE IT.

Lights flared around the edge of what looked like an enormous combination solar and condenser farm, easily six times the size of the biggest one she'd worked on near the City. It filled the entire valley. What looked like an electrified fence formed a perimeter. Inside –

She blinked, rubbed her eyes. Tark wordlessly handed her a pair of the Onlar's goggles.

She put them on. He adjusted them for her. They were night-vision, adjustable zoom. As she tweaked the zoom, it occurred to her that the bright green effect the Onlar used was designed to inspire fear. Because she could see just fine with it off.

She wished she couldn't.

She was looking at rows upon rows of what appeared to be plants. Guards, wearing Patrol uniforms, walked up and down the rows, some kind of weapon slung over their shoulders. People were picking the vegetables and sorting them into bins, nonstop.

But they weren't just people.

They were children.

She looked in increasing horror. The children seemed to range in age from five to about twelve. They worked mechanically, stooped, at least a dozen of them per row. She could see the unnatural bend in their backs as they crouched.

One child, maybe five years old, was crying, sitting back, apparently refusing to pick. A giant Patrol agent stopped before him, shouted some harsh words that Jossey couldn't make out. The man stomped on the ground before the child, gesturing wildly with huge arms. The child jumped, stared at the man in terror, went back to picking the vegetables, face pinched in misery. The child's young neighbor, a girl, flinched and picked faster, looking away.

Jossey took off the goggles and stared at Tark in open-mouthed horror. He was looking at her seriously.

"What – " she finally managed under her breath. "What is this place?"

"This," Tark said quietly, "is why I did not return."

Jossey shook her head, tears threatening. "No, Tark. How – "

She shut her mouth and looked at him. His name had slipped out. Tark's men looked at him in confusion.

He shook his head, just slightly.

"This is what your people have done to mine," he said to her.

"But these must be – this must be a mistake," she said helplessly. "You said the City was dying, maybe this is their way of–"

She racked her brain, trying to make sense of what she was seeing. "Uncle Sokol told me that we were having issues with the electricity, so maybe they're expanding so they don't have to use the grow lights as much – "

The words didn't make sense, even to her. And they didn't explain the children, but her mind could only take in so much at once. She shut her eyes, turning away from the scene below her,

401

trying to unsee the small child's face as the enormous man stomped on the ground and screamed at him. The numbness on his neighbor's young face.

"Jossey."

Tark's voice was very quiet and very serious. She opened her eyes and looked at him.

"Jossey, there are no grow lights."

84

The group headed back down the ridge silently. Tark's men were still looking at him, confusion written on their faces. He did not give them an explanation.

Jossey followed him, still stunned, trying not to trip on the rocks and half not caring if she did. She was trying to comprehend what she'd just seen.

Were those –

The children couldn't have been from the City. There'd have been riots, she thought. So –

Realization hit her like a hammer blow. Those were Onlar children, she thought.

She made a small sound and froze in her tracks. Tark turned around. She looked at them all, their claws, taking in their ragged armor when compared with Patrol's. The aged motorcycles they were using were probably the only ones they had.

She began to weep silently, making no attempt to hide the tears. The men shifted awkwardly.

She walked past them and staggered down the hill toward the ridge, in the direction they'd come.

Tark took her arm. "Jossey," he whispered. His men were

watching him warily again. He ignored them. "Do you under-stand now?" he asked.

"Have there ever been grow lights?" she asked him, face wet with tears.

He slowly shook his head.

85

GAVIN TAPPED HIS MASK IMPATIENTLY AGAINST HIS KNEE. CASPAR was late. After everything, Savaş was late.

They'd gotten a late start, and now Caspar was doing...whatever. Gavin didn't care what it was. He just knew that he wanted to throttle the man. If he had his way, Gavin thought darkly, Savaş would be sitting here in the City until they got back, Delta or no.

He wasn't sure exactly why he hated the man so much. Maybe it was the infuriating smile. Or the way Jossey lit up when she talked to him.

Gavin had taken the liberty of checking Savaş's Patrol records while waiting for the "tracker" to appear, curious as to what Delta's history would look like.

There was absolutely nothing out of the ordinary.

Caspar Savaş, born [REDACTED], eyes light gray, hair dark, identifying marks none. Patrol Service: apprenticed to Unit 3, call-up duty 3 years. Engineer school. Solar crew 35, service 6 months.

Patrol Unit 2-5.

All things Gavin knew already.

Savaş's record had been, in fact, entirely ordinary, featureless, if somewhat impressive in terms of the number of things he'd done, until Gavin had dug further, and found that there was no civilian birth record for a Caspar Savaş.

The Engineer school had no record of Savaş on file beyond the standard graduation certificate. No enrollment. No housing records. No transcript.

In fact, the surname Savaş didn't appear to exist at all.

Savaş. In the Old Language it meant war. Appropriate, thought Gavin.

Gavin would probably get in trouble with Sokol for meddling with the system, but he felt it was his right to know. Right now he didn't care much what Sokol thought, either. It was mission-related, and he hadn't broken any laws.

He tapped his mask impatiently.

He heard footsteps and turned. Caspar was there, dressed in the slightly ill-fitting outfit of an auxiliary Patrol tracker, equipment and all, his face concealed except for his eyes and mouth. His dark hair was still pulled back into a half-ponytail.

Tskoulis almost laughed. Longer hair wasn't that unusual, but there weren't a lot of men on Patrol with both that hairstyle and that build.

Not a great job of being secretive, he thought.

Then again –

His eyebrows went up as Caspar approached the group. The way the "tracker" was carrying himself, he appeared to be an entirely different person. He walked differently, seeming nervous, fidgety, almost clumsy; he was glancing from one member of the team to the other. He was even dangling his assigned equipment bag in one hand as if he had no idea what to do with it.

Just as one faced with the near-legendary members of Unit 1 would be expected to act.

Tskoulis smiled crookedly. The man seemed very good at what he did, he had to admit.

406

"You're late, Tracker," he said.

The others turned, briefly acknowledged the newcomer.

Caspar saluted. "Very sorry, Commander," he said. "I had to be outfitted. I'm ready to go."

Excellent reply too, thought Tskoulis sourly. "Understood," was all he said, donning his mask. To the others, he said, "Move out."

The six men climbed out of the service exit. One of the silent Patrol aboveground vehicles was waiting for them.

The night was almost cool. Tskoulis looked around as they headed for the vehicle. He'd gone over the supplies twice, three times. He counted off the men. Everything was in place.

"Radio check," he said quietly.

"Alpha." "Gamma." "Phi." They went down the list. At the end, Caspar raised his to his lips. He glanced at Tskoulis.

"Tracker," he said.

Tskoulis glanced at his wrist gauge.

They'd gotten a very late start, due in large part to whatever had held Caspar back. Tskoulis knew he had no way to ask at this point, probably had something to do with Sokol, but he was not happy. He'd hoped to leave by the afternoon, get into the tunnels before nightfall.

At least this time they could be somewhat more confident that there hadn't been any change in the roads. They should be able to cut through Uchisar and go straight to Asmalih in their vehicle, rather than deal with the potential snake's pit of ruins that was much of the old city.

Tskoulis climbed into the driver's seat and started the engine.

. . .

As they crawled through Uchisar and on to Gurime, Tskoulis got a spine-tingling feeling.

"Eyes," he said.

Alpha and Rho looked out the windows as they went.

"Two on the left," Alpha rumbled.

Tskoulis kept driving. "How far?"

"Eight o'clock, on foot. Probably can't catch us."

"Keep an eye out. They seem to have some way of communicating with each other."

Coms, Tskoulis thought, but didn't say it aloud. He didn't know what Unit 1 knew about the Onlar, didn't really want Sokol to come down on him for telling them the wrong thing.

As for Caspar, Tskoulis had a good guess what *he* knew.

He kept his eyes on the road.

They had just entered Asmalih. Here there was a steep S-curve that required Tskoulis to slow to barely fifteen miles per hour, not something he preferred to do at night. Just before the curve there were towers upon towers of rock, with caves in the side, and a steep drop to the canyon below.

A great place for an ambush.

"Eyes," Tskoulis gritted out.

They were slowing down, approaching the curve, when he saw something in the road ahead.

A rockslide?

He stopped the vehicle.

"Sir?" Alpha said. "What's going on?"

Tskoulis frowned. "I'm not sure. Cover me. Gamma, Phi, stay with the vehicle."

He got out, listened carefully. The night was silent.

Caspar had gotten out of the vehicle too. "Too quiet," he muttered when Alpha wasn't nearby. "Something seems wrong."

For once, Tskoulis agreed with him.

A large piece of rock looked to have fallen onto the road

ahead. It was half the size of a car. Debris surrounded it. Tskoulis glanced up at the cliffs.

Fallen, or been pushed.

He looked at the road, calculating. They were about two miles from their destination, give or take, and then there was the canyon to navigate. If there were Onlar out here other than the two Alpha had seen, if this was a trap –

If there were Onlar, Patrol was probably in big trouble.

He glanced at Caspar, muttering, "Whatever Sokol told you, this is no time to just be a tracker, got it?"

Caspar didn't respond, but Tskoulis could see the half-concealed knife strapped to his side.

His lips quirked. As far as he knew, trackers didn't normally carry weapons.

He turned back to the vehicle and waved the men out. They strapped on their equipment bags. No point in using the vehicle now.

Alpha turned off the engine and tossed Tskoulis the keys. He caught them mid-air.

"Fan out," Tskoulis said quietly. "If they come at us, run. That's an order. The numbers are probably not in our favor here. That canyon is our priority. Not fighting the Onlar. Unless they follow us in."

"Sir," they said.

"Move out."

They were inching past the base of the houses when the howling began.

86

Tskoulis looked up sharply. He only heard that noise when They traveled in groups. Large groups.

"Run!" he shouted.

The Patrol agents raced down the cobblestoned road.

Green spots flared in the cave dwellings all around them. Tskoulis counted them – ten sets, twelve.

The Onlar streamed out of the houses and began to descend to the road. Below, he could see another three or four ascending from the valley below, walking abreast in the road, long claws out like enormous knives.

He dropped his bag and drew his sword.

Gamma and Phi grinned at each other, and took off into the fray. Alpha had already engaged a couple of Onlar nearby, and Rho, the biggest of the unit and the most heavily armored, made a sound that might have been a roar, stepping toward the largest Onlar.

Tskoulis smiled for half a second. Good.

He blocked the closest Onlar's swipes and stepped forward,

elbowing the creature in the face. It went down, wheezing. He dispatched it with a single stab and looked up, dodging just in time as another one sliced toward his neck.

He took a step backward and watched as Rho threw down his sword and got into a brawling match with one of the Onlar, armed only with a knife.

He shook his head, laughing. So this was Unit 1. He suddenly felt less concerned. This might actually be –

His laughter died as another ten Onlar appeared from somewhere. Patrol was hugely outnumbered.

He looked around for his men.

Caspar was gone.

An Onlar rushed Tskoulis, and he shoved aside its claws with an armored forearm, kicking it solidly in the chest. Where was Savaş? he thought, furious. Was he dead? Had he actually –

Tskoulis had no time to think further. There were now more than twenty Onlar against five men, streaming in groups toward them. Their strategy seemed to be to isolate the Patrol agents and take them down one at a time. Tskoulis looked around, shouting, "Alpha! Gamma! To me!"

The Onlar's claws were easier to maneuver than a sword, and they had two sets each. That made them particularly dangerous from behind. Patrol might be better off if they stayed in a tight group.

Rho had ended his brawl, which had not gone well for the Onlar, and grabbed his sword again. He was fighting another two Onlar at once. Tskoulis watched for half a second before he was forced to dodge a side-swipe from a huge set of claws.

As he moved, Tskoulis saw something strange over Rho's shoulder.

Several of the Onlar had climbed up on a ledge behind their battling companions, seemingly waiting to join the fray.

One began to sway strangely, its green lights tilting, and fell silently off the ledge.

Tskoulis squinted, half-distractedly blocking a blow from the Onlar in front of him. Had it just –

Then he saw something that made him stare.

Caspar appeared out of the darkness.

He moved silently, a curved knife in one hand, moving along the ledge toward the second creature.

Tskoulis cut viciously with his sword at the Onlar ahead of him, which backed off, snarling. This he wanted to see.

The Onlar next to Caspar turned.

Tskoulis had never seen anyone move so fast. Caspar grabbed the Onlar's forearm, twisted it outward, and stabbed between the Onlar's armor so precisely that Tskoulis blinked in shock.

The three remaining Onlar turned. The one nearest Caspar lunged at him, hissing angrily, claws extended.

Caspar dodged. But the Onlar swiped with its other hand, its claws hitting the knife, which flew from Caspar's hand and landed on the ledge between them.

Tskoulis shouted Caspar's name and smashed his current enemy out of the way. As far as he knew, that was the only weapon Savaş had. And he couldn't let the man die.

Caspar only smiled, silver eyes narrowed as he focused on the Onlar. He didn't even bother to look at the knife.

* * *

As Tskoulis watched, Caspar walked casually straight into the Onlar's slicing range. It stabbed toward him with its claws.

In what looked like a single fluid movement, Caspar dodged behind the Onlar, wrenched its right arm backward, then stomped the creature hard in the back of the ankle, adding a vicious blow to the side of the head with his elbow.

The Onlar dropped and lay there. Caspar scooped up his knife.

The fourth ran at him, howling. Caspar ducked underneath the claws, slicing diagonally upward across the Onlar's legs as he rose. The creature staggered. Caspar stood and shoved the creature's left wrist upward against the wall, tossing the knife to his left hand and slicing sideways so fast across the creature's throat, almost surgically precise, that Tskoulis wasn't sure the Onlar had realized what had happened until Caspar kicked its foot out from under it.

The Onlar sank back against the wall and to the ground.

Tskoulis stared openmouthed. It had been less than a minute, and four Onlar were down. One without using a weapon.

Three had even had time to prepare.

The remaining Onlar took one look and fled.

Caspar glanced down at the Onlar next to him, a flicker of something on his face, before he set his jaw, turned, and hurled his knife into the darkness after the fifth Onlar. There was a cry and a thud.

Caspar barely glanced at Tskoulis and went after his knife.

Tskoulis shook his head to clear it. He nearly missed dodging the claws of the Onlar in front of him.

He swiped with his sword. The creature hissed angrily. He was still trying to process what he had just witnessed.

He had just seen Savaş cut down an entire line of Onlar. Five of them, all heavily armed.

On a thin ledge. In the dark. With a knife and his bare hands.

The commander had never seen anything like it.

"Thanks, Sokol," Tskoulis muttered.

* * *

They regrouped at the rocks. Caspar had vanished, which didn't surprise Tskoulis.

The commander glanced over at the ledge. Even in the dimness, he could see that the Onlar were gone. No blood. No trace. Just gone.

He felt a chill.

Rho was wounded. Alpha clapped him on the back and said, "You've got to stop leaving your sword in the grass, Rho, doesn't matter if you prefer brawling. This always happens when you do that."

Rho was grinning as he bound the slice on his arm. "Ehh. No big deal. It's so much more fun," he said. "Besides, I have armor."

Tskoulis raised an eyebrow.

"Where's the tracker?" Phi asked.

"Probably hiding," Gamma laughed. "Not sure why Sokol sent him with us."

Tskoulis almost snorted. If they only knew. But he remembered Sokol's orders. "At least he's probably good at tracking," he said with a grin.

Phi frowned, glancing around. "Am I wrong, or were there more Onlar? Like, a bunch more?"

Tskoulis shrugged. "Maybe they ran. I've never seen someone flat out brawl with an Onlar before." He laughed and slapped Rho on the shoulder. Rho grinned.

Or maybe they tried to run, he thought. He still couldn't get the image out of his head. After the knife throw, he'd seen the occasional green lights just disappear. Vanish from the perimeter of the fight, one at a time. He didn't know for sure it was Caspar. But he assumed.

As far as Tskoulis could tell, none of the other Patrol had seen Caspar in action. It was better, he thought, that they didn't.

He wondered if he himself should have. He remembered Sokol's voice: *"You presumably understand what Delta...does."*

He did now.

"Yeah, but I thought I saw at least – " Phi was saying, scratching his head.

Tskoulis snapped back to the present.

While they were debating, Caspar appeared from somewhere, looking appropriately shaken.

The Unit 1 men glanced at him, looking less than impressed.

"You okay, Tracker?" Rho asked, snickering a little.

"I'm okay." The Tracker half-smiled. "Got any extra weapons?" he asked. "I wasn't quite expecting that."

Alpha snorted, turned it into a cough. "Guess we should have armed you, sorry." He turned to Tskoulis. "Commander, can we give him something, uh, useful?"

Tskoulis glanced at Caspar, trying his best to keep a straight face. Caspar looked expectantly at him.

"Would, say, a knife make you feel better?" Tskoulis asked at last, carefully.

Caspar said, "A knife sounds great, thanks."

"Well," Alpha said magnanimously, "if we're out here long enough, maybe I'll show you how to fight."

Tskoulis bit the inside of his lip so hard he tasted blood.

Caspar glanced at Tskoulis, keeping a much better straight face than the commander was currently doing.

"Thanks," was all he said. "I'd like that."

87

IT WAS TWO MILES TO THE CANYON. THEY DID NOT MEET WITH further resistance. Maybe, Tskoulis thought, they'd gotten rid of all of it.

He wasn't convinced.

They paused for a long time at the entrance, watching silently, waiting for any hint of movement.

The night birds were singing. They took that as their cue that it was safe.

"How come the night birds don't stop singing when *we're* around?" grumbled Rho. "We're dangerous."

"We're human," Gamma said, looking at Rho as if he were stupid.

Tskoulis listened to them bicker. They were like 2-5, but much more skilled. He almost smiled. But it was an interesting point.

Caspar was walking beside him. Tskoulis glanced sideways at the man.

"What kind of training does one need to become a...tracker?" he finally asked, hoping Caspar would get the hint.

Caspar smiled. "Learning to be a tracker takes years," he said.

"I was specially trained. They noticed my aptitude back when I was an apprentice."

"And pulled you."

"Yes," Caspar said quietly.

"Did you want to become a tracker?" Tskoulis finally asked. The conversation was very unlike him, at least out of context, but he was curious.

Caspar glanced at him. "I don't know."

They made it to the end of the canyon with no further incident, and slipped into the cave.

88

THE AGENTS STOOD IN THE CAVE, THE ONLY SOUNDS IN THE darkness their breathing and their footsteps in the dirt.

"This seems too easy, Commander," Alpha said quietly. "Are you sure we weren't followed?"

Tskoulis turned on his red light. The others followed suit. "Phi, you stay here, keep an eye on the exit. If you see any movement at all, use the com, understand?"

"Yes, sir."

Tskoulis remembered the wolf that had attacked them the last time. "Watch out for wildlife too," he said.

"Sir?"

"Wolves. Desert cats. We were attacked last time."

Phi shivered. "Yes, sir."

"The rest of you, with me," Tskoulis said. "Tracker, Gamma, I need both of your eyes here."

Gamma glanced sideways at the supposed tracker, looking skeptical. Tskoulis hoped Caspar was as good an actor as he seemed.

One by one, they slipped into the tunnel at the back of the cave.

Alpha seemed impressed. "How old do you think this is?" he whispered.

"I have no idea," Tskoulis said truthfully. "Given the script I found on the wall, probably long before the Founders. *Long* before."

They turned up their safety lights, and pressed on into the gloom.

It was about twenty minutes, as before, when they came to the large open space he and Pricey had found.

Also as before, it smelled terrible. They cleared the chamber. Tskoulis noticed Gamma was making a small map as they went.

The commander glanced at Caspar. He was checking the ground, deep in concentration.

"I've seen something like this in the OS1," Gamma remarked quietly as they came to the tunnels at the end. "I wonder where that other one goes." He ran his gloved fingers over the carved word. "Ne – " Tskoulis could imagine his forehead furrowing behind the mask. "This is the tunnel Sokol thinks leads to the OS2?"

"Correct."

Gamma made a note on his map. "Wow."

Tskoulis spoke quietly into his com. "Phi. Come in, Phi."

A crackle. "Yes, Commander."

"Anything?"

"No, sir."

Tskoulis smiled grimly. "Good. Permission to rejoin."

They sat and waited for Phi.

Caspar seemed restless. He was examining the ground around the tunnels. He went a few feet into the Nevşehir-marked branch and ran his hand along the walls, taking his time, shining the light over them.

Tskoulis finally looked over and lightly tossed a piece of rock his way. "What are you doing, Tracker?"

Caspar didn't seem to notice the rock. He had stopped and was standing very still, looking at something in his hand. "Commander," he said slowly. "Did you say you found blood last time?"

"Yes." Tskoulis frowned. "Not a lot. We think the wolf scared them, made them run, opened the Onlar's wound. Why?"

"I'm not sure it was from the Onlar," Caspar said.

"What do you – " Tskoulis got to his feet.

Caspar was holding up something small and tan, stained with brown. "This was caught on the side of the tunnel. Around waist height. Looks like they were in a hurry."

They clustered around. It was a small bit of rope.

It was almost completely stained with blood.

Caspar's face was pale. He and Tskoulis glanced at each other.

"Phi." Tskoulis gritted into the com. "Phi, where are you?"

Silence. Then a crackle. "On my way, sir."

"Well, hurry up. We don't have all night." He was trying to stay calm.

"Yes, sir."

Quick footsteps, and Phi entered the cavern.

"There you are," Tskoulis said darkly.

"Sir?" Phi looked confused.

Alpha glanced at Phi and shook his head.

Tskoulis grabbed his pack from the ground. "Ready?"

He didn't wait for an answer. He took off, Caspar close behind.

. . .

420

The tunnel seemed to get narrower as they went. It was hard to see if there was any more blood, since they were using red lights. But Caspar and Gamma both found drops here and there, seeming to get worse as they went on. They were spaced fairly far apart, but that didn't make Tskoulis feel any better.

And these tunnels. He didn't understand how people could have used these in ancient times. They were so close in, so inky black, he felt like he was suffocating. Nothing like the spacious City tunnels. Or even the OS tunnels. They almost had to go single file here.

He didn't know how the Onlar would have carried an extra person without bumping into the walls.

Indeed, Caspar had found spots where something, maybe a wooden stretcher, had scraped the walls. He was good at this, Tskoulis thought. It was with relief this time rather than annoyance.

It was unclear what the marks were from. But everywhere there was a scrape, they found spots of blood on the ground.

Tskoulis forged ahead into the blackness.

89

AFTER WHAT SEEMED LIKE HOURS, THE TUNNEL OPENED UP INTO A cavern. It was empty, but Tskoulis smelled something odd. Faintly sharp.

"Is that – "

"Ashes," Gamma confirmed. He pointed to a small fire pit in the center of the cavern. The top was grayish.

Gamma held his hand over the ashes, stirred them with a stick. A light substance flew into the air. He pointed to a small piece of bone. "Looks like they had a meal. Bird, maybe. I'm not an expert, but these ashes don't look fresh."

Fire was not generally used, even among Patrol, unless they were stuck aboveground at night, and even then they tended to eat preserved food rather than draw attention with the firelight. It was only really used in emergencies.

Caspar smiled a little. "Two days, give or take," he said.

Tskoulis wondered how he knew, but didn't ask.

Caspar waved to Gamma, who looked annoyed, but wandered over. "What do you make of this?" Caspar asked.

There were greenish threads on the ground, mixed in with bits of rope. It looked like it had caught on the fabric.

"A blanket," Gamma said, frowning. "Wait, a blanket?"

Tskoulis could picture the thoughts whirling through his mind.

"Are you sure," Gamma said slowly, "that Agent Sokol was taken by Onlar?"

Tskoulis looked at the threads. They weren't from a Patrol uniform, that was clear. He glanced at Caspar.

"Maybe from her equipment bag," Caspar said. "Commander, does your unit take that type of supply out into the field?" He looked directly at Tskoulis.

"On occasion," Tskoulis said, straight-faced.

They could deal with this all later, if they ever found Jossey, Tskoulis thought. For now, he preferred to stay on Minister Sokol's good side.

Caspar looked satisfied.

So did Gamma.

"Looks like they stayed here for some time," Gamma said. "If she had a blanket, I would guess overnight. They might not be far if they stayed here that long. Especially if one of the party was wounded."

They only found a few more dark spots, by the campfire. Nothing by the blanket. Probably only the Onlar had been injured. Tskoulis felt a wave of relief, and glanced at Caspar, who seemed to be thinking the same thing.

"Let's move on," Tskoulis said. "They still have a two-day head start on us. If one of them is badly wounded, maybe a lot less."

Alpha cleared his throat, glancing at his unit. "Sir," he said. "Might it make sense to stay here for now?"

The Tiger gave him a look.

"Go on," he said, not wanting to hear whatever Alpha had to say, but knowing the man probably had a point.

"We've been traveling for several hours, sir. Rho is injured."

Rho looked offended. Alpha continued. "More importantly,

this place clearly has good enough ventilation that we can build a fire. And as you said, if one of their party is injured, we likely have some time. Besides – " he grinned. "It's probably three of them versus all of us."

Tskoulis thought. Then he said, "All right. Rho, put something on that arm."

They'd dug around a bit and figured out how the Onlar might have been able to build a fire so easily. There was a hidden stash of wood. It was quite extensive, so much so that Gamma made a note.

"They must use this place often," he said to the others. "No other reason to drag so much all the way down here."

"Either that, or there's an easy access to the surface from here," Caspar said.

Tskoulis grinned. Savaş really was playing the part of Tracker well. Or not playing. Either way, it was a welcome development.

The men built a small fire, sufficient to make their food a little more edible, and set a rotating watch. Tskoulis was itching to get going, no matter what time it was or who was injured, but Alpha did have a point.

They sat and ate, talked a little, mostly stared into the fire. Rho applied something unpleasant-looking to his wound. Alpha took the first watch, followed by Rho.

Eventually, lulled by the crackling of the wood and the low conversation Gamma and Alpha were having, Tskoulis lost the battle with sleep. He drifted off, one hand next to his sword.

Just in case.

90

TSKOULIS SNAPPED AWAKE AS A PIECE OF WOOD POPPED LOUDLY, showering the now-orange coal base with golden sparks. He sat up, looking around, wondering how long he'd been out. Phi was on watch, and had set himself across the chamber. He was facing away from them.

Caspar was awake, staring into the flames. He'd peeled up his mask, the orange glow illuminating his features. He stirred the coals.

Tskoulis propped himself on an elbow and turned to look at Caspar. He had an entirely different view of the man now. Still annoying, but intensely capable. Frightening.

And changeable. Right now he was the Tracker. Tskoulis suspected the others hadn't put him on watch for that reason. He was surprised Caspar had even removed his mask, but figured that wasn't his business. Caspar could take care of his own identity, he thought.

Caspar glanced at him. "You're awake," he said very quietly.

Tskoulis sat up and went to join him by the fire. It was warm, and he held his hands out. He wasn't used to feeling warmth as a positive thing. But these tunnels were chilly at night.

"Can't sleep?" he said.

Caspar shook his head, prodding at the coals.

Tskoulis watched them for a while in silence. They were beautiful. The pieces at the base would furl and bloom at the ends like tiny golden flowers, then shatter and fall and crackle into a sea of molten orange.

It helped him think.

Which he needed, because something was bothering him.

He turned to Caspar at last, glanced at Phi, who was far away and probably not paying attention.

"Savaş."

Caspar glanced at him.

"Sokol said you were assigned to protect Jossey, and I've seen what you can do," Tskoulis said under his breath. "Now that I know – in the tunnels, when Jossey was wounded. Nearly died. Why didn't you protect her then?"

There was a very long silence. Caspar didn't look at him, kept stirring the coals, a frown appearing between his eyes.

"She came out of nowhere," he said at last. "The Onlar was injured, and we didn't have weapons, and I was trying to think of a way to fight it without revealing myself. I didn't expect her to take the Onlar on, not by herself. I didn't have time to stop her." He seemed to be looking inward. "I thought she – "

For a moment something flickered across his face. Pain.

Tskoulis glared at him. "You thought you'd failed your job."

Caspar looked up, long silver eyes watchful. "Yes."

The fire crackled loudly, and Phi turned around. Caspar reached up and smoothly pulled down his mask.

"It's not a job for me," Tskoulis said finally. "I made a promise."

Caspar looked at him sharply.

"To her brother," Tskoulis hastily added. "A long time ago."

Caspar smiled a little. "Now I remember. You told me. At the hospital."

Tskoulis looked straight at the masked agent. "Is it still your job to protect her?"

Caspar looked straight back. "Why do you think I'm here?"

They talked of other things, then Tskoulis took watch, and Caspar slept. They were scheduled to leave in three hours.

Something was still bothering Tskoulis. He pondered, keeping an eye out for movement in the tunnel, pacing to keep himself awake.

Then he realized. The look on Caspar's face when he'd heard 2-5 had to stay behind instead of looking for Jossey. The fury in his gaze.

His voice over the intercom when Jossey had been taken.

He might be an excellent actor, Tskoulis thought, but those hadn't seemed faked.

91

THE SMALL GROUP OF ONLAR AND JOSSEY MADE THEIR WAY slowly back to Ilara on the bikes. Jossey was having trouble concentrating on the road, and finally veered far enough to the side that Tark ordered them to stop.

He sat her down, took her by the shoulders and looked her in the face. "Do you understand now?"

She shook her head. "What was that? What do you mean, no grow lights?"

His men were muttering. He turned to them. "What is it?" he snapped.

Altan glanced at the other two. "Bey, how does she know your name? And why – "

He gestured to Tark's hands on Jossey's shoulders.

Tark pulled his hands back. Jossey glanced at him, confused. He was her brother. Surely –

Then she remembered his instructions not to tell them who she was.

Tark stood and looked evenly at them. "Do you support me? And this plan?"

They glanced at each other, looking startled, then at him.

Erkan frowned. "Why do you even ask, Bey?"

Scarface and Altan were silent. Tark turned to them. "You?" he demanded.

"Bey, you know we trust you. You helped rescue us from the farm," was all Scarface said after a long moment, placing a hand on Altan's shoulder. "You saved our lives."

Altan murmured agreement.

Tark looked hard from face to face. The men looked soberly at him.

Then he stepped back and smiled.

"Then," he said, "forgive me for not having told you that this Engineer is my younger sister Jossey."

They stared at her. She shrank back awkwardly. Altan in particular looked stricken.

"I am sorry, Bey," he stammered. "She was a prisoner." He looked at Jossey. "I – " He seemed to be grasping for words.

Tark looked pained. "I know. And we must continue to treat her as one. If Kudret or his men were to know that the Engineer we waited so long to capture was my own family, he would probably have even more ammunition to get rid of me, call me a traitor to the people. And all of you."

Their faces stilled.

He turned to Jossey. "Do you understand now why I said you were in great danger? This is not just about whether you will help us."

She tried to smile.

"This was not my plan," Tark said somberly. He put an arm around her. "But she is here now."

He glanced at Altan and pointedly lifted his arm from Jossey's shoulders. "Thank you, Altan. I must remember to act accordingly."

"And you." Tark turned to Jossey. "You need to make a choice. Will you help us?"

Jossey gaped at him. "What?" She still didn't even fully understand what she'd just seen back there.

"We need to know if you will help us negotiate with the Colony – the City. My father-in-law, Diros Bey, tried for years to come to an agreement with the City, to let us live in what you call the Old Sector 1, what we call Derinkuyu." He grimaced. "We all worked together once, long ago, but the City broke agreements and decided, I guess, that non-City people were best used as free labor. We have been trying to negotiate ever since."

His men seemed slightly lost at some of the terms. He translated quickly.

"Why don't you just leave?" Jossey asked, horrified.

Tark gestured to something in the distance. She squinted but couldn't figure out what he was pointing to.

"Do you see those lights?" he said.

Between the hills, she could see a faint blinking. Tall, thin posts, with lights at the top. Like long matchsticks. There were dozens of them. Based on the scale, she guessed they stretched for miles.

"What is that?" she asked.

"The Perimeter."

"It's – " Scarface seemed to be searching for the word. He finally held up a hand. She could see a long burn mark there. "If you touch it, it can kill you."

She gaped at him. "They've fenced you in?"

Tark looked grim. "Like I said. Free labor. They even sank the pilings deep to prevent tunneling. If you managed to get past the land mines, that is."

She shook her head, uncomprehending. "But why?" *Land mines?*

"It's not just to keep us in," Tark said. "It's – "

Suddenly the wail of an alarm pierced the night air.

They jumped.

"Get to the bikes," Tark hissed. "Now." He looked at Jossey. "Jossey, stay with Altan. Yazar, Erkan, with me."

Jossey looked at the glow in the distance. "Have they found us?"

Tark looked grim. "I don't think so," he said.

He ran for the bike. Erkan and Scarface – Yazar, Jossey thought – were right behind him. They hopped on and took off down the road.

Altan had removed his claws. "We need to get to cover," he said. "Grab the bike." She hurried to obey.

A blinding light had appeared above the mountaintop. It was sweeping the countryside in great circles.

She and Altan drove away from the hillside. She glanced over her shoulder and saw something odd – a small light rising in the air above the glow.

Flying.

She stared, amazed.

"Get off the road!" Altan shouted in her com. She veered off, barely missing the ditch, and leaped off the bike.

"What is that?" she gasped.

"Get DOWN," hissed Altan.

She dropped to the ground beside him. "The bikes – "

"Don't worry about the bikes. Just don't move."

She froze, the thick blades of grass cold and scratchy against her face, stabbing into her exposed hands. She wondered if they could poke out an eye, and tried to keep her head still.

The little light drifted above them, hovering in place for a moment, then continued across the field.

She turned her head, just barely. She could hear, faintly, the motors of the other bikes, returning.

The light turned in the bikes' direction.

Altan muttered something Jossey didn't catch.

"Stay where you are," he whispered to her. He crept up the side of the ditch. She could see him hailing the other bikes.

They zoomed up. Tark took off his helmet and shook his head.

Jossey watched them, confused. Altan seemed to be arguing with him.

"We can't risk it," Tark said.

Scarface looked furious. "Bey," he said.

Jossey saw a flicker of movement to her left. She turned.

A young boy, about twelve, was running through the field about a hundred yards away, staggering. She gasped and pointed.

The flying light was right behind, shining a beam directly on the child.

And on three Patrol agents.

The child kept glancing back, terror written on his features.

Tark jammed his helmet back on his head. "Stay with her!" he hissed to Altan.

Scarface was already on his bike. He took off into the field, zooming through the high grasses.

Jossey watched as the two bikes converged silently on the Patrol agents. Scarface had drawn his sword.

The agents didn't seem to notice the bikes until it was too late.

Tark pulled up alongside the boy and grabbed him with one arm. The boy clung to him desperately as he swung the child up onto the back seat of the motorcycle.

The light still hovered in mid-air, as if confused.

Tark turned, took a knife out of a sheath. To Jossey's amazement, he hurled it at the light. With a small explosion, it disappeared.

Tark and Scarface zoomed back to the road. "Get on!" Tark shouted. "Now!"

He tore a piece from his uniform. "Sorry," he said to the

child. Then he tied a blindfold around the child's eyes, picked the boy up, and set him on the bike behind Altan. "Hold on," he said in the Old Language.

He turned to Jossey. "Get on my bike. Don't let go."

She obeyed.

"Don't fall off," Tark yelled at her. She locked her arms tightly around his chest.

He zoomed onto the highway. Jossey's heart caught in her throat. The night air rushed past her helmet, her uniform. She'd never gone this fast in her life. Had never even imagined going this fast. She clung to her brother so tightly her hands went cold, terrified, feeling as if she might slide off the back at any moment.

"Bey!" she heard over her com. "Beyim, nereye gidiyoruz?" *Where are we going?* She thought it was Erkan.

"The other bike, Bey?" Altan.

"Leave it," was all Tark said.

92

THEY FLEW DOWN THE HIGHWAY.

Jossey was still clinging to Tark, terrified. They zoomed back through the village square and kept going, past the turnoff, straight through the ruins, directly west. She had no idea where they were going, had only a faint idea of where Ilara was relative to them.

"Tark, where – "

He ignored her. "Hold on," he muttered. "Don't let go."

She wasn't planning to.

To her left she could see an enormous dark shape. A mountain. The same one she'd seen from Ilara, she thought. And a vast open plain.

"Is the searchlight still on?" Tark shouted. She flinched as his voice boomed in her ears.

"Yes," she yelled back, looking over her shoulder. It was faint, barely visible from here. But it was still on, blinking in the distance. She estimated they were around fifteen miles off.

"Good," he said. "They probably haven't noticed yet. Yazar, you got them all?"

Scarface's voice. "Yes, Bey."

They turned to the south.

"Bey, where are we going?"

Tark glanced over his shoulder. "The lake," he said.

The land grew flatter as they went. Jossey could see that much of it had probably once been farmland; even now, she could see slight distinctions, faded patchwork, as if the same crops had grown wild after their owners had fled or perished.

She wondered about the young boy on the bike behind her. She glanced over her shoulder, but could not see him. She wondered if he was more or less terrified now.

A ridge rose to their right, and they slowed as they passed through a small village and over a bridge.

"This is our river," Tark said to her. She looked down at the dark water beneath them. As they sped up again on the other side and dropped well below the ridgeline, she could no longer see the light.

Tark sped up and took a sharp turn when they got to the main road.

"You took the long way, Bey," Altan said in Jossey's ear. "Do we have enough fuel to get back?"

"Pray that we do," Tark said grimly.

93

TSKOULIS HAD MANAGED TO SLEEP FOR A FEW HOURS AFTER HIS conversation with Caspar, but it hadn't been a sound sleep. The ground – he'd slept on hard ground before, had never been bothered by it, but this time it seemed like he felt every rock. He couldn't get comfortable, tossing and turning.

He remembered the blanket fibers they'd found and smiled grimly. At least They seemed to be taking some kind of care of her, he thought.

As soon as a reasonable amount of time had passed, he got up and prodded the others awake.

He was impressed by how professional they were about it. There was a minimal amount of grumbling as they got to their feet, mostly from Rho, who hadn't slept well either with his wound.

They sat and had a quick breakfast.

"Here's the plan," Tskoulis said as the others silently ate. "Assuming these tunnels are a straight shot, it'll probably take us until at least noon to get to the OS1. That's barring any accidents or cave-ins or anything else that might block our progress. Gamma, you're in charge of mapping any additional tunnels so we can go back if needed." He looked at Caspar. "And you. Look for sign."

"Yes, sir," they said.

"Supply check," Tskoulis said.

They had three days' supply of water, two days' of food. Food was less of a concern. And it was cool enough down here, Tskoulis thought. But still – better to be prepared. He'd brought extra batteries for the lights, extra tools in case of cave-ins. They were as prepared as could be.

He hoped.

They made sure the fire was completely out, lest it use up more oxygen than was safe, and packed up their small camp.

They headed into the tunnel.

The agents realized there might be a problem when the first branch appeared.

Gamma mapped it, then he and Caspar took a close look at the ground while the others stood well back, making sure not to add their own footprints to the dust.

For a long, tense moment, both trackers were silent. Then Gamma pointed to something on the ground in the right-side branch.

It was a tiny drop of some kind of oil.

They inspected it. It appeared to be either animal fat or maybe some kind of mineral oil – it was impossible to tell. None of them had any idea what it might mean. But it was a physical trace of some kind.

Just to be sure, Caspar went up the left branch a ways and came back empty-handed.

They made a note of the branch and headed to the right.

94

THEY REACHED THE LAKE AS DAWN WAS BEGINNING IN THE EAST. It was very faint, but Jossey could see the gray on the horizon. The stars were scattered across the sky; racing clouds obscured the moon.

The lake was long and narrow, disappearing into the distance toward the east. To the left, on the northern shore, there was a flat area down by the water, a sort of strangely-shaped beach, and then a ridge with what looked like limestone columns. Tark gestured in its direction.

The other bikes followed as he maneuvered around the northern edge of the lake.

They got off at the oddly-shaped beach and removed their helmets. Jossey was chilled from the constant wind, and hopped up and down, shivering. The boy looked the worse for wear too, shivering and blindfolded. She glanced at Tark. He shook his head. "Not yet," he said.

Altan said something quiet in their language, and the boy sat on the ground.

Tark and Yazar had stashed their equipment in their bikes' cargo compartments. In the confusion, they'd even remembered

Jossey's. She gave them grateful smiles.

The lake was very still. She gazed at it in wonder. She'd never seen so much water at once.

Tark said her name, and she glanced up. He was holding up a couple of canteens.

"Here, fill these," he said, tossing them to her one at a time. She caught them and glanced at the water.

"Is it clean?" she asked.

He shrugged. "We drink from it."

Then he winked. "The canteens have filters."

She looked skeptically at the canteens, but picked her way over the rocks to the water's edge and crouched. The water was only an inch or so deep here – even in the darkness, with her Patrol safety light she could see the sand rippling underneath the water. She frowned. Did he want her to go in?

Altan laughed. "Not there," he said. "Over there."

He pointed along the sand to a long narrow section of the beach. There, the drop to the water was about a foot. Water lapped at the rocks as the wind pushed it gently.

"Be careful," Tark said. "It's still dark."

"Thanks." She carried the canteens over to the edge and sat down. Here she couldn't see the sandy bottom anymore, and the lapping of the water against the rocks sounded...hollow. Deep. She shivered.

Making sure her balance was solid, she leaned over, scooped out a full canteen with one arm, and deposited it on the sand, screwing on the lid. She repeated the process and got carefully to her feet.

Tark gestured up the hill. She looked up at the limestone ridge. There were caves where the ridge met the dirt.

"The middle one," he said.

She turned that way and began to climb.

Altan joined her with the boy, holding him gently by the arm. The boy obediently staggered up the hill, wincing a little as he scraped his ankle on a stone. He barely had shoes, Jossey thought. He was wearing tattered clothing, something like a uniform. She realized to her horror that it was very much the wrong size.

Like it had belonged to another child before.

They climbed up, up. The rock columns making up the ridge appeared to have broken over the years, and the dirt hill up to the ridge was a field of boulders, some bigger than Jossey's living quarters. She let Altan lead; he seemed to have been here before.

The path led directly to the cave, which looked like a square hole in the rock columns. At some point, steps had apparently been carved up to it.

Altan helped the boy up the steps. She followed the pair up into the darkness.

She went to switch on her Patrol safety light, but Altan had already reached for an oil lamp in a small carved niche near the entrance and lit it. He took it far back into the cave. She followed him with the water and set it down carefully.

He gestured to a folding screen near the cave opening. "Cover the entrance," he said. "Even a candle can be seen for miles out here."

She did as he ordered.

He went to the boy. Before he removed the blindfold, he turned to Jossey. He was fidgeting. "I – just – "

He looked away, at the ground near his feet. Then he met her eyes and blurted, "I'm sorry. For before." He made a fist of his hair and looked at her again. "I didn't know who you were. And anyway I shouldn't have – "

He trailed off and looked back at the ground, awkwardly, still fidgeting.

She looked at him for a long moment.

He glanced at her, then away again.

He seemed very young at that moment; something about

him reminded her a little of Thompson. That felt so long ago, she thought.

"*Merak etme,*" she said at last in the Old Language. *Don't worry.*

His eyes shot up to hers in surprise.

"I think I said that wrong," she said, giving him a rueful smile. Maybe she'd said "don't be afraid" instead.

"No, you – "

He lapsed into silence, looking carefully at the flame.

"I don't blame you," Jossey said. "Not given what I've seen tonight." She gestured silently to the blindfolded child. "I'm not sure I forgive you for kicking me in the head, though." She gave him a hard look.

He looked away. "Please forgive me," he mumbled, looking miserable.

"Altan."

He looked up at her, eyes searching. He reminded her so much of Thompson, she thought again.

"None of us knew certain things." She smiled gently. "You were doing your job. I was doing mine. And you brought me to my brother, who I didn't even know was still alive."

"Are you su– "

The child in the corner shifted, shivering. They both stopped talking and looked over at him.

Altan said something Jossey didn't understand to him. The child stopped moving. Altan went over and took a blanket out of his bag, then wrapped it around the child's shoulders. He tossed another to Jossey, gesturing for her to cover her uniform. She obeyed.

"*Sağolun,*" the child whispered.

Footsteps outside, then Tark and the others entered the cave, moving the screen out of the way and replacing it with care. Tark looked around approvingly, smiling as he saw the blanket around the child's shoulders.

"Welcome," he said to Jossey. "This is our hideout when things, ah, go wrong."

He walked over to the boy.

"*You're safe, inşallah,*" he said in their language. He crouched and removed the blindfold. The boy blinked at the light, then his big eyes focused on Tark's face.

"*Tark Bey misiniz?*" he asked, looking awestruck.

Tark grinned.

The boy's chin trembled, then he stood awkwardly and flung his skinny arms around Jossey's brother's neck, tears running down his young face. He wiped at them furiously with one dirty hand and held on tightly.

Tark held onto him for a long moment, then held him at arm's length. "*Çok yiğitsin, maşallah,*" he said. His men all clustered around him, looking seriously down at the child.

The boy wiped his eyes. "*I'm sorry,*" he muttered. Jossey smiled a little. He looked torn between trying to appear manly and wanting to just cling to Tark.

The boy finally drew himself up and saluted, looking proudly up at his leader.

Tark gestured for him to sit. The young boy took a seat, wrapping the blanket around himself. Tark gave him water and gestured for one of his men to bring the boy something to eat.

"*What is your name?*" he asked the child.

"Mustafa," the boy said.

"*Mustafa, welcome. These are my men, Yazar, Erkan, Altan. This is – *" He glanced at Jossey, who was following along as well as she could. "*She is with Altan,*" he said after a moment.

Jossey stared at Tark. He shook his head slightly. Altan's face was bright red.

"*Hello,*" the boy said innocently.

Jossey glanced at Altan, then looked at the ground, flushing furiously.

She forced herself to look up and smiled in welcome at

Mustafa, hoping he wouldn't speak to her, then shot Tark a look.

"Not now," he mouthed to her.

Erkan looked extremely amused. Yazar had busied himself putting together a meal for them, but from the way he was studiously avoiding looking at them all, she thought he was trying not to laugh.

Mustafa turned back to Tark, not seeming to have noticed a thing. *"Can they find us?"* he asked urgently.

Tark glanced at the screen covering the cave's entrance. *"I hope not,"* he said. *"We're very far away. Now tell me."* He crouched next to the boy. *"How did you escape?"*

The boy's gaze became far away. He pulled the blanket closer. *"When they changed ---"*

Jossey didn't understand everything he was saying. Altan translated under his breath. He didn't look at her as he did so.

"He says they changed the guard and he got out under the...electric fence, says he dug a hole when he went to relieve himself," Altan muttered.

It made sense. Jossey watched the boy's face as he recounted the escape.

"They didn't notice him because the guard who counts them off in their living quarters was sick, and the others had a plan to cover for him," Altan explained, a bit haltingly, pausing over a couple of the words.

"Thank you," she murmured.

"He was going to get help," Altan added.

"Help from where?" Tark frowned, looking directly into the boy's eyes. *"From us? Ilara was very far."*

The boy looked at him, big eyes solemn. *"I had to try."*

"Çok cesur, maşallah," Tark murmured admiringly. He clapped the boy on the shoulder. The boy beamed.

Then the boy looked straight at Jossey. *"Why does she speak the Colony's language?"* he asked Tark.

Jossey looked wide-eyed at her brother.

"*She is like me,*" Tark said carefully.

Mustafa looked at Jossey. Then he looked solemnly back at Tark. "*Anladım, Bey.*"

The sun was beginning to rise. They had eaten a quick meal, and Tark had dug some old tattered bedrolls out of one of the storage containers the Onlar had stashed in the cave. There were only three bedrolls, so he gave one to Jossey, one to the boy, and the third he laid out for himself and his men to use as a long pillow. Erkan and the others protested that he should use it, but Tark just smiled and shook his head. Jossey suddenly understood why his men seemed to love him so much.

She was very tired, but she couldn't sleep. She went to the cave door and peered out at the sunrise.

It was one of the most glorious things she had ever seen. The lake was filled with sparkling golden-orange light; some kind of water birds glided across the shining waters. Further out, mist rose from the surface. She shielded her eyes, amazed.

She turned at the sound of footsteps. Altan, clearly exhausted, had followed her outside. She smiled as he hovered in the entrance, looking unhappy.

"Don't worry, I'm not planning on running," she said.

"You're my assignment," he said stubbornly. He still refused to look at her.

Tark appeared. "Altan, go sleep," he said.

Altan looked extremely relieved. He escaped into the cave with barely so much as a "Bey."

She tried not to laugh.

Tark sat down next to her. "Beautiful, isn't it?"

She sighed. "Yes. It's amazing. We saw this on solar crew, but only for a few moments. They didn't let us up aboveground until the sun was fully up."

They sat for a few minutes, watching the birds, then she turned to him. "What did you mean when you told that kid that I'm like you?" She had so many questions. "Tark, what about – "

He put a finger to his lips. "Let's sleep. It's been a long night. That poor child has been through – I don't even want to know. But let's sleep now. Ask me later."

"Tark," she said very quietly, "I need to know some things. I *need* to. I thought you were dead."

"I know – "

"No, Tark, you don't understand." She glanced at the screened-off cave, then took his hands, looked into his eyes. He looked very seriously at her.

She faltered. "Gavin – found – what we thought was your body. Your bones." She reached up and touched his hair. "The skull had your – " She stopped and looked away, throat catching. Tark was here before her, but she couldn't get the image out of her mind. She touched his face, trying to convince herself that *this* was real. Her brother was real. He was alive. Not bones in the sand.

He took her hand from his face and held it in his own, gently, eyes traveling over the scar on her face, and she remembered he'd thought she was dead too. For a moment he looked as if he wanted to speak. Then he glanced away, out toward the water. "Is Gavin well?" he asked softly.

"He's probably searching for me right now," she said. "He's my unit commander."

Tark smiled a little. "Good," he said. "There's a lot we need to talk about. But go get some sleep."

"Do you promise?" She examined his face.

"I will tell you everything, God willing."

95

IT WAS BARELY MID-MORNING. THE DAY HAD NOT GONE WELL SO far for Sokol. Or, he imagined, for the flunky who stood shaking before him.

"Repeat that, agent," Sokol gritted out.

"Sir," the flunky said, "I don't know how else to explain it. Karapartei appears to have discovered our farms."

Sokol stood and stared at the man. He took off his glasses and set them on the desk.

"Explain," he said slowly. Dangerously.

The flunky looked determinedly at the wall. "Sir, we received reports of three agents down. One of the young workers escaped last night, around midnight. The three sent to retrieve him never returned. Their companions found them in the morning when the shift changed and the guards were able to go mount a search."

He pointed to the wall, where an image was being projected. "This is all that was recovered, sir."

The footage was blurry, but Sokol could make out what looked like two motorbikes. Black. Zooming through the field right behind the three Patrol agents. Certainly not Patrol's equipment he remembered seeing. He frowned. He'd never seen anything like it.

One bike drove in among the running Patrol agents. There was a flash from some kind of bladed weapon. The first Patrol agent dropped.

Sokol looked away. He didn't need to see any more.

"Can you identify the perpetrators?" His voice was cold.

The flunky trembled. "I'm – that is, we're not sure, sir. The video quality is poor – the drone was able to transmit this much before it was destroyed."

"Destroyed?"

"Some kind of impact," the agent squeaked. "Possibly from a metal object."

Sokol slammed his hands down on the table.

Of all the times. Delta was out in the field with Unit 1 and Tskoulis, and probably unreachable depending on how far out they were, or how deep underground. Sokol's preference would have been to send Caspar out to deal with this. But –

"Good news, though, sir," the flunky added, eyeing Sokol, one foot toward the door as if he wanted very much to flee. "We've recovered one of the bikes. Old military-grade. Founders-era, it looks like. Reworked." His voice grew slightly calmer as he continued speaking without any explosion from the Minister.

Sokol forced a smile onto his face. "Very good, agent."

"Sir?" The man looked hopeful.

Sokol strode around the desk, examined the footage on the wall. "Two bikes, you say? What happened to the other?"

"We're not sure, sir. As I said, the drone – "

Sokol cut him off. "Very good, agent. That's all. Dismissed."

The flunky looked at him, opened his mouth, then shut it firmly. "Yes, sir." He left quickly.

Sokol sat and stared into space.

If Karapartei knew about the farms...

This was a real problem. He rubbed his forehead.

He'd heard nothing from Tskoulis' team. That meant they'd found nothing, he guessed. Or maybe they simply had no signal at the moment.

He paced, thinking. The solar project was still proceeding. But if Jossey had been interrogated –

He sat down and rubbed his forehead again. He hated this. But it was necessary.

If Jossey had been interrogated, and depending on what she had told the Onlar, Delta had his orders.

96

"ARE YOU SURE THIS IS RIGHT?" CASPAR GLANCED AT THE MAP Gamma was putting together. "Something seems wrong."

Gamma glanced at him sideways, looking less than amused. "I've mapped every side corridor I've seen."

"I don't doubt that." Caspar had taken a stick and was drawing in the thick dust. "But I think maybe – "

He glanced up, waved Tskoulis over. "Doesn't it seem like we're a little too far to the east?"

Phi snorted. "How would we have any idea? It's not like compasses work very well this far underground."

"It's math. We've been traveling at a constant pace. If we've been heading – roughly – due south-south-west, based on our assumptions, we should have reached the OS1 by now."

The tunnel system seemed to have bypassed the OS2 – Nevşehir – altogether, and headed directly south from Gurime. No wonder, thought Tskoulis, the Onlar had never been caught. They'd been several miles out of the way. Wherever Tskoulis' team was headed, it appeared to be to a place no one from Patrol had ever thought to look.

Gamma looked annoyed. He sat down on the ground, took a

449

swig from his water canteen. "So where do you think we are now?"

They were sitting in an open chamber in what appeared to be a small version of the OS1 – another underground city. But none of them had ever seen it before. There were no obvious exits to the surface – those that they had seen had been blocked off. Or caved in.

Caspar looked coolly at him, his nervous Tracker's guise slipping for just an instant.

"Why don't you take a guess," he snapped.

Gamma's gaze shot up, and he glanced at Tskoulis.

Tskoulis shook his head. He really didn't need them fighting, and he felt bad for Gamma if they did.

He wasn't sure about Gamma, but he hoped Caspar had better self-control than that.

Caspar looked at the ground. "Sorry," he muttered. "I'm just – I know this is an important mission. Sorry, sir." He glanced at Tskoulis.

He seems to want to find Jossey as badly as I do, Tskoulis thought.

Tskoulis crouched. "What's the situation?"

Caspar held out his hand. Gamma grudgingly handed over his maps.

"We're here," Caspar said. "We should be approximately here if the tunnel goes straight to the OS1 or OS2. As I said, we've been traveling at a reasonably consistent pace since this morning, so that *should* put us here. But instead..." He gestured around them. "This isn't even the same color stone as the Old Sectors. And I haven't seen a well shaft at all. What is this place?"

Even the architecture was different – the arches more fluid, as if the builders had used their tools differently, or hadn't planned to dig quite as deep, hadn't thought to hold up quite as much weight.

"Based on the air temperature and the stone itself, we're probably not that far below the surface," Caspar said. "If we were in one of the Old Sectors, we should be seeing well shafts, stairs. This is – " He glanced around. "I think this is a totally different city."

Gamma spoke up. "I remember learning about a couple of the major ones in the region. But we thought they'd been blocked off after all the bombing. They were too unstable to be used as a location for our City."

They glanced around. Tskoulis was suddenly all too aware of how fragile the arches looked around them.

"If that's so," he said, "where does that put us?"

"Could be just about anywhere." Gamma took the map back from Caspar. "But if the Tracker here is right...we might be directly parallel to the City. Out maybe five, six miles."

"We should keep moving," Caspar said tersely. "Unless you want to try some of the side tunnels."

They hadn't found any sign for quite some time. A drop of oil here and there. That was it. And the occasional fiber on the ground.

They continued.

Eventually they found a place where it seemed the Onlar and their captive had sat and eaten some food. But they'd cleaned up well after themselves. It was only due to Caspar's thoroughness that the team noticed something else.

Bare footprints in the dusty tunnels.

At one point, it seemed They'd taken her boots.

"So she didn't run off," Phi guessed.

Tskoulis glanced at Caspar, not missing the way the man's jaw was clenched as he examined the floor.

"So she's barefoot," Rho said. "That should have slowed them down. Do you think they walked straight the whole way to wherever they were going? We've already been out here for what, twelve hours?"

"I doubt they took her boots the whole time." Caspar was examining the footprints. "Her feet would likely be bleeding."

Tskoulis flinched. But he had a point.

"Let's keep going," Tskoulis said. "Like you said, Rho, that probably would have slowed them down."

They continued on for another hour or so, passing a couple of large chambers that seemed to have been used to store supplies. Or house people. It was hard to tell, the architecture down here was so odd. As they walked, the tunnel slowly widened. Alpha was the first to point out the strange grooves in the floor.

He dropped to the ground and examined them. They were at least an inch deep, parallel lines running the length of the tunnel, with room for a man to pass by on each side. "Are these wagon tracks?"

"Looks like it." Phi walked ahead. "The width doesn't change." He looked to Gamma. "How old did you say the Old Sectors were?"

Gamma shrugged. "As far as I know, about a thousand years."

Tskoulis' eyebrows shot up. "A thousand?"

"Yeah. The people here used them to hide from invaders. Pretty interesting stuff."

"Well, looks like someone used to drag a cart back and forth. A lot." Alpha grinned. "Maybe we have found the Onlar hideout after all."

"Maybe." Tskoulis was skeptical. These looked *old*. He didn't think the Onlar used carts anyway.

There was warm air drifting from somewhere. "Do you feel that?" Caspar asked.

"Yeah." Gamma glanced down at the map he was making. "If the math's right, we should be pretty close to the – "

Tskoulis suddenly held up a hand. Gamma almost plowed into him.

452

"Sir?"

Tskoulis gestured wordlessly to the fork in front of them.

One of the tunnels led to the left, down into blackness. To the right there was a faint glow. A fire? Daylight? It was impossible to tell.

"Quiet," Tskoulis hissed to Alpha and Phi, who were walking behind with Rho, swapping battle stories from the Onlar the night before.

They immediately shut up as he pointed to the light.

They inched along the upper tunnel, which quickly grew narrower, the tracks in the floor disappearing. They could see faint shadows on the walls now.

Flickering. Like fire.

And then they burst around the corner and stared.

They'd reached the surface. Or, rather, they'd reached a level or two below the surface. There was an enormous crater where a bomb seemed to have fallen centuries ago, exposing parts of the tunnel, the rooms in the ancient city, to the sky.

They coughed as they stirred up dust, and looked up into the blue, shielding their eyes.

Tskoulis felt tiny as he stared up at the destroyed cross-section of what he realized was a tremendous architectural achievement. They were standing in what seemed, in its destruction, like a grand hall with three stories or more of arch-ways, spiraling upward toward the empty sky. The sun beat down on them, and immediately he flinched away from the heat.

"Sir," Gamma said behind him, "what's that?"

Tskoulis turned and looked where Gamma was pointing. He froze.

Across the crater, in the shadows, partially hidden underneath a slab of rock, he could see what looked like a pile of bones.

His chest tightened. Trying to breathe, trying to stay calm, he pointed to Phi and Gamma, wordlessly ordering them to stay where they were, then picked his way around the edge of the rock-filled crater. Was that an equipment bag? Was that –

This was a great place to dispose of a body, he thought. The desert rats out here worked quickly. He'd seen it himself.

Who would ever think to look –

He half stumbled, not fully paying attention to where he was going, horrible thoughts flooding through his mind, and caught himself against one of the arches on the perimeter. A faint trickle of dirt came away with his hand. He brushed it off, forging onward.

Caspar was right behind him. Alpha and Rho had their swords drawn, waiting near the tunnel.

In the shade, or what passed for shade down here in this desiccated pit, Gavin could see that the bones were scattered.

Some looked like they had been dragged away.

If she'd been interrogated, left here –

He pushed on, stepping carefully, steeling himself to look, knowing he couldn't allow himself to falter in front of his men.

No matter what he might be looking at.

He peered into the shade, shielding his eyes from the noontime glare.

For a long, horrible moment, he thought he was looking at what was left of a hand.

. . .

Gavin forced himself to be calm, look closer.

The hand was curled, lying face-up. It had...

Pads. Claws.

Gavin realized he was looking at a creature's forepaw. It still had soft tissue attached.

A desert cat.

He crouched and examined the remains, allowing himself a moment to breathe.

Thank God.

Caspar was there before he could be waved back.

"Tskoulis," he said. His face was white, and not from the blinding daylight.

"Tskoulis," he said again.

Tskoulis waved back the men. The bones looked relatively recent. He didn't know how the creature had gotten down here. But they weren't – He crouched to examine them again.

"Sir?"

Gavin looked up. Rho was pointing upward.

Then the commander saw it. The trickle of dirt from the column he'd hit had become a small stream.

He glanced at the desert cat, then back up at the falling dirt, his mind still elsewhere.

"Tskoulis!" hissed Caspar.

Gavin belatedly realized what was happening as Caspar grabbed his arm and yanked him to his feet, pulling him in the direction of the tunnels.

There was a rumbling up above, and the edge of the crater began to slowly give way.

"Go!" shouted Gavin. "Go! Back into the tunnels! Now!"

The crater began to collapse as if in slow motion, the arches on the top levels shattering, the stones tumbling into each other one after the other.

A giant piece of column came free. It smashed into the ground right where Gavin had been standing moments before.

The men sprinted through the dust and rapidly-darkening air, desperately seeking the entrance to the tunnel. Caspar was holding onto Tskoulis' arm so tightly the commander was glad he had armor on.

Rho was still staring, stupefied.

Caspar yanked his arm and pulled the enormous man along with Tskoulis into the tunnel just before a massive piece of stone fell across the entrance.

97

THEY FLED DOWN THE INK-BLACK TUNNEL, FINALLY REACHING THE fork again, crashing into the wall. They huddled in the pitch blackness, groaning.

"We need to get further down the tunnel," Tskoulis coughed, choking on sour-tasting dust. "Anyone have a light?"

"I think I crushed mine," Rho's voice.

After a moment, Gamma's red light flared.

They inspected each other for wounds. Nothing obvious, but they realized half their equipment was gone, probably crushed under rock up above in the tunnel where they'd left it.

"How much water do we have?" Tskoulis demanded.

They counted. Enough for just them, for that day, maybe a second day if they rationed it.

Alpha muttered something angry.

Other than Tskoulis, only Caspar seemed at all calm.

"What's wrong with you, Tracker?" Phi demanded. "How are you not – "

Caspar turned to him. "We have to keep moving," he said. "Do you think I don't know how to find water?"

They looked at him silently.

"Gamma doesn't," Rho said at last, under his breath.

Gamma nudged him not-so-gently.

Caspar said quietly, "We have two clear choices. We can keep going, or we can go back. There's no water supply further up the tunnel, not that we've found."

"There's a potential third choice," Gavin said. "We can make our way up to the surface if we find an air shaft, and go back to the City."

"You're the commander." Caspar seemed to remember he needed to sound appropriately nervous.

Tskoulis looked at all of them. "We're alive. We're relatively uninjured, thank God. We need to keep going."

There was another rumbling. Their heads shot up.

Rocks began to fill the tunnel behind them, sour-smelling dust rushing ahead in a noxious cloud.

"Run!" shouted Tskoulis.

They sprinted down the tunnel that had the grooves. It was the tunnel that led down deeper into the earth. Behind them, Tskoulis could hear what sounded like the tunnel filling up completely.

It was their only way out, and only water source, that they knew of.

They reached what looked like a safe spot and turned around. Tskoulis could hear the grinding of rocks.

"I guess we should go onward," Caspar muttered after a long, horrified moment.

Tskoulis didn't know whether to laugh or slug him.

98

The Onlar all dozed throughout the day. Jossey kept an eye on Mustafa, who seemed more exhausted than was healthy. He tossed and turned on his bedroll, alert to what looked like every single sound, every footstep. She watched him sadly. The poor child.

At one point, Altan stepped close to him while wandering around preparing food, and the child shot bolt upright, shielding his face. Altan nearly dropped the bowl he was carrying.

Mustafa shrank back, hands over his head, then seemed to realize where he was.

Altan set the bowl down on the ground and sat beside the boy, quietly.

"How long were you there?" he asked at last.

The boy drew the blanket up around himself, still trembling. *"Bilmiyorum,"* he said quietly. *"Maybe two years."*

Altan looked into the distance. *"I was there for three."*

Even if she couldn't understand well, Jossey felt like an intruder, and not only because she was Patrol. Face burning, she got up and retrieved the bowl, retreating as fast as possible to the back of the cave, where Yazar was making some kind of meal. She handed it to him and hovered, hoping he'd let her help.

He still seemed less than friendly to her, but it was probably him or that conversation, she thought, and she didn't want to upset whatever truce she seemed to have with Altan.

"Can I help?" she finally asked.

He grunted and gestured to one of the bowls, saying something in his language.

"What?"

He looked at her as if she were stupid and mimed stirring, one eyebrow raised.

"Ah." She grabbed a spoon and went to work.

Altan and Mustafa were still talking when Tark and Erkan returned. They were carrying some kind of small game, several of them in a basket. The late afternoon light slanted into the cave.

Mustafa's face lit up as Tark entered the cave. He tried to get to his feet, but Tark waved him down.

"Please," Tark said. *"Rest."*

"Yes, Bey." The child was beaming.

Tark turned to Jossey. "Do you know how to prepare rabbit?"

She didn't. He looked mildly disappointed. She wanted to make a face at him but remembered the boy.

"It's fine. I'm just not a good cook." He grinned. "Neither are they."

She kept stirring whatever the paste was, until Yazar snapped at her to stop or she'd ruin it. She handed it to him and went to the cave's entrance. Altan watched her warily.

She stood breathing in the evening air. The sunset was glorious, great clouds marching to the west, brilliant shades of gold and purple and pink. She sighed.

Behind her, she heard Mustafa say, *"Altan, your wife seems very nice. She brought me an extra blanket when I was cold."*

Jossey nearly choked, regretting that she understood quite as much of the language as she did. She didn't dare turn around.

She heard Altan stammer some reply as she kept her gaze fixed on the sunset. Tark had some explaining to do, she thought.

She watched the sun disappear beyond the western horizon, the clouds slowly fading from pink to purple and night creeping over the land. Reluctantly, she went back inside, knowing they needed to keep the screen closed once it was dark.

They ate dinner all together. Whatever spices Yazar had used, the food was delicious. It was some kind of wild grain and tahini pepper dish, along with the rabbit Tark and Erkan had caught. She was impressed.

Mustafa wolfed it down until Tark laughingly took it away from him, telling him to be careful so he didn't get sick.

She found herself smiling as the night wore on. Although she couldn't quite follow their low conversation, she could feel the camaraderie. Even Yazar's scarred face seemed less scowling as he looked her way.

She found herself feeling strangely at home, trapped in a little cave on the edge of a lake in the middle of she didn't know where, eating with almost-strangers over lamplight.

Strangers who wanted her dead not two days ago, she reminded herself.

But somehow – seeing Mustafa's young face, her brother's crooked grin as Altan launched into another ridiculous adventure they'd had before Tark became bey...she felt...right.

She excused herself, grabbing a blanket, and got up to sit outside. Altan got up, but Tark waved him to sit back down.

She took off her boots and put them beside the screen, smiling pointedly at them both.

Altan flushed a little; she wasn't sure if it was for not trusting her or because of Mustafa's innocent observation earlier. Indeed, Erkan grinned and whispered something that earned him a not-so-gentle nudge from Altan. She chose to ignore them both and walked outside on bare feet.

The night breeze was warm and the hot stone felt good under her feet as she sat on the little ledge that doubled as a porch of sorts. The stars were already out, to her surprise – she'd forgotten that they seemed to come out more quickly in late autumn.

She wrapped herself in the blanket and sat, feet dangling over the edge, the wind caressing her face, as the last of the light faded and the stars rose over the world.

Looking around, she saw that the end of the lake was suspiciously rectangular, and she realized it was some kind of dam. She wondered whether families had sat here in centuries past, looking at the stars just like her.

She wondered where Gavin was now. Whether he was out under the stars somewhere, looking for her. Thinking she was dead.

She started as the screen behind her opened, and Tark stepped out quietly. He closed it behind him and came over, sitting next to her.

"You didn't run," he joked.

She grinned. "After that meal?"

He laughed under his breath. They had to be very quiet, she knew – sound carried, especially among rocks and water.

They sat in companionable silence for a long time.

He turned to her. "Do you miss it?"

"What?"

"The City."

She thought for a long moment.

In a few short days, she'd seen trees aboveground, real trees, and now this lake. And that terrible place from which they'd rescued Mustafa.

And more landscape than she'd ever seen in her life.

"I don't miss being underground," she said truthfully.

"But?"

"The people," she admitted. "My unit." She looked away. "I'm sorry. I know you hate – "

"They're your friends," Tark said quietly. "Tell me about them. About you. About Gavin. About – " He swallowed and looked down. "About our parents."

She glanced at the screen. He waved a hand. "I told them to keep the child entertained," he said.

"Okay." Patrol at least sounded easy. "My unit is – " She described Zlotnik, Wickford, Ellis and his obsession with protein, Thompson who wouldn't stop staring at her.

Tark snorted.

"I don't know what's up with him," she said. She waved her hand. "Whatever. And then there's – "

She faltered.

"Then there's Caspar," she said.

Tark glanced at her. "Caspar?"

How did she describe Caspar? "He's...he's the one who helped me when our transport was attacked. Then my uncle had him switched to Patrol with me to help me – " She was probably spilling classified information, but at this point she didn't care.

"He's – " She remembered the way Caspar had appeared out of the crowd to stand between her and the Karapartei agent, seeming like a different person, eyes burning with fury. His winning smile as he held up a box of doughnuts in the corridor.

His frantic voice on the radio.

To her horror, she realized her face was burning. She hoped Tark couldn't see that well out here.

"He's probably looking for me with Gavin," she mumbled.

He glanced at her. "Is Gavin – how is Gavin?"

She smiled. "He's bigger than you."

Tark looked mildly disappointed.

"And he still likes stories like you guys used to read." She made a face. "And he's so overprotective it drives me insane. He seems so mad whenever I screw anything up, like he thinks I can't handle things, or like he thinks I might die if I go off on my own or something." She thought. Then she smiled. "And everyone treats him like a celebrity because he's Mr. Tall and Handsome Patrol Commander and I always have to tell him to stop accidentally flirting with people because he 'doesn't do it on purpose.'"

Tark snorted. "I see at least one of us grew up."

She glanced at him. "Oh, he's a grown-up. But you should have *seen* the nurses when I was in the hospital."

"You were in the hospital?" He frowned. "When? What happened?"

"I...one of your people attacked my solar crew's transport a while back. Gavin came and rescued us. I was in the hospital for a while."

He looked away. She squeezed his hand.

"He really grew up," she went on, thinking aloud. "Everyone in Patrol is terrified of him. They call him The Tiger."

Tark stiffened and glanced at her. "The Tiger?"

"Yes."

He pulled his hand out of hers suddenly and looked away, pain shooting across his features. "The Tiger is the reason for half my men's deaths in the last several years."

She reached for his hand again, carefully. She felt him tense, felt him try not to pull away from her.

"Tark. He doesn't know, I don't think, who the Onlar – that is, your people – are."

A thought occurred to her. "If he finds me, I have to tell him. Maybe then – "

Tark glanced up at the stars. "Let's not worry about that for now. I'm not surprised." He smiled crookedly at her. "From what I understand, most of your Patrol doesn't. But the Tiger–"

464

He sighed explosively. "I didn't know. I've almost fought with him a couple of times. Wow."

Jossey shivered a little. "How do you know that they don't—"

"Politics," Tark said shortly.

Then he turned to her. "Do you think Gavin – do you think he would probably believe you?"

She saw a little of the boy he'd been in his face, his eyes. Hopeful.

"I don't know," she said, "but Gavin's pretty much as he was when you disappeared. Honest. Loyal. Fighting for what is right. A little more...obedient." She gave him a wry smile.

"Then, God willing..." He glanced at her. "Don't tell my men you know the Tiger, all right? And especially not that you're in his unit. I think Altan finally doesn't hate you."

"Oh, yes." Her expression changed in an instant. "That boy in there thinks I'm Altan's wife," she hissed. "Want to explain?"

"Just go with it for now." Tark looked appropriately ashamed. "I'm sorry. The less he knows, the better, for now."

She stuck out her tongue at him. If she was acting six, so much the better. He laughed silently.

He sobered. "You haven't told me. How is Mother?"

Jossey looked out across the lake, or what she could see of it.

"Mother – " She clenched her hands. "Father – died, looking for you," she said.

Tark took a deep breath. "I know," he said.

"You know?" She turned to him. "How?"

He looked away. "He was a civilian, so my father-in-law's men tried to save him when they found him in the desert, tried to take him back. But it was too late."

Jossey remembered the funeral. Dehydration, they'd said. Not the Onlar.

But she'd refused to believe it at the time.

"Oh," she said.

"And Mother?"

"Mother hates me," she said in a very small voice.

"Hates you?" Tark frowned, looked into her face. "Why?"

"Because I lost you. And Father. And because of this." She pointed to her scar. "She used to say it was...a good thing I had it so it would keep other kids scared to go into the tunnels," she said bitterly. "She wouldn't even look at me for months. Even now she tells me to cover it up."

"Jossey." He shook his head. "It wasn't your fault."

Jossey frowned at him. "How? I was the one who wanted to see the moon. I made you take me up there." She looked down. "Mother told me – "

She trailed off. She didn't need to repeat them, the cruel things Mother had said. Instead, she said, "I still don't understand why Gavin doesn't hate me too."

Tark stared at her. "Why would Gavin hate you? You said he keeps an eye out for you. Doesn't sound to me like he hates you."

Jossey was quiet for a very long time. Then she glanced at him. "He kept some promise he made to you. He's always helping me. But I never understood how he could help me when I was the reason you were gone." Her mouth twisted, and she looked away, miserable. "I just wanted him to stop. I didn't want to be that kind of burden on him. When he found your bones – that is, what we thought were your – "

She stopped speaking, reaching for her brother's hand and avoiding his gaze. A single tear betrayed her, and she wiped it away viciously.

He smiled a little and squeezed her hand. "Oh, Jossey."

"What?"

He was still smiling, shaking his head, his face half-visible in the starlight. She frowned and turned to him.

He sobered.

"I had a...competition going with Gavin," he said slowly. "He dared me to go up aboveground at night without him.

He's the one that found the elevator. He's the one who came up with most of our adventures, actually. He called me – if I recall correctly – a 'wannabe-Patrol doofus loser,' whatever that meant, and said I wasn't brave enough and made me so mad that I decided to do it. So I took you so you'd be a witness that I *was* – technically – brave enough. I'm sorry. This" – he pointed to her scar – "is his and my fault. Forgive me."

She had to cover her mouth to stop laughing aloud. "Wannabe-Patrol doofus loser?" she repeated, eyebrows raised. Then she stopped as her brain caught up. "Wait. A *dare*?!"

He shook his head. "We were what, twelve? Thirteen? We were so stupid, he and I." He looked at her gently. "But if he hates anyone, it would probably be himself."

Jossey was still staring at her older brother. "You – " She gaped at him. "Really, Tark?"

She clapped her hand over her mouth before she could yell it at him, glancing at the lake below him. She hissed it again. "A *dare*?!?"

She didn't realize she was crying until Tark reached out and poked her face, lightly, the way he had when they were kids. She touched her cheek. It was wet. She smiled through her tears.

"A dare?" she repeated. She shook her head incredulously.

"All this time," she said. "Poor Gavin." *Poor me*, she didn't say.

One of the men poked his head out of the cave. "Bey?" he whispered.

"Yes, Erkan." Tark turned half around.

"Yazar is on first watch. He waits for you."

"Very good. Tell him to take second. Jossey and I have much to discuss."

Erkan saluted and went back inside.

Jossey's face was still wet with tears. For once she didn't try to wipe them away, as embarrassed as she felt. She glanced side-ways at her brother. "Do you forgive me then?"

"Do you forgive me?" Tark smiled hugely. "I told you, he and I were stupid. I'm sorry for...well, a lot of things."

She poked him in the face back. He laughed.

He looked out over the starlit lake and half drew his knees up to his chest. Even as tall and grown-up as he was now, he was still Tark, she thought.

They sat in comfortable silence for some time. She realized Tark was watching her face, and glanced at him. "What?"

"Did Gavin ever get married?"

"Huh?" She turned to him, confused.

She thought for a moment. "He has enough admirers, I'm surprised he hasn't. But I don't think he cares about that. He just reads military stuff and fights. And acts like the world's most annoying bodyguard." She stopped. "That's not fair of me. Anyway."

Tark had a funny smile on his face.

She glanced at him. "Why?"

"That's too bad." He was grinning a little.

"Tark, what are you – "

He was grinning bigger now. "Just curious. Never mind. And you?"

Jossey flushed with shame and looked determinedly at the rocks next to her hand, feeling a cold prickling tightness in her chest. "No," she stammered.

"What do you mean?" Tark frowned.

She looked anywhere but at her brother. "Have you *seen* this...thing on my face?" She touched the white raised scar. "Even your men said I looked like a...*canavar*. A monster."

Tark shook his head. "They can be obnoxious." He still looked faintly amused about something.

"Tark," she said, trying to change the subject, steer it toward more comfortable waters, "now it's your turn. I want to know everything that happened. How you ended up here. Why you are the Bey." She turned and sat facing him. "Is – is that baby I saw your little boy?" she asked shyly.

His face softened. "Yes. He's almost a year old. His name is Muhammed."

She smiled. "He's beautiful. I hope I can meet him one day."

"*Elhamdulillah.* As soon as we can get back to the camp and I can talk to a few people, you will, *inşallah.*" *God willing.* He looked seriously at her. "I know we've put you through a lot. And I'm sorry. But you are my family."

"Thank you." She smiled.

Then her smile faded. "Tark. Please. Tell me. You promised."

His eyes were fixed on hers. Silver, under flaxen hair. Exactly the way he'd been the night he'd disappeared.

"I did," he said.

* * *

"I don't remember much of the first few days," he said, but he looked as if he were holding something back.

"I remembered your...mother's face, screamed about it, for weeks," Jossey said softly. "I wouldn't tell them what I had seen."

He flinched, eyes searching her face, and she realized he was probably remembering seeing Jossey lying there, apparently lifeless, in the sand.

"We thought you were dead," he said at last.

He ran back to the base of the condenser, screaming, "Jossey! Jossey!" The Onlar grabbed him, shrieking something he couldn't understand. "Hadi!" she said. "Hadi!" He fought her, flailing, but she was too strong. "The girl – "

He refused to hear her. Jossey was alive. Jossey was –

Jossey's eyes were closed, blood seeping from her destroyed leg and from the wound on her face, so much blood. Her young face was already going pale, whether from shock or blood loss he could not tell. He screamed her name, eyes wide with horror.

Then there was another Onlar, tall, muscular, who picked Tark up, clamping a big hand over his mouth.

The last thing Tark saw as they carried him away into the night was his sister's small body, crumpled on the ground, under the burning moon.

He woke up in a cell. Everything was dim, and dark, and strangely cold, despite being aboveground in July. He had no idea where he was. "Mother?" he called. "Father?"

Then he remembered.

The small figure lying in the sand. The Onlar carrying him away. It was all he could see. Her little crumpled body. Blood. And it was his fault, all his –

The boy put his face between his knees, arms covering his head, and shook, shivering, crying.

Eventually he fell asleep.

They left food for him, and on the fourth day he decided to see who They were, these creatures that had stolen him away from his home and left his sister to die.

He picked up the metal bowl – not understanding where they had gotten metal, not caring, just wanting revenge, wanting to harm them as much they'd harmed him, harmed his sister. He carried it over to the huddled figure who was sitting by his cell, just within reach.

He nearly dropped it as he found himself looking into the puffy eyes of a woman.

She was not old, maybe his mother's age, maybe a decade older. Her skin was withered. She had light eyes, a pale green in the light from the fire They'd lit at the camp, and she looked like she had been crying.

He lowered the bowl, staring at her. "Who are you?" he finally rasped.

She dissolved into tears again. "You look so much like him," she said softly.

Tark was confused. What was a woman doing at the Onlar camp? And who did he look like?

She took the bowl gently from his numb hands and filled it with some kind of porridge. She handed it to him. He ate greedily, still uncomprehending.

"Who are you?" he rasped again when he could speak.

In answer, she held up a locket. She opened it carefully.

"Her name was Katha," Tark told Jossey, "and she had lost her only son to the farms."

"I hated her at first. I tried to escape, several times, not realizing just how far away from home I was." He laughed shortly. "But then – " He sighed. "I saw her lose another child, a daughter, to the kidnappers. I saw how much she mourned her son. I saw the people hiding in fear, waiting for their husbands and fathers to get back from raids, trying to find a way back into the Old City that was theirs long ago. Living there for part of the year, then being chased out at random intervals. I saw that the City Patrol, or whoever they are that steal children, didn't care if I was City or not. They didn't seem to know who I was. Maybe our uncle" – he looked darkly at Jossey – "maybe he did try to find me. But those men didn't seem to be looking for me. And as I grew older I stopped trying to escape."

He looked at the lake. "I thought you were dead. We found Father and failed to save him. Mother – I thought it might be easier if I just let her mourn rather than see her son turned into an 'Onlar.' Rather than go back and live a lie, maybe be interrogated, maybe have to fight against these people who had treated

471

me as one of them. And then Katha's daughter Aysun grew up, and the rest is history." He smiled a little.

Jossey smiled too. She was watching his face. "Tark," she suddenly said, "whatever happened to your ring?"

He shrugged. "I lost it in a contest. Fighting competition. Someone thought it looked cool and demanded it as a prize. Don't remember. Why?"

She shook her head. "I just remembered. One of those details you remember."

99

GAVIN AND HIS MEN STAGGERED DEEPER INTO THE TUNNELS.

It had been several hours since the ancient city above them had caved in, and they didn't dare try any of the side corridors that now proliferated around them. Gamma was doing his best to make a map in the near-dark, but he finally gave up and just muttered something to himself every time they passed a passageway.

"This is probably the main road," he said defensively when Rho pointed it out. "I mean, why else would they have wagon tracks?"

"He has a point," said Caspar.

They took turns shouldering the packs. They'd managed to scavenge some of their gear from underneath the rocks once the dust settled, but they didn't pull too hard for fear of creating another rockslide. Consequently, they had less than half the water they'd hoped for.

And their radio was –

Tskoulis wasn't convinced it was shot, but he knew they might only have one chance to use it...if they managed to get close enough to the surface for it to even be useful. It was full of gritty dust, and he carefully blew on it to try to get rid of the silt.

He tucked it away, really not wanting to have to make the trek aboveground if it came to that.

He estimated it was about evening. They still hadn't gotten to the OS1.

Gamma's light began to flicker.

Tskoulis tried his. Nothing. He wasn't sure what had happened, but the impact with the wall as they fled seemed to have done something to it.

"Anyone else – "

They all eyed the light and shook their heads.

They gathered around.

"Masks," Tskoulis said grimly. "Try not to walk into the walls. Hold on to the man ahead of you if necessary."

Gamma looked soberly at his light as he reached up and switched it off.

The darkness was total. Suffocating. Tskoulis had occasionally had this happen in the tunnels, but he'd never gotten used to it. At least this particular tunnel was wide enough that it wasn't claustrophobic, but he still inched forward, regretting that he hadn't brought some kind of stick with him.

For all he knew, there could be a hole ahead of them. A cliff. And they might have no idea until they were right on top of it.

They moved forward. He felt with his boots for the ridges in the ground.

They were there. He sighed with relief.

"Keep to the ridges," he said.

He moved ahead one step at a time, slowly getting into a shuffling rhythm. The men behind him were very quiet, following him into the pitch-blackness.

"Water," he eventually said. But they were heading downward. The air was cooler here.

He hoped there was enough oxygen.

He ran his left hand along the wall as he went. It was slimy, as if there were moisture in the air somewhere. Or a water source. It was cold.

Caspar seemed to have noticed it too. He heard the man's breathing change.

Suddenly Gavin stopped. His fingers had just slipped into empty air.

He held up a hand before remembering the pitch-darkness and muttered, "Halt."

He reached out a careful hand, leaned to the left.

His hand disappeared into empty space.

"Tracker," he said. "Go to your right."

"Sir."

Caspar's footsteps moved carefully to the right. Behind him, he could hear Rho groan. His wound, Tskoulis thought.

Caspar's footsteps continued. Then they shuffled back.

"Sir, we appear to be at a crossroads," Caspar said softly.

"Light," Tskoulis commanded. Gamma obeyed and switched on the rapidly-dimming safety light.

They were standing next to an enormous side tunnel, wide enough for two carts and men besides. It extended into blackness in both directions.

"Light," Tskoulis said softly. The red orb disappeared as quickly as it had appeared.

"So," he said into the darkness. "Any ideas?"

100

JOSSEY LAY AWAKE, STARING AT THE CEILING OF THE CAVE.
Across the small room, she could hear Tark's men snoring lightly. Well, not so lightly in one case. She snickered a little.

Mustafa was out like a light. She smiled, thinking how happy he should be to see his family after so long. Then her smile stilled. She didn't know if he still had any family.

She remembered what Tark had told her about the woman who had taken him away.

She couldn't really imagine the cruelty of what he was explaining, but she'd seen it for herself. The small child and the enormous Patrol agent. She still couldn't get his little face out of her mind.

She wanted to take her sword and rush down into the farm, snatch up that child and the others –

And probably be killed on the spot, she thought grimly.

Tark had said the Patrol agents hadn't seemed to be looking for him. And her uncle –

Her expression stilled. Sokol must know about all of this. Must be –

Running it, she thought, horrified. If this was a longstanding policy...

It did indeed *look* longstanding. She'd taken a closer look at Mustafa's uniform when he'd fallen asleep. It looked like it had been patched several times, hemmed to fit various lengths of arms. Several children.

Even one child was enough.

She had no idea what to do.

For the first time, it occurred to her that if her uncle knew she'd spoken with the Onlar, she could be in great danger. It wasn't like she had told them much about the solar project – Tark hadn't exactly asked – but even knowing that they were human, that her brother of all people was in charge...

She could go back, pretend she'd gotten lost. And do what? Accuse her uncle? Get herself jailed or worse? Try to sabotage the project?

Stay here with Tark?

She rolled over and looked at the sliver of pale light coming in underneath the screen.

If the sun was rising, in a few hours the landscape should be a burning desert, unnavigable except by the very skilled, and her City's population relegated underground, a few brave uniformed solar crew members up on the surface, taking care of the solar panels and condenser machines that powered the City, kept it functioning.

Or so Sokol had told her.

She sat up. If there were no grow lights – what was her uncle trying to do with the electricity? Maybe trying to reinstate them? Go fully underground? The only thing the City really used electricity for, to her knowledge, was residential and agriculture.

He'd said he needed a high-capacity low-fluctuation system. Something about keeping Karapartei from finding out. Karapartei with their claims of the government hiding instability and some kind of decline.

But if the City already had farms...

She couldn't figure it out.

The others were still unconscious. She was afraid to get up and accidentally wake them. She thought Erkan was outside standing guard – she didn't want him to think she was trying to escape, either.

She rolled over again and blocked out the light, trying to still the thoughts racing through her mind, trying to sleep.

Maybe Tark would have some answers for her when he woke up, she thought.

They slept late, and woke up around noon. The sleep seemed to have done Mustafa good – he seemed more chatty, following Altan around as the warrior prepared food for them.

The men went down to the lake to wash in the afternoon. Tark tossed her a spare uniform. "Here," he said.

"Thanks." She'd forgotten how gross she felt. But she probably looked awful. And smelled awful.

"Go with Altan and wash that other one." He grinned.

He herded them out of the cave while she changed. Then she went down to the lakeside. She knelt by the water and dipped her uniform in, scrubbing it with some kind of strange sponge Tark had handed her.

Altan was staring at her. She looked at him, shielding her eyes against the still-bright afternoon sun. "What?"

"Nothing," he muttered. He fidgeted. "You look like – "

"A monster?" she said half-jokingly. But he looked away, looking embarrassed.

"One of us," he said.

She glanced down. She was wearing the light-colored robes of the Onlar. She did indeed look like one of them.

"Oh," was all she said.

He sat on the rocks and looked out over the shining waters as she scrubbed.

They headed back up the hill to eat an evening meal, and Tark got straight to business as they chewed away at whatever delicious dish Yazar had prepared for them. Even Mustafa went silent as Tark began to speak.

"We have about half battery left on the bikes," Tark said. "We need to make a choice. Either we go straight back to Ilara overnight, risking Patrol out on the highway, or we go while it's still light and they probably aren't out. It's quite warm out there, but our bikes are better, faster, and the farm is about twenty miles off. They probably won't be looking this far...yet. If they're looking at all." He glanced at Altan. "We left the one bike there, so they may have found it by now."

"Bey, going around sunset makes more sense. They'd be blinded if they tried to head in this direction. We'd have the advantage." Erkan gestured with a leg of rabbit.

Tark turned to Yazar and Altan. "You agree?" He glanced at Jossey.

"Bey, what are we going to tell the people about – " Erkan glanced at Jossey, at the boy.

Tark held up a hand. "Yazar, take Mustafa and refill the water canteens."

"Yes, Bey." He gestured to Mustafa, who looked confused, but hopped to his feet. "*Let's go,*" he said to the boy.

They slung several canteens on strings over their backs and walked out.

As soon as the screen closed behind them, Tark turned to Jossey.

He looked straight at his sister. "Have you decided?"

"I – "

479

She wanted to understand exactly what she was agreeing to.

"If not, you know we can't let you go," Tark said seriously.

"I understand." She did. She just wanted to know –

"Why do you need my help so badly?" she said.

"I told you we need you for negotiations with the Colony – that is, the City. We've been trying to get them to let us settle long-term within the Old City, Derinkuyu, what you call Old Sector 1, for a hundred years, if not longer." He took a sip of water. "I don't know what you know about this region's history, but we did work together once. I wasn't quite telling the full truth when I said there had never been grow lights."

She looked at him. "A hundred years ago?"

"Yes. At least. At one time, the Founders came here saying they were here to settle peaceably in this region. There were some of my – Altan's – people here. They'd survived many invasions, many wars, by retreating underground over a millennium, if not longer. They showed the Founders how to carve into the rock around here, the way they'd been doing for generations. The Founders chose a site directly over the old underground city of Kaymaklı, halfway between Nevşehir and Derinkuyu. They drilled straight down, destroyed the old city, installed their modern-day module system, set up their lab-based agricultural system underground, and that was that."

He stirred his food thoughtfully. "For a while, everything worked fine. The locals had Derinkuyu, and there weren't many of them – not with the extreme heat and the wars and the famine in the region. The Founders were fine too. But then there were – let's just say politics, it's a very long story, and the Founders suddenly decided they needed to expand, make themselves more secure, and they made it very clear that they were planning to take the resources of the locals, 'for everyone. With everyone's help.' Conscripted labor for the grow labs, for the mining, for the construction of large-scale solar panels. Largely from the local population. Some of the locals didn't like that."

Altan didn't seem to be fully following. Tark said a couple things quickly in the Old Language, and Altan's eyes lit with comprehension. He took another bite and kept listening.

"So," Tark went on, "they fought back. Bombed some of the tunnels. Were sealed out into the heat as punishment. Were dehumanized, severely. And, in short order, when the solar panels weren't sufficient to run everything needed for the Founders' fast-growing population, the local people – what you call the Onlar – became a resource themselves."

Altan pulled up his sleeve, showed her horrific scars that roped around his forearm. She flinched. "I got this trying to escape from the farm," he said, in the accent that she'd almost stopped noticing.

"Even the language. Most people never learn English, not well. The only contact we have with the City is diplomacy and the farms, and English is...discouraged there. We all look pretty much the same," Tark said bitterly, "so they had to have an easy way to keep track of us."

She thought of Caspar, his long silver eyes, much like Altan's dark ones. Gavin's surname.

Those who had stayed with the Founders.

She took a bite of food and thought.

It was all horrific. But how could she specifically help?

"What good could I do?" she asked, thinking aloud as much as asking her brother. "I'm just one person."

Tark smiled. "You're a solar Engineer. You and you alone know what Sokol is working on, in all its details."

"And Caspar," she interrupted.

"And your friend Caspar." His gaze was deadly serious. "We've been keeping an eye on Patrols in the last several months. Their patterns have changed. The City seems to be gearing up for something."

"Gearing up?" She glanced between him and Altan. "Gearing up for what?"

Tark and Altan shared a look. "We don't know. But we think it has to do with the solar project you were helping design."

She frowned. "I know Sokol said that Karapartei – the terrorist group – might be interested in knowing about it. He said that the Onlar – you – were attacking the infrastructure and for security reasons they needed a more reliable solar..." She trailed off. He'd said it was a matter of keeping the electricity at normal levels.

"Tark," she said slowly, "what did you say about our City dying? I thought it was about the grow lights. I thought – " Her cheeks burned. "I thought Sokol was worried you would try to disrupt the power to them and starve us out."

He shook his head. "You have too many people," he said. "Without enough electricity, you have to either rely on above-ground farming or you have to add extra labs. And to do that you have to expand. It's why you've had supply issues."

She wondered how he knew.

"We had grow lights once, you said."

"Yes." He poured another cup of water, handed it to her. She took it and drank.

"I'm not sure that's the City's plan," he said. "But if it is – "

He looked at her, expression deadly serious. "If it is about putting more grow lights into play, he would have no reason for us. And do you really think he'd let us live? Why give ammunition to his detractors in the City? Do you really think the entire City would be okay with this happening right under their noses? Slavery and such? What with the 'glorious Founders' and all that?" He shook his head. "If he gets that grid going..."

Jossey gaped at her brother. "Are you saying he'd try to – "

Tark glanced at Altan, translated a couple of things quickly. Then he turned his attention back to Jossey. "What do you think he and his kind have been doing for the past century?" He smiled bitterly. "Do you remember the Founders' motto?"

For the Successful of the Earth. She'd always found it odd, contrived. Arrogant.

"Well, the Onlar are the...unsuccessful, in their way of thinking," he said flatly.

She took a bite of food as what he was saying sank in.

She thought of baby Muhammed, that beautiful little child. Her nephew. In a few years he might be old enough to be stolen away, Bey's son or no.

She thought of Gavin, who went forth every day to defend his City. Who talked about doing right.

Of the Onlar who had attacked them, and the man in the OS1 with Tark's ring. Of Tark's family, and the small skeleton Gavin had found in the canyons.

With horrific clarity, she suddenly understood where the bones had likely come from.

Deposited. Left. No longer useful.

"What do you need from me?" she asked.

101

THEY TOOK ERKAN'S SUGGESTION TO GO WHILE IT WAS STILL light and the sun was still blinding.

They made sure any fire was out completely, stashed away their supplies, then headed out as the sun was nearing the horizon. It was still burning hot, but not unpleasantly so – it was a dry heat, and Jossey squinted toward the west as they stepped out into the late October sun.

She couldn't imagine this place in July.

She looked up, shielding her eyes, as Altan handed her a bundle.

"Take this to the bikes," he said.

She carefully balanced it and took it down to Tark, who stored it in his bike's compartment.

"Are you good with having your own bike?" he asked. "We may have to speed. Or we can switch off when we get closer to Ilara."

She looked back at the approaching men. "I – "

"Remember, you're still a prisoner. We have to treat you as such. I'm sorry. Don't take anything I do personally."

He waved Altan over. The young warrior came jogging.

"Yes, Bey?"

"Remember, Jossey is still your prisoner. Act accordingly. But Altan." He looked hard at the young man. "Don't overdo it."

Altan flushed, and didn't look at Jossey. "Yes, Bey."

Erkan, Yazar, and the boy approached carrying the last of the supplies. They loaded them onto the bikes.

Erkan went back up the hill and swept with a broom of sorts. Then he stashed it in his bike and hopped on, pulling on his helmet. "Ready, Bey."

Tark motioned to Mustafa to hop on his bike. Erkan and Altan paired up. That left just Jossey.

"Ready for this?" Tark asked.

She wasn't. But she had no choice. She couldn't risk the child seeing who she was...yet. And she understood from the Onlar's behavior that most men and women couldn't be in close proximity. So she couldn't be on any of their bikes. At least not before the boy knew the truth.

Tark glanced at her helmet. "Let's go then."

They zoomed down the highway, the sun at their backs. She risked a glance down at the electrical gauge on her bike. Forty-eight percent, it said. She hoped it would be enough.

How far had he said? Twenty miles?

The sun was sinking swiftly toward the horizon, covering the fields with golden light. Jossey had to keep her gaze on the road, stop from staring around her. She'd never seen such color. Had never really bothered to look.

The evening breeze was picking up, too, though she felt it more than heard it. Her helmet blocked out sound.

They turned to the southeast. She became aware of the golden orb of the sun out of the corner of her eye, its rays piercing even the thick glass of her helmet's view field. She blinked, turned away, saw the long shadows of the other bikes tilting unsteadily across the landscape, like giants running, fifty feet tall.

As the sun dropped further, it flooded the entire horizon with burning orange. She imagined anyone coming from the other direction would be completely blinded.

Everything was unfamiliar, orangish, purplish, like an alien planet. She grinned, exhilarated, wanting to take off her helmet and just scream into the wind.

Tark shot past her, giving her a thumbs-up, and it took all her strength not to race him down the highway.

The sun slanted across her face as they headed more directly south. She understood that Tark was just taking the straight route – no darting across fields, no hiding. The fastest route.

Whatever that floating light had been, she hoped that the Patrol farm didn't have any more of them.

Not fifteen minutes later, the sun had dropped below the horizon. The light had gone quickly. The sky was pale, filled with thin clouds that were quickly purpling in the dusk.

She stayed in formation, feeling the need to go faster, faster, realizing that once it was down, they'd probably have no protection from whatever roving technology Patrol had out there.

She sped up.

"Careful," Tark's voice said in her ear. She jumped.

"Stay behind me," he said.

"I'm not trying to run away," she said, offended.

"I'm not worried about that," he said. "We have to make a detour."

. . .

She pulled back. He went ahead, gesturing to the right as they approached what she remembered as the enormous cliff where the Onlar had originally brought her to their camp.

They slowed, and he took a sharp right. It cut straight through what she now saw were ruins, and down to the south, toward the deep tree-filled canyon of Ilara.

"We need to stay below the ridge line now that the sun is down." His voice was taut. "We need headlights."

"How – "

"The button by your left thumb."

She glanced down, glanced back up.

They switched theirs on. She fumbled with the button for a moment before hers worked, wobbling a little. She jerked the handlebars back into line.

The ridge rose against the sky, and she had to slow down so she could see.

They slowed to thirty mph, Yazar grumbling, but the boy seemed afraid too.

"Keep an eye out for animals," Tark muttered into the com. "We can't afford a crash."

Eighteen percent. Her battery gauge was beginning to glow a faint yellow.

"Tark? What happens if we run out of battery?" she asked.

"Worry about it around ten percent," he said.

She frowned. But she said, "Okay."

The road had ruts and rusted equipment half scattered on the asphalt. Jossey slowed her bike still further.

Suddenly Erkan pointed to the sky. "Bey!" he shouted.

They all looked as one. A small light was shimmering in the distance, behind them. It was hovering at a distance of maybe a mile, just above the ridge line.

Tark shouted, "Get off the road! Shut off your lights! Now!"

Jossey fumbled for her headlight button. She couldn't see well even with them. Without them –

"Now!" His voice was frantic.

She shut off the lights.

In the sudden darkness, she couldn't see what she was doing. She hit the brake, skidding sideways, unable to control the bike.

She braced herself for impact or worse, gripping the handlebars as she swayed toward the edge of the road.

Altan shot up next to her, grabbed the handlebar, steadied the bike. She stared at him wide-eyed through her helmet.

"Tap your brakes!" he shouted.

She did so carefully, slowing just enough to recover.

"You okay?" Altan.

She tried to respond.

He pointed to the small light. It was rapidly approaching.

"Turn your bike and follow me," he said.

She swallowed her fear, still shaking, and did as he asked.

They sped directly toward the ruins. The closest building seemed to be an old house, its red-orange roof long open to the elements, judging by the state of the rust and the tree that was growing through the floor.

Erkan was last; he drove the bike directly into the house and shut off the engine as the light made its slow way into the town.

Tark's jaw was clenched as he looked up at what appeared to be a small flying camera.

"Might be infrared," he hissed. "Stay down. Don't make a sound."

Mustafa looked petrified. He hid next to Tark, eyes enormous as he stared up at the light.

It drifted slowly and descended to street level, floating through the ruins of the town, up and down the streets as if scanning for something, not twenty feet off the ground.

They'd put the bikes right inside the wall. But if the drone went above it, and it was infrared...

If the drone went above it, they'd probably be as visible as in clear daylight.

. . .

They huddled, barely breathing. Tark had his hand over Mustafa's mouth.

"*They might have audio,*" he mouthed to Jossey.

Infrared. Audio. Military-grade, Jossey thought. Probably motion sensors too, if she'd learned anything from Gavin's conversations about military tech.

She stayed as still as she could.

The little machine whirred as it passed the open window.

She wondered if the bikes had left tracks in the dust. But there was nothing they could do about that now.

They waited.

After an agonizing several minutes, the light drifted up, up, up, and disappeared beyond the ridge line.

Tark kept his hand over Mustafa's mouth and stood up slowly. Jossey's heart was pounding in her throat.

He kept his other hand up as he looked out the window. Finally, he lowered it slowly, putting a finger to his lips and releasing the boy. "It's gone," he whispered. "But we have to walk – can't use headlights from here on out. We're much too close to Ilara. Can't risk bringing any kind of camera equipment anywhere close to the canyon. Especially not infrared. They haven't found Ilara so far. If they ever did..." He clenched his fists.

"How far are we, Bey?" Erkan asked.

"Around eight miles."

Altan looked sober. "How did they know to search here, you think?"

"I don't know," Tark said. "But they probably figured there was no life below the ridge line, and just double-checked in case. Let's hope so, anyway."

They brushed the dust off their clothing and looked at each other.

"Everyone take your water," Tark said quietly. *"Altan, we need a ---- tomorrow to get these."*

"Yes, Bey."

Eight miles. Jossey was glad they had fresh water. And that the sun was down.

"Let's get out of here," she said.

102

TSKOULIS AND HIS MEN HAD DECIDED TO REST AT THE JUNCTION. They needed to look for water, Tskoulis knew, and the tunnel seemed to lead in the general direction of where Gamma and Caspar thought they could find the OS1.

It was a wide tunnel, and showed signs of older activity – more cart tracks, for one thing. But no sign.

In fact, Gamma and Caspar couldn't find any sign anywhere. It was like the Onlar had simply disappeared.

They sat down and tried to get their other lights to work while discussing their options.

Phi's flickered, and he showed it to the others with a triumphant cry before it flickered off again.

He set it down, groaning.

"At least one of us has a functioning light," he grumbled. "Rho, you smashed into me back there."

"Yeah, well, now my chest hurts," Rho said.

Phi twisted something on the base. "Maybe it's just loose," he said. "A connection or something."

"Keep working on it," Tskoulis said absently. He turned to Gamma and Caspar. "What's the verdict?"

Caspar seemed to be calculating something in his head. Gamma looked slightly irritated.

Welcome to the club, Tskoulis thought, trying not to grin. He was glad he wasn't the only one annoyed by Mr. Good-at-Stuff.

Part of him wanted to see the looks on their faces if they ever saw Caspar *really* in action.

Caspar seemed not to have noticed Gamma's annoyance. He muttered something final-sounding, then glanced up at them. "The right tunnel," he said.

He grabbed one of the charts, scribbled a few numbers on it. "Look," he said.

Gamma shot Tskoulis a look and scooted over.

"We've traveled about...I'd say this many miles, give or take." Caspar pointed to some calculations.

"How do you know?" Gamma looked smug.

"I've been counting paces." Caspar's sharp silver eyes flickered over the paper. He tallied up something else.

Paces, Tskoulis thought, annoyed. But it made sense. Impressive, even, considering the conditions they were in.

He wanted to admire the man. He really did.

He just wished Savaş weren't *quite* so good at, well, just about everything.

He shook his head and focused on what Savaş was saying.

"We're about here. That means we're either directly parallel to OS1 or slightly beyond it, assuming we've been going in a straight line. I don't know where this tunnel continues on to, but it's apparently somewhere important given the grooves in the floor. Then again, so is this other one we've just found." He reached for Gamma's light, shined it on the walls. "See these?" He pointed to niches carved at about shoulder height. "Those are, I believe, for lamps. Oil lamps. At one time – "

" –this was probably an underground highway," Tskoulis interrupted.

Caspar grinned. "Exactly."

Tskoulis grinned despite himself. He held out a hand and pulled Caspar to his feet. He slapped the Tracker on the back, feeling the strength in the other's arm.

"Are you certain?" Gamma asked. "If we run out of water on the way..."

Caspar wet a finger and held it up, concentrating for a long moment.

Then he grinned hugely.

"There's air," he said quietly. "Coming from that direction." He pointed to the right.

Tskoulis did the same, felt the air.

Savaş was actually right.

"I don't know how they trained you, Tracker, but you were worth dragging along." Tskoulis gave him a real smile.

"Keep working on that light, Phi," the commander said over his shoulder. "Let's see where this goes."

The air got cooler and breezier as they moved, and they sped up in anticipation.

Phi even got his light to work, if he held it just right. It seemed one of the wires inside had come half undone. He lurched along, half balancing with the bag and holding his arm at an awkward angle, but it was with a grin on his face.

They still had quite a ways to go, according to Caspar's calculations, but they walked with more energy than they had in some time. The OS1 had water, and fresh air. And they knew how to get to the surface from there.

"Commander," Caspar said as he strode along behind Tskoulis. "What if J – what if Agent Sokol is being held some-where in the OS1? What if our replenishing supplies somehow alerts them to our presence?"

Tskoulis didn't look at him. "Keep looking for sign. In my experience, the Onlar tend to cluster around the third or fourth level. They're familiar with those. We can drop down to the lower levels, get water, see if we can pick up any audio of any kind through the well shafts."

"Yes, sir." Caspar glanced back at Gamma. "And if we don't find her there?"

Tskoulis looked grim. "Then we should come back to this junction and continue where we left off."

103

AT LAST THE TUNNEL OPENED UP INTO A LARGE CAVERN. TSKOULIS grinned. He'd been here before. Many times. Not this specific chamber, but they all had a signature look.

And, of course, there was another word etched in the wall, much more clearly than the other word had been. This one he could read.

He didn't need to know the letters. He'd seen it on so many old maps he recognized it instantly.

It was the ancient name for the underground city. It had probably had other names in its long history. What mattered was knowing where they were.

He turned to the others.

"Welcome," he said, "to Old Sector 1."

They fanned out. Tskoulis had been here more than a few times, but even he got lost on occasion. But he felt he recognized this particular area, if very vaguely.

They went further in. A few chambers in, and they came across a tiny Patrol sign, embedded in the rock. OS1-5-Q3-4.

Fifth level, quadrant three to indicate south, fourth chamber from the center. It was almost like an address.

So they were on the opposite end from where Caspar, Henry, and the rest of 2-5 had fought with the Onlar, Tskoulis realized. The last time he'd been on the southern end, he'd gotten in what amounted to a brawl with a group of lightly armed Onlar. Neither group had ended particularly well off. He'd had to call for Forensics, had to take his men's bodies up to the surface. That had not been a pleasant night.

He cracked his knuckles, remembering.

"Where's the supply cache?" Alpha asked. He gestured to Rho. "I think we need to take a break."

Tskoulis looked back at the big man, who looked pale even in the uneven reddish light.

"This way," he said.

5-Q3-18 and -19 were where Patrol kept some of their hidden supply caches.

They went over to the first cache and uncovered it. It was half empty, but what was left looked worth eating. They shared the preserved food among themselves, sitting down, stretching their legs.

Rho's arm didn't look good. Tskoulis shared a look with Phi, who supposedly had some medical experience.

Their med pack was back at the cave-in, he remembered. But maybe –

Tskoulis dug around in the cache and found a tube of honey.

He tossed it to Rho. "Here."

Rho tore it open with his teeth.

"Hold on a sec." Alpha did not look pleased. "I thought you were keeping that clean, Rho."

The wound was pink and starting to swell. Rho groaned.

"I was," the big man gritted out. "It's probably the dust from the cave-in."

"Wash it out." Alpha tossed him one of the canteens. "Use what you need. Don't waste the honey."

They looked away as Rho poured water over the cut, hissing.

He picked up the tube of honey and applied it directly to his wound. It had antibiotic properties, they knew. But they had no bandages. Tskoulis shook his head. Rho shrugged, wincing.

"You need a doctor." Phi was frowning.

"I've survived worse."

"Yeah, well – " Phi trailed off. "Let's just take the rest of the honey with us, yeah?"

They made their way single file down one of the passages. They kept silent. Tskoulis had ordered them to listen for any sign that Jossey and her captors were there.

"Why would they keep her this long?" Caspar asked at last.

Tskoulis glared at him. But it was a valid point. She'd been gone five days. At that rate they'd probably have run out of food.

"Maybe they have some kind of...den down here," he said at last.

It was the only reasonable explanation, he thought. They'd cleared much of the OS1 in the past, but there were still levels that hadn't been accessible or hadn't been checked recently. And the Onlar seemed to come back, year after year. He tried to remember where the bigger living chambers were. The place was capable of holding thousands of people, after all. It was entirely possible he'd missed some, now and in the past.

Most, as he'd said, were on the third and fourth levels, but that didn't mean They couldn't have gone deeper into the earth, especially if they suspected Patrol would come after them.

The best option seemed to be to sweep those levels, then see if they could hear anything from the air shafts as they went.

It would probably be long, tedious work.

He glanced at the men. They looked exhausted. They'd been traveling in pitch-blackness for hours, half their water gone. They needed to take a real rest.

If Jossey was being held down here somewhere, they needed to be in top condition to find her.

"Let's take two hours," he said. "Get some sleep. Then carry on." He glanced at Rho. "Give your arm time to heal a bit."

"Give me that light," Caspar said to Phi. "Let me see if I can fix it."

Phi looked suspiciously at him. "You're a Tracker. How would you – "

Tskoulis caught Caspar's eye and shook his head a little.

"You're right," Caspar said. "Never mind, don't want to break it."

They took some more of the food out of the supply cache.

"Gamma, you take first watch," Tskoulis said. "Two hours."

104

Jossey's feet were killing her.

She followed Tark and the others down into the canyon, shouldering her bag, refusing to complain, trying not to trip on the roots and rocky ground.

Under the trees, the air was cooler, and she was grateful for the stream that ran alongside them. At least here they could refill their water.

They stopped to rest around the seven-mile mark, climbing up the hill to take shelter in one of the caves. It was a rocky climb, and her leg muscles were burning by the time she reached the top, but it was worth it. They could see much of the canyon from up here.

In the distance, they could see lights.

Fires.

Tark frowned. "There's too many," he said.

He grabbed one of the sets of goggles from his pack and zoomed in. "What are they – "

"Let me see, Bey." Altan took the goggles from him.

"They're..." He removed them from his face, stared at Tark. *"It looks like they're having some kind of celebration."*

Tark grabbed them out of his hand. "What are you talking abou– "

His voice stilled.

Jossey glanced at Erkan.

Mustafa was looking back and forth between them, concern on his young face. *"What happened, Bey?"*

Erkan had his own goggles out. He *tsked* as he looked.

"My guess is Kudret," he said softly.

Tark made a contemptuous noise. "We've been gone barely over two days. That's it."

"We didn't tell anyone we ----, Bey," Erkan said carefully. *"And maybe we're wrong. Maybe it's not what we think it is."*

Tark looked skeptical. *"Does he think we ------- the camp?"*

"He...may think we left to negotiate on our own with the prisoner," Erkan said in English, glancing at Jossey.

Tark took another look. "We need to go," he said. "Right now. If it's Kudret..." His expression stilled.

"Bey..."

"Come on. Rest's over."

"Yes, Bey."

They scrambled down the hill.

Tark turned to Jossey. "I'm sorry," he said.

He tied a rope around her hands.

To Mustafa, who was staring wide-eyed at the rope, he said, *"She is not Altan's wife. She is our prisoner. But she is here to help us, you understand? Stay silent, Mustafa. This is important."*

Mustafa turned his shocked gaze to her. But he did not move away from her.

Altan took the rope and tugged on it, but very lightly. She half-smiled and followed him.

They crept closer to the fires.

About fifty Onlar were seated in a circle. Kudret was standing in the middle.

"*Kudret,*" one of the Onlar was saying. "*This is ----. Do you really think our Bey would desert us and take the prisoner? We have been waiting for this for months.*"

Kudret looked around. "*Well? Where is he? Has anyone heard word?*"

He turned and pointed to Aysun, who was seated at the head of the gathering, chin held high. She looked past him.

"*Has your husband said anything to you?*"

She said flatly, "*No, he has not.*"

Tark's jaw clenched.

"*There.*" Kudret looked gleeful. "*You have heard from the Bey's wife. Tark Bey has some kind of plan that he has not shared with us. Is that right? Is that the way we should be?*"

Altan was translating for Jossey. But she understood the gist from Kudret's face, his gestures.

Kudret frowned. "*Diros Bey's plan was to bring us a prisoner so we could negotiate with the Colony. We were to take a ------ of our leaders to meet with them. In doing this, our new Bey has shown that he does not ---- to represent the people. He represents only himself.*"

"I've heard enough," Tark muttered.

"Wait, Bey." Erkan held up a hand. "Let him..."

He said something Jossey didn't understand. But Tark smiled coldly. Altan grinned.

"*My husband would not have betrayed his people, God forbid,*" Aysun said stiffly. "*He has saved many of your children from the farms. He and my family have been very generous with you in times of hunger and -----. Or have you forgotten?*"

"*No, Lady,*" murmured many of the Onlar.

Kudret stood, hands behind his back, looking at her. His eyes were narrowed. "*And do you even know the name of our prisoner?*"

A murmur raced through the crowd.

"We do not know who she is. Diros Bey's wife, Lady Katha, seems to. Maybe our new Bey knows something we do not."

"That is enough." Tark stepped into the firelight.

The entire crowd turned and stared, dead silent.

Kudret turned too.

Tark took Jossey's rope from Altan and yanked on it. She staggered forward.

"Enough, Kudret." He spoke in English. "The prisoner has been shown the farms. She has agreed to help us, *elhamdulillah.* Do not dare question my authority again." He put his hand on his sword.

Kudret stepped back, put his hands up, smiling. "You make quite an entrance, Bey."

Tark glanced over at Aysun. She was staring at him, at Jossey. He gave her a small smile.

Then he beckoned to Mustafa. "And, thank God, we were able to rescue one of ours."

Mustafa stepped up beside him, silent, looking overwhelmed at all the faces.

There was a scream, and a woman ran out of the crowd, pushing past the guards, embracing him, babbling. Mustafa clung to her, weeping, choking, *"Anne."*

Tark watched them for a moment, smiling. Then he turned back to Kudret. "Do not concern yourself with the details of the negotiation," he said. "As you know, you have not been invited to be part of the negotiating party."

Kudret's brow darkened. "Bey – "

Tark said icily, "Now. What are we discussing, other than my supposed betrayal of the people who raised me?"

An oily smile appeared on Kudret's face. "Bey, I did not – "

"Be quiet," Tark snapped.

Altan put his hand on his sword. Tark held up a hand.

"The prisoner is mine," he said. *"I decide how this works. I, of course, consult my people. But some matters are very delicate. This*

operation has taken months. Do not pry into things you do not lead, Kudret. If we fail now, we may fail forever, God forbid, do you all understand?"

Jossey did not need a translation.

Silence. Kudret looked ready to explode.

"If you have a problem with that, you are welcome to challenge me as Bey."

Aysun's hand flew to her mouth.

Kudret's eyes were dark. But he kept his mouth shut. The men stared at each other for a long moment.

Then he stepped back. *"Please, Bey. Welcome back. And welcome to our young escapee."* He smiled at Mustafa, who clung to his mother and barely acknowledged the man.

"Thank you, Bey." Mustafa's mother turned a tear-streaked face to him.

Slow applause, a trickle, then a roar from the crowd as she took her son by the hand and led him to an old couple who Jossey thought were his grandparents. They kissed him, the old woman's face disappearing into wrinkles as she smiled. Kudret sat down, stone-faced.

Tark handed Jossey's rope to Altan. She looked around apprehensively.

"After dinner, after the camp settles, come to my tent," Tark said to them quietly.

Altan saluted.

Jossey watched her brother join his family. Aysun embraced him, put baby Muhammed in his arms. She shot Jossey a look, then turned back to Tark and gave him a bowl, saying something to him.

Altan tugged on the rope. Jossey turned and followed him over to the side of the camp, where they sat down.

. . .

She entered Tark's tent with Altan. The camp was quiet, the embers of the bonfire still glowing out in the canyon. She was careful not to make any noise. The guard out in front raised an eyebrow at Altan, but otherwise said nothing.

Tark was waiting for them, along with Aysun and his mother-in-law. Aysun had little Muhammed in her arms. He at least did not seem ready to sleep. Katha was yawning, but she perked up as the prisoner and Altan entered the tent.

Aysun shot Jossey an icy look. Jossey flinched.

"Welcome," Tark said. He turned to Aysun. "Would you bring us some tea?"

Aysun looked unhappy, but greeted Altan and fetched a tray.

Altan sat next to Tark. He motioned for Jossey to sit as well. She sank down between them, trying not to overbalance on her bad leg, and clumsily managed to land in a graceless heap. The young warrior shot her a look, and she glared at him.

"Now," Tark said. "You should understand we need to speak very quietly. I want to make everything clear from the start." He turned to his wife and mother-in-law.

Aysun just looked at him.

"As you know," Tark said carefully, "I came from the Colony a long time ago. Ever since Diros Bey...has been gone, I have faced opposition from Kudret and his men, who think I am somehow loyal to the Colony."

Aysun's gaze slid to Jossey.

Tark caught his wife's hand in his. She looked back at him.

"Forgive me," he said. "I have not been fully honest with you. I could not risk telling you the truth until our prisoner agreed to help us."

"*What truth, Tark?*" Aysun whispered.

Tark smiled a little, crookedly. "That of all the people in the Colony..." He trailed off. He glanced at Jossey. "This woman's name is Jossey. She is a solar Engineer, in charge of the project my men saw."

He looked straight at Aysun. "She is also my younger sister, the one I thought dead."

Aysun's eyes opened wide, and she stared at Jossey. Pain flashed across Katha's face, and her hand flew to her mouth. *"Yapma,"* she said, voice quiet, but breaking. *"Do not take my son from me."*

She had dementia, Jossey suddenly realized. Or something similar.

Aysun put her hand on Katha's arm. "Shh. *Hayır, anne.*"

The young woman turned to Jossey. "You – " She stared into Jossey's eyes, really looking at her face. Jossey looked back at her, unblinking.

"The scar," Aysun said flatly, in English. "I know about your scar."

Then she smiled. "I can see Tark's face in yours."

Jossey smiled awkwardly. "It's nice to meet you," she faltered, glancing at Tark. He motioned for her to go on.

She looked at the little boy in Aysun's arms. "Your son is very beautiful."

Aysun glanced down at Muhammed, who was gazing up with big dark eyes. She kissed him on the head and he gurgled. "Yes, *maşallah.*"

Jossey smiled. "He looks like – " She glanced at Tark.

Aysun, too, looked at Tark. "I understand why you did not tell us," she said quietly. "Kudret – "

Tark looked grim. "Kudret looks for chances to harm me. To grab power for himself. I don't trust him to negotiate with the Colony."

Aysun turned back to Jossey. "And you have agreed to help?" Her look was gauging.

"Yes." Jossey ignored the cold look. It was a lot to take in, she knew.

"How?"

"That," Tark said, "is why I have brought her here."

. . .

He gestured to Altan, who went to the tent entrance and waved in Erkan and Yazar. They came in and sat down.

Tark reached over and slipped the rope off Jossey's hands. She stretched her wrists and gave him a grateful look.

Aysun passed the tray of tea around.

Jossey took a cup, still feeling uneasy. Aysun didn't seem to have fully bought the idea that she was Tark's sister. They did, after all, look quite different, she thought. Just in case, she made sure to sit far away from him. She moved in Altan's direction; Altan looked uncomfortable and scooted away from her as she got close.

Katha looked closely at Jossey at one point, green eyes wide. "*You*," she said. Then she lapsed back into silence, smiling at Tark. Jossey flinched, but Aysun seemed satisfied somehow.

Tark glanced around the group. "Jossey is an engineer. She is in charge of the project that the Colony has begun. We suspect that they are trying to...become independent of us. I've been thinking, and we have two clear options right now."

"Two options?" Jossey asked.

"You told me your friend Caspar is also working on the project," he said. "We have no leverage, because he could complete it without you, correct?"

She looked away. "Probably."

His lips pursed. "Therefore your value in negotiations is as a hostage. If we try to trade you, how much do you think...Uncle Sokol" – he said the name with distaste – "would offer for you?"

He waved a hand as Jossey's face started to burn. "Don't answer that. He knows very well that we do not give prisoners up unless we are getting something more valuable than the information they can provide. And you have very valuable infor-mation. But if we give you up, we lose any head start or leverage

506

regarding the solar project. If he's a logical man – which I know he is – he should assume that we would only be willing to give you up once interrogation has broken you. Therefore we still have no leverage, and you are unsafe." He looked at her darkly. "You know what Sokol does to those who fail?"

Jossey shuddered. She'd refused to think about it, but he was right.

"So you are saying she is not valuable?" Aysun hissed.

"Oh no," Tark said, grinning. "She is very valuable. As long as no one knows she was ever here."

Aysun looked oddly at him. "What do you mean?"

"We can try to negotiate." He looked at Jossey. "Or we can try to sabotage their system."

Jossey stared at him. "You want me to be a spy?"

Her older brother winked. "You know how you were always nagging me and Gavin to take you on an adventure?"

"Yeah, but – "

He looked at her soberly. "I'm sorry, Jossey. I didn't mean for all this to happen. My father-in-law didn't share his entire plan with me before he died. But he didn't know about this whole solar upgrade either. The original plan was – "

"Interrogate a random Engineer and figure out how to sabotage the City, then take those secrets with you to the negotiation," Jossey said flatly. "I got it."

Tark blinked. Aysun's eyebrows went up.

"Well, yes," he admitted. "But you – "

She glanced at Erkan. "I'm...valuable," she said. He had the grace to look away.

"You are," Tark said. "Not because you're my sister. We didn't realize the extent of the Colony's plans until we saw what your Patrol team was putting together. We can't just threaten the

City anymore." He looked seriously at her. "We have to stop him from putting that plan into play."

"I understand," she said. She glanced at her nephew. He was asleep, drooling on Aysun's arm.

"I'm sorry," she said suddenly, not quite looking at any of them, gesturing vaguely to the tent, to the things around them. "I didn't know." She looked straight at Tark.

"Sorry," said Katha.

Jossey's head shot up. The older woman reached out toward her face, still smiling that vacant, sweet smile from before.

"Sorry," she repeated, tracing what looked like Jossey's scar in the air.

Jossey stared at her, tears in her eyes.

Altan snuck out of the tent and fetched Jossey's things from the prisoner's area, returning quickly. He deposited them at her feet, murmured "Bey" to Tark, and left.

Jossey laid out her bedroll on the floor near the remains of the small fire. It was pleasantly cool in the tent.

Aysun sat stirring the ashes. She looked up at Jossey, then went back to stirring.

"How old were you?" she finally asked.

"What?"

"When your brother came to us." She kept her eyes on the ashes.

"Ten." Jossey looked away too. "I thought he was dead. Until now I thought he was dead."

Aysun looked up. "And you are willing to give up your entire City for your long-lost brother?" She sat back, stopped stirring. "Forgive me for my suspicion, but – "

Jossey smiled sadly. "My Patrol leader was Tark's best friend when they were young. He found bones in a canyon some time ago on a Patrol mission. He thought it was Tark. He thought he'd found his friend's body after fifteen years. I thought – " Her voice caught and she looked at the floor.

She cleared her throat and went on. "That's why I joined Patrol." She didn't meet Aysun's eyes. "They always told us the Onlar were 'vicious killers,' that sometimes Patrol would only find bones. That your people could see in the dark. Nonsense like that. It turns out *we* are probably the ones leaving the bones."

She looked down. "I don't know who Gavin really found in that canyon. But if that's what the City does to survive, then maybe we don't deserve – "

She trailed off, unable to speak. Aysun was looking at her solemnly.

"I hope you are prepared for this," was all she said.

105

Tskoulis rolled over on the hard stone and groaned, looking at his wrist gauge. He blinked, confused, focusing on the time.

6:03 AM. They'd slept for five hours, he thought. Not two.

He sat up. Gamma was unconscious at his post. Alpha was standing motionless by the door.

Tskoulis shot Alpha a look. "Anything?" he asked.

Alpha came over and crouched next to the commander.

"No, sir." Alpha jerked a thumb toward Gamma. "He woke me up first, don't –"

Gavin waved his hand and glanced around the room. The others were in varying states of unconsciousness. Caspar was muttering something. Rho was sprawled on his back, snoring loudly.

Gavin tossed a pebble at his foot. He snorted, then went back to sleep more quietly.

"Sir, it should be after dawn up aboveground. If she is indeed down here, they'd probably be trapped for now. I'd say let's give the men a little more sleep. They've earned it."

Tskoulis smiled a little as Phi curled up into a tight ball, reaching as if for an invisible blanket.

"How much time is left on your watch, Alpha?"

"I was about to wake him." Alpha gestured to Phi.

Tskoulis sat up. "I'm awake. I got it."

"Yes, sir."

Alpha stretched, made his way over to what passed as a bedroll.

Tskoulis took his place, seating himself on an uncomfortable boulder by the chamber doorway.

It was so quiet. He wasn't unnerved by it, but it forced him to think. And he didn't want to think.

Didn't want to think what might be happening to Jossey right now, didn't want to think what orders Sokol had given Delta.

He glanced over at Caspar. The man was still unconscious, still muttering something in his sleep. Tskoulis couldn't make out what it was.

The Tiger turned back to the empty corridor.

If she had been interrogated, and she confessed it to Sokol–

Gavin shivered. He'd seen Sokol's flat eyes, the way he'd looked at Jossey when she signed on for Patrol. Like he'd won a prize.

The commander wondered yet again why what Jossey was doing was *so* important.

What her tormentors might be doing to her to get the information.

He put his head in his hands, trying to block out the thoughts.

He remembered an unfamiliar voice in the tunnel. *"We need medical attention."*

511

Looking up to see Jossey of all people lying on a stretcher. Feeling his heart almost stop.

Racing over to her, not knowing what had happened, if she was badly injured. Maybe worse.

Her expression when he took off his mask.

Like she was almost...frustrated. Disappointed. She had that look on her face a lot. He'd never been able to tell if it was directed at him or at herself – if she was mad that she'd gotten herself into hot water *again*. Or if she was mad that *he* was helping her.

He'd never understood it. But he'd made a promise to Tark, and as the years went on and they grew up, he'd silently made one to her too.

She'd probably kill him if she knew, he thought, smiling a little. Or at least try. She was so defensive, so independent. Her mother had never really recovered from the whole incident, so Jossey had been working almost since her father had disappeared.

Working, and trying to do it on her own, not profiting from the Sokol name.

He smiled. Tark had had no such inhibitions.

His smile faded.

"Why don't you hate me?"

He hadn't understood before why she was so bothered by his help. But now he thought he was starting to.

She seemed to think he was doing it out of obligation, helping someone she thought he should detest. And her scar. Her mother had made very sure Jossey had seen the scar on her face as a mark of what she'd done. That she thought she was tainted somehow. Ugly and frightening.

Jossey was extra nice to strangers to make up for how she thought she looked.

He almost laughed.

On that last front, she had no idea how wrong she was.

Thompson, for example. The young man could barely speak around her. Tskoulis had taken pity on him and privately told Henry not to pair Jossey with Thompson, lest the poor young man manage to injure himself with his own weapon.

Yet somehow it had all gone straight over Jossey's head. He smiled crookedly. As for detesting her –

He glanced around the room, his mood souring as his gaze fell back on Savaş.

What he didn't understand was why Jossey seemed to have no problem accepting Savaş's help.

It didn't matter, Gavin told himself firmly. That was between her and Savaş. They were teammates, after all. They were working on a high-security special project. Of course she should want his help. It would be of concern if she didn't. And Savaş seemed very professional. Respectful.

Tskoulis crossed his arms and stared into the pitch-dark corridor.

He eventually awakened the men. The wrist gauge said 10:00 AM. They seemed refreshed, other than Rho, but even his wound was better than it had been. He washed it again and applied extra honey.

They packed up their gear.

"Let's clear the third level first," Tskoulis said. "If they're here, that should hopefully force them downward, give them less room to escape."

He made sure his sword was strapped to his side. "Weapons check. Water check."

"Sir, we need to get more water," said Phi. "We're low."

"Understood. Let's sweep the floors, then see where the nearest well is."

106

THEY SLEPT MOST OF THE DAY, THEN JOSSEY PACKED UP HER
things and changed back into her Patrol uniform.

As she strapped on her boots, she heard Altan's voice in the
other room, and Tark's. They seemed to be arguing.

She stepped out from behind the curtain. Altan stared
at her.

"I'm ready," she said flatly.

"I don't like this." Altan looked at her, then back at Tark.
"What if she fails?"

"She has no choice," Tark said. He looked straight at Jossey.
"If she fails, my uncle will probably kill her."

Jossey felt very cold, deadly calm, as she met Altan's gaze. He
looked back at her.

"Do your best," he finally said.

"We have to go," she said. "The window of...presumed innocence may be closing, and fast."

Altan frowned. Tark said something in their language.

"If I don't return soon, they may guess something is wrong,"
she explained.

Tark turned to her. "What are you planning to tell them?"

She'd thought about this while the others slept. "Altan, give me your knife."

He looked startled. "What? Why?"

"I need some kind of proof that I fought you and the others off, left you for dead, escaped from the tunnels. Came across the farm, thought it was Karapartei and illegal, feared for my life, so I stole a bike from them and headed back to the City as best I knew how. They do have bikes, yes?"

Tark appeared to be thinking. "They do. So you're planning to head across the desert by yourself."

"I don't see another way to do this."

He hunched his shoulders. "Neither do I. Do you even know how to get back to the City from the farm?"

She shook her head. "I was hoping you did. I have Gavin's com code. If I get within range he should be able to come find me."

He shook his head too, but it was in admiration.

"It's simple," he said. "Let's discuss on the way."

"Okay. Altan? The knife?"

Altan glanced at Tark. Then he slowly unsheathed his knife and gave it to her.

"Thanks," she said. "I hope you don't want this back."

Tark laughed. "Here, take mine."

She smiled. "Thanks." She handed back Altan's. He grabbed it. She laughed a little. "You can keep the one your men confiscated from me," she said.

Then she looked at Tark evenly.

"Now," she said. "I need you to make me look like I got in a fight."

Tark shrank back. "What?"

"I need to look like I was wounded. Bruises. That type of thing."

Tark shook his head. "No. Jossey – "

"If they don't believe me – " She turned to Altan. "You do it."

Altan looked stricken. He looked to Tark, who shook his head, eyes dangerous. "Don't," Tark hissed.

"Tark. Please. You know I have to convince – "

"Jossey, I forbid it."

She snorted. "You forbid it? How old are you, eighty?"

He gave her a look.

"Fine," she said. "I can do it a different way."

She lifted the knife.

In a second Tark had closed the distance between them and wrested the knife from her grasp, holding her wrist behind her back in a tight grip. "Jossey," he hissed.

She winced. "Trust me," she hissed back. "And ow, Tark, let *go*. You're not thirteen anymore." She turned to Altan, who seemed to be trying not to look at her.

"Altan," she said. He looked at Tark, dark eyes wide.

"Altan," she repeated. "Are they cooking rabbit for dinner? Do they...drain them first?"

Altan stared at her for a moment, uncomprehendingly. "Drain," she said again, miming.

Then his eyes lit up.

Tark seemed to understand at the same time. "Go," he said, looking relieved. Altan disappeared.

Tark took the knife from her, stepped back. "Jossey, what are you doing?"

"Trust me," she said again. "Do you have a set of those claws?"

"Yes, why?"

"Bring them here."

He gave her a look, then, still holding the knife, he moved toward one of the boxes on the floor and opened it. He carefully lifted a forearm sheath out of the box.

"Put it on," she said.

Tark eyed her, putting the knife on the ground, well out of her reach.

She sighed. "Tark, hurry up."

"Oh, hurry up and stab your sister," he said, glaring at her.

"No." She grinned. "I'm not *that* bad at fighting. Stab my armor."

Altan returned and hovered, awkwardly holding a bowl of blood.

"Don't ask how I got this," he muttered.

Jossey was holding up a piece of her armor. Tark stood in front of it. He strapped on his claws, extended them, swung his wrist around in a circle. It looked practiced. Precise.

For a moment, Jossey shivered, looking at her brother.

"Brace yourself," he warned her. "Don't move a muscle."

"Make it look good," she retorted.

He gritted his teeth, as if trying not to think about what he was doing, and swiped.

They splashed her Patrol uniform with rabbit's blood. Then they set the knife in the bowl and let it soak.

"You've ruined my armor," Jossey said, grinning, looking at the clean score marks straight across the chest. "Impressive. Looks like I barely survived."

Altan looked impressed, arms crossed. "Looks like it."

"Yeah, well – " Tark looked traumatized. "Let's not do that again."

She took a little of the rabbit blood, smeared it across her face. Altan flinched.

"Okay," she said. "Let's do this."

. . .

She and Tark left the tent carefully, just the two of them. She'd used a rock to scrub parts of her uniform raw, rubbed dirt into it. She was, literally, a bloody mess.

If Kudret or anyone else asked, Altan had been instructed to say that the Bey had been very clear and that no one was to speak to the prisoner while Tark arranged negotiations with the Colony.

Then, at some point, when it seemed politically safe, Tark planned to share with the people what he had done.

Meanwhile, they had to get out without being noticed.

The smell of woodsmoke was heavy in the air as they moved through the dark. Every footstep seemed too heavy, too loud. She kept glancing back at the grass to see if they were leaving a trail.

As they neared the edge of the camp, she heard footsteps. Jossey jumped back and pulled on Tark's arm, yanking him behind one of the tents.

Just in time. Kudret and one of his men strolled by.

She and Tark froze, and she realized how ridiculous they looked. She had blood on her uniform and destroyed armor; he looked like an oversized bodyguard with about five empty canteens stashed in his bag.

She tried not to laugh at the memory of Aysun's face as she'd sent them off.

Now Jossey turned to Tark.

"It's like the tunnels again," she whispered. All that was missing was Gavin and some stupid overblown story about giant tunnel bats with massive claws. She'd never understood what was up with Gavin and tunnel bats. She shook her head, smiling.

Tark shushed her, but his eyes were bright.

They made it into the canyon and jogged to the wall.

He helped her up. Her leg was still sore, but she could do it – she just had to be careful.

At one point, near the top, she slipped on a handhold and slammed her arm into the wall. She groaned, and he grabbed her wrists before she could drop, but she just smiled. "There," she said. "Now I should have real bruises."

He grimaced at her. "Not funny," he said.

She scrambled up over the top of the ledge and rested for a long moment.

She could still see the fires of the encampment. From up there they were like small embers in the vast darkness. She smiled.

After a few minutes, she got to her feet. "Let's go."

Tark had sent a retrieval team to get the bikes. One was waiting at the top of the ridge. He and Jossey climbed up.

"Are you sure you want to do this?" he asked, glancing over his shoulder.

"I don't have much of a choice," she said. "You already told your people that if I didn't, the penalty was death."

He looked away.

She wrapped her arms around him and held on as he turned onto the highway.

They had to walk through the fields again to get to the farm. This time, Tark led her to the houses where she'd seen lights before.

They stood in waist-high grasses just outside the ruins, examining the small village.

"There," he whispered. "There's HQ. They usually have extra bikes there. The guards circulate out of there every hour and walk the boundary. You should have a fifteen-minute window once the guard leaves the station." He pointed to the north. "Do you see that road? When you get there, take a right and head due east. Don't leave the road. The Old Sector 1, where you 'escaped from,' is at the end. It's about twenty-five miles away. You can't use headlights, understand?"

"Got it. East."

"Their bikes – well, you've ridden them." He looked at her. "Jossey, I should stay until you get one."

"What if you get caught?" she whispered.

"Don't worry about me. I don't want to leave you here alone."

She smiled. "You always were a great big brother."

He reached out and pulled her close, kissing the side of her head.

"There's a garrison of my men to the northeast, in the canyons," he muttered. "If you need help, they patrol near that elevator every two days. You can leave a message in one of the caves, the one with the stump near the entrance."

She didn't need to ask which elevator.

"What if I can't get out to the caves?" she asked. "They have codes on the elevators now."

"Make an excuse. Say it's for the solar project," he said.

Then he smiled. "See if you can convince Gavin," he said. "Carefully. But Patrol is the real power in that place, after Intelligence. If we could get them on our side..."

He trailed off. Took a breath. "And Jossey – "

She looked at him.

"Be careful."

The door to the HQ building clicked open, and Tark and Jossey froze. A guard stepped out into the night. He spoke into a radio for a moment, then started to wander in their direction.

At the last minute, he took a sharp turn and headed along the boundary.

She sighed under her breath.

"Go," said Tark.

She started walking, then turned, took two steps and flung

her arms around her older brother, clung to him. His face was dark with pain as he wrapped his arms around her.

He held on for a long moment, then held her at arm's length. "Go," he said. "Do your best. Convince Gavin if you can."

She smiled through tears. "Goodbye, Tark."

107

She crept toward the building. It looked like someone had refurbished an old house, adding a living suite to a large garage. In the guard shack itself she could see warm lights and papers scattered all over a desk. It was empty.

She glanced in. A radio. She needed a radio.

She turned back for a moment. Tark was gone.

She sighed and turned to the task at hand.

There were keys all over the wall, and a tangle of cords. She noticed the shack was heavily air-conditioned, with extra-insulated walls. She wondered where the "workers" stayed during the day. There didn't seem to be enough caves around here to house all of them.

No radio. She poked around a bit more.

She'd have to make one, she thought. Ideally, she could steal one of theirs, but that likely meant accosting a guard, which was too much of a risk.

She left the office quietly and headed for the back of the building.

The garage was unlocked, to her surprise. But her mouth twisted. Who but the Onlar could possibly steal a bike out here?

She inched her way into the garage. There were two rows of motorbikes, all standard Patrol-issue. She'd used those before.

She smiled, looking for the key, and realized they'd all been on the wall in the office.

Guess they have to sign them out, she thought.

How much time had Tark said? Fifteen minutes?

She darted back out the door, ducked below the office window, and peeked in. Still empty. She wondered if they had cameras. It seemed pretty low-tech here, considering the fact that they had an entire probably-illegal farm that she'd never heard of.

She stared at the board. There had been ten bikes, but there was an entire wall of keys, which she guessed were for storage units and the like. Maybe food storage.

There. Bike keys, all in a line. One was missing.

She grabbed keys 4 and 5 and made her way back to the garage.

Something felt odd as she stepped into the small room. She froze, looking around, smelling the air. Nothing.

Jossey moved through the shadows. The bikes loomed eerily in the half-light from the windows. Bike 4. She sat on it, tried the key. Nothing. Bike 5.

It rumbled. She grinned.

She turned it off and maneuvered it carefully out of its spot. She was positioning it to leave the garage when a voice sounded behind her.

"Identify yourself."

She jumped and whirled, looking at a Patrol agent.

He was young, tall, and stood leaning on one of the bikes across from her.

The missing key. She mentally smacked herself.

"I was assigned to patrol the boundary," she said, hoping she sounded confident.

He stepped into the light. He had a cruel expression and flat blue eyes. She shrank back.

"You're not Patrol," he said, smiling. "And I was just about to go do that. Care to join me?"

"I'm – "

"We don't have any female agents out here." He sneered, wrinkling his nose. "Why are you covered in blood?"

"I – "

He took another step closer. She didn't like the way he was looking at her. The way he was smiling.

She jammed the key into the bike's ignition and turned it on, flooding the garage with light.

He shouted and stumbled backward. She twisted the throttle.

He dove out of the way.

She saw him reach for his radio. She'd forgotten about it. Of course he had a radio.

No no no no. She turned the bike, staring him right in the eyes, as if daring him to do it.

The agent put his finger on the button, drawing his sword as he grinned.

She got off the bike, drew her knife, shaking as she took a step toward him.

He grinned at her, lowering the sword. "Well, well. You're a fighter, I see. I like that." He looked her up and down. "Shall we play?"

She felt her skin crawling at his tone, backed toward the bike, wishing she knew how to throw a knife.

He walked lazily toward her. "Come back, sweetheart. I thought you wanted to join me."

He grinned.

Jossey tripped, steadied herself against the handlebars. She tried to climb back on, shaking.

The Patrol agent lunged and grabbed her by the boot,

yanked her forcefully off the bike and to the ground. The bike toppled. She shrieked and tried to roll away, tried to scramble back to her feet.

He stepped over her, sword drawn, and put the tip to her throat, stepping hard on her wrist, forcing her to let go of the knife.

She froze, wincing in pain as he dug his boot further into her wrist.

He grinned. "Well now. How impolite." He crouched next to her, eyes raking over her face. "I wasn't done with our...conversation."

She tried to sit up. He pushed her back down with the sword tip.

She shrieked for help.

"Shh," he said. "No one can hear you." He clicked off his radio. "See?"

He reached for her. She backed away frantically, only to run into the bike.

He grinned and tossed his sword to one side.

"NO!" she shrieked.

Suddenly he glanced up and his face changed, eyes wide. Jossey turned her head, peering around the bike.

Tark stood in the doorway, sword in one hand.

The man stumbled to his feet, backing away, his sword still on the garage floor.

Tark stepped toward him, glancing down at Jossey for half a second, tossed her something. She caught it. A radio. It was covered in blood. She looked at it, stupefied, and stuffed it into her uniform pocket. She grabbed her weapon.

"Go," he gritted out. "Get out of here."

He drew his knife, silently. The Patrol agent's eyes were huge.

She shakily righted the bike and hopped on.

Behind her, she heard the man draw his own knife.

She shot out of the garage, cutting the lights, but not fast enough to miss the body of the other guard. He was lying on the ground, near the edge of the field.

He'd been coming back to the office early, she thought. Maybe he'd forgotten something.

She bounced over the ground and toward the north, as Tark had said.

The boundary was extensive. No one seemed to notice her as she sped along. But she kept scanning for holes, stumps, anything that could slow her down. It was very dark, other than the faint glow from the farm itself.

Behind her, she thought she heard shouts.

She accelerated into the darkness, praying she wouldn't crash.

She shot out onto the highway and flew along toward the east.

It was just past the new moon tonight, and she was grateful for it as she zoomed along, pushing the bike as fast as she dared. The road was a grayish white and sprinkled with debris, but she was able to maneuver around most of it.

He'd said about twenty-five miles. She realized that she had no idea how she was going to get down into the OS1 if she did manage to find it.

Or how she was going to call Gavin.

There was nothing for it. She had to try.

To the north, a mountain loomed, more like a large hill. She thought she vaguely recognized it, but she couldn't be sure.

With a jolt, she realized she hadn't taken her water with her. It had fallen when the man had attacked her.

At least she had the radio.

She gritted her teeth and carried on.

Another mountain rose to her right. She'd been driving for about fifteen minutes.

She should be within range –

Behind her, she thought she heard a noise.

She whipped around. In the far distance, she saw headlights.

She started and took a sharp left into the ruins of another small village.

She abandoned the bike inside a building and fled on foot, looking for something suitable. Shelter. Something with water. But someplace they wouldn't think to look for her. She hoped.

As she ran, she tripped over a rock, and went flying. She felt her bad leg twist sharply, and bit her lip to keep from crying out. She got to her feet and stumbled onward, her knee bleeding.

Her leg was killing her, but she had no choice.

There was a large cemetery to her right. She headed past it, up toward the dark hills that ringed the city.

One of the buildings on the outskirts had what looked like a supply shed. The door was off its hinges.

She darted inside.

She was several blocks from where she'd left the bike. She hoped if they found it, it would give her time to run.

To where, she had no idea.

Suddenly, the radio in her pocket crackled.

She jumped and turned down the volume, fumbling with shaking hands.

They were talking about her. Hunting her.

"Suspect, maybe Patrol," said the voice. "No definitive visual information, probably a woman. Killed two men."

So Tark had escaped. She smiled.

They were listing off their locations into the radio. She wasn't far off the search grid. She sat, radio right next to her ear, straining to make sense of the words while also mapping things on the ground using her knife.

She flipped the radio. It was standard-issue.

1120 was Gavin's number.

But if she pressed the button now, they might all be able to hear her.

She peered at it in the dark. She was an Engineer. A solar one, but still. She should be able to make this work, she told herself.

She had no choice.

They were calling out radio locations again. She was afraid to even breathe, lest they hear her over the radio and figure out where to find her. Eventually they seemed to give up and regrouped at their bikes.

She took a moment and looked at the radio. It seemed to be set to a different set of channels than the ones Patrol used. She'd never even heard of these.

She pried off the back and made a few adjustments, praying this would work.

She dialed in 1120. The time was around midnight.

"Gavin," she said quietly. "Gavin, do you read me?"

108

GAVIN SAT DOWN HARD, STARING IN FRUSTRATION AT HIS HANDS. They'd swept the entire third and fourth levels. It had taken them hours, and all their food, and most of their water.

Nothing. Absolutely nothing. No sign. And it was evening on the sixth day. She'd been gone almost a week.

He groaned. If the OS1 was clear, that meant they'd probably either have to abort the mission or continue back down the tunnel that led to...somewhere, he hoped.

Caspar flopped down next to him.

"I'm out of ideas," he admitted. "Either she was on a different level, one we haven't checked before, or she wasn't here. Or they're really good at clearing their tracks."

Gavin put his head in his hands.

"If they do anything to her – " he said.

He sat up. Caspar glanced at him.

"You take very good care of your people," he said neutrally.

Gavin looked away.

The others entered the chamber. "Nothing, sir," Alpha said.

Tskoulis got slowly to his feet. "Let's take a break. We need more water. And we're out of food."

"There should be water down on the eighth level," Caspar said. "We can access it via the wells."

Tskoulis gestured, no longer caring how Caspar knew these things. "Lead the way."

They walked single file down several flights of stairs. Down here the air was colder, drier. He could hear a faint sound of lapping water in the distance.

Tskoulis glanced at his gauge. Midnight. Six days missing.

He closed his eyes.

They were very deep underground. He didn't think they could use their coms at this level. "Stay close," he said to them.

The well was in front of them. They could hear the water, but it was hard to tell how far down it was.

"Does anyone have a rope?"

They emptied their bags. Phi came up with one. It wasn't thick enough to hold a man easily, but it might hold a bucket.

His light was working. Somehow overnight the connection had apparently set.

Tskoulis glanced at Caspar. Caspar gave Tskoulis an innocent look.

Phi took the rope, tied it around his hand, and lowered it into the well. He leaned down and pulled it back up.

The strands on the end were wet.

They quickly tied one of their metal mess tins on the end and lowered it into the well. One cup at a time, they filled their water canteens, then drank their fill. It was slow going, and they had to switch off. Rho, with his bad arm, was exempt.

Eventually, all their canteens were full and ready to go. Phi went to pull up the makeshift bucket.

He frowned, yanked on it. "It's stuck," he said.

"Leave it," Tskoulis said.

"I don't have another mess kit. Hold on."

"Phi – "

He was already leaning over the edge of the well. He turned on his safety light.

He yanked on the rope. It didn't come loose. He reached further down.

His sword slipped out of its scabbard and fell, clanking.

There was a splash.

Phi yelled and climbed up over the lip of the well. Then, as Units 1 and 2 watched, he climbed down into the shaft and disappeared.

They raced to the side of the shaft. "Phi!"

They could see him. He had his light around his neck, and he was descending rapidly.

"Phi, get back here," Tskoulis shouted. "That's an order."

Phi looked up at him. "I'm almost to the bottom, sir. It's moving fast, but it's not deep. I can see the sword."

So could they. It was leaning against the wall, in the river that flowed beneath OS1.

"Phi – " Tskoulis' voice was dangerous.

The man reached into the river and grasped the sword. He grinned up at them and put it in his scabbard. He began to climb.

He was halfway up the shaft when he slipped.

Phi fell, striking his head against the side of the well, and did not move.

They stared in horror.

The only rope they had was with him at the bottom.

As they looked around for something to use as a harness, Caspar was up and over the lip of the well.

Tskoulis didn't even try to stop him.

Caspar descended like a madman. Phi was beginning to sink beneath the water.

"Phi!" Caspar shouted. He jumped down into the swiftly-moving current, slapped Phi, shook him. Phi didn't respond. His temple was bleeding, a stream of red joining the water.

Caspar seemed to be muttering something, then, in the tiny cramped space, still illuminated by Phi's light bobbing in the water, he swung Phi over his shoulders and secured the man to his back with the rope.

Then he began to climb back up the shaft.

Five feet. Ten. Twenty. All they could see behind his mask were silver eyes, burning into the air ahead of him. He didn't make a sound as he climbed, just doggedly continued upward.

Phi was not a small man. They all stared. The kind of strength necessary...

Four pairs of hands helped them out of the well and untied Phi from Caspar's back.

Rho and Gamma stood back, looking stunned, as Caspar collapsed against the side of the well, breathing heavily. Tskoulis silently handed him a canteen of water.

"How – " Alpha was gaping at the Tracker.

Caspar shook his head. "It doesn't matter," he said. "We need to get him to the surface. Right now."

Gamma was already trying to stem Phi's bleeding, tearing a piece of his uniform to do so.

Caspar turned to Tskoulis. "I'm sorry, sir, but if we don't abort the mission and get aid immediately..."

Tskoulis didn't blink, "Do it," he ordered.

Alpha and Gamma put Phi on a makeshift stretcher and lifted him carefully. Gamma had managed to staunch the bleeding, but they couldn't afford to jostle him.

They climbed up through the endless stairs, twisting and

turning, pausing when needed. Caspar had tossed their meager equipment on his back and followed up the rear with Tskoulis. Rho went ahead, holding the one functioning light among them.

The surface was four levels away. Three.

Then they carefully lifted a hatch that had been put in place by Patrol and stepped out into a sea of endless stars.

They sat down, and Tskoulis tried the radio.

"Patrol base, come in," he said quietly.

They were out in the middle of what was half-fields, half-ruins: the old aboveground city of Derinkuyu. The Onlar could be anywhere.

Probably not this far south, but just in case.

"Patrol," he repeated. "This is Commander Gavin Tskoulis of Unit 2. We have a man down. Repeat, we have a man down. Come in, Base."

Silence. The only sound was the wind blowing across the flats.

Gavin sat back on the ground, keeping an eye on Phi. The man was pale, breathing steadily but unconscious. He lay limply on the stretcher.

Gavin's radio crackled. He picked it up. "Patrol. Come in," he said.

A faint voice. He turned up the volume, blew dust out of the speakers.

"Commander. This is Base."

"Base." He saw Caspar perk up next to him. "We are outside the OS1. Requesting immediate pickup. Medic team. Do you copy?"

"Copy, Commander." The voice was silent for a moment. "We can have a team there in twenty-five."

"Make it twenty," Tskoulis snapped. Phi might not be able to wait that long.

"Yes, sir."

The radio clicked off.

Gavin looked up at the stars. *Aborted.*

He wanted to go back down into the tunnels, keep searching on his own. From Caspar's posture, he seemed to feel the same way. But they couldn't.

Gavin looked out across the plains. Six days. She'd been gone almost a week.

For the first time, the thought occurred to him that they might never find her.

He squeezed the radio in his hand. He couldn't even imagine.

He remembered her first day on Patrol. Getting knocked down by her roommate, multiple times. On the final time, when he'd stood there observing silently, she'd been knocked down hard, gasping for breath, her strange eyes tearing up. The impact would probably leave a bruise. She'd looked at him as he'd stood there, and it had taken all of his self-control to walk away.

Now he looked out over the deserted landscape, looked up at the stars.

Maybe she was dead.

It would make sense. Maybe they'd realized she couldn't help them, or wasn't useful in some way, and they'd killed her.

It was rational. But his mind refused to accept it, refused to think about it.

He needed to get her back, he thought angrily. She was supposed to finish the solar project.

She was supposed to give him annoyed looks and stop him from accidentally flirting with the nursing staff.

He stood and paced, needing to move, needing to stop thinking.

Patrol had said twenty minutes. It had been ten.

He thought he saw lights in the distance, to the west, and

squinted. But they disappeared, winking out as quickly as they'd come. He blinked, wondering if he was seeing things.

Caspar had seen them too, apparently. He sat up, looking hard toward the horizon.

He and Tskoulis glanced at each other.

For a long moment they watched. But the lights did not come again.

Caspar seemed on edge, and went over, checking on Phi. Tskoulis sat down again and looked up at the stars.

He wanted to shut off his mind. Stop thinking about the last time he'd seen her.

"Promise me," he'd said. He'd tried.

"Don't worry, Gavin, my uncle probably won't throw you off Patrol if anything happens to me." She'd smiled.

She really had no idea, he thought. And now –

The radio crackled in his hand. Patrol, he thought, and turned up the volume. They were late.

Base had better have a good explanation. He glanced over at Phi.

Savaş gave him a thumbs-up. "He's stable," he said.

"Good." Gavin lifted the radio to his lips. "Where are you?" he demanded.

Another crackle. Maybe they were in the tunnels.

The button was stuck. He pressed it a couple of times, freeing an extra bit of gritty sand. It flaked off into his hand.

Then he realized something was odd as he looked more closely at the display.

It was a Patrol frequency, but an unfamiliar one.

Gavin frowned, turned up the volume.

"Gavin."

He almost dropped the radio.

Caspar's head shot up next to him.

"Gavin, do you copy?" A tinny voice, crackling, as if it were far away. A very familiar voice. She sounded small, lost. Terrified.

He blew the dust off, praying the thing would work. He pressed the button.

There was a hiss as the radio connected, then silence.

Tskoulis said, "Jossey?"

Her voice crackled through the airwaves, elated, faraway. "Gavin?"

Caspar scrambled over, staring at the radio. Tskoulis ignored him.

"Jossey!" Tskoulis shouted into the radio. "Jossey, where are you?"

"Gavin!" She sounded like she was crying. "Oh thank God. Gavin. Help me. I'm – they're – "

Her voice cut out.

"Jossey, tell me where you are."

"The – " It crackled, and he resisted the urge to shake it.

He made out the word "ruins." And the word "west."

His head shot up. He looked toward the horizon.

"Bikes," he heard. She was saying something else, but he couldn't make it out. "Help," she pleaded. "Please."

"Jossey, wait," he said.

The signal faded, and with a last crackle she was gone.

"She said 'ruins to the west,'" Caspar said quietly after a long moment, looking stunned. "Where those lights were."

Tskoulis was still staring at the small box in his hand.

Then he lifted it to his lips. "Base, come in," he said.

One of the Patrol aboveground vehicles came shooting across the desert, sending a dust plume several feet into the air.

Tskoulis flagged them down.

A medic hopped out, followed by two Patrol agents. "Sir. Where's the patient?" she asked.

"Are there two of you?" Tskoulis demanded. "And bikes?"

"Just one." She looked confused. "Two bikes. Why?"

"Load Phi here into the vehicle and wait for us."

"Sir?"

"Do as I say," he snapped. She blanched and saluted.

He waved to Caspar and Alpha. "Come with me. Grab the bikes. And your weapons."

Alpha glanced back at his agent.

"Sokol's made contact," Tskoulis said shortly. "We may need backup."

Alpha's eyes widened behind his mask. "Yes, sir. Understood." He turned to Gamma and Rho. "Rho, stay here. Gamma, with me."

Tskoulis took a bike from one of the agents. They had a pair in the back of the vehicle. "Get on," he said to Caspar.

Alpha and Gamma took the other bike.

"Sir, where – "

"Just follow me." He looked over at the medic. "As soon as he's stable, follow us. Wait for my signal."

He started the bike, Caspar hanging on behind him, and wrenched the throttle, flying over the landscape in the direction of the lights he'd seen.

They skidded to a stop in the center of the town, dust billowing.

Gavin and Caspar jumped off, left the bike where it was. Alpha and Gamma followed suit.

They grabbed their weapons and spread out.

The ruins were dark, no signs of life whatsoever. But they crept along the walls, listening.

If Jossey was here, she was probably hiding.

Was it Onlar? Gavin thought. But she'd said something about bikes.

The only people he knew of with bikes were Patrol.

He frowned.

"Tracker," he said quietly. "Look for tire marks."

Caspar shot him a look, but said, "Yes, sir."

Hills rose behind the town. The men followed what looked like the main road.

It headed up into the hills, and appeared to vanish. Gavin shook his head. "If there were...bikes, as she said, they had to have come from somewhere. There's nothing authorized out here."

Caspar and Alpha glanced at each other.

"Maybe further to the west?" suggested Gamma.

Gavin frowned. There was nothing out that way. Just more desert.

But the road was serviceable enough. He glanced down as they walked. It looked like it had survived the worst of the wars.

"Sir," Caspar said quietly. "I think I've found something."

Gavin turned. Caspar was pointing to tire marks.

Recent-looking tire marks.

Gavin crouched and inspected them. It looked like a bike had zoomed to a halt.

He looked at Caspar, stunned.

"Jossey," he said quietly into the radio. "Jossey, can you hear me?"

Silence. A slight crackle.

"Jossey?"

Nothing.

He kicked the tire marks in frustration.

"Looks like they turned around," said Gamma. "That way."

He pointed down one of the main roads, next to what appeared to have once been a school.

"Eyes," Gavin said.

The ruins were deathly silent as they walked. If the biker or bikers had been here, they seemed to be long gone. Gavin unsheathed his sword, clapped on his mask.

They made their way down the main road.

The road curved gently to the left, and at the end they could see that it forked, each branch appearing equally wide, equally likely.

They came to the gates of a cemetery.

Gavin raised the radio, tried again. "Jossey, come in."

Maybe she was trapped. Maybe the people on bikes had found her, and she was afraid to speak in case they heard her.

"We are at the cemetery," he said. "Tell us if we are close. Anything. Please."

Alpha shot him a funny look.

Silence.

They kept going, taking the left fork. It looked slightly bigger than the other. There was a faded road sign that said "GAZ." Probably heading to the highway.

They'd traveled about a mile when they came to the end of the road.

It had been a major intersection once, it seemed. Two crumbling gas stations sat opposite one another.

They looked along the crossroad in both directions.

Blackness. Starlight.

Gavin shook his head.

But Caspar was grinning.

"What's so funny, Tracker?" Gavin snapped.

"Look down, sir."

Gavin looked.

Five lines of tire marks.

Four in a group, skidding as if at high speed.

One alone, as if the rider couldn't control the bike well.

The four men turned around.

They walked back up the road, searching carefully for any sign of life.

To their right was what looked like a farmhouse compound.

Gavin waved Alpha and Gamma to search it. He and Caspar took the house on the opposite side.

He was walking through the high grass when he heard a shout.

"Sir!"

Alpha was standing, waving to him. "Sir, we found a bike!"

Gavin and Caspar ran.

Trees lined the road. The rider had shot right through the line, judging by the tracks in the grass.

The bike was lying on its side in the garage. Whoever had ridden it hadn't even bothered to take the keys with them.

"She's probably close," Gavin said. "Not a lot of places to hide here. And she should know that she has to get belowground once the sun comes up."

They searched the compound and found nothing.

They took to the road again, heading back up.

"She'd probably cut through the fields," Caspar pointed out.

"That'd slow her down," Gavin said. "And she'd probably leave a trail through the grass. If she was being chased – "

He looked ahead, up the road.

The bike had had no supplies with it. Nothing.

They kept going up the road. "Jossey," he said into the radio. "Jossey, come in."

When they reached the cemetery again, Gavin saw something.

The rocks on the side of the path looked as if they had been disturbed, as if someone had tripped and crashed to the ground. He saw blood on one of the rocks.

He'd barely seen it. He hoped the mysterious people on bikes hadn't.

"Tracker," he said.

Caspar saw it too.

They turned, and headed toward the hills.

There was a field across from the cemetery. The road had more tire marks. Oil droplets from bikes, as if they'd idled in place, waiting for something.

Orders, maybe.

He tried again. "Jossey, come in. We're in the town. It appears clear. No one searching. Where are you."

A faint crackle.

He held the radio up, listening carefully.

It crackled again. "The shed," Jossey's voice whispered. The signal was stronger now. "---- the hills." Her voice broke. "Please hurry."

Then he heard a faint gasp, and the radio went silent.

They broke into a run.

The house on the left – there was a field, several outbuildings. He shouted, "Gamma, Alpha."

They broke off, headed that way.

Caspar pointed to the right. "That one?"

It was a small compound with overgrown trees, dozens of them. Beyond, there was a dilapidated house.

And what might be a shed.

Gavin ran.

As he ducked under the trees, he saw bent grass, as if something or someone had staggered through. This place was like a jungle.

Beyond, he could see a small outbuilding. The doors were lying on the ground, as if they'd fallen long ago.

Caspar had followed him. He turned and held a finger to his lips.

They approached the shed carefully. Gavin turned up the contrast on his mask.

He could see no movement inside, and the thermal setting wasn't working. He edged closer.

"Jossey," he tried into the radio again. "Come in. Please."

Then he heard a small voice from the darkness. "Gavin?"

He and Caspar stepped into the shed. In the corner he could just barely see a figure.

"Jossey."

He didn't have a light, he remembered.

"Jossey, do you have a light?"

A red light flared.

She stood there in the dimness, staring at him. Her strange eyes were wide, her scar extra-visible in the red light. She was back against the wall, holding a knife out in front of her like a sword.

Her face – he winced. Her face had dirt and blood on it, half-scrubbed, as if she hadn't realized it was there. Her uniform had a massive set of claw marks down the front. Her leg was oddly twisted, dried blood running down her uniform.

What did they do to you? he thought.

Beside him, Caspar's silver eyes were fixed on her. Then, with what appeared to be great effort of will, Delta turned his masked face away.

"Jossey," Gavin said softly.

She was staring at them in the darkness, as if unable to believe what she was seeing, the knife still held out in front of her.

He took off his mask to make sure she knew it was him. Beside him, Caspar left his on.

She sucked in a ragged breath.

Gavin took two steps forward, reached out, and took the knife very gently from her shaking hands.

Her strange eyes were wide, focused on his face, and he realized she was weeping.

"You came," she rasped, her voice barely audible.

Gavin tried to grin, say something flippant, but could not.

Could not tear himself away from her face.

Alpha and Gamma entered the shed. She jumped, staring at them, pressed herself further against the wall, looking frantically at Gavin. He remembered their masks. Their unusual uniforms.

"It's okay," Gavin said. "They're with me."

Alpha stepped out, said something into his com. "Medic's on the way, sir," he said to Tskoulis.

She looked at them all, not seeming to recognize Caspar, who had moved to the back, silver eyes directed at the floor. She looked back at Gavin. "You came." Her voice cracked.

"Are you injured?" He looked carefully at her face, her eyes. She had blood on her cheek. It wasn't hers, he saw.

Her leg wobbled, and she sank to the ground, leaning back against the wall and closing her eyes. Her face was pale.

"Water," Gavin snapped. Gamma tossed him a container.

He held it out to her. She took it and drank carefully with shaking hands. "I'm okay," she said.

He crouched beside her. "Medic's on the way."

She smiled sadly up at him. "Gavin – I mean, Tskoulis – the others, are they – "

She trailed off.

"2-5 is fine." He carefully didn't mention Liam. "Don't worry about that for now. We need to get you back to the City."

She took another sip of water. "Did you find the men who were searching for me?"

He got to his feet. "Who was searching for you?" His voice was dangerous.

She looked dead-eyed into the darkness.

"They tried to kill me." Her voice was little more than a whisper.

"Who, Jossey?"

"I – I don't know." She started shaking again. "I escaped from the Onlar, made it to the surface. I didn't know where I was, so I traveled overland. I – " She shut her mouth suddenly, looking around at the others. "I – Commander, I need to speak to the Minister."

Commander. That's right. He couldn't keep calling her Jossey. No wonder Unit 1 seemed so bothered.

"You can tell me, Sokol." He stepped back, away from her.

Her startling eyes fell on him, pleading. "I – don't know if I should share this."

Tskoulis thought for a minute, then turned to his men. "Go outside," he said. "Down the hill."

They saluted and left.

He turned back to Jossey. "What happened?"

"I found some kind of farm. Something illegal, I think. They had...uniforms, like Patrol uniforms, but they weren't Patrol."

She took a deep, shuddering breath. "They were growing vegetables, a lot of them, aboveground."

Something flashed across her face. Pain. She looked away from him.

"Jossey," he said very quietly.

"I – I killed two of them," she said. "I didn't mean to. I hid in the hills and snuck to their office after nightfall, seeing if I could figure out what was going on. They had – they had their own military setup and everything. And then when one of them saw me – "

544

She closed her eyes and shivered.

"He saw my Patrol uniform. He tried to kill me. He – " She stopped and looked down, still shivering, and curled up, wrapping her arms around her knees. "I – fought him off. Stole one of their bikes."

Gavin got the distinct impression she wasn't telling him everything.

But he didn't push. She looked terrified.

He hadn't missed her reaction to his men a few minutes ago.

"I didn't even know how to find the City," she said after a moment. "I just rode as far as I could, and kept trying your com. They came after me, searched this village." She wrapped her hands around her shoulders, rubbed them. "I heard them on the radio. They had orders to kill me on sight."

"Let me see the radio."

She handed it to him. He frowned, examining it. "It's Patrol," he said flatly. "A separate channel." His eyes flicked up to hers. "How did you manage to override it, get to me?"

She smiled a little. "I'm an Engineer."

He turned it over. The back was gone. He grinned at her.

Then his smile faded. "Your armor. You say you fought the Onlar?"

She looked away, face spasming in pain.

"What did you do with the bodies?"

She covered her eyes with a hand. "I don't know. I left them in the dark and ran. I don't even know where I was. We traveled through so many tunnels – "

She started to weep. His hand hovered over her shoulder awkwardly.

"Jossey," Gavin said quietly. "Don't think about it. You're here now. With me. And Unit 1," he added hastily.

She smiled a little. "Thank you," she said. "For rescuing me."

He grinned. "Did you think I wouldn't?"

Footsteps approached, crunching loudly on the gravel outside. "Can I come in, sir?"

Gavin turned. "Come in."

Alpha stepped into the shed. He glanced at the weeping woman and cleared his throat awkwardly.

"Sir," he said. "The medic is here."

As the medic worked on Jossey, removing her armor carefully and preparing her a stretcher, Gavin sat and thought.

Her leg was badly injured. He knew she had an old injury from when Tark had been taken, and running seemed to have exacerbated it. She winced when the medic helped her onto the stretcher. Her face was bloodied, but as he'd thought, it wasn't her blood.

She had been carrying an Onlar knife. He turned it over in his hands. Beautiful craftsmanship. The handle was bound in some kind of leather. The weapon looked very old. He hadn't seen this type of weapon in a while.

Who exactly had taken her? he wondered.

The medic had removed her armor. He picked it up and examined it. The claw marks across the front were deep. Precise.

Brutal.

Whoever had done this, it looked like they'd been aiming to kill, he thought.

Whoever had done this to her, the Tiger thought, if they were alive, they'd just secured themselves a death sentence.

109

THE REST OF THEM PILED INTO THE PATROL VEHICLE, AND IT zoomed back toward the City.

Jossey lay on the stretcher with her arm over her eyes, as if trying to block out the light. She'd been underground for several days, barring the last, Gavin remembered. He turned to the medic. "Can we turn down the lights?"

"Yes, sir."

He sat beside her, ignoring the looks Alpha was giving him. Caspar had chosen to sit up front with the medic.

Good, Gavin thought grimly.

Both because Delta's identity could not be compromised, and because part of Gavin didn't want Savaş there at all.

He looked back at Jossey as the vehicle bumped over the ground. She winced. The medic turned down the lights and she uncovered her eyes, blinking up at Gavin.

"You said 2-5 is all right?" she rasped.

He smiled. "Yes. Zlotnik had to have surgery, but she's doing okay now."

She closed her eyes. "Liam."

Gavin didn't respond.

"How did you find me?" she asked at last.

He glanced at Alpha. "We – found some tunnels the Onlar appear to have been using. Your captor was wounded, evidently. We followed the blood trail."

She looked away. "How far did you go?"

"The Old Sector 1," Gavin said. "Then Phi got injured." He glanced at the medic.

"He's unconscious, but doing all right," the woman said. "He seems to have hit his head pretty hard."

"Thank you," Gavin said. He turned back to Jossey. "You weren't that far from the City."

She shivered. "It felt like we traveled for days."

"Were they holding you underground?"

"At first. I woke up underground. One of them had kicked me in the head. I don't know how long I was out." She pointed to a fading bruise on her cheek. He hadn't seen it under the dirt.

Gavin's jaw tightened.

"Then – " She gestured vaguely. "I escaped. And...got lost." She closed her eyes. "There's no light down there, Gavin. And they were chasing me."

She turned away again, curled up on her side. "I killed the biggest one," she said in a small voice. "And then – "

She stopped talking.

"Save it for now, Sokol," Gavin said. "You're back now, that's what matters."

"I have to talk to the Minister," she repeated.

"I believe he's waiting for your return," Gavin said. "And I'm giving you a temporary discharge."

She looked at him, shocked. "No," she said. "I – "

"I can't let you back into the tunnels," he said firmly. "And especially not aboveground. Not again."

"Tskoulis," she pleaded. "I'm still working on my solar project. Don't take that away from me."

548

He glanced at the others. "That's for the Minister to decide," he said at last.

They transferred her stretcher down into the tunnels, to an ambulance, and she disappeared into the City along with Phi.

Gavin stood staring after the vehicle.

He turned and stalked down the corridors with Unit 1 and Savaş in tow.

They took the back route. No need to cause a scene. He smiled twistedly. Five enormous masked men would probably not go unnoticed.

They made their way to the Patrol headquarters.

He'd called ahead. It was the middle of the night, but Minister Sokol was there waiting for them.

They went into the conference room and closed the door.

None of them removed their masks. Caspar hovered in the back.

"Commander," Sokol said. "Is she safe?" He looked exhausted. The clock said 2:45 AM.

"Yes, sir. Injured, but safe."

He smiled. "Thank God." Then his face took on a cruel look. "Did you find her captors?"

"No, sir. She says she escaped from them somewhere underground, she's not sure where, but I believe somewhere near OS1, then she killed at least one of them when they came after her. She – " He glanced at Unit 1. "She requested to speak with you, sir."

"Thank you, Commander. Were you – able to map the tunnels?"

"Yes, sir." He gestured to Gamma. "Gamma has prepared a thorough map, up until we had a cave-in. We lost all visual somewhere to the east of the OS1. But we know the tunnels go at least that far, and appear to continue beyond."

Sokol took the map and examined it. "Excellent work," he said. "Your City is indebted to you." He glanced up at Tskoulis. "So they took her into OS1?"

"That was my understanding, sir."

"Very good." Sokol carefully placed his glasses on his face. "Gentlemen, you have done truly commendable work these past several days. I hope I need not call on your services again for some time. Please, enjoy the next week off." He glanced around. "Where is Phi?"

"Injured, sir. An accident."

"Well, I must visit him to thank him in person as well." He smiled. "I assume you have not yet informed 2-5?"

"No, sir. We came straight here."

"Very good." Sokol looked straight at Tskoulis. "Unit 1, you are dismissed."

They saluted and left.

Savaş remained.

The moment Unit 1 closed the door, Savaş straightened up, stood at ease, no longer the Tracker. He looked like an entirely different person. He removed his mask, cool silver eyes on the Minister.

Tskoulis had stopped being surprised.

"Do you have instructions for me, Minister?" Savaş asked.

Sokol turned to him, waved to Gavin to have a seat. "Indeed, Savaş. 2-5 has been told you have been temporarily assigned to do some...academic work on our solar project for the last week, in my niece's absence. I've prepared some things for you to go over."

"Yes, sir."

"You may return the day after tomorrow to regular training, as I assume you would like to sleep. You may act as you see fit, keeping in mind that as far as you know Jossey has not been found. Until that report has been delivered by Tskoulis, you may not visit my niece in the hospital."

Caspar's expression was neutral. "Yes, sir."

"Try not to be insubordinate once I tell them," Tskoulis said lightly.

Caspar glanced at him and actually smiled.

"Several days is enough for a temper to cool," he said.

Sokol turned to Tskoulis. "As for you, you may also have a day to rest, and then you may inform 2-5 at training that my niece has been found. Of course, no detail is necessary."

"Understood, sir."

"Very good. Now. Is my niece conscious?"

"She was when she went into the ambulance, sir." Gavin frowned a little.

"And you said she wanted to speak with me?"

"Yes, sir." A warning was going off in the back of his head. Sokol's orders to Caspar.

"I believe I should go speak with her now, then."

"Sir, let me come with you." Gavin started to get up.

Sokol waved him to sit down. "No, no, my boy. It's quite all right."

"If it's a matter of City security, I should be there," Gavin said carefully.

Caspar was glancing back and forth between them.

"He's right, sir," Caspar said. "Best to have everyone on the same page. Besides, I believe Jossey already spoke to him."

Gavin's eyebrow shot up, but he didn't protest.

Sokol looked at Savaş, then Gavin. "Very well," he said. "Commander, you may accompany me. But please, the two of you – please clean up first." He wrinkled his nose. "I do not mean offense, but you seem to not have bathed in days."

Caspar and Gavin glanced at each other, then down at their filthy uniforms, and burst out laughing.

. . .

Gavin changed into a clean uniform. He tucked the Onlar weapon away and headed for Sokol's office.

Sokol was waiting for him.

The Minister looked approvingly at him. "Let us go, Commander."

As they walked, the older man said, "She is injured, you said? Badly?"

"Injured, sir, but she appears to be in good enough condition considering her captivity. She – " He closed his mouth. Jossey could tell Sokol about the bikes herself.

The hospital was the only thing lit in the City Square. Everything was dead silent – curfew was in place.

They crossed the Square quickly. Tskoulis almost had to speed to keep up with the much shorter Minister, which part of his mind noted was amusing.

Sokol must really be in a hurry to speak to her, he thought darkly.

Warning bells were sounding in his mind again, and he shoved them away. Sokol's niece had been kidnapped by Onlar. Of course he was concerned, Tskoulis thought.

They entered the side door, where a glowing sign said EMERGENCY. A nurse looked up.

"Minister Sokol." Her face brightened. "How may I assist you?"

She glanced at his companion and her face went a deep pink. "And Commander Tskoulis."

He said, "Good evening." She turned pinker. Like Jossey's solar crew woman, he thought. He'd done nothing, but all Tskoulis could hear was Jossey's annoyed voice, telling him off. He grinned to himself.

The woman in front of him smiled brilliantly. He looked away.

"We're here to see Jossey Sokol," the Minister said smoothly. She glanced at him, eyes wide.

"Oh, yes, she's in recovery room 1A." She pointed down the hall.

"Recovery room?" Tskoulis turned to the woman, startled. "She had surgery?"

"No, sir, not at all. We simply call the rooms in the emergency ward that."

"Thank you. That is all." Sokol smiled flatly at the woman. He strode off in the direction she had pointed. Tskoulis followed him, not looking at the woman again.

Jossey was awake when they entered the room. She smiled faintly at her uncle, but her eyes lit up as she saw Gavin. He hovered in the back of the room, hands behind his back, like a bodyguard, eyes on her face. The light was dimmed, but he could tell she was still pale.

Sokol sat beside her and took her hands in his. "My dear niece," he said warmly. "Thank God you are alive. And relatively well, I see."

She smiled wanly at him. Gavin wanted to speak, but kept his mouth shut. Now was not the time, he told himself.

"Commander Tskoulis has informed me that you escaped from and killed your captors, is that so?"

"Yes, Uncle." She tried to sit up. They'd put an IV in her arm, a saline drip.

Sokol shushed her. "Please, don't," he said. "We can speak just fine this way."

She gestured to Tskoulis with her free arm. "I told him about it. We – we were somewhere underground, maybe the OS1, maybe somewhere else, I don't really know. We'd been traveling for days." She pointed to her bandaged feet. "They took my boots at one point, and I couldn't run away."

Gavin stared at the floor.

"I woke up at one point and they were all asleep. I managed

to flee. They came after me, and I – " She trailed off, gestured mutely to Gavin.

He produced the Onlar knife. There were still flecks of rusty blood on the blade.

She looked away.

Sokol took the knife with distaste. "You trained her well, Commander," was all he said.

"Thank you, sir," Tskoulis murmured.

Sokol handed the knife back to Tskoulis. Then he leaned back in his chair and looked at Jossey.

"My dear," he said quietly. He hesitated. Then he said, "Did they at any point...question you? Tell you where they were taking you?"

Jossey looked at him. "No," she said, frowning, looking lost in thought for a moment. "I was unconscious for some time. When I woke up, they had me bound. They did not speak." She peered at him. "How could – "

Tskoulis glanced at Sokol. *She does not know they are ordinary humans*, he thought. *What is he doing?*

Sokol smiled, waved a hand. "Of course," he said. "How silly of me not to explain."

He looked calmly at her. "My dear, do not be alarmed. I had cause to believe you had been kidnapped by enemy agents posing as Onlar."

Tskoulis kept his face frozen.

"*Certain information is...partitioned,*" he remembered Sokol saying. Well, this had clearly been partitioned – from him as well.

"The Onlar do not appear to speak our language," Sokol said smoothly. "But Karapartei is another story. I did caution Patrol that Karapartei might be interested in our solar project." He looked carefully at Jossey, glanced back at Tskoulis. "Do you understand that this conversation must not leave the three of us?"

"Yes, sir," Tskoulis said.

"Yes, sir," said Jossey.

"Very good." He turned back to Jossey. "As I said, Karapartei – I believe they may represent an off-branch of Patrol. Someone within Patrol may have reported our project to them, giving Karapartei a chance to kidnap you, the head person involved."

Jossey's eyes widened.

Tskoulis' did as well.

It would make sense, Tskoulis thought. But he did not appreciate all of this being withheld until now. Especially not as a unit commander and the head of her rescue mission. He stood taller, put his hands behind his back.

Jossey seemed to be thinking. Then she glanced up at Sokol. "Uncle," she said, "I think you're right. When I was attacked at Founders' Day – the man who kicked my pole, he bent it. He was wearing steel-toed boots, it looked like. And if they are trying to use the OS1 for supplies, as Henry told us, they must know how to fight the Onlar, otherwise they probably wouldn't risk it."

Sokol's eyes sparked with anger. "Who else knows about the solar project?"

"Just 2-5, sir," Jossey said quietly. She glanced at Tskoulis. "And possibly Unit 1."

Sokol shook his head. "It can't have been your unit. But maybe they have general spies. Someone who monitors equipment check-out, maybe." He touched his chin. "Thank you for that valuable insight, my dear."

"Uncle," Jossey said, "There's something else."

"Something else, my dear?"

"Yes." Jossey lay back, closed her eyes. "I – "

She kept her eyes closed as she spoke. "I escaped aboveground. I didn't know where I was. I had water and a knife, that

555

was all. I ran – it was so dark – I ran, and I finally saw light in the distance."

Tskoulis frowned.

"I had never seen light aboveground," she continued. "Not artificial light. I came upon – "

Her face contorted. "It was – some kind of farm." She opened her eyes, looked at her uncle. "Some kind of large vegetable farm. And there were men there, on the boundary. They wore – it was like Patrol, but the uniforms were off somehow. I thought maybe you were expanding agricultural work aboveground. But then – "

Her fists clenched, and she took a shuddering breath. Sokol's brow was knitted.

She seemed to steel herself. "I did not get close," she said. "I realized maybe I was seeing something I...should not. I thought maybe they would spare me if I didn't have anything to pin on them. But I found what looked like an office, thought I would try to find a radio, see if I could either turn myself in or – " She stopped. "They tried to kill me," she said in a small voice. "One man – "

She began to tremble.

Sokol took one of her hands.

"I stole a bike and fled," she said softly. "One man – " She closed her eyes. "I can't stop seeing his face. He looked cruel. He'd gone to get a bike and caught me. He – " She shuddered.

Her voice got very small. "I was trapped. He laughed and said I was a fighter. Said he liked that." She bit out the words. "He actually said, 'Shall we play?'"

Gavin's head shot up.

She wiped at her eyes viciously, pulling her blanket closer around her with one hand. "'Come back, sweetheart.'" She imitated a man's voice.

She looked at them, tears starting. "I – tried to get back on the bike, and he yanked me off, and – stood over me with his sword, and – " She started shaking violently, eyes shut tightly. "And then – he – "

She trailed off.

Sokol glanced at Gavin, frowning, then looked back at Jossey and squeezed her hand.

Gavin was imagining the multiple ways in which he'd like to use his sword on the man.

She opened her eyes at last and looked away. "Well, whatever he was trying, he's dead now," she said flatly.

Sokol glanced at Tskoulis again. Then he turned to Jossey.

"And then, my dear?" he asked quietly.

"I drove the bike to the highway and headed toward where I thought the City was," she said mechanically, still looking away from them. "Another guard...was in my way. I got as far as some ruins when I saw they were chasing me. So I abandoned the bike and – "

She pointed to Gavin. "Then I called for help."

"Called for help?" Sokol's face changed. "How?"

Gavin had the radio with him. He'd cleaned it of blood.

He handed it silently to the Minister.

"She rewired it," he said as the Minister turned it over.

Sokol looked impressed. "Isn't this a Patrol radio?" he asked.

"Yes, sir."

"It's on the wrong channel," Jossey said. "I had to open it up."

"I see." Sokol smiled. "You have just provided me with further ammunition in our fight against the Karapartei," he said. "Thank you, my dear."

She smiled wanly. "Uncle Sokol, why would Karapartei have a farm?"

His face darkened. "I believe they are trying to set up an independent government," he said. "There are more under-ground cities in this region than we had known. Maybe they are trying to feed their own population, recruit others." He glanced at Tskoulis. "I can...take care of it."

Tskoulis did not move.

Sokol smiled gently at his niece. "My dear, you have once again proven your bravery. You risked your life to expose Karapartei. I would like you to continue working on the solar project to which you have been appointed – after some vacation. Your unit should be pleased to see you return."

"My unit." She looked at her uncle. "Gav-Tskoulis says they are all right. What about Caspar's people? Did they – "

Tskoulis felt his mood sour.

"Everyone in Mr. Savaş's group is fine," Sokol said.

She closed her eyes.

"Now, my dear," Sokol said, "you should rest. The Commander as well. You have both had a very long past few days." He gave Tskoulis a look.

"Thank you, Uncle." She smiled past him, at Tskoulis. "Thank you," she said.

Gavin tried to smile.

"Good night, my dear." Sokol got to his feet, squeezed her hand once more. "Please do not hesitate to call for the nurse. And if you think of anything else pertinent, please do not hesitate to call for me."

"Yes, Uncle. Good night."

As they left, Tskoulis glanced over his shoulder.

Two days later, Tskoulis returned to Patrol duty.

He entered the training area. Immediately, 2-5 jumped to their feet and lined up, saluting him.

Even Savaş looked nervous. Tskoulis grinned inwardly.

"Good morning," he said to them.

"Good morning, SIR!"

"At ease. I have some good news." He smiled and told them.

They started cheering even before he finished speaking. Thompson and Ellis fist-bumped each other.

558

"Sokol should be returning within a couple of weeks, I hope," Tskoulis said. "I cannot discuss her condition for privacy reasons, but she has asked about all of you."

"In the meantime," he said, "we need to resume regular training. Karapartei appears to have upped its activities within the agricultural sector."

Caspar gave him a look.

Tskoulis didn't elaborate, simply said, "We need to stay at peak preparedness for now. Thank you for your patience during this time. I assume you have all been productive?"

Henry stepped forward. "Sir, we've put some of the wiring into place, but Savaş was called away by the Minister for some kind of additional research, so we haven't finalized it."

"I see." Tskoulis looked at Caspar. "And you've finished what you needed to?"

Caspar looked evenly at him. "Yes, sir."

He added, "It's a relief to hear Sokol is alive, sir."

They all glanced at him, suddenly tense. Tskoulis remembered the last time.

But Caspar smiled.

110

Jossey awoke and stared at the ceiling.

Her leg was still killing her, but she ignored it as best she could, thinking furiously.

Did her uncle believe her? He'd said that he thought it was Karapartei. Of all ridiculous things. From the look on Gavin's face, he hadn't been very convinced by Sokol's answer either.

But Sokol had seemed genuinely shocked when she'd mentioned the farm. Maybe –

She didn't know what to think. She had no doubt that he knew about the farms. But she assumed it was something he'd never intended for her to learn. Maybe her saying it in front of Gavin had been what had made him look so disconcerted.

She wondered where Tark was now.

* * *

Sokol paced up and down his office, glaring at Delta, who sat patiently, watching him wear rows in the carpet.

"Karapartei knows about our farms," Sokol gritted out at last.

Caspar's eyebrows went up.

"How, sir?" he asked after a long moment.

Sokol slammed his hand down on the projector button. The grainy footage of the bikes appeared.

Caspar leaned forward, frowning. "What are those?"

"Why do you think I employ you, Savaş?" Sokol snapped. "That is what I want you to find out."

Savaş sat back, face unreadable. "Yes, sir."

"And now two of our agents are dead, due to my beloved niece."

Savaş smiled a little. "You did well in choosing her for Patrol, sir."

"Yes, well, it was all well and good until she talked about it in front of Tskoulis. Now I have yet another problem to deal with. You know Karapartei is on his top list of...threats to squelch."

"Sir, he may have already suspected," Caspar said.

The Minister's eyes narrowed. "How?"

"He saw the farm Patrol's bikes too, I think – the lights, that is."

"I hope he can be counted upon to stay silent."

"He's your ideal commander, sir," Caspar said quietly. "Most likely. But if you'd prefer me to speak to him..."

Sokol sighed.

Caspar started to get to his feet.

Sokol held up a hand. "Wait. You need to see this."

"Sir?"

The Minister pressed another button on the projector.

Jossey's face filled the screen.

"My dear niece," Sokol's voice said warmly. The recording sounded tinny. "Thank God you are alive. And relatively well, I see."

Caspar frowned. Her face was cleaned up, but he could still see a bruise on her cheek. She was pale, faded-looking. Her scar stood out on her face.

She kept glancing past the camera. Tskoulis, he assumed.

She narrated her escape, and Sokol's voice asked if she had been questioned in any way. She appeared confused.

Then Sokol's voice: "I had cause to believe you had been kidnapped by enemy agents posing as Onlar."

Caspar's eyebrows shot up.

"I did caution Patrol that Karapartei might be interested in our solar project," Sokol's voice said. The camera turned, showing Tskoulis, who was watching, face expressionless.

On the screen, Jossey was saying how she'd figured out that Karapartei might be Patrol based on the man who'd tried to attack her on Founders' Day.

Caspar smiled a little.

Sokol's voice said that the spy or spies couldn't be Unit 2-5. He mused aloud about where they could have come from.

Caspar glanced at the real-life Sokol. "Spies?"

"Yes." Sokol paused the recording. "How else would they have known about the solar project?"

Caspar shook his head. "2-5 appears clean, sir. Maybe the Onlar – "

"Maybe," Sokol said darkly.

He turned the recording back on.

They listened to her description of the farm. Sokol paused it. "Do you think she saw the workers?" he asked Caspar.

"I doubt it." Caspar looked closely at the screen, at Jossey's face. "I don't think she'd be this calm."

Sokol seemed to think for a moment, then pressed play.

"...But I found what looked like an office, thought I would try to find a radio, see if I could either turn myself in or – " She stopped. "They tried to kill me," she said in a small voice. "One man – "

She began to tremble.

On the screen, Sokol's point of view glanced down and he took one of her hands.

The camera focused back on her face. She had gone pale, her eyes elsewhere.

"I stole a bike and fled," she said softly. "One man – " She closed her eyes. "I can't stop seeing his face. He looked cruel. He'd gone to get a bike and caught me. He – " She shuddered.

She looked terrified. Caspar frowned.

"I was trapped. He laughed and said I was a fighter. Said he...liked that." Her voice was tiny. "He actually said, 'Shall we play?'"

Caspar's eyes narrowed.

He watched her wipe at her eyes, drag her blanket up, as if protecting herself.

"'Come back, sweetheart,'" she said in imitation of a man's voice.

Caspar got to his feet.

"I've seen enough, sir," he said.

"Sit down, Savaş." Sokol's voice was cold.

On the screen, tears rolled down Jossey's face. "I – tried to get back on the bike, and he yanked me off, and – stood over me with his sword, and – " She started shaking violently, eyes squeezed shut. "And then – he – "

Caspar's fists were clenched as he stared at the screen.

The camera turned toward Tskoulis, whose expression was murderous. Caspar smiled bitterly.

"Well, whatever he was trying, he's dead now," Jossey said flatly.

"And then, my dear?" Sokol's voice was saying. Caspar wanted to hit him.

"I drove the bike to the highway and headed toward where I thought the City was," Jossey said, voice flat. "Another guard...was in my way. I got as far as some ruins when I saw they were chasing me. So I abandoned the bike and – "

Sokol clicked off the recording. The screen vanished.

"This is what she and Tskoulis know," Sokol said. "You were there for the rest."

Caspar was looking at the wall where the screen had been. "I understand. Sir, before I go, I'd like to visit Agent Sokol."

Sokol looked at him for a long moment, then smiled. "Your dedication to my niece is admirable. Make sure she continues to think of you as trustworthy. I hope to...bring her in soon."

Caspar's face didn't change.

"Yes, sir," he said after a moment. "Do you have excuses for any absence I may...incur?"

Sokol tapped the TOP SECRET folder on his desk. "It is here."

"Thank you, sir."

* * *

There was a knock at Jossey's door. She rolled over and smiled at the nurse.

"Good morning, Miss Sokol. Excuse me – Agent Sokol." The nurse fixed her bedsheets. "How are you feeling today?"

Jossey shrugged. "I've been better. My leg still hurts."

"We can adjust the medication."

"It's all right. It's a good reminder to me not to run too fast on it." She grimaced. "Anything good for breakfast?"

"Your favorite." The nurse winked. "And you have a visitor."

"A visitor?"

"Yes. Agent Savaş, from Patrol Unit 2. Should I show him in?"

Jossey sat up, flustered. "Yes, please."

"Yes, Agent." She pushed the breakfast tray over to Jossey. "Let me know if you need anything."

She went out into the hallway, holding the door and speaking to someone.

Moments later, Caspar entered the room.

He was smiling as he thanked the nurse.

Then his gaze fell on Jossey, and the smile dropped from his face.

He crossed the room in three strides and sat next to her bed.

"Jossey." His long silver eyes were fixed on her face. He looked horrified.

She smiled widely. "Caspar. It's so good to – "

"What did they do to you?" he demanded, cutting her off.

She frowned. "What?" Then she reached up, felt the bruise on her face, winced. "Oh. That. One of them kicked me in the head."

Pain flashed across his face.

"I'm so sorry," he muttered. "I tried to get there in time."

"It's not your fault," she said gently. "They were too fast. Besides – " She looked away. "They're dead now."

"How did you escape?"

"I – " She looked away from him. "Caspar, I'm sorry. There are some things I – can't tell you. I've spoken to my uncle."

He sat back, looking earnestly at her. "If I can help – "

She smiled. "You're helping just by being here."

He cracked a grin. "I'm more than happy to...regale you with some more of those, um, classic novels."

She snorted. "Weights sound better than suffering through that again."

He looked hurt. She laughed. "I'm kidding. They're awful, but that's the fun of it."

"So – which do you want? The Desert Rider II?"

"There's a SECOND book?" She looked horrified.

"No, I'm kidding." He smiled. "Can I get you anything?"

"Just – " She looked at him. "How is the solar project?"

"It's – your uncle's had me doing some extra research. Boring stuff. We haven't made a lot of progress. Been too worried about you." He winked, then his smile sobered. "Are you sure you're all right?"

He didn't seem able to stop looking at her face. Her bruise, she thought.

"I'm okay." She smiled. "My leg – I think I screwed it up running from – " She clamped her mouth shut. "Escaping," she said at last. "The Onlar wounded it years ago. I still can't use it the way I'd like."

"And your head?"

"I can think pretty straight." She laughed. "I hope, anyway. Tskoulis wanted to pull me off the solar project. I yelled at him a little."

Caspar snorted. "That was brave of you."

"If he's not going to let me into the tunnels, the least he can do is let me do something interesting." She huffed. "He's so overprotective sometimes."

Something flashed across Caspar's face. "He...takes good care of his people," he said after a moment.

She smiled. "How is 2-5?"

"They anxiously await your return, milady."

"Please tell them hello for me." She lay back against her pillows, looking up at him. "Sorry," she said. "I'm exhausted."

He looked concerned. "You should sleep," he said.

Jossey smiled wanly. "Thanks for coming, Caspar. I'm so glad to see you again."

His answering smile faded. "I was worried I – " He clamped his mouth shut. "I'm glad you're here," he said quietly.

He got up. "I have to go," he said, silver eyes warm. "I'm sorry. I'd love to stay longer."

She lifted her free hand in a half-wave and smiled.

He disappeared, glancing at her once more over his shoulder.

111

DELTA SHOT ACROSS THE DARKLANDS, MASK DOWN OVER HIS FACE, dark hair streaming behind him.

He turned onto the highway heading west, cutting through the ruins he'd searched two days ago.

Then, without hesitation, he turned right at the gas stations and sped through the night.

In the distance, he could see the faint glow of the farm. It was well-disguised – not noticeable until you were within a mile or so.

The highway skirted a large series of rounded hills, mainly rock, like giant domes in the earth. Centuries ago, people had lived scattered along the sides, their farmlands filling the flat areas below.

There was a long fence built across the land now.

Caspar approached the gate, slowing to a crawl. Spotlights flashed on as he crossed the outer boundary.

A guard stepped out, heavily armed.

"Identify yourself," the man shouted.

Caspar said nothing. He removed his mask.

The man stood back immediately, face going pale. He saluted and gestured to the figure in the guardhouse.

"Notify Kobol of my arrival," Delta said.

The man saluted again and spoke into his radio. The gates swung open.

The road wound along the base of the hills and beside a small round lake. Heat had made it into an algae dump. He could smell it from here.

He sped down the road to the main headquarters.

They were waiting for him outside.

"Sir." Kobol, a short, squat man with pale blue eyes, saluted. "Please, come in."

Caspar left his bike where it was.

He strode into the office.

Six men sat around a table. They'd apparently been summoned from their beds; they were yawning, and one was clutching what looked like an emergency cup of coffee. Caspar grinned a little.

"Wake up," he snapped.

They sat up as a man, scooting their chairs up to the table, making horrible grating sounds.

His grin disappeared.

"I should not have to tell you that I do not want to be here," he began slowly. "I prefer never to be here."

They flinched under his icy gaze.

"But as I am here – I can tell you that Intelligence is...not pleased. Unidentified foreign agents have infiltrated our boundaries, made off with one of our workers, destroyed our equipment," he said. He strode around the room, staring at them all. "And two nights past, there was yet another breach, the importance of which you appear not to understand, based on the...report I read." He raised his voice. "We trust you with very valuable work, agents. Vital work. Am I to understand that you have failed TWICE to – "

A man shifted in his chair. It squeaked.

Caspar stopped talking.

The room froze.

"Do you have something to say?" Delta said coolly.

Dead silence. The others stared.

Sweat appeared on the man's forehead. He swallowed and opened his mouth.

"Go on," Caspar said.

"Sir, we think them to be Karapartei," the man stammered.

Delta's face remained expressionless.

"You *think* them to be. Intelligence does not brook incompetence," he said at last. "You were all chosen for your ability to *maintain* the boundary."

He glanced down and casually adjusted the armor at his wrist. A knife, strapped to the underside of his forearm, gleamed there.

He looked up at the men, gaze probing. "But I am willing to...give second chances."

They stared back at him, deathly silent.

"Now. Why don't we go over the situation from the beginning," Caspar said lazily. He gestured to the man. "You were saying?"

The man glanced around. No one else appeared willing to volunteer. He stood up, straightened his uniform.

"Sir," he began, "one of our workers escaped a few nights ago. We sent three of the guards after him. They did not return. We could not afford to go after them, sir, until the guard changed. When we went – "

His face was pale. "They'd been killed by swords, sir."

"I know all this," Caspar snapped. "Do you have anything useful for me? I've been informed you have one of the bikes?"

"S-sir. We do, sir. And one of our men – witnessed the attack the other night."

"And?" Caspar said sharply.

"Well, sir, there was...another of the figures. Our man thinks he saw two."

Caspar sat down. "Explain." His eyes bored into the man.

"The woman who stole the bike – she got away. But there was – "

Caspar laughed. It was not a kind sound.

"Do you know who that woman was that you almost killed?" he asked.

The men looked at one another, then back at him. "No, sir," another said. "She was wearing a Patrol uniform. We have orders to – "

"Kill on sight, I know," Caspar said. "However." He put both his hands flat on the table. "Possibly you have been informed that Jossey Sokol, niece of Minister Sokol, was missing?"

They suddenly looked stricken.

"Maybe it occurred to ANY of you that a woman, alone in the desert at night, IN PATROL UNIFORM, just *might* have been the same missing woman?" He was standing now, shouting at them.

All six military men stared at him, pale as death.

"Sir, we – " one began.

Caspar waved him into silence. He rubbed his forehead with his left hand. "Happily for you all, she escaped alive." He glanced at them.

A shudder ran around the table.

"Now," Caspar said quietly. "What was this about a second figure?"

Silence.

"We – might have been mistaken, sir," said the same man who had spoken. "It was dark. We – " He looked ashamed. "We did not believe that a woman could have inflicted those wounds."

Caspar grinned crookedly. "You might be surprised," he said. "Were there any tracks? Any evidence of a second figure?"

"N-no, sir. Just – our man had blood on his sword. Quite a bit of it."

"I have recently spoken to Agent Sokol," Caspar said flatly. "I can assure you she had no sword wounds."

"The other figure – "

Delta smiled. "You found no blood, no traces of this 'other figure,' correct?"

"Correct, sir."

"If your man wounded someone with his sword, I would think there would be obvious traces," Caspar said dryly. "Maybe even a wounded person somewhere within range. You have a drone, after all, do you not?"

They squirmed.

He glanced around, watching them closely.

"Sir." One man had a stubborn set to his jaw. "Pardon me, sir, but are you really saying that you think a *woman* could have taken Taurin's sword from him and killed him with it?"

Caspar looked up, eyebrows raised. "If sufficiently frightened, yes, I think she could. The information she gave me – "

They seemed to be trying to process something.

"Sir," one said, "it's possible we saw a shadow, not a second figure. The bike's lights were on in the garage. We saw the agent, and our man, and – " He trailed off. "The lights moved quite a bit. I think she tried to run him over. So maybe – "

Caspar had a slight smile on his face.

The man held something up. "Also, we found this in the garage, sir."

Caspar took it, looked at it. It was a ring. With the Sokol crest.

He started laughing. They glanced at each other.

"Now," he said. "Show me the bodies. And bring me that bike."

. . .

They took him to the morgue. It was a small room with a refrigerated unit. Very expensive to maintain, but necessary.

They pulled the men's bodies out on trays.

Caspar examined them, looking with particular distaste at the larger man. He did indeed appear to have been killed by a large blade. It did not look like a pleasant death either.

He frowned. Jossey hadn't been trained to kill this way.

But he'd seen her face on the video. Heard her voice. She'd sounded desperate, terrified. And if the man had attempted to do what Caspar thought he had –

Yes, he thought, she could have done this. There was no evidence to indicate otherwise.

The other had met his demise by what appeared to be a knife.

"Sir, again, not to belittle Minister Sokol's niece, but the strength required – " One of the agents had appeared, was pointing to Taurin's body.

Delta glanced at them. "I can assure you she is more than capable of this kind of action."

They grumbled a little, but stood down.

"Now," Caspar said, "leave me. Kobol, meet me in your office in ten minutes. We have things to discuss."

"Yes, sir."

The agents left and shut the door behind them.

Caspar stood staring down at the body of the larger man.

He remembered Jossey's expression as her face filled the screen.

"I was trapped. He laughed and said I was a fighter. Said he...liked that. He actually said, 'Shall we play?'"

Caspar stared down at the dead man, Jossey's voice filling his mind.

"I – tried to get back on the bike, and he yanked me off, and stood over me with his sword, and – and then – he – "

Caspar's fists clenched.

Something was burning inside him.

He took his knife out of the forearm sheath, toyed with it for a moment, eyes fixed on the dead man's face.

Then he turned and hurled the blade across the room, burying it in the wall.

Outside, one of the men stood waiting for him, standing beside a black motorcycle.

He examined it. As the Minister had told him, it was a very old model – he was impressed it had worked at all. He waved in thanks to the agent, and crouched beside the bike.

He frowned. It was electric. That meant it had to have somewhere to charge.

Solar panels, was his best guess.

"What have your men found?" he asked quietly. The agent stood straighter as Caspar glanced up at him.

"It's an older model, former Turco-Russian army, sir," said the man. "Probably 2200s. We're not sure."

"Any idea who could have been driving it? Or where they could have come from?"

"No, sir. We sent out a drone after the prisoner, but found nothing. If the other bike is out there, they either rode very fast, or disappeared underground." He laughed nervously. "The drone found no heat signatures."

Caspar smiled wryly. "These bikes are not designed to heat up."

"Sir?"

"Never mind. Let me get a copy of that drone footage."

"Sir."

Kobol opened the door to his office. Caspar entered, tall figure barely clearing the doorway.

573

"Sit down, please, sir," Kobol said. "What can I do for you?"

Caspar smiled. "Relax, Kobol."

Kobol looked anything but relaxed. But he half-smiled.

"Coffee, sir?"

"No thank you, Kobol." Caspar looked around the office. "I see you've...decorated."

Kobol had a small kitchen unit near his desk, with a countertop. It looked oddly like one of the underground living units. The room was completely bare except for a single painting on the wall.

"My daughter," Kobol said, smiling at it.

"Quite an artist." It was a fuzzy landscape, with the sunrise pouring gold across a tan desert. Fat pink clouds floated above the earth.

Kobol sobered. "Yes, sir."

Caspar made himself comfortable at Kobol's kitchen counter. "Feels like my mother's kitchen," he said lightly. "Now. Kobol. It has come to my attention that there has been...Karapartei activity recently."

"Yes, sir."

"At Founders' Day. And now this. Do you believe they are related?"

"It's hard to tell, sir. We have no idea where the bikes came from. Footage was inconclusive, but we don't believe we've seen them before."

"Understood." Caspar frowned. "Do you...believe that more caution is warranted within the City? If they have bikes..." He glanced at Kobol. "As you know, the agricultural expo is scheduled for a few weeks from now. We already have enough supply disruptions from workers escaping and Onlar attacks and whatever else. It would be...less than ideal if Karapartei were to disrupt things."

Kobol looked soberly at him. "I understand, sir."

"Is there anything else to report?" Caspar took a sip of water from the canteen offered to him.

"Not of interest, sir."

"Everything here is of interest to me," Caspar snapped.

"Yes, sir." Kobol shrank back. "Nothing to report."

"Good. If that changes, you know how to reach me. And Kobol – "

"Yes, sir?"

"You may wish to get better trackers. This 'second figure' nonsense...it...may deplete confidence. *My* confidence in this farm's ability to correctly respond to security breaches. Wild speculation undermines that ability. Do you understand me?"

Kobol swallowed. "Yes, sir."

"Very good." He strode toward the door, replacing his mask. "Bury those men."

"Yes, sir."

Caspar stepped out into the darkness.

He sped back toward the City.

The night was very dark, the stars sparkling across the sky, the Milky Way a brilliant band of dust and light. He looked up at it.

Something was still burning. Rage. Emotions he couldn't identify.

He pulled over, looking up at the stars.

He couldn't get Taurin's face out of his mind. Couldn't stop thinking about Jossey's words. The way she'd pulled the blanket up around her, shivering.

The murderous look on Tskoulis' face.

The knife in the wall hadn't been nearly enough, thought Caspar, but the man was already dead.

Caspar sank to the ground, putting his head in his hands. He took a deep breath and looked up at the glittering stars, elbows on his knees.

Calm down, Savaş, he told himself.

But his chest was still burning.

He'd been assigned to protect Jossey Sokol. A Council kid, he'd thought. He'd been impressed by her abilities as an Engineer, but he'd just gone along, done what was necessary. It was an assignment. A boring one. He'd barely stayed awake during the day.

At least he'd known enough about solar engineering to be of use on the crew. But he'd longed for action, wanted to be out in the field, as much as he disagreed with some of the Minister's assignments.

They'd never even spoken. She hadn't appeared to notice the silent young man with the glasses.

And then they'd gotten in that crash, and he'd watched Jossey almost single-handedly save the lives of nearly three dozen people.

And now –

He shook his head. What was he thinking?

Her voice on the radio, shrieking. *"No! Please! Don't!"*

The sudden silence as it had gone offline.

He'd thought she was dead.

In an instant, he'd thought she was gone.

And then Patrol had found traces of her, and he'd nearly strangled Tskoulis when the commander told him that 2-5 was to remain behind.

He'd been surprised by the intensity of his rage. He felt responsible, he told himself. Responsible for keeping her safe, responsible that he hadn't told Tskoulis he felt uncomfortable splitting up the group.

Responsible.

But it wasn't just that, he thought.

He buried his head in his hands, staring at the idling bike, its headlight illuminating the rock. The stars above.

He couldn't. He had a job to do.

And there were Delta's orders. They were ironclad. If Jossey had been interrogated, had revealed anything...

For the first time, Caspar wondered if he could do it.

If he did, he thought wryly, Tskoulis would most likely kill him.

Or try.

Part of him thought it might be well-deserved.

He stared out across the fields. The burning hadn't gone away.

He shook his head violently.

He had to get back, had to report to Sokol. Had to –

Caspar staggered back to the bike. He glanced one more time across the fields, toward the farm.

He clapped down his mask. He had a job to do.

He shook his head again and accelerated down the highway.

112

J OSSEY GROANED AND ROLLED OVER, UNCOVERING HER EYES
groggily. She had been asleep for she didn't know how long. Her
vision was a blur of shapes, dimmed light. She didn't know
where she was.

She looked around her, half-conscious. Her eyes fell on an
enormous figure nearby.

Come back, sweetheart. The voice repeated in her head. The
memory of the man, standing over her, tossing his sword aside,
grinning.

Reaching for her.

She jumped back, gasping, scrabbling for something to fight
with, some kind of weapon.

"Jossey!"

She shrank back, terrified, squeezing her eyes shut, and then
the voice sounded very close to her. "Jossey, calm down."

She opened her eyes to see Gavin staring down into her
face.

She stopped squirming, looked up at him, blinking in confusion. "Gavin?"

He didn't bother to grin. "Are you all right?"

She curled up, turned away from him. "Sorry," she muttered. "I can't stop thinking about that man. The one who – "

She trailed off, still shivering.

Gavin sat back down, heavily, and looked at her, dark eyes shadowed.

She turned back and looked at him, pulling her blankets up around herself.

His posture – he looked like he hadn't slept, maybe in days. He was slumped in the chair.

"How long have you been here?" she asked.

"It doesn't matter," he said very quietly. "I thought – I'd lost you."

He looked like he had the first time she'd been rescued from the tunnels.

Only this time something seemed different. There wasn't even the trace of a grin on his face.

She sat up a little, pasted a smile on her face. She hated to see him unhappy. "I'm here. I'm back. No claw scars this time, not on me, anyway." She grinned lopsidedly. "I suppose you won't let me into the tunnels for the next month."

He shook his head, dark eyes full of pain. "Jossey. I – "

He paused.

She gave him a quizzical look.

After a long moment, he looked away. "Never mind."

She frowned.

"How's your leg?" he said lightly.

"It's okay. Like I said, you probably won't let me go back into the tunnels for a couple months."

He looked directly at her. "That's fine with me."

She laughed for a moment before realizing he seemed entirely serious. She glared at him. "No. Tskoulis. I have to do that solar project. I have to – "

He cut her off. "Sokol. Do what you want, but I don't want to ever have to...come find you again. Do you understand? Ever."

She looked at her hands.

"Understood," she muttered. "Sorry." Then – "Thank you. For saving me. For coming to find me." She looked up, meeting his eyes.

He flushed. "Don't be sorry. I made that promise, don't forget." He flashed her the Tskoulis grin.

Jossey smiled a little.

Then she looked seriously at him.

"Gavin, you don't have to keep that promise if you don't want to."

His expression changed, became guarded. "What are you talking about?"

She looked away from him.

"I was thinking about it while They held me captive," she said. "When I was hoping you would come rescue me. If you blame me for what happened to Tark, you shouldn't still have to–"

He ran a hand through his hair, dark eyes full of something she couldn't read. "Jossey, stop. Of course I – "

She went on. "I never understood why you didn't hate me. Why you keep trying to rescue me," she said.

She allowed herself a tiny glance at him.

He was shaking his head.

She took a deep breath. "I need to know, Gavin. Please. Do you blame me still? For what happened to my brother? Your best friend?"

He looked at her incredulously. "Why would I blame you? And you already said that about hating you when I told you we found – " He trailed off, staring at her. "You really think I hate you?"

She looked around, away from him, face going hotter. "N-no," she stammered, "not exactly, but I always thought you should, because I – "

"Jossey. Look at me." His voice was not calm.

She looked up. His gaze was locked on hers, something in his dark eyes. Frustration. Or something else.

"You were a child," he said. "You even told us you didn't think the Onlar were really real. Tark was old enough to know the danger. It was his decision to take you up there. It wasn't your fault."

"Yes, but – "

At her expression, he took a deep breath. "Besides. If it's anyone's fault," he said slowly, "it's mine."

She didn't move.

"I...encouraged him. Dared him," he said quietly. His face darkened with what looked like some long-ago pain. "It was stupid. I told him to go aboveground without me. Just to see if he was brave enough. I guess he decided having you with him counted."

She looked at him silently for a long time.

He flinched away from her gaze. "Don't look at me like that," he mumbled.

"A dare?" she finally said. "Why didn't you just tell me?"

"I thought you knew. You really didn't know? Tark didn't – " He stared at her. "This whole time, you didn't know?"

She shook her head slowly. "That's why I always felt terrible about being helped. I thought you were helping someone you should hate. Out of obligation."

She stared at him. "But it was out of *guilt*? Seriously?"

He didn't quite look at her. "A little. And doing right by my best friend. But now it's – "

He shut his mouth, his handsome, tanned face flushing deeply.

She stared at him, unsure whether to laugh or cry. "Why didn't you just tell me months ago when I asked why you didn't hate me? Didn't you figure it out then? Gavin, are you serious? I've spent *years* feeling guilty. I still feel guilty, but – "

He looked stunned.

"Don't tell me *now* you're angry at me," he muttered. "I've spent years trying to make it up to you. And I honestly thought that you knew – "

She started laughing.

Gavin just looked at her.

She grinned. "Oh, Gavin. The last time I was truly angry at you, you had taken my ice cream and run around the Square until it dripped everywhere, calling me Bossy Jossey while I shouted and my stupid brother laughed."

Gavin's lips twitched. He cracked a grin.

"You *were* bossy," he snorted. "And I bought you a new ice-cream cone, thank you very much."

And then the two of them were laughing.

They managed to regain their composure, and Gavin glanced at the time.

"Almost curfew," he said. "I should go."

"Gavin, you *enforce* curfew." She gave him a look.

"True. But you should get some rest, Sokol. I haven't given you *that* much vacation time." He grinned.

She made a face at him.

"Get some rest, Sokol," he said again, smiling.

She saluted.

He walked out, glancing back, and made his way through the hospital corridor.

As he left the building, bidding good night to the guards, he looked up at the City's half-lit "night sky." It was nothing compared to what he'd seen aboveground.

He sighed deeply, looking at the "stars."

She didn't hate him. She'd thought he hated her. That, he thought, was why she'd always looked so bothered when he'd come to her aid.

She didn't hate him.

He grinned hugely and strode across the City Square.

* * *

Caspar sat in his quarters, examining the ring the men had given him.

He frowned. It was a man's ring. He'd never seen it on Jossey.

It was the kind of thing passed down from father to son in the City. Sokol was one of the older families, from the time of the Founders.

He pulled up a set of Forensics records on the terminal in front of him, chewing on a piece of plant jerky.

SOKOL, he typed in. RUPERT.

A man's face appeared on the screen. He looked vaguely familiar. Caspar frowned.

The man had eyes like Jossey's – almost, both pale blue.

But the chin –

Caspar looked closely at the face. He'd seen those features somewhere before. But he couldn't put his finger on it.

He shook his head. That was like Jossey's chin too, he thought. Sort of.

DECEASED, said the file. It gave a date. Fourteen years ago.

POSSESSIONS RECOVERED.

Shoes. Half a shirt. Empty canteen. Solar goggles. Navigation equipment.

No ring.

Caspar frowned.

The Onlar weren't really scavengers, he knew. They tended

to treat the dead with respect. He didn't imagine they would have taken a ring from a civilian found dead in the desert.

If Rupert Sokol had passed on the ring to his son, that meant it would most likely have been on Tark's hand when he disappeared.

SOKOL, TARK.

Caspar pulled up another photo.

A young boy beamed, gap-toothed.

He could see the resemblance.

He flipped through file photos. Intelligence had been ruthless about cataloging all sorts of photos from City life.

Tark, and Gavin Tskoulis. Running. Fleeing, apparently, from a Patrol guard. Walking through the Square, carrying what looked like an entire crate of soda, grinning.

Sitting with identical ice-cream cones, what looked like chocolate smeared on their faces, arms around each other, up on a high fence, skinny legs a blur.

Gavin was a scrawny kid, dark-brown tousled waves sticking up every which way. His grin in the pictures rivaled Tark's.

Caspar smiled crookedly.

Tark had a mop of blond hair and silver eyes. He was maybe nine, and missing a tooth in his photo. But something – again, Caspar felt a twinge of something. Some memory.

He flipped through the file on the screen.

SOKOL, TARK. DISAPPEARED. ONLAR. SERVICE ELEVATOR ----.

A new entry, recent:

NOTE – DECEASED. OFFICER: GAVIN TSKOULIS, COMMANDER.

He stared at the face again. Something...

Suddenly, he heard footsteps in the hall. Voices. Ellis and Thompson.

He slammed the terminal shut, shoved the ring into a box of

equipment he kept under his bed, grabbed one of the terrible novels.

The Desert Rider again. He groaned.

They opened the door, laughing loudly. He pretended to be absorbed in his novel.

"Hey, Savaş." Thompson. He grinned hugely. "You missed dessert."

Caspar glanced over the top of his book, as if just realizing they were there. "Oh. Oops. What'd they have?"

"Pie." Ellis looked gleeful. "I – "

"Ate three?"

Ellis tossed a pillow at him.

Caspar grinned and dodged. "Watch the book. This is a classic."

Ellis looked skeptical. Thompson flopped onto his bed. "Freedom," he sighed.

Ellis glanced over at Caspar. "Yeah, not like Savaş here. He still has to do...what, like homework for the Minister?"

Caspar raised an eyebrow. "Something like that." He kept reading.

"Well, other than pie, you're missing out on *life*. Like me and Thompson here. We're planning to go visit Sokol in the hospital. Wickford too. Wanna come?"

Caspar lowered the book half an inch.

Thompson had a huge grin on his face. "Yeah."

Caspar lowered the book. "Right now?"

Thompson was changing into a clean civilian shirt. "Yeah, gimme a minute." He looked in the mirror, fixed his hair.

Caspar snorted. "Thompson."

"Yeah?"

Caspar eyed him for a moment. "Never mind," he finally said. "Yeah, all right. I'm in. Got to keep you from embarrassing yourself."

Thompson tossed something at him, not lightly. Caspar dodged without thinking.

"You realize that's really creepy how you do that." Ellis was giving Caspar a look.

Caspar grinned and slung an arm around Thompson's neck, ruffling his hair. "Don't worry, Thompson."

Thompson jumped and re-flattened his hair in front of the mirror, mumbling something about not liking her that way. Ellis was laughing in the background.

"I don't," Thompson insisted, glaring at them. "I'm just glad she's back."

They shoved him out the door. Caspar tossed the book behind him. It landed on the carpet, and the door shut with a click. Wickford was waiting for them in the corridor.

They left Patrol quarters, swiping out, and Caspar wandered after the trio.

At the hospital, he half-leaned against the wall, arms crossed, observing, as Thompson and Ellis inquired about Jossey.

"One moment," the nurse said. She disappeared down the corridor. They plunked themselves down in a couple of chairs. Wickford wandered over to the water machine.

Caspar took a seat across from them and picked up a magazine. There wasn't a huge selection, but they tended to have funny stories.

The nurse reappeared a few minutes later. "She's awake," she said. "She said you're welcome to come visit."

Thompson got to his feet at once. Ellis and Caspar followed suit. Wickford hurried over. They walked across the room to the nurse and down the hallway in the direction she was pointing.

Jossey's room was on the right. They entered.

. . .

Jossey looked up from her magazine as the men entered her room. She sat up carefully, smiling brightly at them.

Ellis and Thompson stood blocking the doorway. Over their heads, she could see Caspar in the background, hanging back a little. Wickford too, red hair visible as he glanced around her room.

Ellis and Thompson wore identical grins. Wickford smiled shyly. Caspar she couldn't see fully. But she imagined he was smiling.

They sat down by her bed.

Ellis was closest to her. She grinned at him. "Ellis! You look...healthier than ever. Have you been eating my portions?"

He looked semi-offended. "I – " he sputtered.

Thompson threw an arm around him. "Ellis here is the picture of innocence."

Ellis grinned. "Precisely."

Caspar looked amused at the pair of them. She turned to him. "And you."

He sat up.

"Bring me any more novels?" She grinned.

"Sadly, I forgot." He glanced at Thompson. "I was reading one when these two suggested we come visit. Left it there. Sorry." He grinned. "You've already read it anyway."

Jossey made a face at him. Then she turned back to Ellis and Thompson. "How are things? How's...how's Zlotnik?"

Ellis sobered. "She took a pretty hard hit," he said. "She had surgery – broken collarbone, they think, and some pretty nasty slices from the claws. But she's recovering."

Thompson added, "We're glad you're okay."

She smiled warmly at him. "It's good to be back," she said quietly. "I missed all of you."

"Are you feeling any better?" Wickford asked.

Caspar was remarkably silent as she chatted with Thompson, who for once was being friendly. Not awkward, not afraid of her. Just friendly. It was refreshing. Apparently he'd gotten over...whatever the problem had been.

Ellis said something that made her nearly choke on her water.

Thompson was smiling like a little kid on Founders' Day.

Caspar was –

Caspar was staring at her, silver eyes looking almost frightened.

Like before.

She felt her face heating up and looked away. Why would he be frightened? She was in the hospital, true, and she had a bruise on her face and hadn't really slept in days, but she didn't think she looked *that* –

She turned quickly back to Thompson, who said something goofy that made her laugh.

Out of her peripheral vision, Caspar shifted in his chair, and she heard the harsh sound of leg on metal. He flinched but said nothing.

Whatever he'd done, he seemed very focused on it, looking down at his leg.

Jossey turned to ask him if he was all right when suddenly Ellis turned to her.

"If you don't mind," the big man said, voice serious, "I'm really curious. How did you escape?"

Jossey felt her hands go cold. The blood rushed out of her face.

Ellis looked mortified. "I'm – sorry, I didn't mean – "

She sat up straighter, adjusting her blankets carefully. "It's okay," she said softly. "I – there's certain things I shouldn't talk about. But – "

She faltered, and glanced at Caspar. He was looking down at his leg.

"Tskoulis wouldn't tell us anything," Ellis said apologetically.

She smiled a little at Gavin's name.

Then she looked away. "Do you remember the Onlar in the Old Sector?"

Thompson looked slightly queasy.

"It was like that. I...I got away, and then they came after me," Jossey said slowly. "They chased me. In the dark. I thought they were going to – "

She trailed off, clasping her hands together so hard they went white around the edges. "Anyway," she said in a low voice. "I – I took care of them. I'd rather not – "

She hoped they wouldn't ask further. Hoped her discomfort would be sufficient to stave off questioning. Like it had with her uncle, to her amazement.

"It's okay," Wickford said sweetly. "You don't have to tell us."

Jossey looked gratefully at him, gave him a big smile.

Caspar had an odd look on his face.

113

"COME IN." SOKOL GESTURED EXPANSIVELY. "ANY CHAIR." HE grinned a little.

Caspar didn't laugh. The joke was tiresome.

The agent tossed his cloak onto one of the chairs and stood easily before the Minister.

He'd been the Tracker for nearly a week, and his shoulders still ached from hunching, his entire back burning a little in strange places from second-guessing every bit of instinctive movement, slowing himself down, even walking differently. He grimaced. It wasn't something a workout had easily taken care of. When Sokol turned the other direction, Caspar pulled his shoulder blades together, feeling everything crack into place.

Sokol flinched at the sound. Caspar ignored him.

It had felt good, so good, to get back out to the farms as the mysterious man from the City. To be able to really drop the act and just be Delta.

Which – he thought, grinning a little – was a bit of an act in and of itself.

Not even Kobol, with whom he'd worked for years, knew his real identity.

The farm Patrol just knew his face, and that was enough. Enough to make a guard go instantly pale. It was...not gratifying, not the way that some of them seemed to take pleasure in frightening people, but very useful for Delta's ends. He encouraged their fear. It kept things in line.

And that branch of Patrol almost never left the farms, so identifying Delta was highly unlikely.

Sokol's predecessors had designed it that way.

Now Caspar stood before Sokol, removing his traveling gloves slowly. He glanced up, long hair falling in his eyes, as Sokol spoke at length about the mission, about how the fools at Farm C had nearly ruined everything...

He knew all this. Had seen it. He half tuned it out until Sokol ranted about how they couldn't even be trusted to keep their boundary secure against a lone woman armed with a knife...

"She's your niece, sir," Caspar said dryly. "You approved her for Patrol."

Sokol rounded on him. "Yes," he hissed, "and I'm quite proud of her. But that does not rectify the situation."

"You're right, sir."

Caspar went back to removing his gloves.

"Are you listening, Savaş?"

Caspar smiled a little. "Yes, sir." He glanced up. "I'm here to report to you that your men are indeed grossly incompetent, but I have gone over everything, and there does not appear to be a security threat, at least not from your niece. On the contrary, she is...impressive."

He set his gloves down, procured a small data stick from his pocket. "Here, sir."

He tossed it to Sokol. Sokol put it into the projector.

An image of Taurin's body filled the screen.

Sokol looked disturbed. "Why are we looking at this?"

Caspar strode over to the desk. "Your men seemed...convinced that there was someone helping Jossey. However, these

591

wounds." He traced the wall with his finger. "Done by your man's own sword, it appears. Quite feasible for someone with Jossey's training. Note also the knife wound, here. Your man Taurin appeared to have been attacked by a knife first, then his own sword used on him. I've seen her fight, sir. She is...inventive."

He snorted. "I spoke with your men. Their entire rationale for a second figure was that they did not believe a woman could fight this way."

"And? You are certain?" Sokol's flat eyes betrayed nothing.

"There were no traces whatsoever of a helper, sir." Caspar grinned crookedly. "Which is good, because you and I both know she's the real scientific brain behind this solar project of yours."

Sokol looked at him coldly. "So your investigation – "

"Negative, sir. Her story checks out. I have no doubts." Then his expression darkened. "As for your foolish men who chased her halfway across the desert and tried to hunt her down..."

He realized his fists were clenched. He carefully unclenched them.

Sokol sat down at his desk. "They followed orders. Admittedly their judgment..."

"I'm just worried they will expose us, sir," Caspar said quietly. "As I said, Tskoulis saw signs that they'd been there."

The Minister paced. "We need to contain this, Savaş." He looked at his agent. "Tskoulis seemed...bothered when I suggested to Jossey in the hospital that her kidnappers might have been Karapartei. But he did not bring it up with me."

"Do you think he is likely to push for the information?" Caspar looked seriously at the Minister.

Sokol appeared to be thinking. Then he shook his head. "I think we can likely trust him to work with us and leave well enough alone. He seemed to accept my statement that 'Karapartei' were trying to set up an independent government." He scoffed. "He is – it seems he understands when not to ask questions. Tskoulis is a deeply loyal man, from what I've seen. And for what it's worth, he's doubly loyal: to this City, and to Jossey."

Sokol laughed at the look Caspar was giving him. "That boy – I'm surprised he even let her join Patrol. Not that he had any say in the matter."

"Sir?"

The Minister shook his head, looking highly amused. "Nothing, Savaş." His smile went cold. "So my beloved niece believes she is exposing Karapartei, was even willing to risk her life to bring them to my attention. Admirable. I would say – "

He stood for a long moment, then reached over and switched the projector off. The image of Taurin's body vanished, replaced by a blank white wall.

"It seems to me that it is time to move to the next stage of the solar project," the Minister said.

"Sir," Caspar said. "I agree with you. But I think we need to consider the possibility that Karapartei is out there and has the capability to disrupt our project. You said yourself to Tskoulis that you thought it possible that they were the ones who kidnapped Jossey."

Sokol shot him a look. "You believe that nonsense?"

"No, sir, but I do think it's worth considering that they are stronger than we had anticipated. How else would they be operating anywhere near the farms? On those motorcycles? You know as well as I do that there's nothing out there. Their attacks seem to originate from within the City, sir, but what if – "

Sokol sat at his desk, smoothing his jacket. "What are you suggesting, Savaş?"

Caspar sat down across from him. "I'm suggesting, sir," he said, "that Karapartei may be in league with the Onlar."

Sokol started laughing. "What on earth would make you think that, Savaş? The Onlar kill Patrol on sight. Even...rogue

Patrol." He bit out the words. "No, that would be truly ridiculous."

"You have...allies among the Onlar," Caspar said carefully.

"That despicable man Kudret?" Sokol's flat eyes narrowed. "You really think he would endanger his miserable quest for power by attempting to stir up his people's worst enemies against me?" He snorted. "Savaş, Savaş. Sometimes – "

Caspar sat back, face neutral. "It was only a suggestion, sir. Or maybe – "

"Maybe?"

"Karapartei is displeased with the status quo, as it were. I have heard no such disgruntlement among the farm Patrol, but it is possible that Karapartei...originates there." His face was expressionless. "I would be happy, sir – "

Sokol glanced at him. "You've already done a thorough investigation of the farms, is that not so?"

"Farms C and B, yes, sir. Not Farm A. Not yet." Caspar grinned. "And Farm A, as you know, is closest to the Onlar canyons."

"Ah, yes. Farm A. That would make most sense, as they deal with the miserable creatures on a more...regular basis." Sokol waved a hand. "Take care of it."

"And sir."

"Yes?"

"Have you given any more thought to mi– "

"Savaş." Sokol's voice was dangerous. "If you say 'migration' one more time in this office..."

"You know that we've received another, ah, diplomatic inquiry, sir."

"Yes, I'm well aware of that, Savaş." Sokol's eyes burned with fury. "If that...creature actually thinks we plan to cave..."

Savaş looked coolly at him. "Sir. They sent us one of our own men's heads."

"And I believe that Patrol suffered a similar end for their

incompetence in sufficiently guarding the Perimeter," Sokol snapped.

"Correct, sir." He looked up. "Again, sir – "

"This is why we are upgrading our infrastructure, one vulnerability at a time. And this is why I believe it may be time to bring my niece on board."

Caspar sat again in his room, alone, watching the drone footage. He'd sent Thompson and Ellis out on some errand. Find cookies in the mess, he'd said. He figured they'd be gone for some time. Thompson was a glutton for sugar.

He clicked on the video.

Fields, endless fields. The sun looked to have just slipped below the horizon, and twilight illuminated the land.

The drone flew out from the hill above the farm. It seemed to be a natural launch point – he'd seen many videos from this spot.

It followed the highway for some time, then the landscape disappeared below a steep ridge, at least a hundred feet high. The drone hovered in place, then descended into the valley.

The view changed to infrared.

There was nothing. The ruins below were completely dark.

The drone hovered, then sank, falling rapidly until it was twenty feet or so off the ground.

Still nothing.

Caspar wasn't surprised. There was no life down here, not beyond the ridge, as far as he knew.

The drone eventually pulled up and away.

But where had the bikes gone? Where had they come from?

The landscape out there was extensive, he knew. Plenty of ridges and canyons to hide out in.

Maybe Kudret would know, he thought, his smile twisting. What a disgusting man. But he might prove useful.

114

"SUIT UP!"

The call came down the corridor.

Jossey staggered out of bed, made herself relatively presentable.

She was still limping, had really done a number on her leg, but her bruises were mostly gone, and she felt stronger than she had in some time. She'd been allowed an extra week to recuperate in the hospital.

She'd been ridiculously bored. A daily visit by various Patrol members hadn't been nearly enough.

And they kept asking her uncomfortable questions about her escape. At least Thompson of all people had had the common sense to realize she didn't want to talk about it.

In the bunk above her, Zlotnik rolled over and groaned.

"Get up," Jossey hissed. "It's my first day back. One of us has to look functional."

Zlotnik muttered something, but sat up, blinking.

"You're back," she said.

Jossey snorted. "You let me in last night."

Zlotnik rubbed her eyes, yawning hugely. "Oh yeah. Sorry.

It's been a lot these couple weeks. I haven't slept a lot. I honestly thought you were Olivia."

Jossey laughed. "So you *were* sleepwalking."

Zlotnik looked vaguely ashamed. "Maybe."

"Don't fall off the bunk." Jossey sobered. "Are you better?"

Zlotnik looked straight at her. The new scars had faded somewhat, but she still had thick red slashes across her face. "Henry has orders to go lightly on me in training. None of your sneaky attacks." She winked.

Jossey made a face at her. "Well, my leg isn't doing so great either."

"Sorry I didn't come visit you in the hospital," Zlotnik mumbled.

"It's okay."

"No, really. I – "

Jossey smiled. "I know you were doing rehab. Caspar told me."

Something flickered across Zlotnik's face. She opened her mouth.

"TEN MINUTES TO MESS!"

She shot out of bed.

"Wait!" Jossey ran after her. "I haven't – "

The bathroom door closed in Jossey's face.

The pair of them wandered into the mess hall, only to be greeted by cheers.

The entire table of Patrol stood up, clapping. The other tables turned around, looking bemused, then joined in.

Jossey flushed. Zlotnik just grinned and threw her long arm around her roommate.

"Welcome back, Sokol." Tskoulis was standing there, his famous grin on his handsome face. She flushed even more.

He gestured to a seat. "Please. I believe we've...made sure Ellis has left your portion alone."

Ellis just laughed. "I'm even guarding them," he said.

Jossey sank into her chair, feeling nearly as red as the tomatoes on her plate. Zlotnik thumped her on the back.

Tskoulis sat down with all of them. They went silent.

He smirked. "Oh, carry on," he said. "At ease." Then he helped himself to a small pile of fake eggs.

Breakfast was a blur of laughter and conversation. Eventually they got up and headed toward the training room.

Tskoulis was all business again. But he gave Jossey a half-smile before he went up to the front of the room.

Once he had finished addressing the other subunits, he came back over to 2-5.

"All right, people," he said. "Now that Sokol's back, we need to move to the next stage of our training. As you know, we are partway through a major project commissioned by the Minister of Intelligence." He turned and looked each of them in the face. "We've been ordered to complete the wiring. When Sokol was...kidnapped" – he paused – "the Onlar did not manage to get to the installed switches, but it is possible that they may try to do so in the near future. As far as we know, all those involved in the attack were killed, so we may be safe for now. But as a precaution, a small team may relocate one of the switches, per the work Savaş has been doing over the last week while we searched for Sokol."

Tskoulis looked over at Caspar. "Anything to add?"

"No, sir, not at the moment." Caspar stood tall.

"Very good. And Sokol." The commander turned to Jossey. "To bring you up to speed, the wiring project is slated to begin tomorrow. Our goal is to connect one panel at a time, run tests, make sure everything is working."

She glanced at Caspar. "That seems..."

Caspar spoke up. "Inefficient," he said. "But Minister Sokol wanted to make sure that the grid could handle the adjusted load as we brought each one online."

Jossey frowned thoughtfully. "That makes sense. That would take – " She did some calculations in her head. "At least ten days, maybe longer."

Tskoulis said, "Longer is what we've planned."

"Why, sir?"

"There's an agricultural expo scheduled in a couple weeks. We've received credible threats against it, as was the case with Founders' Day. This expo is a very public event, with the various players interspersed with civilians. We can't afford to be lax on security."

She frowned. "Understood, sir."

"That's enough for now." Tskoulis gestured to Henry. "Henry, take 2-5 through some basic warmups. We have some injured parties here. Use your discretion. But I want everyone as close as possible to fighting form by the end of this week."

Jossey stood taller, ignoring the pain in her leg. "Yes, sir," she shouted along with the room.

As Tskoulis walked off with Pricey, she let herself wince.

She lined up opposite Zlotnik. They grinned at each other.

"We're like the two injured newbies," Zlotnik said. "Go lightly, Henry said. Sounds like a plan to me."

Henry strolled by. "I heard that. Tskoulis said fighting form by the end of the week. Think you can handle that?"

Zlotnik gestured to her arm sling. "Wanna teach me to sword fight with the wrong hand?"

Henry cracked a grin. "I have just the instructor for you."

"Savaş!" he shouted across the room. Caspar's head shot up from where he was sparring with Ellis. Henry waved him over.

Caspar jogged over to them. He shot Jossey a grin.

"Zlotnik here needs some speedy instruction in sword

fighting with the wrong hand," Henry said. "Since you seem to have a natural talent for the sword..."

Caspar grinned. "With pleasure, sir."

He led Zlotnik a little ways away. Henry and Jossey stood watching.

He was an excellent teacher, Jossey thought. He seemed to have an intuitive grasp of how people learned. And of their weak points. She watched Henry's expression as he observed. He seemed surprised at times.

As she had been.

She still hadn't said anything to anyone about the way Caspar seemed to hold back, but Henry seemed to see it.

Finally Henry turned to her. "Shall we?"

She put on her gloves and helmet. "What should we work on?"

He tossed her a wooden sword. "Advanced blocking techniques," he said. "And a few sneak attacks."

She grinned. "Sounds like fun."

Jossey and Zlotnik staggered back to their quarters after dinner.

Zlotnik climbed up and flopped on her bed while Jossey changed into her night uniform. The tall woman watched lazily as Jossey wandered to and fro brushing her teeth and preparing to sleep.

"You're learning faster," Zlotnik remarked.

Jossey rinsed her toothbrush and wiped off her face. "Thanks," she said.

"No, really. It's impressive." Zlotnik smiled. "I'm amazed you survived those six days out there. Clearly you learned something from Patrol. And now that you're back...you seem...fine. It's like you never left."

Jossey smiled, but it was a faraway smile. Zlotnik sat up. "Hey, sorry. I didn't mean – "

"It's okay. It was...it feels like it was weeks ago. Like it almost didn't happen," Jossey said thoughtfully. "Like I disappeared and everything was dark for a long time and then suddenly I was back."

She smiled a little. "I hoped they would come for me. Especially Tskoulis. He – "

She trailed off, not sure if she wanted to share with Zlotnik the promise Gavin had made. Besides, she didn't want it to sound like –

"We all wanted to come after you," Zlotnik said. "But Tskoulis told us that we had to stay, had to work on the wiring, direct order from the Minister."

Jossey smiled. "Thanks. I'm not surprised – it's a vital project. Besides, my uncle – that is, the Minister – sent Unit 1 after me. Elite of the elite. No offense to our unit of course."

Zlotnik snorted. "None taken. We – " She stopped for a moment.

Jossey glanced at her.

The tall woman looked as if she wanted to say something, but should not.

"Ellis told me Caspar stood up to Tskoulis," Zlotnik said quietly after a long moment.

"What?" Jossey froze. She turned and stared at the woman.

"When they were told about the wiring project. I guess Savaş looked like he wanted to fight Tskoulis right then and there." She rolled onto her side, looked seriously at Jossey. "Ellis said he's never seen anyone do that. Ever. They all know what can happen if you challenge Tskoulis."

Jossey was gaping at her. "Fight him? Are you serious? Why?"

Zlotnik just looked at her, face unreadable.

"Anything I say would probably be speculation," she said. "Just – I think he...has your best interests at heart." She smiled a little.

Jossey flushed. "He's my partner," she said. "On our solar project. Of course it would make sense for him to come after me."

Zlotnik's lips twitched.

She rolled over. "I'm tired," she announced. "I have to sleep."

"But – "

"Night, Sokol."

Jossey sighed. "Fine. Good night." She turned out the light and stumbled her way over to her bed.

She stared into the darkness for some time, then sank into a deep sleep.

115

JOSSEY MADE HER WAY ALONG THE CORRIDOR, CAREFULLY PUTTING her full weight on her bad leg. It held. She smiled and continued on, holding her heavy bag in her other hand, balancing the weight.

They'd been working hard on basic drills, and she'd started to get some of the strength back in her arms. It was depressing how quickly she'd lost it when she'd been imprisoned by the Onlar. She grudgingly gave Gavin credit for having pushed them hard – he was right that they needed to keep on top of things.

She wondered where he was. She hadn't seen him much on the training floor.

Probably had a mission, she thought. He was always off on secretive high-level things.

She smiled, remembering his confession that he had been responsible for the situation with Tark.

She wasn't angry at all. She was relieved.

She'd hated herself for years, thought that she was to blame. She'd never imagined that *Gavin* was to blame.

And angry at him?

"I've spent years trying to make it up to you," he'd said.

She smiled.

She stretched her arms as she walked. They'd been let out of training early today, she assumed to start working on the solar project again.

She turned the corner and almost ran smack into Caspar.

He blinked and looked down at her, eyes wide. She jumped back, wincing a little as she landed on her bad leg. Her cheeks went hot.

"S-sorry," she stammered.

He grinned. "You okay?"

"Sore," she admitted. "Tskoulis really pushes us in those workouts."

He shrugged. "I guess."

Jossey shot him a look. "Yeah, well, at least one of us isn't used to everyday workouts."

He laughed, silver eyes alight. "Let's go, Sokol."

He held up a folder. The corners were dog-eared, as if he'd been studying it daily. She raised her eyebrows. "Been working hard?"

"You could say that."

He fell into an easy stride as they walked together down the corridor, Jossey still limping a little.

"Here," Caspar said, glancing down at her. "Let me take that."

"What?

Before she could protest, he'd scooped her bag up and slung it easily over one shoulder.

Her leg did feel better without it. She smiled at him. He didn't look at her, but there was a slight smile on his face as he kept walking.

They opened the door to the classroom. Minister Sokol stood there waiting, hands clasped. He smiled widely as he saw Jossey.

"Welcome back, my dear," he said to her. "Mr. Savaş." He gestured to the chairs. "Please, have a seat."

They sat. Caspar slid the folder between them.

"I am afraid I may have very little time this afternoon," Minister Sokol said. "However, I have some important announcements."

Jossey sat up, looking expectantly at her uncle.

He glanced at Caspar. "First, Mr. Savaş has been studying some additional material on solar networks."

Jossey frowned.

Caspar turned to her. "The Minister has asked us to expand our original vision. We need to incorporate some additional power capability."

"Okay." Jossey glanced at the folder. "Uncle – that is, Minister, should I read all this as well?"

"Yes, my dear. All in good time. But first – " Sokol smiled. "Allow me to express my increasing admiration for your actions these past several months. And, indeed, years. You have long worked to the betterment of this City."

Jossey shrank into her chair. Her family knew how she felt about praise.

He ignored her discomfort and went on. "You saved the lives of nearly three dozen people, underprepared and untrained, something we have taken into consideration as part of our new training program for Engineers."

Jossey's head shot up.

He smiled. "Indeed, my dear. You joined Patrol at my request, despite a difficult personal situation. And now, despite a truly terrible situation in recent weeks, you not only have returned to your duties on a vital security project, you have also risked your life to expose one of our City's worst enemies. You have shown resourcefulness and great mental strength. I know very few Patrol who would likely be able to take on what you have, my dear niece. I say this from my heart."

Sure you do, thought Jossey.

But her face was burning regardless.

She glanced at Caspar, who was smiling at her.

"It is because of all of this, my dear niece," Sokol said, "that I would like to...bring you in."

Jossey looked up, confused.

"Bring me in?" she asked, getting slowly to her feet. "What do you – "

Sokol did not appear to have heard her. "Sit down, my dear. You are not in trouble. This...invitation is extended to only a very select few. Do you understand?"

Dumbfounded, Jossey stared at him.

"What invitation?" she asked.

She remembered Tark's voice. *"If she fails, my uncle will probably kill her."*

"It is my great honor to ask you to consider taking on a more...classified role."

Sokol's expression was dead serious.

She glanced at Caspar, unsure how he looked so calm. Unsurprised, even. She looked back at her uncle. "Excuse me?"

"My dear, you have proven yourself over and again these past several months. As you know, this project is vital to our City's security, but due to certain...incidents which I have not been previously able to discuss with you, we need to speed up our timeline. As such, I need you to be able to handle classified material."

She glanced at Caspar, who gave her a look she couldn't read. Was he working on classified material too? Her head was spinning.

"However, I need to be comfortable that you are likely capable of handling such classified material," Sokol said. "Understand that there is a penalty for revealing such material to the wrong person. It is not a light penalty."

"I understand, sir," she said carefully. "And if I refuse?"

"If you refuse, my dear, I have another agent in mind to continue the project with Mr. Savaş. You may, of course, remain on Patrol, but no longer in an Engineering capacity. Any Engineering information regarding this project can no longer be discussed. And – " He paused. "Mr. Savaş will likely be transferred to that agent's unit."

Caspar didn't look at her.

She remembered the day she'd signed on to Patrol. *Life and limb.* This was no different. Besides, she'd already signed away any of these considerations the day Gavin had told her he'd found those bones.

And she'd agreed to help Tark.

She looked firmly at her uncle. "Yes," she said.

Caspar glanced at her. She smiled at him.

"Excellent," Sokol said. He paced at the front of the room, hands clasped behind his back, a big smile on his face. Then he turned and looked at her.

"My dear," the Minister said, "before we proceed, allow me to introduce to you one of my Intelligence agents."

Silence. Jossey looked expectantly at the door, at the back of the guard's head outside.

Sokol laughed a little.

"He is sitting beside you," Sokol said.

Jossey turned, confused. The only person –

Caspar was sitting there, not quite looking at her.

Caspar.

Her mouth dropped open.

She sank into her seat, eyes glued to Caspar's face. He finally looked back at her, long silver eyes filled with something she couldn't identify.

"Your what?" she managed.

"Caspar has worked with me for many years," Sokol said, still smiling. "I have assigned him to work with you as well."

She felt herself beginning to flush with anger. "You – " She turned to Caspar. "You *spied* on me?"

She didn't care how she sounded right now. Or if Sokol got angry. *Caspar* of all people.

Caspar flushed, just a little. "Not spied," he mumbled.

She turned furiously to Sokol. "You said you'd kept an eye on my work. Now I see how."

Sokol looked amused at her anger. "Indeed," he said. "And it was excellent work, I must say."

Jossey sank into her chair in a huff. "Well," was all she said.

A brief pause, then Sokol said dryly, "Shall we continue?"

"Yes, sir," she mumbled.

"One more thing, Jossey." Sokol's amused look was gone. "I have told you that I have brought you in. This is a very small elite circle. No one outside of it must know about the work we do here, or this group's existence. As far as the outside world is concerned, you are an auxiliary Engineer, working with Patrol, on projects you are not at liberty to discuss."

He looked carefully at her. "Including to your commander. In particular, you are not to speculate with him on anything related to Karapartei. If you do speak with him about Karapartei, you are to report any conversations you have with him on the subject. He already knows more than I would prefer, based on your conversation in the hospital. Do you understand me?"

Jossey swallowed the lump in her throat.

Caspar was looking at her with that unreadable expression again.

They were asking her to spy on Gavin? This wasn't at all what she had signed up for. *Sokol* had brought him to the hospital. *He* hadn't sent Gavin out when she began speaking. Not her. And now Sokol –

She didn't understand. But the thought of betraying Gavin in any way...

If she couldn't spy on him, she could at least avoid him, she thought. Try to keep him safe from whatever her uncle was planning. She almost smiled. As he'd always tried to keep her safe.

She glanced at Caspar.

She looked at her hands. "Yes, sir," she finally said.

After what felt like hours, she left the conference room, her mind reeling. Caspar followed her.

She walked as fast as she could, but her bad leg wasn't cooperating, and Caspar had several inches on her anyway.

He caught up to her quickly, stepped in front of her. "Jossey," he said. "Jossey, look at me."

She glared at him. "Don't talk to me, Caspar. How dare you. After what my uncle just – "

"Jossey, please." His eyes were pleading. "I didn't – " He glanced around, kept his voice down. "I didn't do what you said in there. I was sent to protect you. Keep an eye on you."

"Protect me?" She glared at him. "From what? Really? The Onlar? The one in the tunnel nearly killed me, Caspar!"

He groaned. "I know. You were too fast. By the time I found a way to attack the thing without drawing attention to myself..."

"What do you mean, drawing attention to yourself?" She folded her arms, eyeing him suspiciously. "You mean – *instinct*?"

He looked evenly at her. "Yes. Exactly. An Engineer shouldn't be able to – well, you know."

Jossey huffed and stepped around him. "Great. Leave me alone."

He stepped back in front of her. "Jossey. Please. Don't."

"Don't what?" she hissed. "What do you care? This whole time, has that been the reason? Keeping tabs? I thought – "

"Jossey, keep your voice down." Caspar glanced around. "If you're heard..."

"Even the hospital visits?" She half-laughed.

"No, not at all, I – " His eyes were unreadable. "Jossey, please don't be angry, I can explain – "

"Then explain!" she nearly shouted.

Suddenly her eyes widened. Tskoulis was walking down the corridor toward them.

"Caspar," she hissed.

Caspar turned around.

"Commander," he said shortly, body language instantly calm.

Tskoulis had stopped walking. He looked past Caspar to Jossey, who gave him a tense half-smile, unfolding her arms and pressing them to her sides. He looked back at Caspar.

"What's going on?" he asked. The look he was giving Caspar could almost have melted lead.

Caspar looked completely unfazed.

"Nothing, sir," Jossey said between gritted teeth. "A disagreement over some...Engineering methods."

"Is that so, Sokol?"

"Yes, sir." She looked away.

Tskoulis paused. Then he looked at Caspar. "Be careful, Savaş. She's dangerous when she's mad. I advise giving in."

He grinned a little, but his eyes held a warning.

"Noted, sir." Caspar's eyes were dark. "Permission to go."

"Granted."

Caspar glanced at Jossey, then stormed off down the corridor.

Jossey numbly watched him go.

Tskoulis stood there, looking a little confused, but immediately turned to Jossey. "Are you sure that was just about Engineering?" he asked.

She didn't look at him. "He's..." She groaned and shook her head. "It's just stupid work stuff. He's being obnoxious. Never mind."

"If you're sure..."

Jossey smiled. "I'm sure. Sometimes punching things is easier than dealing with fellow scientists. Are there any punching bags available?"

Tskoulis laughed. "Help yourself."

She saluted, then stomped off in the direction of the training room without looking back.

116

"LINE UP!" SHOUTED HENRY.

2-5 obeyed. Jossey was still not looking at Caspar. It had been three days. They were civil in public, and no one else seemed to have noticed, but she avoided his glances whenever possible. He seemed to have given up trying to get her to talk to him.

She got into line beside Zlotnik.

"The agricultural expo is held every two years," Henry said, striding back and forth like her old teacher. "As you know, Karapartei has made credible threats against certain members of the agricultural industry, notably the Minister of Agriculture himself." He looked at them one by one. "This is a major event and draws much of the City's population. We have been instructed to place security within the general crowd, as there is no spatial separation between civilians and officials."

"Great," muttered Ellis.

"Given the credibility of the threat, you are to wear your full armor and weapons," Henry said.

Jossey and Zlotnik glanced at each other.

The threat must be very serious, Jossey thought.

"Any Karapartei you encounter are to be taken alive and reasonably unharmed."

"Yes, sir," they said.

"Pair up. I want you to all practice taking an enemy down: disarming, specifically."

Jossey stood opposite Zlotnik. This time she felt no fear.

"I know you're good at this," she said. "I've seen you. Teach me."

Zlotnik grinned.

Jossey's arms were killing her. Zlotnik was *too* good at disarming her. She groaned. She'd tapped out for the fifth time, wincing in pain, when Henry had ordered a break.

She sat and drank from her canteen, nursing what she thought might be a bruised elbow.

Caspar sat down next to her. She looked straight ahead.

"What?" she said flatly.

"Twist her arm the other direction next time," he offered under his breath, not looking at her. "And – " He demonstrated in the air. "Not too hard if you want her to still be able to grip things."

Jossey turned away, not wanting to know how he knew these things. "Thanks," she muttered.

He didn't say anything.

She tried it on their next round, and Zlotnik went down, howling. Jossey jumped back, startled.

When she reached for Zlotnik's hand to help her up, the woman glared at her for a moment. Then she lay back on the ground and grinned. "I don't know how you did that, but nice work, Sokol." She took Jossey's hand. "Don't ever do that again."

"Sorry," Jossey muttered.

"Not to me, at least. Save it for Karapartei."

. . .

Jossey stretched at the end of training. She watched the other Patrol refill their canteens one at a time, then trickle out of the room, she guessed heading for the showers and the mess.

She leaned forward, groaning. Her entire back was killing her.

"You have to be faster. All the disarming in the world doesn't work if you get caught in their grip."

Caspar's voice sounded behind her. She jumped and shot him an angry look.

"Can you not sneak up on me?" she hissed.

He laughed and sat down next to her. "I'm just trying to help. You're inventive, Jossey, but probably not *that* inventive. Not if they catch you. There's a big size difference. And strength difference. Are you still mad?"

"What do you think?" she said under her breath.

His expression sobered. "Jossey." He looked seriously at her. "I have a job. One that I take very seriously. But I also – "

She groaned again and stretched. "How am I supposed to believe you? You could just be a great actor for all I know."

He looked almost hurt. "I didn't do anything wrong, Jossey. I just – "

"Looked out for me? Pretended to be someone else?"

"I am, in fact, an Engineer," he said dryly.

"Well. Fine. But that doesn't excuse – "

"What? Looking out for you? Since when is that a bad thing?"

She glared at him. "At least Gavin is up-front about it. He can be annoyingly overprotective but *at least I know*."

Caspar gave an exasperated sigh. "What do you want from me, Jossey?"

Jossey finished stretching, looked at him square in the face. "If we're equal now, or whatever, I want to know a few things. About the Onlar. About Karapartei. About what's really going on."

His eyebrows shot up. But he looked seriously at her for a long moment.

She looked at him, refusing to flinch away from that gaze.

"Sokol can – " he said.

Jossey shook her head. "Not him. You. If I'm really on your team now..."

She watched his face. He seemed to be making a decision.

Caspar watched her strange eyes. They looked solemnly at him. Her scar was a vivid white against her flushed face.

Every part of him was screaming at him to ignore her request. There were certain things that only he had been authorized to know. Certain things that it was...not ideal for her to know.

Especially if Sokol were to ever find out.

And yet.

He needed her to trust him. Not just because of the work they were doing.

Maybe it would be better if...

His instincts were screaming at him to be careful.

But he was having trouble saying no to those eyes. He wanted to kick himself, much like he had in the hospital.

She was looking at him still.

He sighed inwardly.

Then he smiled a little.

"All right," he said.

Caspar lay on his bed, staring up into the darkness, trying to wipe the last several hours out of his mind.

"You could just be a great actor for all I know."

He couldn't stop thinking about it.

He'd agreed to give her information. He wasn't too worried

about that. Whatever she asked, he probably had a dozen ways of answering. He was good at keeping secrets. Too good, he thought. It was what he did. But –

"You could just be a great actor for all I know."

As opposed to who, Tskoulis? Who was terrifying, a beast of a man, but an excellent commander. Honest. Ethical. No doubts where his loyalties lay, unless he was an even better actor than Caspar.

Caspar doubted Jossey had ever wondered about Tskoulis' loyalty to the City. Or to her.

He grimaced.

Caspar knew what his own loyalties were. But what he didn't know, hadn't wanted to consider, was just *what* he was willing to do in order to achieve what was necessary.

He'd fought, spied, and killed for the Minister for years, ever since Sokol had plucked him from a Patrol apprenticeship and sent him for training. He'd done unspeakable things. Things he blocked out of his mind.

But Jossey –

There were some things he was starting to doubt he could do.

And he didn't want *her* to see him the way Sokol likely saw him. The way he suspected Tskoulis saw him.

As he was starting to see himself, if he were being honest.

He remembered her gaze as she'd looked straight at him.

She'd been most upset, as far as he could tell, that his friendship might be false. That he'd only seemed concerned about her. That he would pretend to care.

Of course he would, he thought disgustedly. He'd done it so many times he'd lost count.

But he didn't want to do it to *her*. He wasn't sure he even could. Not anymore.

He flinched, remembering the somber look in her eyes as she'd waited for him to respond. She'd seemed so...naive.

She was so mature in many ways. But in other ways –

For example, she apparently had no idea that *Thompson* of all people had been interested in her when they'd started on Patrol. Thompson, who couldn't seem to keep his heart off his sleeve. Or, rather, off his face.

Caspar snorted.

Thompson was snoring above him in the bunk, sounding happily oblivious to the room.

Caspar ignored him and went back to thinking, staring at the glowing dial on his wrist. 3:00 AM.

He wanted her to trust him, he realized. Really trust him. And not just because Intelligence required it.

Thompson made a strange honking sound above him, still snoring. Caspar nudged the mattress with his foot. Thompson stopped snoring.

Caspar covered his eyes and sighed in relief. He had to deal with this nightly. At least Ellis was quiet. But Thompson was...Thompson. He liked everyone, it seemed. Jossey was just one of the latest. He seemed to have moved on, probably to that new recruit in 2-7. Caspar nearly laughed. He couldn't imagine Jossey ever –

And yet. Thompson had made her smile. Laugh. She seemed to trust him. Feel safe around him.

And the way her eyes softened when their commander was mentioned.

She'd known Tskoulis since they were children, Caspar thought. It was natural. It would be strange if she didn't –

He groaned and buried his head under his pillow.

———————

117

THEY SAT AGAIN BEFORE SOKOL, FOLDERS OPEN, NOTEBOOKS ready.

Jossey took the chair next to Caspar this time. He didn't look at her, keeping his gaze on Sokol, but she could see him smile slightly.

Sokol was pulling down the projector screen. "Today," he said, "I have brought the full plans for the upgraded project." He glanced at them. "I assume you have familiarized yourselves with the material required?"

"Yes, sir." They both looked at him.

"Good."

An image appeared on the screen. A map.

He took out an erasable marker and drew directly on the screen.

"We are here," he said, pointing to the City. OS1 and OS2 were circled in dotted lines. To her surprise, Jossey could see other small circles. They were marked with letters. M1. K2.

"What are those?" she asked.

Sokol pointed to the image. "Those, my dear, are the other known underground cities in this region."

Her face seemed to have betrayed her surprise, because Sokol smiled. "This entire region," he said, "is pitted with underground cities, pardon the pun. The Council hopes to...make use of them as we expand our agricultural capabilities."

He stood before the image and wrote a series of numbers on the wipeable screen. They meant nothing to her.

Her uncle turned to her.

"Jossey," he said. He glanced at Caspar, then back at her. "There are a few things I have not shared with you about our agricultural system."

Jossey sat up, keeping her face carefully neutral.

"Yes, sir?" she asked.

Sokol smiled. "First, I would like to congratulate you on your discovery of the Karapartei-run farm out beyond the OS1. You don't know what a relief it was to me to uncover their operation. We have long wondered where Karapartei was getting their resources. We suspected it was inside the City, but now – " He waved his hand dismissively. "I have...taken care of the problem."

Jossey watched him carefully.

"My dear, this is a complicated matter." He strode to his desk and leaned against the edge, hands clasping the marker. "It may take some time to explain. Mr. Savaş has been fully informed, and can answer any questions you may have."

"Yes, sir." She had quite a few questions. But she kept her smile neutral.

"First, you should understand a brief history of our agricultural industry. We tried using grow lights underground for some time, but as the population expanded, that became infeasible. So we expanded aboveground as well."

She raised an eyebrow.

"We have workers drawn from...a pool of candidates," he

619

said. "Several farms, located above the various underground cities marked on this map." He gestured to the spots marked K2 and K3, both to the west and northwest of the City. "They are well guarded against the Onlar, not that those creatures would likely make their way across that wasteland anyway. But I digress." He gestured to K3. "Our brave workers remain underground in the ancient cities during the day, and harvest food at night."

She tried to look surprised, brow furrowing. "I didn't know much could grow aboveground anymore."

She glanced at Caspar, then back at her uncle. "Why couldn't you use the grow lights?"

"Insufficient capacity," Sokol said. "That is why we are upgrading our solar electricity infrastructure. That is what I have not told you until now. We need to significantly enhance our calculations to include" – he glanced at Caspar – "an entire new underground level of grow lights. Two farms' worth."

She stared at him. "How many grow stations is that?"

He began to write figures on the screen. Her jaw dropped.

"That's – Minister, that's enough to – "

"Enough grow stations to feed an additional five thousand people." He smiled.

"Uncl – Minister, why haven't you told me all this before now? I don't understand."

He sighed. "I apologize, my dear. We thought it was unnecessarily vulnerability-inducing to inform anyone that there are open-air farms, especially with Karapartei now apparently operating aboveground as well as belowground. Additionally, we are facing a potential population crisis. We need to expand our food-growing capability."

"*Her City is failing,*" she remembered Tark saying.

"I remember you said it was an issue of water?" Jossey frowned.

"Yes, my dear. We cannot use the underground river for

hydropower, hence we must upgrade our solar power system to account for a massive additional electrical load. And we must make it defensible, which you so well incorporated into your original design. Happily, the underground cities each have their own water supply, much as the Old Sector 1 does."

She thought for a moment, eyeing the figures.

"What is the overall capacity target?" she asked.

He cited a number. Her eyes widened. She'd never worked with numbers like that, ever.

She glanced at Caspar.

He smiled at her encouragingly.

"How much capacity does a single grow station use?" she asked. "I don't see that in there."

"It varies," Sokol said. "Don't worry about that part. That's what Mr. Savaş is for." He smiled at Caspar, but the smile did not reach his eyes. "We just need to make sure we reach that overall target."

She shrugged and scribbled down a set of numbers.

She glanced back up at Sokol.

"And the workers?"

"We are hoping to...bring them in," he said.

"No wonder I never see anyone from Agriculture," Jossey muttered. Caspar half-laughed.

"Now," Sokol said. "Are there any questions? I apologize for the rush. We do have the agricultural expo on the table as well, but I would like to see a final set of calculations and plans drawn up before the end of the week."

She stared. "That's not much time, sir."

He looked coolly at her. "As Mr. Savaş has said, you are...inventive. If you must, you may take additional time away from your training."

"Sir – " Caspar sat up. "If Karapartei is an actual threat to the expo, Jossey needs to be prepared. Tskoulis has asked that we bring any of them in unharmed. She isn't trained to – "

Sokol glanced at him. "I have given you an assignment, Savaş. Tskoulis has sufficient agents to handle the expo."

Jossey had stopped scribbling.

Caspar had a point. If she weren't prepared, if she came face-to-face with another one of the terrorists...

She looked at her partner. She might not fully trust him, but she trusted his abilities.

He looked back at her, seeming to be thinking the same thing.

"I can't train you, Jossey," he said. "But I can protect you."

"Why can't you?

He shook his head. "There are some things you...shouldn't know. Besides." He grinned. "Your fellow Patrol might wonder where you suddenly gained your abilities. Might blow my cover."

She groaned. "Fine. Just – "

"My assignment isn't over," he said, expression suddenly deadly serious. He glanced at Sokol. "Isn't that right?"

Sokol smiled. "Correct, Savaş."

She flushed a little. But she went back to scribbling.

Later that evening, Jossey sat alone in the mess, chewing thoughtfully.

She'd kept her expression as neutral as possible when her uncle had talked about the workers. And maybe – just maybe – the other farms' workers really were pulled from Agriculture.

She doubted it.

He'd said there was a crisis of population. That, as she understood, was what was driving the attacks by Karapartei. She grimaced. Her uncle was trying to keep a hold on power by expanding, and wiping out existence of the brutal slavery she'd seen at the same time. How disgusting.

She shook her head, trying not to think about it.

She ran the numbers in her head again. Something seemed off.

Grow lights – there was almost no way they required *that* much power. Not the enormous number that Sokol was asking for. It boggled her mind.

It was almost as if he were asking for an entire other City to be powered. She'd never even considered such a large amount of power generation. Let alone stabilizing such power demand.

"That's what Mr. Savaş is for," her uncle had said.

Fine, she thought.

He'd agreed to tell her what she wanted. Well, this was something she wanted to know. Needed to know. And it was work-related.

She got up and wandered toward the training room.

Sometimes he would be in there after hours. It seemed to relax him.

As she'd guessed, Caspar was training in the dimness.

He seemed to have no idea she was there. Seemed to have even forgotten that the training room door was open, that people could walk by. Not that there were likely to be people around at this hour.

Her mouth fell open as she watched.

She hadn't imagined things back in the tunnels, apparently. Or the Old Sector. The way he moved – the speed, the brutality–

She winced as he slammed his fist into one of the biggest heavy bags, carrying the punch through.

If that were a man, she thought, he'd probably be dead before he hit the ground.

She took a step back, automatically, frightened.

Caspar's head shot up, and he looked in her direction.

He grabbed the bag, stabilizing it. He wiped his forehead and started toward her.

She took a hasty step backward.

He held up a hand, looking startled, and stopped.

She stared at him, wide-eyed.

Caspar looked...she wasn't sure what. Upset. At himself, she thought. He unbandaged his hand and stood there, just looking at her.

"The door was open," she said quietly. "I was trying to find you. I had a question."

"About that – " he gestured to the bag. "I – "

She looked down, away from him. "I knew," she said. "About you. But I didn't really realize – "

He walked carefully past her, and she flinched away from him.

"What was your question?" he asked, not looking at her.

"I just wanted to know how much capacity a grow light station uses," she said woodenly.

"It varies," he said, glancing up, removing the other bandage. "Some are bigger than others, or designed for different types of crops. Why are you asking?"

"How much, Caspar? The biggest kind."

He looked her in the eyes.

His breathing was steady. As if he'd simply been walking. Not beating the stuffing out of a heavy bag that she could barely move.

He said a number.

She did a quick calculation in her head. Even at maximum numbers, the desired load fell well short of what Sokol had cited.

"That doesn't add up," she said very quietly.

"Sokol wants backup capacity," he said.

"For what?"

Caspar looked slightly frustrated. "Security," he said. "Over-planning is standard for these types of projects."

"Fine," she snapped.

"Jossey, what's wrong?"

She shook her head, still looking warily at him.

"Jossey," he said carefully, not looking at her. "Please don't be afraid of me."

"How can I not?" She stared at him.

His silver eyes met hers. She forced herself not to look away.

"Are you afraid of Tskoulis?" he asked her after a moment.

She laughed. "Gavin? No."

"Why not?" He looked frustrated. "You know what he's capable of." He ran a hand through his hair. "What's the difference?"

"You know what the difference is, Caspar. Gavin is – " She smiled a little. "I've known Gavin since we were children."

"Gavin Tskoulis is a killer," Caspar said flatly.

"He's a warrior." She glared at him. "There's a difference. He's doing what he thinks is right. As for being afraid of him – " Her expression softened. "I can't imagine Gavin ever hurting me."

Caspar had a strange look on his face.

"Neither can I," he muttered.

"I liked you better when you were just an Engineer," she said. "I'm sorry."

"What's that supposed to mean?"

"You were – " She looked pleadingly at him. "I knew who you were, or thought I did. I didn't have to wonder about anything. You were just Caspar. You read stupid books and made me laugh. You were brave. Zlotnik told me you stood up to Tskoulis when he told you all to stay behind while he searched for me. And now you're..." She gestured mutely.

"I searched for you," Caspar said suddenly.

She looked at him. "What?"

"I'm not supposed to tell you this. Sokol could – " He looked somber for a second. "This is between us, all right?"

Jossey eyed him.

"I did stand up to Tskoulis," he said, eyes dark. "But your

uncle assigned me to go on the expedition anyway. As a tracker. I was there in that shed when we found you."

Jossey crossed her arms. "Were you. Prove it."

"You were standing with your back against the wall, a knife in your hands. Tskoulis asked if you had a light. You had – " He looked away, pain flashing across his face. "You looked half-dead, Jossey. One of the Onlar – it looked like you'd barely survived an attack. You had claw marks on your armor. You had blood on your face. I – "

His fists were clenched, she noticed.

He paused for a long moment. "I...wanted to kill whoever, or whatever, had done that to you. But I couldn't even tell you I was there. Even Unit 1 didn't know who I was. Because of who I am. Who I *really* am. Sokol's head Patrol agent. Delta."

She stared at him. Delta?

"Now do you believe me?" he asked, eyes searching her face.

She turned away, unable to look at him as her face heated.

There had been another man with Gavin, she recalled, but –

She strained to remember. He'd been tall, about Caspar's height. He'd been looking toward the ground. She couldn't remember much about him. It had been dark.

She looked up at Caspar.

"If you were there," she said, "where exactly did you find me?"

"A shed in the southwest corner of the town," he said immediately. "About two blocks past the cemetery. You left your bike in another garage, near the gas stations to the south."

She looked into his eyes.

"When Sokol introduced me by my real identity and said I'd been assigned to the mission, Tskoulis seemed...less than pleased," he said, smiling a little.

Jossey smiled. "So Gavin – Tskoulis – knows about you," she said. "Your identity."

"Yes. He was the only one. And now you. If you tell anyone–"

"Why are you telling me this?"

Caspar looked straight at her. He didn't speak for a long moment.

"I don't want you to be afraid of me," he finally said. "Not you."

She looked quizzically at him.

He grabbed his equipment bag and tossed it over his shoulder. "It's been a long day," he said. "I need to sleep." He headed for the door.

"Caspar," she said.

He turned around.

"Thank you," she said.

He smiled a little. "Good night, Jossey."

He wandered down the hallway, smiling hugely, even saying good night to one of the random flunkies who happened past.

Part of him wondered what he was doing. He'd never voluntarily given up his identity. Ever.

But the other part of him ignored the misgivings. He needed her to trust him, on a number of fronts. Sokol could deal with any fallout. She was part of the team anyway, now, and they'd seen enough to trust her, and Caspar had legitimate reasons.

If one of those reasons was personal, it didn't make the others any less justified, he told himself.

118

Jossey was exhausted. She'd stayed up late doing the calculations for the presentation she was supposed to give to Sokol.

But she had to be on top of her game. Henry had told them to be ready to deploy at eleven sharp for the agricultural expo.

She stumbled into the mess hall.

Zlotnik and Thompson were sitting there, looking half-alive, sipping coffee. Wickford too. He brightened and waved at her, smiling.

She smiled back.

"Good morning, sleepyhead." Zlotnik grinned at her. "You look half-dead."

"Thanks," Jossey grumbled. She glanced at Thompson. "Good morning," she said.

He shoved the pot of coffee toward her. "Drink," he said.

"Thanks." She poured a cup.

"Ready for today?" He pushed the sugar toward her.

She tried to smile. "I guess."

She wasn't. Not at all. Henry had said they were to use their swords, and she still didn't feel particularly confident with that weapon. It was too long, too unwieldy. She still hadn't managed to disarm Zlotnik either, other than that one time.

She'd been too busy working on the project. Her brain was half-melted, it felt like, and she didn't even know how she was going to finish it in time.

But to the expo they had to go.

She drank a second cup of coffee.

"Whoa there, Sokol." Zlotnik pulled back the coffee container. "Slow down."

Jossey groaned. "I'm barely awake as it is."

"Yeah, well, this is for your own good."

She snorted and reached for the coffee. Zlotnik pulled it further away.

"Thompson would probably let me," Jossey said sourly.

Thompson looked slightly guilty. Zlotnik laughed.

Caspar and Ellis sat down beside them. "Good morning, team!" Ellis looked quite awake.

Jossey gave him a sidelong glare. "What's with you?"

He grinned. "I'm in the mood for a fight."

She smiled. "That makes one of us."

"Can I have your eggs – "

"No."

Caspar and Zlotnik cracked up. Ellis wilted. "It was worth a shot," he muttered.

The metal screen clanked upward, and they sprinted to the food line. Ellis grumbled and stalked after them.

They ate quickly and headed for the training room.

Henry stood there in full uniform. Pricey was there as well.

Tskoulis was nowhere to be seen.

The other units had already been briefed. They had been assigned various duties, Henry explained. 2-5 was to be on reserve guard, walking through the crowd, looking for any suspicious behavior. 2-3, the group of gentle giants, was to perform what Henry jokingly called intimidation duty up at the front near the stage. 2-4 and 2-2 were to man the perimeter of the City Square.

"Any questions?"

Jossey's hand shot up.

"Yes, Sokol."

"Can I use a knife instead?" she asked.

She didn't look at Zlotnik, embarrassed.

"You may carry it with you, yes. Do as you see fit. But Sokol. Don't forget who you may be facing."

"Yes, sir."

"And remember," he said loudly to the group. "The idea is to *disarm*, with minimal injury." He glanced at Jossey. "Is everyone prepared?"

She swallowed and said nothing.

They fanned out into the crowd. People parted in front of them, varying degrees of fear on their faces. Some of the older City residents looked completely unaffected by their presence. One old man gave them a thumbs-up and pointed to his veteran badge.

Jossey smiled at him, thinking how ridiculous she must look with a sword strapped to her waist.

She stood silently, watching the crowd. The expo was similar to the career fair the City held once a year. She remembered fighting with Tark for a seat on one of the Patrol bikes. A Patrol agent had let her ride around the Square, clinging on, a child's helmet jammed on her head.

That had been the day Gavin had ruined her ice cream.

She smiled fondly at the memory.

She still didn't see him. Maybe he'd been assigned to some other duty.

She turned to see Caspar standing near her, outwardly relaxed. But his eyes were alert.

A family wandered by, holding toys and sample bags. There were all sorts of interesting things – plant clippings that you could grow in a jar of water in your living quarters, tiny model farming implements, a textbook for sale on how to grow plants in an underground environment. Fresh tomatoes. A little boy meandered past, a bright-red one in his hand, chattering with his friends.

She flinched, remembering another small face.

"Over there," Caspar said quietly, appearing at her side. She jumped.

He was looking toward the corner of the cavern. Jossey squinted. Everything seemed fine. Just some workers unloading boxes of tomatoes from a pallet.

"What?" she asked.

"Look how they're handling the boxes."

The boxes were slightly off-balance. As if they were leaning a bit to the side.

"Those men are armed," he said under his breath.

"How do you – "

He gave her a look. She shut her mouth.

Of course he could tell. She glanced over at Zlotnik, who was on the other side of one of the tomato stalls. "Should we say something?"

Caspar lifted his wrist, activated his com. "Henry. Come in, Henry."

Henry's voice. "Henry here."

"Suspicious activity, quadrant 1, by the boxes."

"I see them." Henry started heading that way. "Pricey. With me."

He and Pricey started through the crowd, slowly. He gestured to Ellis, who moved sideways, then headed in the direction of the boxes.

Caspar looked at Jossey. "Stay here," he said.

"What? No."

"Don't – " He turned to her. "Just trust me. Stay here. You want me to protect you. I'm trying to do that. If anything happens, I want you to run, all right? Run. Don't fight. You're not prepared."

"You know I can't run away. And you want Henry to yell at me for hanging back while you go investigate?"

He sighed. "You're not hanging back. You're keeping watch with Zlotnik. Completely valid."

She glared at him. "Fine."

He gave her a look, then melted into the crowd.

She scooted closer to Zlotnik, who looked at her in surprise. She gestured across the crowd to Henry and Pricey. "Armed men," she whispered.

All around her, noises suddenly seemed louder. She heard children screaming with laughter, the yelling of booth vendors, even the clanging of that stupid game with the mallet that someone had seen fit to bring down into the City with them centuries ago.

She lost sight of Caspar.

There was a flash, and she jumped.

Zlotnik jumped too.

Just one of those expo games, Jossey realized. It was just an expo game.

She sighed, feeling shaky. Last time they'd –

She couldn't think about last time.

She looked for Henry. He had reached the men. They seemed to be arguing with him.

"False alarm," his annoyed voice said over the radio. "They're guards with the Agricultural Minister. Our own people. Agriculture forgot to warn us."

Jossey sighed in relief. She turned to Zlotnik, who smiled.

"I could do with some cotton candy right now," Zlotnik said.

"Yeah," Jossey said. She glanced around. Something seemed off.

The hair stood up on the back of her neck.

She turned around. There was no one there, just more crowds. A woman jumped, staring at her, and she smiled in apology.

More screaming children. She tried to calm her nerves.

Bright outfits sailed past. A man wandered past, wearing a hideous shade of neon yellow. More of a brilliant green.

He stood there, waved to them, looking at them a little too long. Jossey half-smiled at him, thinking maybe he was just a bit off. Some people were overly fascinated by Patrol.

He gave them a big thumbs-up.

Jossey glanced at Zlotnik, not sure what to do. They didn't have time to deal with odd civilians.

She started to return the thumbs-up, feeling silly.

There was a deafening bang, and all the lights went out.

Pitch blackness in the cavern. The crowds around her started screaming. Jossey felt as if she were back in the tunnels again, trapped in the shuttle, with three dozen people shrieking and no air and complete blackness. Only this time there were hundreds of voices.

Maybe thousands. She didn't know.

The man in yellow – it might have been a signal, she thought, trying to force her brain to focus.

She automatically reached around her neck for her light, forgetting she was Patrol now. She grabbed for Zlotnik's arm, grabbed for her own sword, hyperventilating.

Dozens of safety lights flared around her.

The entire City Square was soon a sea of bobbing red lights, streaming toward the exits. She shouted at people, trying to impose some kind of order.

Suddenly the lights flared back on.

The Agricultural Minister, looking shaken, stepped onto the

stage and shouted into the microphone, "Remain calm! Remain calm, Citizens! We apologize deeply for the inconvenience – "

The Citizens did not remain calm.

They stopped running, but she could see the terror in their eyes. Power outages were not common. When they did happen, it almost always meant that someone had pulled the switch, no matter what the Minister of Agriculture might tell the public.

Jossey was an Engineer. She knew exactly how the system functioned.

And she knew that no one would generally pull the switch unless –

She turned around.

And then the shrieking began again.

There were at least twenty of them, all dressed in black, faces half-covered, all carrying swords.

People started stampeding toward the exits.

Zlotnik shouted at the nearest Karapartei. Her scarred face was red with fury. He grinned and drew his sword.

They both faded from Jossey's mind as once again, a man wearing all black came toward her. But this time, he had a sword with him.

And this time, Caspar was nowhere nearby, she thought.

"Disarm them," Henry had said.

She shook her head. She wasn't prepared. Not for this.

Caspar was on the other side of the cavern, she thought. She could run. And probably be thrown off Patrol. But she might live.

Thinking cost her precious seconds. The man was steps away. And he looked like he could outrun her anyway.

She drew her sword, trembling. If she could keep him at arm's length –

The man smiled cruelly.

Then he sliced downward with the blade in a chopping motion.

It was like a boulder crashing into her as she held her blade up with all her strength, feeling like the bones in her hands were going to shatter. She gasped in pain, tears coming to her eyes.

He grinned under his mask and raised the sword again. His teeth were stained. "Wanna play?" he taunted.

She felt her face go pale with *that* memory.

Her hands began to sweat. The sword slipped in her grip, just enough.

He hit her sword again, hard. He seemed like he wasn't even trying.

Her blade jumped from her grip. She leaped back, terrified, scrambling for her knife.

For the first time, it occurred to her that being resourceful, being fast, might not be enough.

"Zlotnik!" she shouted. But Zlotnik was in her own fight.

Jossey was on her own.

She backed up. The man moved toward her, lazily, seeming to enjoy this. He threw aside his own sword and drew his knife, tossing it from hand to hand, as if toying with her.

If she ran, he might hit her in the back. If she didn't run –

Suddenly the man's face went white. He was looking past her.

She turned.

Caspar was there.

He didn't bother to draw a weapon.

In two strides, he sidestepped the man faster than Jossey could follow, striking him hard in the side. The man crumpled. Caspar wrenched the knife from the terrorist's hand, flipped the man's arm backward at the elbow, and forced him to his knees, holding the man's own knife to his throat.

The whole thing had taken seconds.

The man stared up at him, gasping, dark eyes terrified. Jossey stared, incredulous.

Caspar leaned down, hissed something in the man's ear, yanked his elbow up higher, hard. All Jossey caught was "terrorist scum."

The man was deathly pale, eyes darting between Jossey and Caspar.

Caspar hauled him to his feet, then looked at Jossey, silver eyes still furious. "I told you to run!" he shouted at her.

She gaped at him. "I – I – "

"I told you to run. Not fight. Jossey, you have to listen to me. I can't *protect* you if you don't." He glared down at the man, wrenching the man's arm further backward as he said the word "protect." The man howled, going even paler.

"Caspar, no, Henry said – "

"I know what Henry said." Caspar glanced down at the man.

"I couldn't run," she protested. "He was too close."

Caspar sighed. "I should have stayed here. I should have just trained you. You're sure you're – "

"Please, you're hurting him."

He loosened his grip on the man's arm, pressing the knife to his back. "Don't even think about it," he hissed to the man.

The man barely shook his head.

Zlotnik's man appeared to have fled. She joined them, gasping for breath.

"He – I couldn't disarm him, so I wounded him instead," she said. "Sorry." She glanced at their prisoner, looking impressed. "How did you – "

Jossey shook her head. "Wasn't me."

Caspar looked grim. "Looks like the others have fled."

He glanced over toward where Henry and Pricey were making their slow way back through the crowd.

"Rope," he said to Zlotnik. She was pulling some out of her

equipment pack. She tossed it to him. He tied the man's hands tightly behind him.

"Impressive," Henry said as he reached them. He grinned widely. "This is the first time we've actually managed to catch one of them." He spat at the man's feet.

The expo was in shambles. 2-3 and 2-4 went around with the cleaning staff, fixing stands where people had trampled through them, waving injured civilians toward the hospital.

Henry rubbed his forehead. "Good work, everyone." He shot the Karapartei a look. "Whatever you people want, is it really worth this?"

The Karapartei looked back at him, stone-faced.

They frogmarched him down into the Patrol headquarters.

Tskoulis was there, talking to some of his men.

He took one look at the incoming party and his face darkened.

The terrorist stood straight as Tskoulis walked up to him.

Caspar and Tskoulis shared a look. Jossey remembered suddenly that Tskoulis knew about Caspar.

"Come with me," was all Tskoulis said.

Caspar had an iron grip on the man's wrists. He shoved him after Tskoulis.

Zlotnik was watching them go. "What's gotten into Savaş?" she asked.

Henry just shook his head. "I have no idea."

Caspar and Tskoulis took the man into an office. They pushed him into a chair.

Caspar turned to Tskoulis. "Listen to me carefully," he said. "I understand that this is something near and dear to you. But–"

Tskoulis rounded on him. "No," he said. "You can't interrogate him yourself. I've worked too hard to capture one of them. You have to at least let me observe. I don't care if – "

"Watch what you say." Caspar shot him a look.

Tskoulis clamped his mouth shut. "I have to observe," he said stubbornly.

"Fine. You may not like what you see."

Tskoulis' jaw twitched. "At this point, very little surprises me," was all he said.

119

"I THOUGHT YOU SAID YOU HAD TAKEN CARE OF THE KARAPARTEI farm," Tskoulis said quietly to Sokol. They were observing the interrogation on a screen.

"We did," Sokol said.

"Then what farm is this man talking about?"

Sokol frowned, turned up the volume. The man was indeed talking about a farm.

"We were recruited," the man said quietly. "By – I don't know who. A...a large man. Older, I think. He would always meet with us in the dark. He told us his name was Jones, but I never believed that. Please," he said, looking up at Caspar. "I have a family."

Caspar glanced at the camera. "Recruited how?" he snapped.

"The man said – said something about us splitting off, making a more just government."

"Were you hiding in the City? How long? How did you get here from the farm?"

He showed the man what appeared to be a photograph.

"What's that?" Tskoulis asked.

Sokol was staring at the Karapartei. "The farm."

Tskoulis turned to him. "When you said you took care of it," he said carefully, "what exactly did you mean? Were there women and – "

Sokol didn't answer.

Whatever the man was looking at, all resistance seemed to suddenly go out of him. He sank back into his chair.

Caspar stood over him. "Where did the others come from?" he demanded.

"Do what you want to me," the man said quietly.

"That's not an answer." Caspar stepped closer, grabbed the man's chin, forced the man's face up toward him. "Tell me."

The man smiled a little and shook his head.

Caspar glanced up at the camera, then switched it off.

When he emerged at last, even Tskoulis winced at his appearance.

"He's useless," Caspar spat. "Nothing."

Sokol looked coolly at him. "Get rid of him."

"Yes, sir." Caspar glanced at Tskoulis. "I told you you might not want to see this."

Tskoulis looked coldly at him.

Caspar looked back at Sokol. "Permission to dispose of the prisoner."

"Granted, Savaş. Make it clean."

"Sir." Caspar disappeared.

Tskoulis felt slightly ill.

"Permission to go, sir," he said.

"Granted."

He left.

. . .

He ran into Jossey in the mess. She looked cleaned up from her ordeal and was eating. She looked famished.

He looked away from the food.

"Sokol," he said. "I need to talk to you."

"Yes, sir." She stood up.

"Not here."

She looked confused. "Yes, sir."

She followed him out into the hallway. He led her further down the corridor.

There was an office. He motioned her inside. He left the door slightly open and listened for footsteps.

"Jossey," he said. "I heard what happened today."

She looked away. "I should have run. Caspar was right. I wasn't prepared."

"Yes. About that." His voice was deadly serious.

She looked up at him.

"I want you to – stay away from Savaş."

"What?" She laughed. "Caspar? You – do realize I work with him, right?"

He looked earnestly at her. He couldn't tell her what he'd just seen. Couldn't reveal Caspar's identity.

"I – he's...he may seem like a fun Engineering partner, but – " He faltered. She was giving him a quizzical look. "He's...he's dangerous, Jossey. I don't want you to get too close to him, do you understand?"

She frowned. "Of course he's dangerous. You trained him to be dangerous. So am I."

"Not like that. I mean he's really – " He struggled with the words. "Just – be careful, all right?"

"Tskoulis," she said. "What happened?"

He shook his head.

"He was protecting me," she said. "Whatever he did to that man, he was protecting me."

He looked at her, startled. "Protecting you? How do you know that?"

"He told me." She looked confused.

Gavin sighed. "Just – I don't trust him, okay, Jossey? I can't order you not to spend time with him, but just – please consider it, all right?"

She smiled a little, not a happy smile. Then she looked straight at him. "You're so overprotective, you know that? I'm an adult, Gavin. Please treat me like one."

He stared at her as she got up. "Permission to leave, sir."

"Granted," he mumbled, watching her as she went.

When she was out of sight, he slammed his fist down onto the desk.

Elsewhere, Sokol was also slamming his fist down on his desk.

Caspar stood, calmly watching him.

Sokol turned blazing eyes on him. "Useless, you said. After all that, we finally catch one of them, and – "

"I did as ordered, sir. I'm sorry. There was nothing useful. He didn't talk. All he mentioned was – "

"That 'older man' from the farms," Sokol gritted out. "I know. There's no one over the age of forty out there. So who could he – "

Savaş stood looking at a point on the wall. "Sir, if I may make a suggestion – "

"Suggest away, Savaş. I'm listening." Sokol's eyes were frightening.

"Sir, as I said earlier, are you certain that the Onlar – "

Sokol laughed. "I'm a keen student of people, Savaş. I told you, it is in no way in Kudret's interest to – "

"Yes, sir, but hear me out."

Sokol sat behind the desk and stared daggers at his agent.

"Go on," he said slowly.

"Sir, if Kudret is really seeking power, why would he try to ally himself directly with you? There's a clear imbalance there. Much easier to try to destabilize you."

Sokol frowned. "But that doesn't make sense, Savaş. He would need to convince his people to accept help from Patrol, which these Karapartei quite obviously are."

"Yes," Caspar said. "But you have, I assume, heard the phrase 'the enemy of my enemy is my friend.' These are no ordinary Patrol the City is fighting. It would make sense that they would accept any help in order to take down the City." He looked at Sokol. "They say they want justice and peace. You know very well what the Council is really doing out in those farms. Maybe if Kudret had managed to reach out to the Karapartei, realized they had a similar agenda..."

Sokol looked closely at him. "I regret that I did not listen to you before, Savaş. Please accept my apology."

Caspar half-smiled. "I understand, sir. Apologies are unnecessary."

"I think maybe we should contact Kudret." Sokol picked up a decorative letter opener on his desk. He ran his finger along the blade. "As soon as possible. See to it, Savaş."

Caspar saluted.

Delta handed a message to the Onlar. The Onlar disappeared into the tunnel.

A meeting scheduled at Avanos, five days hence. Caspar didn't understand the need for the delay, but whatever Kudret preferred. He was in no hurry. Sokol was the one foaming at the mouth.

He was quite happy to let Sokol stew, he thought.

As he walked back to his motorcycle, Caspar pulled the ring out of his pocket. He'd taken to carrying it with him everywhere, hoping he'd remember whatever was nagging at the back of his mind.

And right now something was nagging.

He sat on the bike and looked at the ring in his palm.

It wasn't the ring, he thought. It was something he'd written in the letter.

Avanos.

His eyes narrowed.

A memory. Years ago. Five, to be precise.

A group of Onlar, meeting with Caspar's delegation at the river-crossing of Avanos.

A young man, sitting slightly behind Diros Bey, his face half-covered as was common with Onlar royalty, the firelight illuminating his eyes.

Those eyes.

The Bey's son. Or son-in-law, maybe. Caspar hadn't really bothered to learn all their names.

He strained to remember.

At one point, they'd sat down to eat together, as a gesture of goodwill. This had been before everything had gone south again, Caspar thought, grimacing.

The young man had removed his face cover. Caspar had caught a glimpse of his face as he ate, his silver-gold hair. Unusual among the Onlar. Like his eyes.

Caspar's head shot up.

Tark Sokol was alive, he thought.

The shock nearly knocked him off the bike. He steadied himself.

His mind was racing. The ring had been discovered at the farm.

The mysterious second figure that they'd insisted had been there. The one he'd laughed off.

The precision of the wound on the guard. The other, killed by his own sword.

Killed in a way Jossey'd never been taught.

And that meant –

If Tark was alive...if Jossey had been kidnapped by his men, had been helped by him...then Jossey had lied to them.

Caspar stared down at the ring.

"Jossey," he whispered, "what have you done?"

120

JOSSEY SAT AT HER DESK, LOOKING OVER THE FOLDER'S CONTENTS again. She'd been working for three days on the presentation, had barely slept, even after the exhausting agricultural expo and the fight for her life.

She'd also avoided Gavin. He had seemed hurt, but she didn't know what else he had expected.

She'd been very distracted, and maybe she'd missed something, but she couldn't figure out what Gavin was suddenly *so* upset about. After everything Caspar had done for her. Gavin even *knew* that Caspar had searched for her. Had spent six days, mostly underground from what she'd gathered, fighting Onlar and doing whatever else to come find her. Had apparently practically fought with Gavin in front of the entire unit before being assigned by Sokol to go along on the mission.

Yes, Caspar hadn't been entirely honest with her, but he'd been constrained by her uncle.

She didn't know what to think. Didn't know whether Gavin was right and she should be wary of Caspar, or whether Caspar had finally fully opened up to her. She was inclined to believe the latter. Caspar had trusted her enough to tell her his real identity, she thought. After that, what could she possibly fear from him?

She wondered if Caspar knew the reality of the farms, or if that were too high above him — a state secret, maybe. He'd seemed unsurprised when Sokol had said that she'd risked her life to expose Karapartei. And she couldn't imagine him being okay with the things she'd seen out there, even if she didn't know him as well as she'd thought she did. She shook her head.

And –

She stopped herself from thinking it. Whoever Zlotnik had been referring to, she couldn't imagine it was either of them. Especially not Gavin, who had much of the City practically in love with him. Not the way she looked with her scar.

She flushed, feeling ashamed for even wondering. Out of her league was putting it mildly, she thought.

She shook her head. It was easier to just avoid Gavin than deal with whatever new mess was going on. She was sick of defending them to each other, she realized. She had work to do.

They could fight out whatever problem they had directly.

She huffed and turned back to the material in front of her. She didn't want to have to deal with that on top of all the stress she was already having with this...monstrosity her uncle was asking of her.

She didn't care about the presentation. She cared about finding out what her uncle was planning to do with it.

Her uncle had put everything in here, it appeared. She just hadn't realized what she was looking at.

She looked again, surveying the data with mounting horror.

The grow lights? They were real, apparently. These ones, anyway. Sokol was planning to move everything belowground and expand into the nearby underground cities, as he'd told her in their previous "class."

But there was only enough room – enough food – for the

population of the City and estimated twenty-year growth, plus whatever the overflow electricity was for.

Somehow she doubted it was for additional grow lights to feed the slaves.

Speaking of –

She wondered where exactly the City got its slaves, since they had never found Ilara, according to Tark. He said that his people only lived in Ilara around wintertime, when it was cool enough to be outside. The rest of the year they holed up underground, just like the City, moving from spot to spot to stay out of reach. Yet somehow the farm Patrol knew just when and where to strike, carrying off children and young adults.

She shook her head. She had no idea how to figure that out. But this –

It was so...systematic, she thought. Sokol apparently planned to set the grow stations up a piece at a time, moving each farm underground. She assumed he'd move all the existing slaves onto the last remaining farm, harvest the final crop – indeed, there were what appeared to be transport orders in here if she read carefully enough, what else could "fuel cell" as a line item refer to – and then, what, leave the slaves out there in the desert? Return them to their families? Let the Onlar retrieve them?

Sokol had specified that he wanted the new solar panels – the full grid – to be defensible. She'd known that already. But it seemed from these documents that he wanted the solar network to be defensible from underground.

She'd never seen anything like it. It was like he wanted to be able to seal out the entire world if necessary. Like he was hiding away from...something.

She sat and thought. If she managed to get this information to Tark, maybe he'd know what to make of it. Or, at the very least, maybe he'd be able to prepare for what might be coming.

Caspar wandered in with a cup of coffee. He looked very tired.

She sat up and smiled, trying to get Tark and her little nephew's face out of her mind.

"You look...half-alive," she said in greeting. She pushed some of the papers aside to make room for his coffee mug. "Are you okay?"

He groaned. "Didn't sleep very well the last couple of days. I hope you're ready for this presentation."

She grinned. "Not really."

He sipped the coffee and stretched his legs out under the table. "So what's the plan?"

He seemed cheery, if exhausted. She glanced sideways at him. "I can do the talking if you want."

He smiled crookedly. "Thanks."

"That was half an offer. I know nothing about – "

"Yeah, yeah." He snorted. "You do most of the talking. I can handle the bit that requires my actual expertise."

She smiled. "The caffeine seems to be working."

He sat up, looking soberly at her. "Jossey."

"Hmm?"

"About the other day."

She looked down. "I should have run. I'm sorry. Thank you for – protecting me. I'm sorry you had to."

He didn't say anything.

She traced a finger over one of the maps on the table. "I still don't understand why they attacked us," she said. "If my uncle is planning to expand the farms, doesn't that mean more food for everyone? Doesn't Karapartei care about...I don't know, resources or something like that? Shouldn't they be happy with this new setup?"

"Karapartei...they think that we would be better off migrating elsewhere, from what Intelligence has gathered," said Caspar.

Startled, she turned to him. "Migrating? What are you talking about?"

He put a finger to his lips. "Your uncle...dislikes the topic. But you said you wanted to ask me some things. So, between us."

"Okay. Tell me, then."

He pulled the map over to him. "As far as we've been able to tell, Karapartei are part of a group that feels that the farm labor has been...unfairly allocated to those who are less well-off."

She kept her face neutral. It was true, after all.

He continued. "They think that, based on certain economic indicators, and based on increasing Onlar attacks and whatnot, we are better off striking out on our own and heading north, toward the mountains and the sea."

She hadn't even known there was a sea to the north.

"That seems...very far to go on just the idea that conditions *might* be better," she said. "Are you saying we probably can't grow enough food even with the new grow lights?"

"Those are their calculations, yes." He glanced at her. "Is the system truly defensible?"

"From the Onlar? Theoretically." She frowned at him.

"Not just them. From the – "

He suddenly closed his mouth, holding up a warning hand. Sokol was visible coming down the hallway.

"Caspar – " she began.

"Not now," he said.

He was acting strange, she thought. But she smiled as her uncle came into the room.

"My dear," he said. "Mr. Savaş. What do you have for me?"

"Very, very good." Sokol looked thrilled, actually clapping as the presentation ended. "Wonderful. Your people owe you a great deal, my dear niece. And Mr. Savaş, of course." He winked at Caspar.

Caspar smiled. "She did most of the work."

Jossey flushed. "Not really."

"Yes really."

"I'm just trying to help."

"And a fine job you've done." Sokol stood up. "I believe the wiring is proceeding well."

Oh yes. The wiring. She'd forgotten about that. She hoped Tark had been observing out there, somehow.

"My dear," Sokol said, "I hope you will have a finalized version to me the day after tomorrow. I must take a trip, I'm afraid, to survey some security issues near Onlar territory, and need to take Mr. Savaş with me. I would like to have a copy of this in hand."

"I should be able to do that, sir." She glanced at Caspar. "You too?"

"Yes," he said.

Sokol smiled. "Once this is complete," he said offhandedly, "I hope we will have no further concern with the Onlar."

Caspar didn't say anything.

Jossey's smile stiffened.

She took a deep breath and looked between the two of them. "Minister," she said, "if it's all right with you, I'd like to have another look aboveground at the canyons. Last time we were...interrupted. I want to do another security assessment of the switch placement. I'm worried They might know where – "

"Mr. Savaş and I have taken care of that," Sokol said. "Don't worry, my dear."

She felt something cold in her chest. But she smiled. "Thank you. That's wonderful to hear."

"Now. I must take my leave. Mr. Savaş, please accompany me."

Caspar pushed the map back toward her and stood, picking

up his coffee cup. As he left, he gave her a look over his shoulder.

Jossey put the final touches on the report and handed it over to Sokol with a smile. He and Caspar then immediately went to board a shuttle to whatever security mission they were scheduled to go on.

She hadn't had a chance to talk to Caspar again. He'd seemed distant, distracted. And every time she'd wanted to, Sokol had been there.

So she'd handed over the document, hating herself, but having no other choice, and no way to tell Tark what she'd done. No way to warn them what might be coming, short of going aboveground alone and probably being killed.

She felt something cold inside again. Far from sabotaging the project, she'd all but completed it, she thought angrily.

She had to warn Tark somehow, she thought.

She just didn't know how.

121

JOSSEY WAS SO DISTRACTED IN TRAINING THE NEXT DAY THAT Henry finally took her aside.

"Look, Sokol," he said. "I realize that you're working on something important for the Minister. But you have to focus here. Got it?"

She flushed. "I'm sorry," she said. "I'm thinking about too much."

"Take a water break, then come back and try again."

"Yes, sir."

She jogged over to the water, gulping down half a canteen's worth. She watched the water burble into the canteen and smoothly come to rest near the top as she turned off the tap.

Water. If they forced the Onlar out of the underground cities, where would her brother get water? What about her baby nephew? Her sister-in-law? Altan and Yazar and Erkan? All those people?

She pushed away the tears. She needed to go over the data again. And she had to get a message to Tark somehow.

She'd promised to do her best. And right now –

"*Convince Gavin if you can,*" Tark had said.

"Patrol is the real power in that place, after Intelligence," he'd also said.

She smiled a little. He was right.

But convince Gavin?

She didn't even know where to begin.

"Gavin, the Onlar are human, and my brother's alive, and my project has possibly just sentenced them all to death, and I need your help."

She almost snorted. He'd probably look at her like she had three heads.

The ring. She could –

She'd kept it in her equipment bag, where no one would likely dare to look. She'd have to look after training.

"Sokol! Hurry it up. We're waiting."

She quickly screwed on the cap and ran back over, apologizing.

She did her best to focus for the rest of the session.

The others wandered off toward the mess. She heard a mention of ice cream later on. Thompson and Ellis high-fived each other.

"You coming, Sokol?" Ellis asked.

"I have to grab something first," she said. "Don't eat all my food."

Ellis made a face at her. She laughed. "I'm kidding. Sort of."

The second she got out of there, she made a beeline for her room.

She tossed the equipment bag down on her bed and rifled through it.

Socks. Old uniforms that needed to be washed. She wrinkled her nose. Random pieces of a broken wrist gauge she'd been trying to put back together.

No ring.

Unconcerned, she flipped the bag, dug through one pocket at a time.

Still no ring.

She tried to remember the last time she'd seen it. Was she sure she'd put it in here?

Then she remembered. It had been in her pocket, along with a string. She'd been meaning to wear it around her neck. Tark still didn't know she had it. She'd been ashamed to show it to him. She hadn't wanted him to see her as a killer, even in self-defense.

But now it was gone.

She had a faint memory of something hitting the ground when the Patrol agent had yanked her off her bike.

Her head shot up, her face feeling suddenly pale.

If they found it at the farm –

She tried to calm herself. They already knew she had been there. There was little chance it could be traced back to Tark. If any of the farm Patrol found it, even if they turned it in –

Her mind was racing. If they found it, they'd probably just think it was hers, she told herself.

No, she thought, probably they'd turn it in and her uncle would figure out that she'd been in touch with the Onlar and –

Part of her brain told her she was tired, stressed, wasn't thinking clearly, and should sit tight until she had a plan. That she didn't need it to convince Gavin.

The other part of her brain was screaming at her to find that ring, and find it NOW.

She got up and shook the entire contents of the bag out onto the floor, sorting frantically through it, not caring that her disgusting socks were touching her clean uniform or that Zlotnik was probably going to wonder why the room smelled rank.

Nothing. No ring.

She put her head in her hands.

She took deep breaths to calm herself. Maybe Gavin knew something. Maybe she *had* had it on her, and they'd just taken it at the hospital, and forgotten to give it back.

She had to find out.

She stumbled out of her room and down the hall, jostling a flunky in the process. She apologized and kept going, jogging toward the main office.

She burst in. Tskoulis was there alone, poring over some maps. He looked up, looking startled.

"What's wrong, Sokol?" he asked.

"Gav- Tskoulis," she gasped. "Where – did the medical crew remove anything from me when I was in the hospital?"

Tskoulis frowned. "Like your armor?"

"No. I – did they find anything on me?"

"What specifically?"

"I – I can't tell you," she said miserably. "Please. If you can get the list – "

He didn't ask further. He went to the computer terminal and typed in a few things.

He scanned the list. "Armor. Uniform. Boots. Onlar knife. Canteen cord." He mentioned a couple of other standard-issue items, then turned to her, frowning. "Nothing unusual. Why?"

She was very still. His expression grew even more concerned.

"Jossey?"

She closed her eyes. "It was something very precious to me," she finally said.

"What was it?" Gavin got up, came over to her, dark eyes searching hers. "Jossey, are you all right? You've been acting – "

"I'm sorry about the last couple of days," she muttered, sinking into a chair. "A lot's been going on. I thought you were being unfair to Caspar, and – "

656

His gaze hardened. She sighed. "Anyway. That's not the issue. The thing I lost, I – I was hoping it could help me."

"Help you with what?"

She looked down at her hands. "I – "

She started to tear up. "Gavin," she said, "I'm in big trouble."

He shut the door. It had a glass window, and he faced her away from it. If anyone walked by, he thought, it would probably look like an ordinary conversation.

Tears were streaming down her face. He had no idea why she was so upset.

"Jossey, tell me what happened."

"Gavin, I need to know something. Right now." She looked directly at him.

He'd never been able to say no to her. But he didn't understand the intensity on her face.

She seemed to be making some kind of terrible decision.

"Gavin," she finally said. "Your promise to Tark. To me. How far are you willing to go to fulfill it?"

Gavin looked at her, and she could see the shock clear as day on his face. "What do you mean?" he finally asked.

"I mean exactly that. If I told you something that could cost me my job, my life – would you turn me in?"

Gavin half-laughed. "Jossey, when would you ever do something that – "

"Gavin. Tell me."

He sobered immediately. "No," he said, dark eyes on hers, full of some strong emotion. "Not if it would cost you your life. Never, God forbid."

Gavin Tskoulis, the ultra-loyal soldier. The City's most-respected commander.

He'd said it without any apparent thought at all.

She smiled and burst into tears.

For a moment she couldn't even breathe, his response had been so unexpected.

"Please, Jossey, what happened?"

"I – I thought you would say it was your job," she admitted. "That you had to. Even if – "

He looked into her eyes, expression earnest. "Please tell me you don't actually believe that."

She wiped at her tears.

"You can have my job," she said. "You can even have my life, if necessary." At his reaction, she held up a hand, wiping away tears with the other. "But please, believe what I have to tell you."

122

A FEW DOZEN MILES AWAY, AT THE RIVER-CROSSING, SOKOL HAD been waiting for an entire extra day in a very uncomfortable cave for the miserable creature known as Kudret to show up.

They were twenty-four hours behind schedule, and Sokol was ready to simply order the Onlar's arrest and interrogation. But...politeness...demanded that he wait just a bit longer. He couldn't imagine what was taking the Onlar so long.

He glanced at Caspar, who seemed strangely quiet, looking out across the twilight landscape.

"Savaş."

Caspar turned to him. His gaze was faraway, but he focused on the Minister. "Yes, sir."

"Any sign of them?"

"No, sir."

"Half an hour more," Sokol sighed. "Then you may proceed."

"Yes, sir."

"Oh, stop it with the titles. Keep your mind *here*, Savaş. I need you at peak form."

Caspar smiled. "Don't worry about me, sir. I'm just thinking."

"About the solar project, I hope."

"Indeed." He went back to surveying the landscape.

They saw lights in the distance, and Caspar stood up, waving the red light he'd attached to a long pole.

There were three Onlar.

The image was strangely poetic, Sokol thought – three figures, carrying lamps, crossing an endless expanse of bluish wasteland. Too bad they'd probably crawled out of some hole somewhere. He sneered.

Caspar greeted them in their language. Sokol did not bother to stand.

Kudret seemed to have been expecting this. He gestured to his men to back off, and seated himself across from Sokol. Caspar stood beside the Minister, a blade visible in his hand.

"How may I assist you, Minister Sokol?"

Kudret's voice always surprised Sokol a little. It was cultivated, smooth. His command of English was rather extraordinary for someone who had spent his entire life living among the Onlar.

Then again, Sokol thought, it only made sense that his head slave-procurer should be an educated man.

He smiled. "Welcome, Kudret. We would offer you something to drink, but sadly all we have is our own water supply, although you are welcome to that. We have, however, brought along some food if you would like to partake. There is, of course...less of it than was available *yesterday*." He looked hard at the big man.

Kudret smiled coolly. "A thousand pardons, Minister. I was...detained. Quite literally."

"Detained?"

"Yes. I believe you are aware of our new...political situation."

"Do tell. I regret that I have had other priorities."

"In the aftermath of Diros Bey's...sad death, his son-in-law was elected Bey, as you know."

"Yes, of course." Sokol smiled thinly. "My associate here has kept me apprised from a distance, as it were, but we have not had the time to sit down and fully discuss this transition with you. My apologies."

"Not at all, Minister." Kudret's expression was oily. "There was not much to tell until recently. The new Bey is not much more than a boy. However." He frowned. "He has taken matters into his own hands of late, refusing to consult with me, to the point that he accused me of attempting a coup these past weeks and had me held against my will for quite some time. I apologize that it was so difficult to reach me, sir. I also apologize for any lack of – "

Sokol waved a hand. "Our farms are running sufficiently. Do go on."

Kudret smiled.

"I was glad to receive your message, Minister. I have much to discuss with you. Shall we?"

They ate a short meal. Caspar did not partake, but sat watching the Onlar. They knew who he was. They kept their hands on their swords.

At length they finished eating.

Kudret smiled. "Well, Minister. I thank you for the food. As I said, I have much to discuss with you."

Sokol examined him with flat eyes. "And I with you, Kudret."

Kudret opened his mouth. Sokol held up a hand. "A moment, Kudret. I apologize for any rudeness, but I have been waiting here rather a long time and must return as soon as feasible. I would prefer to begin."

Kudret smiled unpleasantly. "Please, Minister. After you."

The Onlar guards eyed Caspar. He did not bother to look at them.

Sokol returned the smile. "It has come to my attention that a certain...faction of unhappy members of our City has been recruited by...someone whom they describe as older, a big man, such as" – he gestured – "yourself. You know nearly as well as I do that there is no one over the age of forty at our farms. I do not mean to insult you, of course, my dear Kudret. But it has been suggested to me that the Onlar might find certain...commonalities with Karapartei. Other than your bey, you are the only figure among the Onlar that might conceivably have the means to – "

He stopped. Kudret was staring at him. His men had their hands on their swords.

Then the Onlar started laughing loudly, his voice reverberating off the rocks, filling the blue desert night.

He slapped his knee, crying tears of mirth.

Eventually he stopped. Even Caspar's eyebrows were raised at the display. Wiping away the tears, Kudret looked at Sokol, smiling. "Forgive me, Minister. I – " He started laughing again. "You suspect *me*? Me."

He waved down his two bodyguards, and turned to the Minister.

"I find it very amusing that you would suspect *me* when it is one of your own people who is being used against you."

Sokol's face went very still. He stood up. "What are you saying?" he hissed.

This time Kudret remained sitting. He smiled up at Sokol.

"Oh yes," he said. "I believe that is why I have been kept in captivity all this time. So that I would not betray our *wonderful* Tark Bey's foolish plan to capture one of your people and use them to sabotage whatever plans you have. You know my loyalty, Minister. I have offered you my people as warriors. As slaves, when needed. I have nothing to hide from you."

Caspar kept his face as expressionless as possible.

Sokol was staring at him. "Did you say Tark Bey?"

"Yes, Minister. Tark the Orphan. From your people, I

believe." He spat on the ground. "Captured as a child to 'replace' my bey's son who, ah, was taken by the slavers. Apparently they looked alike. But the first boy was at least respectful."

Sokol's face betrayed nothing. In fact, he seemed to almost be smiling.

"Tark always was a brave child," he said.

"You know him?"

Sokol did not answer the question.

Then his face changed. "And the one who is being used against us?"

Kudret smiled cruelly. "They never told us her name. She was strange-looking. Odd eyes." He held his hand up, dragged a finger across his face.

"A scar," he said. "Like this."

123

GAVIN WAS STARING AT JOSSEY. "ARE YOU – JOSSEY, ARE YOU insane? Are you all right? What are you *saying*? We found Tark. I – I gathered his bones. What on earth do you mean, he's alive?"

She was weeping. "Yes, I'm sane, Gavin. I'm telling you. I found the ring on the Onlar. I broke Protocol. I didn't think much of it because – anyway. Then when they captured me – I already knew they were ordinary humans. They took me – " She glanced at the window, spoke hurriedly. "They took me to their camp, their leader, and when he demanded my name I looked up and I saw his eyes and I – "

Gavin stood up, pacing the room. "How could you not tell me this, Jossey?" he all but shouted. "How could you – "

He, too, glanced at the door. He sat back down, hard, staring at her, dark eyes burning. "Go on," he ordered.

She wilted. "I – at first I thought I would just try to escape, even though he was there. They wanted to use me against the City. Against you, and Patrol, and all the rest. But then – " She wiped at her eyes again. "Gavin, Tark took me to that farm. It wasn't the first time I was there. Gavin, they were using *children* to harvest those plants. Children." She started crying again. "Onlar children."

He stood up again, running a hand through his hair.

"Jossey, *why* didn't you – "

"Because I was afraid my uncle would have me killed," she said flatly. "That's why. The only reason I'm telling you all of this now is because I believe he's planning to kill the Onlar once this solar project is done. And my brother and his family along with them."

She burst into tears again. "You have to help me, Gavin."

He had his head in his hands. "How am I supposed to believe you, Jossey? I want to. I want to help you. But I – I'm a commander. I need proof. I can't just take your word for – "

"Go to Ilara," she said.

He looked oddly at her. "What?"

"Ilara." She ran to his desk, grabbed a piece of paper, scribbled the word on it, turned and thrust it at him.

"Look at the old maps," she said. "The tunnels you found. Follow them to the end. To the southwest, below the ridge line. Please. You have to trust me."

He looked at her, mouth open.

"Don't show that to anyone," she said frantically. "If they find it – "

He mechanically folded the paper and put it in his pocket. He was still staring at her.

"I need proof," he said again.

She sank into the chair. "I don't know what proof I can give you," she said. "Believe me, I've tried. The ring – it's gone. I think I must have dropped it somewhere." She looked pleadingly at him. "Why would I ever lie to you, Gavin?"

He looked away. "Apparently you have for the last several weeks."

"But – "

She thought.

"The Onlar dagger," she said suddenly. "That belonged to Tark."

"That proves nothing," he said flatly.

"The claw marks," she said. "Didn't you wonder how I survived that? Did you really think I was skilled enough to fight off three Onlar in the dark and still make it back to the surface alive?"

He didn't look at her. "Sokol seemed to think so."

"Sokol is not a combat veteran," she snapped. "Do *you* think I'm capable of it?"

He smiled a little. "I wanted to," he said.

"I made Tark put on his claws and swipe as I held the armor up," she said. "He was not happy." She laughed a little. "He's even more overprotective than you. I guess he was worried he was going to miss."

He shook his head. "Jossey, I want to believe you. I do. But if you tell anyone – "

She shook her head. "You still don't believe me, do you? What else can I – "

Then a memory came to her, and she started laughing with joy. *Oh, thank God.*

"Gavin," she said. "You told me it was a dare. Between you and Tark. You thought I knew before."

"Yeah," he said slowly.

"I did know, sort of, but only because Tark told me when I was with them a few weeks ago. You know what you didn't tell me? The exact words you used when you were daring him. He told me, Gavin. He told me you called him a... 'wannabe-Patrol doofus loser.'" She smiled hugely. "Did I get that right?"

Gavin looked dumbstruck for a long moment.

Then he sank slowly to the chair opposite her.

"Tell me everything," he said.

124

SOKOL AND CASPAR HEADED BACK TO THE CITY SHUTTLE IN silence.

Sokol looked like he was chewing on something exceedingly nasty. Caspar was completely expressionless.

Kudret, at least, had looked pleased.

As they got into the shuttle, Sokol turned to Caspar.

"You have your orders, Savaş," the Minister said. He looked away, straightening a wrinkle in his uniform.

Caspar looked straight ahead. His expression did not change.

"Yes, sir," was all he said.

They entered the City. Caspar headed toward Patrol head-quarters.

Sokol headed for his office, in the same direction. "Bring her to me," he said as they parted.

Caspar did not respond.

. . .

Jossey had finished telling Gavin about the bikes, the farm Patrol that had chased her, everything up until the point where they'd brought her back to the City.

She'd explained everything – the rabbit blood, the way she'd rewired the radio, her plan to contact him.

At this point, she had dried her tears. She was even laughing a little. She told Gavin how Tark, out of desperation, had hinted that she was Altan's wife.

He looked less than amused, but cracked a smile as she said how the others had teased Altan.

"I think he hated me for a while," she said, snorting.

She told him about Katha. About Aysun. Tark's little boy. How Tark had seemed annoyed when she said Gavin was even taller than him. Gavin smiled at that.

And Kudret.

"I'm worried he might do something," she said. "He seems to really hate Tark. My guess is he was thinking he would be their leader when Tark's father-in-law died. They said they were planning to eventually tell their people why I had gone back, but–"

She stopped talking. She thought she heard footsteps in the hallway.

They were silent for a moment, frozen. But the footsteps continued on.

She turned to Gavin and quickly explained the final details about the solar project, what she and Tark thought it could mean for the Onlar. Under her breath, she said, "I have all the documentation in my quarters. I made an extra copy. Behind the panel in my wall, next to my pillow. Don't ask. I found a way to unscrew it. If anything happens to me, Gavin – "

He laughed sharply. "If they really think they can do anything to you – "

She looked away. "Thank you. But – "

Footsteps in the hallway again.

"Let's talk about something else," Gavin said. "You've been in here a while. If anyone suspects – "

She glanced at the door. The footsteps sounded like they were getting closer.

Gavin's expression seemed tense. He kept glancing at the door as well.

"You're right," Jossey said. "I know I've been sort of delinquent lately with my...project. Catch me up on the training I need to go over."

"Right," he said. "Henry has been trying to focus more on hand-to-hand disarmament. If we catch any more Karapartei – "

She heard the door behind her slide open.

Gavin glanced up. His eyes darkened.

"Savaş," he said coldly. "What can I do for you."

Caspar's voice sounded unfamiliar. Tense.

"Tskoulis." He didn't even bother with the "sir."

Jossey forced herself to turn around, hoping her smile appeared natural. His answering smile was warm, any tension gone. She wondered if she had imagined it.

"There you are," he said. "I've been looking for you."

Tskoulis was not relaxed, but Jossey couldn't tell if it was their conversation or something else.

"Sorry to interrupt. I need to borrow Jossey for a bit," Caspar said. "Sokol has some additional material he wants to go over with us before we formally launch things for the project."

He glanced at her. "Don't worry." He grinned. "I get to do the homework this time."

She looked at Gavin. Caspar seemed...normal. She looked back at him.

In fact – she frowned a little.

Caspar's expression – there was something faintly wistful

about it as he looked at her. She'd never seen that look on his face before. "Want me to wait outside?" he asked.

"Okay," she said.

He stepped outside and closed the door. She looked at Tskoulis.

He shook his head. "Go ahead," he said. "Let's go over catch-up later."

"Thanks," she said.

She got up to go.

"Jossey," he said.

There was something in his eyes as he looked at her. Something veiled.

"Be careful," he finally said.

She smiled at him and walked out the door.

They headed slowly down the corridor. Caspar didn't seem to be in much of a hurry.

"What else do we have to go over?" she asked.

He shrugged. "Probably some formalities. He didn't really tell me."

They were heading in the direction of Sokol's office, she noticed. The Ministry.

"Not the conference room?"

Caspar didn't look at her. "He's in a bad mood," he said. "His meeting didn't really go as planned."

"Oh." She lapsed into silence. "Well, hopefully this'll be short."

He didn't respond.

"You okay?" she asked.

"Huh? Yeah. I'm fine." He smiled a little. "Just thinking. Sorry."

"It's okay."

"What were you talking about with Tskoulis?" he asked suddenly.

She turned too quickly. "What? Oh. He was talking about some of the things I've missed in training. This whole solar project has taken a lot out of me."

"I should probably do that too," he said thoughtfully.

They had crossed through the various security points and arrived at Sokol's office. Caspar held up his hand as if to type in the code.

As he did, he hesitated, looked at her again with that same wistful smile.

She looked quizzically at him. "What?" she said.

He shook his head. "Nothing." He looked away, something flashing across his face.

Then he keyed in the code.

125

She stepped into Sokol's office.

Immediately she realized Sokol wasn't alone.

Two enormous guards flanked his desk. They stood silently, glowering at her. She swallowed.

"Uncle Sokol?" she asked.

Sokol was seated behind his desk.

"My dear, do come in," he said.

She glanced at Caspar, who wasn't looking at her.

She walked forward timidly, unsure what was going on. Had they found out about the ring? Had they –

"Please, have a seat." He gestured to the chair in front of his desk. She sat carefully, looking around her, looking at the guards.

"What's going on?" she asked.

"A formality."

"A – "

She went silent as one of the guards unfolded his arms. He reminded her of the Patrol agent in the garage. Similar eyes. Similar build. She shrank away from him.

Caspar was standing near the door. He avoided her gaze as she looked at him pleadingly.

"Look at me, my dear."

She looked up, into her uncle's flat eyes.

"We have reason to believe that there may be a...traitor among us."

"A traitor?" Her heart began to pound, but she kept her face as neutral as possible. "What are you talking about?"

"I assume by now that you are aware that the Onlar are not mute creatures, monsters of the aboveground world."

She shook her head. "What?"

Sokol snarled. "Don't play silly with me, my girl. One of my...Intelligence assets informed me that you were seen in the company of the Onlar. Were recruited by them."

She shook her head frantically this time. "Uncle Sokol, Minister, what are you talking about? The Onlar – the ones who captured me, they did not – I killed them, Uncle. I escaped. I told you."

"Did you." He smiled coldly. "My asset seems to think otherwise."

"Who is this asset?" she demanded, shrinking back as one of the guards took a step toward her.

He waved back the man. "At ease," he said. He turned to Jossey. "I believe you are familiar with one Kudret."

Her eyes opened wide. She tried in vain to keep the expression of shock off her face.

He sat back, smiling. "As I thought."

Jossey shook her head again, terrified. "Uncle Sokol, I can explain." She started babbling. "I was afraid. They told me they wanted to use me against the City. They told me they'd kill me if I didn't cooperate. They said – "

"Yes, you'd better explain. I would particularly like to know why my *dear nephew* Tark Sokol has been living among them all this time, has been *leading* them."

She gaped at him in silence.

He waved to his man, who jerked her to her feet. She cried out as he wrenched her arm backward and forced her toward the door.

"That's enough." Caspar's voice had an undercurrent of something dark.

The man glanced at him and removed his hand from Jossey's arm. She gripped her wrist, wincing in pain, tears coming to her eyes. He'd twisted it badly.

Sokol glanced up at Caspar. "Mr. Savaş here has been tasked with...questioning you. I do not particularly like or trust Kudret. And possibly you do indeed have a reasonable explanation for...such a large omission, especially while tasked with such a deeply sensitive project for the City, my *dear* niece. I suggest you cooperate with him."

She looked pleadingly at Caspar. He was looking straight at Sokol.

"Let's go," he said, not looking at her.

She flinched away from the big guard and walked out.

Gavin, she thought. Maybe she could warn Gavin –

"Tell Tskoulis that training is to go on as usual with or without Jossey," she heard Sokol say behind them. "He is to know nothing for the moment."

"Yes, sir."

They walked along the corridor, the two enormous guards behind her, Caspar ahead of her.

"Where are we going?" she asked quietly.

"I have to ask you a few questions," he said. "Don't worry, I hope this won't take long."

He took out a key and opened a side door. A staircase led down, into the dark.

He walked ahead of her.

The staircase seemed to descend forever. She could hear her footsteps ringing on the metal steps.

674

The guards were silent. They hadn't tried to touch her again.

"This should be just routine questioning. Sokol is – mistaken, I believe." He glanced at the guards, as if sizing them up.

Her heart was beating rapidly, but she tried to keep her breathing calm.

Maybe he'd try to rescue her, she thought. She'd seen him take on bigger opponents. Maybe he was trying to –

They reached the bottom of the stairs, and he took out another key. She'd never seen physical keys for these types of doors, and stared in fascination, even as her heart pounded and she felt faint. Her mind seemed fixated on detail.

She looked into Caspar's eyes, looking for some kind of sign that he believed her, was planning to help her.

She realized he was looking back at her, silver eyes filled with something she couldn't identify. Warmth. Something more. And – sadness?

She blinked.

"I'm sorry I have to do this, Jossey," he said quietly.

He glanced at the guards again. She followed his gaze, opening her mouth to tell him it was okay.

Then he stabbed her.

126

THE BLADE FELT WHITE-HOT, PAIN LIKE JOSSEY HAD NEVER FELT before lancing through her.

All she could see were Caspar's silver eyes looking into hers. She crumpled.

"Take care of the body," was all she heard. "Do it right, unless you want to be next."

As her vision faded, she saw him wipe the blade on his uniform. He stepped over her and walked away.

127

GAVIN PACED BACK AND FORTH. SOMETHING SEEMED WRONG. Savaş had seemed fine, but he had an idea just how good of an actor the man was.

And that look he'd given Jossey. Gavin wasn't the best at reading expressions, but that had been –

You didn't look at someone like that unless –

He shook his head, not wanting to think about it.

Jossey hadn't seemed concerned when she'd left, even given everything she'd told Gavin.

Her quarters. She'd said she had something there.

Behind a panel. One she'd unscrewed. He shook his head, grinning crookedly.

Maybe they'd gone to the conference room. He could walk by on his way there, check quickly through the window.

Just in case, he rifled through his desk drawer, grabbed the master key ring.

Just in case.

He walked out the door, striding purposefully toward the conference room.

On the way, Pricey passed him. "Sir," he said. "We're having an impromptu ice-cream night in the mess. Celebrating capturing the Karapartei. Want to join?"

Tskoulis shook his head. A celebration over someone who was now dead at Savaş's hands, he thought darkly. He was fine skipping that.

But he was glad. That meant Zlotnik and the other woman probably wouldn't be in their room.

"Pricey," he said, "I need you to do me a favor."

"Yes, sir."

"It's a personal favor. Not just an order. One that needs to stay between us."

Pricey looked carefully at him. "Understood, sir."

He spoke quietly to the man. Pricey saluted. "I'm not asking, sir."

Tskoulis clapped him on the shoulder. "Thank you, Pricey."

Pricey grinned crookedly. "What are friends for?"

Tskoulis shot him a grin and kept going.

As he approached the conference room, he noticed the lack of a guard. They always had a guard.

He peeked in the window.

It was empty.

Tskoulis turned on his heel and headed directly for Jossey's quarters.

He let himself in after knocking briefly. As he'd hoped, the room was empty. Dark.

He went quickly to what he guessed was Jossey's bed, based on the equipment bag upended next to it, items strewn everywhere. She'd been hunting for the ring, he remembered.

He located the panel and used a key to unthread the screws. It came off easily, and he carefully set it on the ground.

Among the pipes, he saw a folder.

This looked bad, he thought. If anyone else discovered this hiding place –

He pulled out the folder.

GAVIN, it said at the top. He half-smiled. Not Tskoulis. Just his first name.

He thought he heard footsteps, and quickly replaced the panel, screwing it back into the wall.

He smiled a little at what he was doing. Gavin Tskoulis, Patrol enforcer.

As commander, his job was to protect the City. But his *life* – Gavin Tskoulis the man tried his best to do what was right.

And if she was telling the truth, he'd been helping the City do something terrible for a very long time. Something he could barely imagine without seeing it for himself.

He stuffed the folder inside his uniform top and carefully locked the door again from the outside, making sure he'd left no trace in or near the room.

He went back to his office and shut the door, drawing down the curtain.

He flipped through her explanation, then looked carefully through the materials she'd gathered. She'd hand-copied many of them, but it looked as if she'd at some point sneaked into the office and made photocopies. He smiled at her daring.

She'd already gone over much of it with him, but as he looked over the papers his eyes widened with horror. It really was all there, as she'd said.

And nearly every page bore the signature of Minister Pyotr Sokol, her uncle.

He knew that the City had been somewhat ramshackle from its inception – founded by ultra-billionaires who wanted their families, their way of living, to survive the heat that human recklessness had helped to overwhelm much of the world.

They'd done their best, imposing a stringent order on society, imposing Protocols for each branch – Patrol, Agriculture, and whatnot. It had worked for several centuries. They'd had conflict with the Onlar, two half-armies thrown together in combat by necessity, very few people actually knowing how to fight, both sides becoming expert at war by fighting for so long, but he'd never imagined anything like *this*.

No wonder the Onlar hated them.

It was bad enough that they'd been forced out to survive on their own. Being shut out of the cool underground environment, with its abundance of resources, its hospitals, its schools, must have seemed like a terrible betrayal to the Onlar, he'd thought. Had not been happy when Sokol had explained the extent to him. But they had their own society, their own rules. And people had survived in the desert and other inhospitable landscapes for centuries. Sokol had acted as if they'd chosen to remain "uncivilized," picking fights simply over space and resources, which the City could not afford to give up.

A terrible calculus, but Gavin had understood how they could have adopted it. It was what his teachers had called utilitarian. The greatest happiness for the greatest possible number of people.

People who did not, apparently, include the Onlar.

When Sokol had explained things to him, saying that some difficult decisions were necessary as a leader, he had been glad it was a decision he, Tskoulis, had not had to make.

But this. Sokol, and apparently his predecessors, had been stealing the Onlar's children and killing their men indiscriminately. Like animals. For he didn't know how long. And all to maintain order and keep the City functioning.

He put his head in his hands as he thought. Ilara, she had mentioned. She had said Tark was there.

Part of him still thought she had to be making that up. But this was Jossey. He'd never seen her be dishonest about anything. Until now. And she had absolutely no reason he could think of to make up an entire story about Tark and the Onlar.

The intercom clicked on.

"Commanders, to the training room." It was Sokol's voice.

His head shot up.

He took the folder and quickly refilled it. He looked around his office. If they came to search for any reason, they could not be allowed to find it.

Almost laughing at the ridiculousness of what he was doing, he rolled it carefully and wrapped it in waterproof material that they used for the rare aboveground expedition, vacuum-sealing it. He made it into a tube.

Then he carefully threaded the hollow tube down into the office sink.

* * *

They walked into the training room. It was him, Alpha from Unit 1, and some others from the various Patrol units. He greeted them.

Sokol stood there, flanked by two giant guards. Gavin eyed them warily. There was no sign of Jossey.

Or Caspar.

Maybe they were still working on the project, he thought. Caspar couldn't directly be seen with the Minister anyway. Maybe Jossey was at the ice-cream social.

But his heart told him something seemed very wrong.

He didn't want to even meet Sokol's gaze, but he had to act as if everything were normal.

As if almost anything about Sokol were normal after what Tskoulis had read just now.

"Commanders," Sokol said. "Thank you for joining me."

Tskoulis looked him up and down. So this was the man who was truly in charge of Patrol. He'd never fully understood what that meant until now, to have Intelligence and Patrol linked together.

What it meant, he realized, was that Sokol could use the military might of the City to pursue whatever aims he saw fit...without telling anyone.

He wondered how accountable Sokol even was to the Council.

"You may wonder why I have gathered you here." Sokol smiled. "I see your agents are busy celebrating the capture of the Karapartei, as they should. Sadly, we were not able to find out much from that...individual." He glanced around, hands behind his back. "However, there was one happy result of the man's interrogation. We were able, tangentially, to discover a traitor among us."

Murmuring among the commanders. Tskoulis jammed his fist into the small of his back to keep any expression whatsoever off his face.

"Yes," Sokol said quietly. "A traitor. My...Intelligence assets were able to ascertain that a traitor has been living and working among us for quite some time. This individual has been working with" – he paused – "Karapartei."

Tskoulis bit the inside of his mouth and tasted blood. The man didn't even have the honesty, apparently, to tell his own commanders the truth.

One of the commanders looked like he wanted to speak. Sokol shook his head. "I am not able to offer details at this time," he said. "But I wanted to make you aware that Intelligence may be conducting a thorough sweep of Patrol in the near future, as Karapartei appears to have originated there."

Shock. They all began speaking at once.

He held up a hand, and they fell silent.

"What I can tell you, however, is the identity of our traitor. Given recent circumstances, this may come as a shock. It certainly did to me."

For a moment, Tskoulis detected what looked like a hint of sadness on the man's face.

But it vanished as quickly as it came.

"Sir – " another commander said.

"The situation has been dealt with," Sokol said. "Again, I am unable to share specific details at this time."

Gavin dug his knuckles even further into his spine, willing himself not to react.

He watched the man as if at a far distance. His entire body felt like ice.

Sokol opened his mouth.

"I regret to inform you," Sokol said coldly, "that Jossey Sokol, my niece, has been executed for treason."

Gavin felt as if all the air had gone out of his body.

He was still standing, he knew. He was still breathing.

He felt an immense pain in his chest.

They all knew who Jossey Sokol was. The entire room erupted.

Gavin just stood there.

Sokol waved for silence.

They slowly stopped speaking and looked at him.

"At this time, there is to be no discussion of this with your agents. Sokol is not to be mentioned whatsoever. As you know, Commander Tskoulis, she had been working on and off on the project I had assigned her to; any absence can initially be explained that way. I am sorry to be the bearer of this news. Our solar project must continue; Commander Tskoulis, I am still using Caspar Savaş's expertise, and may be calling on other members of Engineering to supplement the work that my niece did. At the appropriate time, I – "

Sokol's speech faded from Gavin's awareness. All he heard was one word.

Savaş.

"Yes, sir," they all said.

"Dismissed," Sokol said.

Gavin all but staggered from the room.

Executed. Jossey.

Gone.

And this wasn't like when she had been kidnapped by the Onlar.

She'd been executed, he thought.

He made it to his office.

He pulled the shades. He locked the door.

He sat in the dark, staring at nothing.

Executed.

He remembered her smile as she left his office.

"Be careful," he'd said.

He'd never been able to say anything further to her. It was always "be careful."

He'd never been able to tell her that he –

He bit down on his knuckle, hard, tears streaming down his face in the dark.

When they were young, she'd been an annoying tagalong, his best friend's bossy little sister. Tark had always had to convince Gavin to let her come along, even though he too had looked annoyed.

And then Tark had disappeared and Gavin had reluctantly kept an eye on her for years. He'd promised, after all.

And then one day he'd realized she wasn't annoying anymore.

She'd never seemed interested in him, never seemed to fall for his celebrity or the blinding grins he tossed her way, the ones that worked so well on everyone else. Had never seemed to even notice the way he went out of his way for her, beyond what was necessary to keep her safe.

Had seemed to resent it, in fact.

He'd been confused, upset, but had manfully kept up his end of the deal, keeping her out of trouble as best he could, rescuing her on more than one occasion. Had hidden his feelings behind "be carefuls" and laughed off people like Thompson, pretending he didn't care and taking solace in the fact that she didn't seem to notice them either.

He'd eventually, belatedly, understood her attitude toward him had been because she thought she was to blame for Tark.

And that stupid scar of hers. She had been convinced she was ugly. Maybe she *had* noticed how he felt, and had just thought he wouldn't –

He shook his head. As if something tiny like that –

He'd been more than willing to wait for her to notice. And they'd gone along fine until Savaş had showed up and destroyed everything.

He wondered what had happened, although his brain screamed at him not to think about it.

He didn't know who had been the executioner. Not for sure. Had Savaş –

A knife, Gavin thought.

Savaş fought best with a knife.

Gavin buried his face in his hands.

He lay on the couch in the dark, staring sightlessly up at the ceiling, still numb.

He couldn't move. Didn't care if they were looking for him. They'd taken from him the one person in the City that he truly cared about.

Their solar project could sink into the sands for all he cared.

As he lay there, something started to burn within him.

Orders, Sokol had said.

Orders.

The Tiger sat up in the dark. The clock said 4:00 AM.

If Savaş had been the one to execute her...

He stood up.

His sword was on the desk where he'd left it. He didn't need light to put it on.

He stormed through the corridors. The entire City was under curfew, and probably asleep. Patrol had almost an hour before they were scheduled to wake up for training.

He pounded on Savaş's door.

Ellis opened the door, peering out sleepily. He straightened, looking shocked. "Sir," he said.

"Where's Savaş," Gavin gritted out.

"He's not here, sir. I think he's staying up working on that project he and Jossey – "

"Where?" Gavin kept his voice low, casual. Inside, he wanted to rip the door off its hinges.

Ellis' gaze went to the sword at Gavin's side.

"What's wrong, sir?"

"Nothing's wrong," Gavin said coldly. "I need to speak to him about today's training. We may have to reschedule something and I need to talk to him. I apologize for the hour. It's urgent."

"Oh. Well in that case, I think they usually use that conference room on – "

"Got it. Go back to sleep, Ellis. If you see him, send him by my office." He kept his face neutral.

"Yes, sir." He looked confused, but began to shut the door.

"Oh, and Ellis. This is a security matter. You say nothing about this. That's an order." Behind Ellis, Tskoulis could hear Thompson snoring. "Including to your roommate."

Ellis saluted, looking slightly pale.

He shut the door.

Gavin stalked down the hallway.

The conference room.

Jossey had been so excited to work on this project.

His heart was clenching in his chest.

There was no guard. But he saw a dim light inside the room. He glanced inside.

Savaş was in there.

Gavin pushed open the door.

In seconds, he had crossed the room and slammed Savaş up against the wall, sword to the agent's throat.

Caspar didn't even resist.

"Give me one reason I shouldn't kill you right now," Gavin hissed. He pressed the blade tightly against Caspar's throat.

Caspar didn't seem to react. Didn't try to move. He almost looked resigned.

"How did you do it, Savaş?"

"Sit down," Caspar finally said.

"You really think I'd let you walk out of here alive?" Gavin was putting all his strength into not shouting in the man's face. "I don't need this sword to kill you."

"She's gone, Tskoulis."

Gavin's sword began to shake. He pressed it closer to Caspar's throat. It drew a thin line of blood. Caspar didn't even flinch.

"She's gone," he repeated.

"I know that," Tskoulis snapped. "Sokol told me."

"No," Caspar said. "You don't."

He glanced down at the blade. "I probably deserve this," he whispered. "But put it down. I have something you need to see."

"Don't tell me what to do," Tskoulis hissed. He couldn't understand how the man seemed so calm. Wanted him to be angry. Needed him to react. Feel *something*.

Caspar reached into his uniform, ignoring the sword, and held something out to Tskoulis.

It shone dully in the dimness. Tskoulis didn't look at it.

"She's gone," Caspar repeated. The words dug into Gavin's mind.

Gavin stared into those emotionless silver eyes, then glanced down at the object in the man's hand.

A ring.

Jossey's ring. The Sokol crest.

"Where did you get that?" he bit out, furious eyes going back up to Caspar's face.

"If you're planning to kill me, I probably can't stop you." Caspar smiled a little. "But you should know I had every chance to turn her in, and I didn't. As far as I know, Sokol doesn't know anything about this ring."

Gavin's sword hand steadied. He stared at the man.

"What do you mean?" he said slowly.

"I didn't betray her," Caspar repeated. "I tried to save her."

Gavin pressed the sword against Delta's neck again. He had several inches on the man. "Do you think I'm stupid?"

Caspar closed his eyes. "No, but I don't think you're thinking clearly. You know what I'm capable of. I was waiting for you here. I wanted you to find me." He smiled crookedly. "The last time someone managed to pin me to the wall, I was fifteen and an apprentice. Do you understand, Tskoulis? And if you kill me, you really think no one could guess who had done it?"

Gavin stood back, lowering his sword.

"I should kill you all," he said. "The lot of you. She wasn't a traitor."

"You're right," Caspar said. "And I told you already. She's gone."

"Stop," Gavin said.

"No, Tskoulis. You don't understand. She's *gone*." Caspar looked seriously at him.

Gavin took another step backward. His eyes narrowed.

Caspar rubbed his neck. "I told you, I tried to save her. I did what I had to. She's not here anymore. But she's not dead, as far as I know."

Gavin stared at him. "What?"

"And I believe you also know the truth about her. Her and the Onlar." Delta smiled. "Do you really think I thought you were talking about training? Again, I didn't turn her in, Tskoulis." His face registered pain. "Believe me, I didn't."

Gavin sank into one of the chairs, put his head in his hands. "I don't understand. What do you mean, she's not – "

He looked daggers at Caspar. "If you're lying to me, Savaş – "

"I'm very good at that," Caspar said, looking down. "But not this time, no."

"Then where – "

Caspar put the ring back into his uniform pocket. "Come with me. Quietly. Before Patrol wakes up."

128

GAVIN FOLLOWED CASPAR DOWN THE HALLWAY AND OUT INTO one of the outer tunnels, not fully believing the man, but not having much of a choice. They got into a tunnel shuttle and Caspar keyed in a code.

They were heading toward the service elevator, Gavin realized.

He saw Caspar take out a small black stick and click it every so often as they flew through the tunnel.

"What are you doing?" he hissed.

"The cameras," Caspar said calmly. "No one needs to know what we're doing."

They got out and walked. Gavin kept his hand on his sword.

"I'm unarmed," Caspar said. "You can stop doing that."

"How do you know," Gavin snarled.

"Your footsteps. They're uneven."

Gavin glared at Caspar's back but took his hand off his sword.

They got into the service elevator. Caspar entered a code.

"1-1-2-5-3." He showed it to Gavin. "Use this if you want to override the system. It doesn't retain any record of the elevator's use. Or the shuttle's."

"Why are you showing me this?"

"I want you to save her," Caspar said shortly.

They went up to the surface. Caspar pointed to the sandy ground. In the light from the elevator, Gavin could see traces of blood there. His stomach clenched.

"They left her here," Caspar said. "My men came and retrieved her. They should be sending a message to the...new bey of the Onlar shortly."

"Your men – "

"Karapartei." Caspar smiled. "I'm in charge. How do you think they escaped Sokol and Patrol for so long? That interrogation you saw? That man is one of my spies. He didn't die in that room. I just had to make Sokol think he had." He looked soberly at Gavin. "The things I think Jossey told you. The things we were working on. The children at the farms. I couldn't do it, Tskoulis. You can hate me. You can try to kill me. I likely deserve it. But I've been trying to destroy Sokol's disgusting system since the day I was brought on board."

Gavin felt like his brain was going to explode.

"Who are you?" He gaped at Caspar.

Caspar smiled bitterly. "Delta," he said.

Gavin looked back at the bloodstains on the ground. "What proof do I have that she is alive?"

"That I was the one who – " Caspar looked away. "I'm very...precise," he finally managed. "A competent doctor should easily be able to save her, or at least that's my hope. The Onlar are more...advanced than you may realize."

Gavin put his hand on his sword again.

"I put something on the blade," Caspar said. "She should appear to be dead for some time. Enough to fool the men who accompanied me, I hope."

"Why didn't you just kill the gua– "

"Some things are bigger than us, Tskoulis," Caspar said coldly. "I had no choice. Not if I wanted to right the wrongs Jossey and I have both risked our lives for. Do you understand?"

"You stabbed her," Gavin said quietly.

"Yes," Caspar said. Gavin saw terrible pain flash across his face. "The guards were probably nothing. But I couldn't risk Sokol bringing all of Patrol down on her, or finding out my real plan for Karapartei. I need Sokol to trust me. Do you understand? They had to believe she was dead, and at my hands."

He looked down. "No matter how I would otherwise want it," he said quietly. "At least this way she'll be safe eventually, God willing."

"You're in love with her," Gavin said after a long moment, staring at Caspar.

"That doesn't matter."

"It does to me."

"I know." Caspar looked straight at him. "That's why I'm telling you to go. Find her. Find the proof you need. Tear down this system. Patrol listens to you. The City listens to you."

Gavin just looked back at him, uncomprehending. "You would give up Jos– "

Caspar rubbed his forehead. "Don't fight me on this, Tskoulis. Please. Just go. After what I've done – " He trailed off.

Gavin suddenly thought he understood the wistful look he'd seen on Savaş's face.

"It's almost five," Caspar said quietly. "Patrol duty calls."

Gavin stood there watching the man silently. "If I go after her and you're lying, they'll probably execute me for treason too," he said flatly.

Caspar smiled. "I've thought of that. I have a plan."

They made their way back into the tunnels. Caspar clicked the little black stick again.

692

"It blanks out the cameras," he said. "Repeats a minute or so of footage. Allows you to walk past undetected."

Gavin was impressed, but he didn't show it.

"Here." Caspar tossed it to him. "I have another one."

Gavin caught it. "Thanks," he said after a moment.

They headed back to the conference room. Caspar opened the door and glanced inside.

Then he beckoned Gavin in.

He pulled a folder out from underneath the table.

"I assume you've seen this," he said.

Gavin just looked at him.

Caspar smiled. "I knew she was inventive."

Gavin said nothing.

Caspar pulled out a mobile terminal. "Here," he said. "This is my passcode. I use this terminal for travel. It's yours now."

Gavin stared at him. "You're giving me access to the Intelligence terminal?"

Caspar looked deadly serious. "I'm not lying to you, Tskoulis. Everything on the project is in here. Everything on Jossey. It's yours. This is what I've been doing for the past...decade and a half, nearly. Every shred of evidence I've collected on Sokol, the Council, all of them."

He put a hand over the terminal. "Wipe the log every time you plug it into the wall, understand? They can see the search history. Sokol may or may not trust me *that* much."

"Got it."

Caspar turned on the terminal and entered the code. He opened a file. "Here. Start with this one. I've organized it."

Gavin's eyebrows shot up. "You've done..."

"A lot of work? Yes."

"Who exactly were you planning to report this to?"

Caspar smiled. "You. Others like you. Patrol is the real power here, you know. They just need the right information."

Gavin looked at him. "You never cease to surprise me, Savaş."

Caspar didn't respond. He glanced at the clock. 4:53 AM.

"Now," he said. "How to get you out of here, should you choose to go. Let me explain."

ACKNOWLEDGMENTS

First and foremost, thank God for everything.

I owe a great deal of thanks to many people: Raahil S., for being a huge source of support throughout…Molly W., for her enthusiasm and for providing me with resources to check on things like moon phases…Amanda A., whose enthusiasm has floored me, and to whom I am deeply grateful for sticking with me through this process, especially for our extensive conversations…Vera K., for checking the Turkish and having long discussions with me…my mom and brother, for their support…Stephanie M., Beth S., Shahyan S., Meryum K., Susan S., Vicky A., Guy W., Khalid T., Sadia A., Lobna A., Esra A., various members of my family, Le Huong H. and Walter T., Sarah G., Samia O., Erin D., Matthew T. and Lindsay M., and many others.

I'd also like to thank other people and institutions that helped make this work:

The amazing people at one of my favorite cafes in Brookline, with its amazing masala chai. Additionally, another favorite cafe in Brighton, which provided a space for many a long afternoon of writing on the weekends. I hope to go back soon and present them with copies of these books.

Another dedication that I didn't put in the front due to spoilers: *Onlara*. To Them. The Others of this place and time: those who continue to suffer injustice.

WANT MORE?

Aestus, Book 2: The Colony is available now!

Did you enjoy Book 1? Please leave a review! This can help other readers find the book — and means a lot to me as an author!

Join my mailing list at www.szattwell.com/signup

ABOUT THE AUTHOR

S. Z. Attwell is a science writer with an M.A. in media studies. *Aestus, Book 1: The City* is her first novel. She lives in New England.

www.szattwell.com

Join my mailing list at www.szattwell.com/signup

f facebook.com/szattwellauthor

⊙ instagram.com/szattwellauthor